SHERRYL WOODS

Winter Vows

The Cowboy and the New Year's Baby and
Dylan and the Baby Doctor

mira

mira™

ISBN-13: 978-0-7783-6948-6

Winter Vows

Copyright © 2023 by Harlequin Enterprises ULC

The Cowboy and the New Year's Baby
First published in 2000. This edition published in 2023.
Copyright © 2000 by Sherryl Woods

Dylan and the Baby Doctor
First published in 2000. This edition published in 2023.
Copyright © 2000 by Sherryl Woods

For questions and comments about the quality of this book, please contact us at CustomerService@Harlequin.com.

Mira
22 Adelaide St. West, 41st Floor
Toronto, Ontario M5H 4E3, Canada
www.Harlequin.com

Printed in U.S.A.

Recycling programs for this product may not exist in your area.

CONTENTS

THE COWBOY AND THE
NEW YEAR'S BABY

One

Country-western singer Laurie Jensen kept her gaze fastened on her husband as she sang her latest megahit at the End of the Road Saloon in Garden City, Texas. It was New Year's Eve and she and Harlan Patrick had taken over the bar and were hosting a private bash for the ranch hands from White Pines. The bar was packed with members of the Adams family, hands and their guests, but based on the adoring look on Laurie's face and the rapt expression on his, she and Harlan Patrick might as well have been all alone. Married for over a year now, they were still besotted with each other.

Hardy Jones watched with a disgusted shake of his head. It pretty much seemed to Hardy as if every male he knew was succumbing to love. First his boss and Laurie, then his buddy, Slade Sutton, and Laurie's assistant, Val. Watching the two couples tonight was giving him a first-class case of hives.

Not that he had anything against romance. Far from it. He loved women. He loved the delicate, feminine scent of them. After a long day with a herd of cows, just the soft, floral aroma of perfume was enough to kick his hormones into overdrive. The shimmering silk of long hair glistening in the sun was enough to conjure up thoughts of a fragrant curtain of curls teasing his flesh while making love. Beyond that, he appreciated the way a woman felt in his arms, the sheer wonder of all those lush curves.

Tonight, in a roomful of available, sensuous women, it seemed to him that irresistible temptation lurked everywhere. In fact it was a little worse than usual tonight because he was all alone and determined to stay that way.

Not five minutes ago a gorgeous redhead he'd been out with a few times had sidled up to him and whispered an indecent suggestion in his ear. He'd swallowed hard, fought off a surge of testosterone and turned her down.

"Not tonight, darlin'." It had taken an act of will to get the words out.

Looking disappointed, she'd run a vivid red fingernail along his cheek. His temperature had skyrocketed, but his willpower had remained firm.

"Another time, then?" she'd suggested. "Count on it."

There had been others. From the moment he'd walked into the bar, it had been like seeing his past flash before his eyes. Los Piños, where White Pines ranch was located, and Garden City were hardly major metropolises. He was pretty sure he'd met—if not dated—most of the single women in both cities at one time or another.

The truth was he'd made it a point to be thorough. At least half of the women here tonight were listed in his little black book, a virtual *Who's Who* of his bachelorhood. It seemed as if his buddies had invited every available female from a hundred-mile radius just to torment him.

As for his little black book, it was dog-eared and invaluable. He touched his pocket just to be sure it was safely tucked there. There were phone numbers in those pages for hot, sultry women who could make a man's vision blur with a kiss. There were numbers for all-American women who liked hiking and sports, for some who could cook a mouthwatering gourmet meal, and for some who could simply make him laugh. He'd slept with fewer of them than most people thought, but probably more than was wise.

Some he'd only been out with once or twice. A handful had lasted longer, until he'd started to notice the way their gazes lingered on the diamonds every time they strolled past a jewelry store. He'd crossed out any who were inclined toward jealous rages.

Yes, indeed, that little book was worth its weight in gold. The men in the bunkhouse at White Pines had offered him all sorts of incentives just to get a peek, but he kept it private. His social life was nobody's business but his own, even though an awful lot of people thought otherwise.

Of course, seeing so many of the entries gathered in one place tonight was a little disconcerting. He'd been walking a tightrope for the past couple of hours, exchanging friendly hellos and not much in the way of encouragement, trying to dodge some of the more persistent, clever females who weren't inclined to take no for an answer.

Ever since his arrival he'd been asked to dance to every song. Drinks had been sent over. A blonde named Suzy with long and very shapely legs displayed to midthigh had brought over an entire bottle of champagne. If he'd been in the market for a date, all of the attention would have been very flattering. As it was, it was making him jittery. His willpower was only so strong, and some of these women were doing their best to destroy it. Alcohol, cleavage, caresses—it was enough to test a saint.

But over the years Hardy had discovered that there were two days of the year on which a dedicated bachelor had to be on his guard: New Year's Eve and Valentine's Day. For 363 days a man could pretty much date whomever he pleased without worrying too much about the consequences. Pay a woman a little too much attention on either of those occasions, however, and a man could all but kiss his freedom goodbye. New Year's and Valentine's Day were meant for lovers and commitment, at least that's how the women he knew saw them.

At 29, Hardy still valued his freedom. Even surrounded by some of the most enthusiastic proponents of marriage in the universe at White Pines, he remained a staunchly determined holdout. He had his reasons. Good reasons. Reasons rooted deeply in the past, a past he never talked about and tried not to remember. He lived in the moment, not the past, and never the future.

He fended off another admirer, took a long swallow of the sole beer he'd been nursing, and tried to relax and get into the spirit of the party. It was hard to do when the only other bachelor not on the dance floor was the grizzled cook, who only had half a dozen of his own teeth left and forgot his plate with the fake ones more often than not. Sweeney was a whiz with a skillet, on the trail or off, but he wasn't much of a talker. He didn't seem to care much about women one way or the other.

"Hey, Hardy, what's your New Year's resolution?" Slade Sutton shouted across the bar, his arm wrapped tightly around the waist of the petite woman with him. "Aren't you creeping up on thirty? Is this the year you're finally going to let some lady catch you?"

Hardy scowled at the teasing. "Not a chance, Sutton. Just because you've got the prettiest woman in Texas by your side these days doesn't mean the rest of us intend to fall into that trap."

The very recently wed Val Sutton regarded Hardy with feigned indignation. "And just what is wrong with marriage?"

Hardy pretended to think really hard. "Let me see if I can count that high."

"One of these days," Slade taunted, "you are going to fall so hard you'll knock yourself out."

"Never happen," Hardy insisted.

"If you had a woman, you wouldn't be sitting all alone at the bar looking pathetic on New Year's Eve," Slade persisted. For a man who'd taken his own sweet time acknowledging how he felt about his new wife, Slade seemed awfully eager to see Hardy follow in his footsteps. He had all the fervor of a recent convert.

"I guess you've missed all the women who've been over here tonight. Val must have put blinders on you," Hardy retorted.

"Watch it," Val warned. "I may be little, but I pack a mean punch."

Hardy grinned at her. She was a spirited little thing. All woman, too. He fondly recalled all the times she'd sashayed around the ranch on outrageously spiked heels just to catch Slade's attention. The other hands had appreciated it, even if Slade hadn't.

"Oh, if only I'd seen you first," he said with an exaggerated sigh that was only partly in jest. Val was a keeper, all right. Even he could admit that. If he'd been a marrying man—and if it hadn't been so plain that Val fit with Slade and his daughter, Annie—Hardy might have made a pass at her when she'd first turned up at White Pines.

"One date with me and you'd never have settled for a broken-down cowboy like Slade," he told her. She gave him a thorough once-over, then turned to her husband and did the same. When her survey ended, she regarded him with exaggerated sorrow. "Sorry, Hardy. Slade's the man for me, has been ever since I first laid eyes on him."

"Yeah, we all noticed that," Hardy conceded. "Took him a long time to catch on, though. He must be real slow."

"Since it's New Year's Eve, I'm not going to take offense at that," Slade retorted. "But I may make it my personal mission this year to see to it that you're the next White Pines bachelor to fall. If the word just happens to get out to Harlan Adams that you're looking to settle down, he'll take a personal interest in seeing you married. The man's got quite a success rate. Now that his son Cody and grandson Harlan Patrick are running the ranch, the old man's got a lot of time on his hands to dedicate to matchmaking. He's made it a full-time hobby."

Hardy shuddered, a reaction he didn't have to feign. "I take it all back," he said quickly. "Just stay the heck away from my love life—you and Harlan."

He'd already resolved to start the millennium by sampling as many women as he possibly could. Playing the field suited him just fine. He figured his life couldn't get much sweeter. A new woman every night pretty much kept boredom at bay. He played fair with every one of them. Treated them like queens. Respected them. Laid his cards on the table right up front, too, so they wouldn't go getting ideas that would result in hurt down the road.

Yet it never ceased to amaze him how many of those

same women—smart as whips, most of them—could ignore what a man said when it didn't suit them. They seemed especially deaf on a night like tonight.

Yes, indeed, New Year's Eve was a marital minefield, and Hardy had no intention of having his firm resolution to remain a bachelor blown to bits.

He checked his watch, saw that he had an hour to spare before the clock struck midnight, then slid off the barstool. "Think I'll be heading home," he announced.

"Hey, it's not even midnight," Slade said. "You turn into a pumpkin if you stay out too late?"

"Maybe I've got a hot date waiting," he retorted, wishing it were true. As it was, he intended to get the best night's sleep he'd get until February fourteenth.

Famous last words.

Trish Delacourt was on the lam.

She had planned to be tucked away in a cozy little bed-and-breakfast with a fireplace in her room on New Year's Eve. She had it all picked out. She'd made the reservation the minute she'd seen the brochure. Her father, who had standing accounts in every luxury hotel in the world, would never think to look for her in some stranger's home.

And Bryce Delacourt was looking for her. She didn't doubt it for a minute. He was too controlling, too convinced he knew what was best for everyone around him not to be. He'd probably put half a dozen of his best private investigators on her trail the instant he'd realized she was gone.

Fortunately for her she was resourceful and her father was a workaholic. She had managed to sneak out of Houston while he was away on a business trip he'd sandwiched between Christmas and New Year's. The head start had been critical. Even a couple of days might keep her out of his reach as long as she kept moving and steered away from all the big cities where her father would be likely to concentrate his search. He was probably combing Dallas at this very minute, dead certain that she'd go somewhere where she could be pampered.

But at 25, Trish was tired of being the pampered, only daughter of an oil tycoon with four headstrong sons, who also treated her as if she were made of spun glass. She was tired of her father's condescending attitude toward her work. He acted as if the business she loved was no more than an indulgence, a cute little hobby to keep her occupied until she married someone suitable.

Of course he knew precisely whom she should marry. He'd handpicked the man for her, then all but coached him into proposing. For a time she'd been caught up in the whirlwind courtship, blinded by Jack's good looks, dimpled smile and easy charm. She had almost fallen in with her father's plan.

Then, with all the force of a bolt of lightning, her vision had cleared and she'd seen Jack for what he truly was—a weak-willed opportunist and a ladies' man. Heaven protect her from the type. If she ever dated another man, he would be ugly as sin, acerbic and completely unfamiliar with the legendary Bryce Delacourt. For now, it was enough just to be out of Jack's clutches.

She'd plotted her escape like a prisoner scheming a breakout. Everything had been going swimmingly up until now. She'd felt the tension of the past few months sliding away. She'd felt in control of her own destiny, at least until a few minutes ago.

Unfortunately a couple of wrong turns and the weather

had conspired against her. Just when she'd been counting her blessings, her car had skidded into a snowdrift and sputtered to a stop on a stretch of deserted highway in the middle of nowhere in West Texas. By her calculations, she was miles away from her destination. Images of that cozy little B&B were fading fast, and the new year was rapidly approaching. Snow was falling outside in a blinding swirl. Inside the car the temperature was dropping at a terrifying clip. Her hands and feet were already freezing.

And, unless she was very much mistaken, she was in labor. Apparently her baby was going to follow in her footsteps and not do anything right.

After another unmistakable contraction, she rubbed her stomach. "You know, kiddo, you could just settle down and go back to sleep. You don't want to come into the world in the middle of a blizzard. Besides, you're not due for two more weeks." That news didn't seem to impress the baby.

Trish's body seized with another contraction, hard on the heels of the last one. This one left her gasping for breath and near tears.

Angry now, she declared, "I am not having this baby on the side of the road all by myself." She stared hard at her stomach. "Understand?"

She was rewarded with another contraction. Obviously the kid had another of her traits: he or she wouldn't listen to reason, either.

Convinced by now that nothing she could say was going to change the course of events, she yanked her cell phone out of her purse and punched in the number for the State Highway Patrol. A blinking red light on the phone reminded her that in her haste to leave Houston and stay one step ahead of her father's detectives, she hadn't taken the time to charge the battery. The phone was dead.

"Stupid, stupid, stupid," she muttered, tossing the useless phone on the floor. How could a woman who'd bought, built up and sold her own business for a tidy profit—the last without getting caught by her father— be so dumb?

"Now what?" she asked, not really expecting an answer. She was fresh out of ideas and, goodness knew, there was no one else in sight.

A quick survey out the window was not reassuring. There wasn't a house or a gas station within view. The last road marker she'd seen had been for Los Piños, fifteen miles away. Too far to walk even under the best of conditions.

The name of the town triggered a memory, though. One of her father's business associates lived in Los Piños, all but owned it from what she could recall.

Jordan Adams was head of a rival oil company. He and Bryce Delacourt had been friendly competitors for years. The one honorable man he knew, her father always said. They'd even been fishing buddies for a time when Jordan had lived in Houston, and they continued to trade tall tales about the one that got away. They still got together from time to time at business functions and at fishing lodges, where no wives were allowed.

Trish had no doubt that Jordan and his wife would come to her rescue, if only she could figure out some way to contact them. Unfortunately she also had a hunch that if he were even half the straight arrow her father described, Jordan would blab her whereabouts to her father the first chance he got. With the circumstances getting more desperate by the second, she was almost willing to take that risk.

"Why here?" she asked, gazing heavenward for answers that weren't forthcoming here on earth. "Why now?"

As if in response to her murmured questions, headlights cut through the pitch-black darkness. In such wide-open spaces, there was no way to tell just how far away they might be. She had to act and act quickly. There was no time to worry about the dangers of attracting a stranger's attention when she was all alone in the middle of nowhere. She needed help. She had to take her chances. Her baby's life was at stake. She'd already made a lot of sacrifices for the child she was carrying. This could be the most important one of all.

She jabbed frantically at the button to turn on her blinking hazard lights, then awkwardly heaved herself out of the car to signal to the oncoming driver.

Her feet skidded on the icy road and she clung to the car door to keep herself upright. More cautious now, she managed to slip-slide her way into the middle of the road, waving frantically, praying that the driver had at least a smidgen of the Good Samaritan in his soul.

At the last possible second what turned out to be a late-model, fancy pickup swerved, then skidded to a halt. The driver emerged cursing a blue streak. He ate up the distance between them in three long strides. Naturally he didn't slip. In fact, he didn't even seem aware that the ground was six inches deep in fresh snow on top of a sheet of slippery ice. She had to admire his agility, if not his choice of vocabulary.

When he was practically toe-to-toe with her, he scowled down, looking as if he would like very much to shake her. "Lady, are you out of your mind? I could have killed you."

Trish gazed up into eyes blazing with anger and what she hoped was at least a tiny hint of worry. Hoping to capitalize on that concern, she opened her mouth to explain her urgent predicament, but before she could, another wave of pain washed over her.

To her chagrin, she crumpled to the ground, right at the feet of the most gorgeous man she'd ever seen. If she hadn't been panting so hard, she might have sighed, maybe over him, maybe over the indignity of it all. Her only consolation was that, like Jack, this guy probably had women fainting at his feet all the time.

Two

"What the devil?"

Hardy dropped to his knees, oblivious to the biting cold wind and the six inches of wet snow that had made driving treacherous. What had happened to the woman? Had he hit her after all? Or was she some sort of insurance scam artist who was only pretending to be injured?

Or maybe just a nut case with a death wish? After all, she had planted herself directly in front on his oncoming truck on an icy road, all but asking him to run her down.

Whatever she was, at the moment she was clutching her stomach and writhing in pain. No matter which way he looked at it, that was not a good sign. If she was faking it, she was doing a really fine job of it. He was certainly buying it, and he was about as cynical as any man could be.

"Miss, are you okay?" he asked, gingerly brushing silky, blond hair back from a face streaked with tears. He couldn't quite bring himself to try to slap her back into consciousness.

"Come on now, darlin', wake up for me."

Finally, wide, blue eyes fluttered open, then promptly

glazed over with unmistakable pain. Any lingering doubts he'd had about her faking it vanished.

"Are you okay?" he asked again, conducting a quick visual survey to try to determine if there were any cuts or broken bones.

"No, dammit, I am not okay," she snapped.

The words were ground out between panting breaths that might have been alarming if he hadn't just noticed the size of her swollen belly. How he could have missed it was beyond him. Maybe he'd been too entranced by that delicate, angelic face of hers, too distracted by the tears that smudged her cheeks. He cursed his ingrained tendency to get all caught up at the sight of a pretty woman and lose control of his common sense. He had a feeling the occasion called for really clear thinking. A pregnant woman in pain and flat on her back in the snow was not a good thing.

"You're having a baby," he said in a bemused tone, which was not exactly the brilliant observation of a man who'd gotten a firm grip on reality.

"Great deduction, Einstein," she said, clearly not impressed with his quick wit.

He continued to grapple with the implications. "Here?" he asked uneasily. Surely she wasn't in labor. Surely she'd just slipped and landed a little too hard. This wasn't the time or the place to be having a baby, and he definitely wasn't the right person to expect to assist in the delivery.

"Not if someone would get me to a blasted hospital." She glanced around in an obviously exaggerated search of the barren landscape. "Looks to me like you're elected, cowboy."

Sweet heaven, it was every bit as bad as he'd feared.

She didn't seem any more overjoyed about the circumstances than he was. In fact, underneath that smart-mouthed sass of hers, she was probably scared to death. He couldn't say he blamed her. He was bordering on real alarm himself.

"Well, are you going to stand here all night or are you going to do something?" she demanded, rubbing her belly.

The movement of her hand all but mesmerized him. He'd never felt a baby move inside a woman before, never thought he wanted to, but for some reason he had to fight an urge to do so now. His willpower, already tested to its limits tonight, was called into play to restrain him from covering her hand with his own. As he struggled with himself, she scowled.

"Wake up," she snapped. "You aren't drunk, are you?"

"Stone-cold sober," he assured her. More was the pity. If he'd had more than one beer, he'd still be in Garden City, a long way from this woman and her problem.

"I hate to rush you, but I really think we need to get going," she said with renewed urgency. "Unless you'd like to loan me your truck and let me go on my own."

"Nobody drives my truck," he said tersely. "Why am I not surprised?" she muttered. "Then how about we hit the road, cowboy? This situation is only going to get worse with time."

Her cheeks were damp with tears, which she brushed at impatiently. Clearly, she wasn't used to having to count on someone else, and even more clearly, she didn't like it.

Although in a practical way he could see her point, Hardy was not overjoyed with the plan. Tears rattled him. He hated to see anyone or anything in pain. And the mere thought of babies gave him hives almost as severe as the thought of marriage. He sincerely regretted being so anxious to flee the End of the Road Saloon. Normally cool and calm in a crisis, for some reason he couldn't seem to snap into action the way the situation required. No wonder she was losing patience.

"Where's your husband?" he asked, aware that he sounded just a little desperate. It was clear enough that the man wasn't close enough to help them out of this jam.

"No hus...band." She bit the words out between gasps.

Before he realized what she intended, she seized his hand in a grip that an ex-rodeo star like Slade Sutton would have admired. There wasn't a bull on the circuit that could have thrown anyone hanging on that tightly. Hardy gently tried to extricate his fingers.

It was finally beginning to sink in that he had two choices: he could turn around and drive her to the hospital in Garden City or he could deliver the baby himself right here on the side of the road.

Over the years he'd delivered his share of calves and foals. He supposed he understood the rudiments of giving birth to a baby, but it seemed like an awfully personal activity to engage in with a complete stranger, especially one who was eyeing him as balefully as if he were the one responsible for her being in this predicament.

He figured this was no time for asking all the million and one questions that occurred to him, such as what she was doing out here all alone with a baby due any second. Terrified that the decision might be taken from him, he reached down and scooped the woman into his arms.

"Don't panic," he soothed. He figured he was panicked enough for both of them. "I'll have you at the hospital in no time."

"How far is it?"

"Not far," he reassured her. Too blasted far, he thought. Contractions as hard and fast as she was having them were not a good sign. Even he had sense enough to recognize that.

"Don't push," he cautioned as he settled her into the cab of his truck. "Whatever you do, don't push."

"Easy for you to say," she muttered, clinging to the door with a white-knuckled, viselike grip as another contraction washed over her.

Hardy leaned down and gazed into her eyes. "Sweetheart, you are not going to have this baby in my truck." It was part reassurance, part command. Apparently the baby didn't get the message, because a scream ripped from the woman's throat.

"Oh, my God, the baby's coming." Tears streamed down her cheeks, unchecked now, as she gave in to panic. "Do something. Please."

Hardy sucked in a deep breath of the chilly night air and reached a hasty conclusion. Like it or not, he was about to be midwife to this woman's baby. He touched her cheek with a soothing caress, trying not to notice how soft it felt to his callused fingers. She'd already proven beyond a doubt just how much trouble she could bring into a man's life. The last thing he needed was to be attracted to her. This was about helping her out of a jam, nothing more. He'd get this over with, deliver her to the hospital and wash his hands of her. It sounded like a sensible plan to him.

She turned those huge blue eyes of hers on him, blinking back a fresh batch of tears. "Help me, please."

The plea cut straight through him and propelled him into action.

"Shh," he whispered. "It's going to be just fine. I'll

just spread a couple of blankets on the seat here so you'll be more comfortable, and we'll get this show on the road."

"Do you have any idea what you're doing?" she asked hopefully, struggling to stretch out in the cramped confines of the pickup.

"Enough," he promised. Calves, foals, babies. Nothing to it, he reassured himself. Just concentrate and help nature along.

After that, everything happened so fast he could hardly catch his breath. The next thing he knew, he was holding a tiny baby girl in his arms. She was screaming her lungs out, but she was the most beautiful sight he had ever seen. Tiny fingers and toes, every one of them perfect. A swirl of soft brown fuzz on her head. Eyes as blue as her mama's.

Amazing, powerful, unfamiliar feelings swept through him. He felt exhilarated, even more satisfied than he ever had after rambunctious sex. He had a hunch nothing he ever did would match the experience he had just shared with a woman he was never likely to see again.

He gazed into her anxious eyes. "You have a daughter," he told her, his voice filled with awe.

"Is she okay?" the woman asked, struggling to sit up. "She's not too little, is she? She's early, not by much, but still it would have been better if she'd waited."

"You're telling me," Hardy said dryly. "Let me see."

"In a second. Let me clean her up a little, get her warmed up in something comfortable. Not that I'm any expert, but she looks just about right to me," he reassured her.

He stripped off his flannel shirt and wrapped the baby

in it. She snuggled in, looking as contented as if this weren't her first minute in the real world. He glanced at his watch. It was midnight on the dot. This little one had been in quite a rush to greet the new millennium.

Grinning, he placed the little sweetheart gently in her mama's arms. "Happy New Year, darlin'."

Hardy had a feeling it was going to be a long, long time before he got this New Year's out of his head. Next year he might even break tradition and have a date. Surely a date couldn't complicate his life any more than this stranger had.

"Oh, my God, she's beautiful," the woman whispered, then glanced at him. "Isn't she the most beautiful baby you've ever seen?"

"A real knockout," he concurred. "Now what say we bundle the two of you up and get you to the hospital?" He regarded her worriedly. "Sorry about the accommodations, but you'll have to sit up and hold the baby. Think you'll be able to?"

She nodded, her gaze never leaving her baby's face. She had to be uncomfortable, but with his assistance she struggled into a semi-upright position, then settled the baby in her arms.

When he was satisfied that she and the baby were as comfortable as they could be, Hardy eased the truck back onto the highway, turned around and headed toward Garden City. Although the condition of the roads required his full attention, he couldn't keep his gaze from straying to his companions. After a few, slow-going miles, both of them fell asleep, clearly exhausted by the whole ordeal.

Hardy, however, felt as wired as if he'd just downed a full pot of Sweeney's coffee. Normally he liked to tune in a country music station while he drove, but he didn't want to risk waking either mother or baby, so he hummed quietly. Christmas carols seemed oddly appropriate, so he went through a whole medley of them.

He calculated the time it would take him to get to the hospital, glad that his grown-up passenger wasn't awake to notice just how far away it was and just how big his lie had been when he'd told her before the birth that he thought they could make it. It had taken him better than half an hour to get from the party to where he'd been intercepted. The roads were worse now. Aware that he was carrying precious cargo, he was creeping along even slower than he would have been normally.

It was nearly one by the time he saw the lights of Garden City, another fifteen minutes before he saw the turn-off to the hospital. All that time and there hadn't been a peep from either of his ladies. He regarded them worriedly as he drove to the emergency entrance. What if they weren't okay? What if he'd done something wrong? What if the mama was bleeding to death? What was wrong with him? He should have driven faster, found a phone and called for help, something.

The roads around the hospital had been sanded. Even so, with the snow still coming down, the truck skidded when he tried to stop behind an ambulance, barely missing the back bumper of the emergency vehicle. Hardy bolted from the cab. Perfectly aware that he was acting a little like a crazy man, he raced into the emergency room shouting for help.

A nurse came flying out of a cubicle in the back, followed by a familiar face. He'd never been so glad to see anyone in his life as he was to see Lizzy Adams-Robbins, daughter of Harlan Adams and, far more important, a full-fledged doctor.

"What on earth?" she said when she saw him. "Hardy, what's wrong? Has there been an accident? You were at the White Pines party, weren't you? Did somebody get hurt?"

"Outside," he said. "My truck. A woman and a baby." For a man known for his glib tongue, he was having serious trouble forming sentences.

"Is the baby sick?" she asked, already moving toward the door at an admirably brisk pace.

"Newborn," he said, then drew in a deep breath and announced, "I delivered her."

Lizzy stopped and stared. So did the nurse who'd been running alongside.

"You delivered a baby?" Lizzy echoed. "Where? Why?"

"Just help them. Make sure they're okay," he said. "Don't you need a stretcher or a wheelchair or something?"

"Got it," the nurse said, grabbing a wheelchair. Lizzy raced past him. Outside, they found the baby squalling and her mama just coming awake. Hardy helped Lizzy get the two of them into the wheelchair, then stood back as she whipped them inside.

Suddenly feeling useless, Hardy stayed where he was. He sucked in a deep breath of the cold air and tried to calm nerves that suddenly felt strung tight as a bow. It was over now. The woman and her baby were in the hands of professionals. He could go on home, just as he'd planned.

But for some reason he couldn't make himself leave. He moved the truck to a parking space, then went back inside. He grabbed a soda from a vending machine, then settled down to wait for news.

He watched the clock ticking slowly, then stood up and began to pace. There was no sign of Lizzy or the nurse. Seconds ticked past, then minutes, then an hour.

Hardy was just about to charge into the treatment area and demand news, when the nurse returned.

"Everybody's doing fine," she assured him. "They've checked the mother and the baby from stem to stern and there are no complications. You did a great job, Dad."

Hardy started at her assumption. "I'm not the father," he informed her quickly. "I don't even know the woman."

The nurse didn't seem to believe him. She regarded him with amused skepticism that suggested she recognized him and that she'd heard tales about Hardy Jones. Since he'd dated quite a few people on staff at the hospital, it was entirely possible she had.

"Really," he insisted. "I found her by the side of the road. Her car had skidded into a snowdrift."

"Whatever you say."

"No, really. I'd never seen her before tonight."

She grinned. "Young man, you don't have to convince me. I believe you." She winked. "Of course, I also believe in the tooth fairy and Santa Claus."

Hardy sighed. Word of this was going to spread like wildfire. He could just imagine what the rumors would be like by morning. He'd never live it down. "I have some paperwork here," the nurse said. "If you'd just fill out these forms for me, I'd appreciate it."

His frustration mounted at her refusal to take his word for the fact that he didn't know the woman in the back room. "I can't help you. I don't know her. I don't even know her name. I don't know where she's from. I don't know what sort of insurance she has. Ask her."

"She's pretty well wiped out," the nurse said. "Then

look in her purse. She probably has ID in there, an insurance card, whatever you need."

"I can't go through her purse," the nurse retorted with a touch of indignation. "I just thought, given your relationship, that you could provide the necessary information."

"There is no relationship," Hardy said tightly. "None. What about that word don't you understand?"

The nurse withdrew the papers with a heavy sigh. "They're not going to like this in the billing office."

Hardy whipped his checkbook out of his back pocket. "How much?"

The nurse blinked. "What?"

"I asked you how much. I'll write a check for it."

"I don't know the charges, not yet. She'll be here overnight at least. There will be routine tests for the baby."

"Then give me something to sign and send me the bill."

"You said you don't know her."

"I don't, but I wouldn't want your precious paperwork messed up. Just send me the bill, okay?"

The bright patches of color on the nurse's cheeks suggested embarrassment, but she popped some papers in front of him, anyway. Hardy signed them all. He knew, even as he scrawled his signature in half a dozen places, that he was dooming himself. After all, what kind of fool would pay for the hospitalization of a woman he didn't even know? Obviously everyone was going to jump to a far different conclusion.

Well, so be it, he thought as he jammed his checkbook back in his pocket and headed for the exit. What was it they said? No good deed goes unpunished. Between his reputation and his bank account, it looked as if he were going to take a real hit.

Then he thought of the baby and the sassy woman who'd been forced to trust him with their lives. What if they did cost him a few bucks? What if he took a little ribbing for a few weeks? It would pass soon enough.

And in the meantime he could remember forever that he'd been part of a miracle, the kind of unexpected miracle that a bachelor was unlikely to experience, the kind of miracle that assured a man of God's presence. What price could he put on that?

Three

The last thing Trish remembered was falling asleep, her baby in her arms, as the stranger rushed her to the hospital. She'd been exhausted, but she had never before felt such contentment, such an incredible sense of accomplishment.

She woke up to bright lights and chaos as three people swept her from the truck, wheeled her into the emergency room, then took her baby from her arms and clucked over her bravery. Once she was inside, there was no further sign of her reluctant hero. He vanished just as quickly as he'd appeared earlier. She hadn't even had time to thank him properly, to apologize for the grief she'd given him.

No one seemed to stay still long enough for her to ask a single question. Finally she latched on to the sleeve of a pretty, dark-haired woman whose bedside manner had been gentle, cheerful and briskly efficient. She read the name printed on her tag: Lizzy Adams-Robbins, M.D.

"Doctor, is my baby all right?" she asked. "She was a couple of weeks early, and I was in the middle of nowhere when she decided to come. The man who helped was wonderful, but he wasn't a doctor…" She realized she was babbling but she couldn't seem to stop.

"Your baby is perfectly healthy," the woman assured her. "She weighed in at a respectable seven pounds, three ounces. Terrific lung power. Despite the circumstances of her untimely arrival, I'd say everything turned out just fine."

Trish remembered the baby's wails and couldn't help smiling. "She already has a lot to say for herself, doesn't she? No wonder she was so anxious to get here."

The doctor grinned, then patted her hand sympathetically. "Right this second you may find that charming, but take it from me, you won't feel that way a week from now when she's been waking you out of a sound sleep a couple of times a night. By the way, have you decided on a name for her?"

Trish hadn't given the matter of naming the baby a lot of thought. Despite the increasing size of her belly, the routine of prenatal visits and regular kicks from an active baby, she had somehow gotten the idea that she had forever before she had to decide on anything as important as a name. She'd been too busy trying to plan her escape and steer clear of her father, who was dead set on having her marry the baby's father.

Even now with the baby a reality and the future uncertain, she still knew with absolute certainty that she wouldn't marry Jack Grainger if he were the last man on earth. On the same day she'd found out she was pregnant, she had also discovered that he'd been seeing at least two other women—intimately—while he was supposedly engaged to her.

Even if those two pieces of news hadn't collided headfirst, she would have wriggled out of the engagement.

She'd discovered that Jack bored her to tears, maybe because he was so busy with his other women that he hadn't had time for her. She suspected he hadn't been any more overjoyed by the prospect of marriage than she had been. He'd just been too much in awe of her father—or her father's fortune, more likely—not to go along with Bryce's plans for the two of them.

Very methodically she had gone about quietly selling her business to a friend who'd expressed interest in it. She'd put her furniture in storage and slipped out of Houston. She'd been heading west to start the new year and a new life...someplace, when she'd gone into labor. The fact that her daughter had arrived early did not alter her determination to move ahead with her plans, and they definitely did not include Jack or any of the Delacourts.

The baby was her responsibility, and she was going to do right by her. That started with giving her a name she could be proud of, honoring someone who deserved it. Certainly not Jack. Certainly not anyone in her own family, since they'd all been far more concerned about convention than about her well-being or the baby's. Assuming that the marriage was a foregone conclusion, her mother had pleaded with her more than once to rush the wedding so that her pregnancy wouldn't show. When Trish had made it plain that there was to be no wedding despite her father's wishes, her mother had been appalled.

"What will we tell people?" she had demanded. "That your daughter had better sense than to marry a man she didn't love."

"What does love have to do with it?" her mother had asked, genuinely perplexed. "I thought the two of you got along well enough. Jack is suitable. You've known him for years now. He has a place in your father's company, the promise of a vice presidency after the wedding."

That, of course, had been Jack's incentive. She'd had none, not any longer. "I've only known the side of him he wanted me—wanted us—to see. I certainly didn't know about the other women."

Ironically, her mother hadn't seemed nearly as surprised or dismayed about that as Trish had been. "You knew, didn't you?" Trish had charged, stunned that her mother would keep something like that from her.

"There were rumors," her mother admitted, then waved them off as unimportant. "You know how it is. A handsome man will always have women chasing after him. It's something you get used to, something you just accept."

"True," Trish agreed. "The difference is an honorable man, a man who actually cares about his fiancée, doesn't let them catch him."

"You're being too hard on him, don't you think? He was just having a little premarital fling."

"Or two," Trish said, wondering for the first time whether her father's behavior was responsible for her mother's jaded view of marriage. As far as she'd known, her father had never strayed, but maybe she'd been blind to it.

"Never mind," Trish had said finally. "It's clear we don't see eye-to-eye on this. Bottom line, hell will freeze over before I marry Jack. I'm sorry, but you'll just have to get used to the disgrace of it, Mother."

Of course she hadn't. Straight through until Christmas Day, with Trish's due date just around the corner, Helen Delacourt had remained fiercely dedicated to seeing Trish and Jack married. Without informing Trish, she had even included him on the guest list for the family's holiday dinner. When he'd arrived, Trish had promptly developed a throbbing headache and excused herself. Even as she went to her room, she could hear her mother apologizing for her. If she hadn't already been planning to leave town, overhearing her mother's pitiful attempts to placate the louse would have spurred her to take off.

"Hey, where'd you go?" the doctor asked gently.

Back to a place she hoped never to set foot in again, Trish thought to herself. "Sorry. I guess my mind wandered for a minute. What were we talking about?"

"Naming your baby."

"Of course." She thought of the man who'd helped her. He might have been caught off guard. He might not have wanted any part of the crisis she had thrust him into, but he'd pulled through for her. She and her baby were fine, thanks to him. "Do you happen to know the man who brought me in?" she asked the doctor.

"Sure. He works at my father's ranch." She chuckled. "I've got to tell you I've never seen a man so relieved to get to a hospital in my life."

"What's his name?"

"Hardy Jones. I'm not sure where the nickname comes from. I've heard Daddy say it has to be short for hardheaded because he's resisted every single attempt that's been made to get him married off. You'd have to know my father to understand how annoying he finds that. He's not happy unless he's matchmaking and he's not ecstatic unless it's paying off."

"Well, I certainly can't name the baby that," Trish said, disappointed. "Do I have to decide right now?"

"No, indeed. We'll need it before you leave the hospital, but it can wait. You take your time and think it

over. Get some rest now. I'll be back to check on you
later, and the nurses will bring the baby in soon so you
can feed her."

Trish lay back against the pillows and let her eyes drift
shut. The image that came to mind wasn't of her baby,
but of the cowboy who'd delivered her.

"Hardy," she murmured on a sigh. A strong man with
a gentle touch. She could still feel the caress of his work-
roughened hands as he'd helped her in one of the most
terrifying, extraordinary, wondrous moments of her life.
No matter what happened in all the years that stretched
ahead, she would never forget him, never forget the miracle they'd shared.

"Hey, Hardy, I hear you're a gen-u-ine hero," one of
the men taunted at the bunkhouse the next morning.
Hardy grimaced and concentrated on spooning his oatmeal into his mouth.

"Yes, indeed, our boy has delivered himself a baby
girl by the side of the road," another man said. "Is that
some new technique of courting that I missed? No wonder I'm still crawling into a cold bed all alone at night."

"Oh, go to blazes," Hardy snapped, sensing that there
was no let-up to the teasing in sight. He grabbed his coat
off the back of the chair and stormed out of the bunkhouse.

It had been like this ever since the word of his good
deed had spread at dawn. He'd barely crawled into his
bed, when it had been time to crawl out again. Lack
of sleep had left him testy. By the time everyone had
come back in from their chores for breakfast, he'd been
the nonstop subject of their good-natured taunts. Even

the untalkative Sweeney had thrown out a sly comment while he'd dished up the oatmeal.

Outside, Hardy drew in a deep breath and tried to clear his lungs of the smoke that permeated the dining room.

"Hardy, could I have a word with you?" Cody Adams called out, poking his head out the door of his office and beckoning for Hardy to come inside. Hardy walked over and followed his boss into the cluttered office, wondering what his boss wanted to discuss. For the last year or so Cody had let his son, Harlan Patrick, deal with the hands more often than not. Cody ran the business side of things, analyzing the market for beef on his computer, determining the best time to take the cattle to market, tracking down the best new bulls for breeding. Harlan Patrick knew the land and the herd. He knew which men he could rely on and which were capable, but lacked initiative. He and his father had arrived at a division of labor that suited them.

"Congratulations! I hear you delivered a baby girl last night," Cody said, proving right off that the conversation had nothing to do with ranch business. "Did a right fine job of it from what Lizzy tells us."

"Lizzy had no business blabbing," he grumbled. "I just did what had to be done. Dropped mother and child off at the hospital, and that was the end of it."

"I'm sure that's how you see it, but the new mama's mighty grateful. Lizzy phoned a little while ago and said she'd like you to come see her. If you'd like, take the morning off and drive on over to the hospital."

The very idea of seeing the woman again panicked him. He'd felt too much while he was delivering that baby—powerful, unfamiliar emotions that his bachelor's instincts for self-preservation recognized as way too risky. "I can't ask the men to take on my chores," he hedged, grasping at straws. "We're short, anyway, because a couple of the men aren't back from their holiday break."

"I'll pitch in," Cody said. "I still have a rough idea of how things work around here. Go on. Let the lady deliver her thanks in person. Get another look at that baby. Wouldn't mind getting a peek at her myself. Did you ever hear how my brother Luke delivered Jessie's baby, when she turned up on his doorstep in the middle of a blizzard?"

Oh, he'd heard it, all right. It was the stuff of Adams legends. Every man on the ranch had heard that story. He also knew how it had ended, with Luke and Jessie married. That ending was warning enough to him. He wasn't about to risk such an outcome by spending a minute more than necessary with the woman whose baby he'd delivered. He ran a finger around his collar, as if he could already feel the marital noose tightening around his neck.

"I've heard," he said tightly.

Cody chuckled at his reaction. "I suppose a bachelor like you would find that scary, seeing how they ended up married. Well, you go on over to the hospital just the same. Take your time. With so little sleep, you won't be much use around here, anyway. Besides, you deserve a break after what you went through last night."

No, what he deserved was to have his head examined, he thought as he reluctantly climbed into his truck and headed toward Garden City. He was asking for trouble. He could feel it in his bones.

As if the reaction at the ranch wasn't bad enough, he

was greeted like a hero by the staff in the emergency room, too. The response made him queasy, especially since he'd dated quite a few of the admiring women in there at one time or another. Thanks to that paperwork he'd filled out, he figured half of them were speculating on just how close he was to the new mother. The other half were probably hoping this would make him more susceptible to the idea of marriage. He couldn't get out of the reception area fast enough.

Rather than going to the mother's room, though, he detoured to the nursery. An infant—female or not—was a whole lot less risk than a beautiful mama.

That's where Lizzy Adams found him, peering in at that tiny, incredible little human he'd brought into the world the night before.

"Amazing, isn't it?" she said, standing beside him to look through the glass. "I never get over it. One minute there's this anonymous little being inside the mother's body, and the next he or she is out here in the real world with a whole lifetime spread out before them. It surely is a miracle."

Hardy nodded, wishing he'd managed an escape before getting caught. "Yes, ma'am, it surely is."

"Are you here to see Trish? She's been asking for you. To tell you the truth, grateful as she is about your help last night, she's mad as spit that you agreed to pay her hospital bill. I thought I ought to warn you."

"I only agreed because that barracuda of a nurse panicked over the paperwork," he said defensively.

"Whatever. I'm sure the two of you will work it out."

"Maybe I'll wait to go see her, though," he said, seizing the excuse. "She's got a right sharp tongue when she's riled up. I wouldn't want to upset her."

Lizzy grinned at him. "Want to hold the baby first?"

Hardy was tempted, more tempted than he'd ever been by anything other than a grown-up and willing female. That was warning enough to have him shaking his head.

"I don't think so."

She regarded him knowingly. "You're not scared of a little tiny baby, are you?"

He scowled. "Of course not."

"Come on, then," she said, grabbing his hand and propelling him into the nursery. "You can rock her. Look at that face. You can tell she's getting ready to wail again. She's been keeping the other babies up."

Before he could stop her, Lizzy had him gowned and seated in a rocker with the baby in his arms. He stared down into those wide blue eyes and felt something deep inside him twist. Oh, this was dangerous, all right. If he'd been able to thrust her back into Lizzy's arms without looking like an idiot, he would have.

"She's beautiful, don't you think?" Lizzy asked, gently smoothing the baby's wisps of hair.

A lump formed in Hardy's throat. He was pretty sure he couldn't possibly squeeze a word past it without making a total fool of himself. He nodded instead, rubbing the back of his finger along the baby's soft cheek. She was…amazing. It was the only fitting word he could think of. Since he'd never considered marriage, he'd figured fatherhood was a moot point. Holding this precious little girl in his arms, he was beginning to realize that he was actually sacrificing something incredible.

"Here comes her mama now," Lizzy said brightly. "Don't you two be fighting over her."

She beckoned to the woman who was gazing through the window. Hardy took one look at the baby's mama and wanted to flee. She was every bit as beautiful as he'd remembered, every bit as much of a shock to his system. If he hadn't been holding her baby, if Lizzy hadn't kept a hand clasped on his shoulder in a less-than-subtle attempt to keep him in place, if it wouldn't have been the most cowardly thing he'd ever done, he would have leaped up and run like crazy.

Lizzy made the formal introductions that had been skipped the night before, gave them both beaming smiles, then took off and left them alone, clearly satisfied by a sneaky job well done. Hardy awkwardly got to his feet, then gestured toward the rocker.

"After what you went through a few hours ago, you should be sitting down," he scolded.

Trish gave him an amused look, but she dutifully sat. He all but shoved the baby into her arms. For a moment, with her attention riveted on her daughter, neither of them spoke. Eventually she sighed.

"I still can't quite believe it." She looked up at him. "Thank you."

"No thanks necessary."

"You handled it like a real pro. Are you in the habit of delivering babies by the side of the road?"

"No way. This was a first for me. Can't tell you how glad I am that I didn't foul it up. What were you doing out on a lonely stretch of highway in a snowstorm, anyway?"

"Running away from home," she said wryly. "It's a long story."

And one she clearly didn't want to share. Hardy pondered why a woman in her twenties would need to run away from home. Was it that husband she'd said didn't exist that she was leaving? If so, getting to know her any better would just be begging for trouble. He twisted his hat in his hands, then asked, "Does that mean you're not from around here?"

"Yes. I'm just passing through."

To his surprise, her reply actually disappointed him. Because he wasn't wild about the reaction, he backed up a step. Entranced by the daughter, intrigued by the mother, he was likely to do something he'd regret. In fact, if he wasn't very careful, he might be crazy enough to suggest that she stay on just so he could sneak an occasional peek at that little girl growing up. The words might pop out despite his best intentions to steer as far away from them as possible from this moment on.

"Ought to be going now," he said in a rush.

She reached out a hand, but he was too far away for her to make contact. The gesture was enough to bring him to a halt, though.

"Oh, no, you don't," she said firmly. "You and I need to talk."

"About the bill," he guessed, based on Lizzy's warning. "Don't get all worked up over it. I was just trying to keep the nurse from having apoplexy. You know how hospitals are about their forms these days."

"Oh, I'll admit that threw me, but I figured out what had probably happened. It's settled now. I've already explained to the billing office that the bill is my responsibility," she said. "No, what I wanted to talk to you about is more important."

Hardy regarded her warily. He didn't like the sound of that. "What's that?"

"The baby needs a name. I was hoping you could help me choose one. Something that would be special to you." Her gaze met his. "Your mother's name maybe."

Hardy froze at the mention of his mother, a woman

who'd run out on him so long ago he could barely recall what she looked like. It wasn't a betrayal he was ever likely to forget, much less honor.

"Never," he said fiercely.

The fervent response clearly startled Trish, but unlike a lot of women who'd have taken that as a sign to start poking and prodding, she didn't pursue it.

"Another name, then. Maybe a sister or a girl you've never forgotten."

Hardy thought of the older sister who'd left home with his mother. Neither of them had ever looked back. He'd go to his grave resenting the fact that his mother had loved his sister enough to take her but had left him behind.

Then he considered the long string of woman whose memories lingered. None were important enough that he wanted to offer their names.

Finally he shook his head. "Sorry."

"Surely there's a girl's name you like," she persisted. "Or even a boy's name that we could change a little to make it sound more feminine."

He squirmed under the intensity of her gaze and her determination to pull him into a process that was by no means his to share. Naming a baby should be between a mother and a father. A stranger should have no part in it. But he recalled that she'd told him the night before that there was no father. Well, obviously, there was one, but he wasn't in the picture. That still didn't mean that Hardy had any business involved in this.

"Can't think of a single name," he insisted, hoping that would be the end of it.

"Well, then, I guess it will just have to be Hardy, after all."

He thought at first she was teasing, but he could see from her expression that she was flat-out serious. "Oh, no," he said adamantly. "That's no name for a pretty little girl. Not much of one for a man, if you think about it. Comes from Hardwick, an old family name on my daddy's side. At least one boy in every generation had to be a Hardwick. Just my luck that I came along first in my generation. You would think after all those years of saddling poor little kids with that name, some mother would put her foot down and insist on something ordinary like Jake or Josh or John."

"What were the girls in your family named?"

He chuckled as he thought of his cousins, every one of whom had been named after flowers. They'd viewed that as being every bit as humiliating as Hardwick. "Rose, Lily, Iris," he recited, ticking them off on his fingers. He watched her increasingly horrified expression and kept going for the sheer fun of watching the sparks in her eyes, "I believe there might even have been a Periwinkle a few generations back."

Testing her, he said, "How about that for your baby? I really loved hearing about old Peri. To hear my father tell it, she was ahead of her time, quite the feminist."

Trish laughed. "You're kidding."

"About Peri?"

"About all of it."

He held up a hand. "God's truth. I swear it. Somebody, way back when, had a garden thing. Nobody who came after had the imagination to stray from the theme." He finally dared to look straight into Trish's eyes, which were sparkling with little glints of silver that made the blue shine like sapphires. "Okay, forget Peri. What's wrong with naming her after yourself? Trish is a pretty name."

"Short for Patricia," she explained derisively.

"It's a fine name, I suppose, but too ordinary. I want something that will make her stand out."

"Take it from someone whose name was a constant source of teasing, ordinary has its merits."

He paused for a minute, suddenly struck by a memory of the one woman in his life who'd been steadfast and gentle, his grandmother Laura. She'd died when he was only ten, but he'd never forgotten the warmth she had brought into his lonely life on her infrequent visits. She'd smelled like lily of the valley and she'd always had little bags of candy tucked inside her purse. She was the one person on his mother's side of the family who'd ever bothered to stay in touch.

"There is one name that comes to mind," he said, still hesitant to become involved in this at all. His gut told him even such a tenuous tie to this woman and her baby was dangerous.

"Tell me," she commanded eagerly.

"Laura. It's a little old-fashioned, I suppose. It was my grandmother's name."

"And she meant a lot to you?" she asked, searching his face.

"A long time ago, yes, she did."

Trish's expression brightened then. "Laura," she said softly. "I like it."

Hardy liked the way it sounded when she said it. He liked the way her voice rose and fell in gentle waves. Even when she'd been snapping his head off during the baby's birth, there had been a hint of sunshine lurking in that voice.

He liked everything about this woman a little too much. She and her baby were the type who could sneak into a man's heart—even his—before he knew what hit him. Just thinking that was enough to have him heading for the exit from the nursery.

"You're leaving?" Trish called after him, clearly surprised by the abrupt departure.

"Work to do," he said tersely, not turning around. "I meant to go a while back."

"Maybe I'll see you again."

"Since you're not from around these parts, I doubt it."

He hesitated, then turned and took one last look at the two of them, sitting in that rocker with the sunlight streaming in and spilling over them. He had a feeling that image would linger with him long after he wanted to banish it.

"I'm glad everything turned out okay," he said. "You all have a good life wherever you go."

Not until he was out in the hallway with the door firmly closed behind him did he begin to feel safe again.

Four

Trish had no idea what to make of Hardy Jones. He wasn't like any other man she'd ever known. He was brusque and tough one second, a little shy the next. As gorgeous and enigmatic as he was, she could imagine women falling at his feet, wanting to unravel the mystery of him. She had no intention of being one of them.

He'd done her a huge favor. She'd thanked him. There was no reason for their paths to cross again. In fact, he'd made it plain that he'd prefer that they didn't. Given some of the gossip she'd heard in the hallways about his active social life, she'd concluded he was a little too much like Jack. She certainly didn't need another man like that in her life. After Hardy had gone, her doctor magically appeared in the nursery as if she'd been waiting just outside the door.

"So, what did you think of Hardy?" she asked.

It seemed to Trish that she posed the question a little too casually. Her watchful gaze suggested she was very interested in the answer. Alarm bells went off. Between her father and her big brothers, Trish had spent her entire life with overactive meddlers. She knew one when she saw one. She phrased her reply very carefully.

"He's very sweet, but he seemed nervous. He must be awfully shy around women, or is it just me?" she said, testing what she'd overheard about Hardy's womanizing.

The doctor's mouth gaped predictably. "Hardy, shy? That has to be a first. If you asked a hundred women around this part of Texas to describe him, I doubt there's one who would come up with that."

The doctor's description confirmed her worst fears. "You said you've known him for a while, Doctor. How would you describe him?" Trish asked curiously.

"Forget the 'Doctor,' okay? Call me Lizzy. I think we're going to be friends. As for Hardy, well, I'd have to say he's a hunk. The general consensus rates him as sexy, handsome and charming," she replied without missing a beat. "A real ladies' man. The word around here is that he can accelerate a pulse rate faster than a treadmill."

All the traits Trish had vowed to avoid in a man, she thought. It was strange, though. Obviously she had noticed that the man was gorgeous, that he exuded masculinity, but she'd been more struck by his gentleness, by his uneasiness around her. Not once had he tried to charm her. Of course, she doubted any man on earth would be inclined to flirt while delivering a baby, but what about today? Was she that much of a wreck that he hadn't even been inclined to try? And why did she find that so annoying? It was probably just some weird hormonal shift. "I hadn't noticed," she said, aware that she sounded ever so slightly testy about it.

The doctor pulled up another rocker and sat down, clearly ready for a friendly chat. "I'm amazed," she said.

"Flirting's as ingrained in Hardy as breathing. Are you telling me he never so much as winked at you?"

"Nope."

"Hmm. Isn't that fascinating?" Lizzy said. "No little innuendoes, no flattery, no sweet talk?"

"Afraid not." She grinned. "Of course, I have just had a baby. Not many men would flirt with a brand-new mother. What's he going to say? You look pretty good for someone who's just had a baby in my truck?"

"You don't know Hardy. The guys say…" She hesitated. "Well, never mind what the guys say. Let's just leave it that Hardy likes women. Correct that. Hardy loves women. Big, small, old, young."

Trish studied her intently. "Why are you telling me all this?"

"Just sharing information," Lizzy insisted. "In case you're interested."

"I just had a baby," Trish reminded her. "I'm passing through town. Why would I be interested?"

Lizzy shrugged, unperturbed by her response. "I just thought you might be."

Trish recalled what Lizzy had said about her father's matchmaking on Hardy's behalf. Obviously she shared the trait. It just seemed a trifle misplaced under the circumstances. "It hasn't occurred to you that I could have a husband somewhere?"

"No mention of one on your hospital forms," Lizzy said. "I checked."

Trish stared. "You didn't."

"Of course I did," Lizzy replied unrepentantly. "You have to admit that having a baby together—"

"He delivered the baby," Trish corrected impatiently. "We didn't have one together."

"Still, it had to be an incredibly intense moment. That's the kind of moment that creates an enduring bond, don't you think?"

Friendly chitchat was rapidly turning into advice for the lovelorn. Trish figured it was time to put a very firm stop to it. "Oh, no, you don't," she warned. "Stop it right there. Obviously you have your father's matchmaking tendencies. I am not in the market for a man. Hardy clearly wasn't the slightest bit interested in me. Even you have to realize that, since he didn't even bother to try to charm my socks off."

"But that's what makes it so interesting," Lizzy insisted. "For a man like Hardy not to flirt, for him to actually act all shy and tongue-tied around you, I think that's very telling."

"And I think you've been at the hospital too long without sleep," Trish said. "You're hallucinating."

"We'll see," Lizzy said, undeterred.

"Afraid not. As soon as I'm back on my feet, the baby and I will be moving on. I'll probably never see Hardy Jones again."

Famous last words.

Not an hour after she'd made her very firm declaration to Lizzy, Jordan and Kelly Adams appeared. Trish wasn't dumb enough not to realize that there was a connection, especially when they suggested she come and stay with them.

"We have lots of room, and you need to get some rest. Having a brand-new baby is exhausting. You'll need help, at least for a while," Kelly said. "Don't even bother making excuses. I'm not taking no for an answer."

"It's the least we can do for Bryce's daughter," Jordan added. "Your father…"

Before he could get the rest of the words out, Trish cut him off. "My father is not to know I'm here," she said firmly. "I can't come with you, unless you agree to that. If you feel you have to tell him, then I'll just take the baby and move on."

Kelly squeezed her hand and shot a warning look at her husband. "I'm sure you have your reasons, though I hope you'll reconsider. I'm sure he must be worried sick about you. In the meantime, we want you here with us. Isn't that right, Jordan?"

He looked uncomfortable with the promise, but he finally nodded. "It's your decision."

"By the way, how did you even know I was here?"

"Word travels fast in a small town," Kelly Adams said. "It's hard to get used to, if you've lived in the city most of your life."

"And in this family, word spreads like wildfire," Jordan added. "Never known a worse bunch of gossips. My father's the worst."

"Then you and Lizzy *are* related?" she asked, trying to reconcile the age difference.

"She's my half sister," he said. "We share the same impossibly nosy father. No doubt you'll meet him. He's chomping at the bit to get over here and get a look at you and the baby. With luck we'll be able to keep him away until you move into the house, but don't count on it. He's not a patient man."

"He's also looking for a new project," Kelly warned her.

Trish managed a wan smile. "I've heard about the matchmaking. Lizzy seems to have inherited the trait."

"Yes, well, I don't know about Lizzy, but he certainly

does seem to have a flair for it," she said. "He did well enough by us."

Jordan frowned at her. "I'm the one who courted you, remember? My father had nothing to do with it."

Kelly patted his hand. "You go right on thinking that, sweetheart."

Trish was fascinated by the byplay between them. There was so much obvious affection, so much love.

Her own parents were not especially demonstrative. She'd assumed it was that way between all couples after many years of marriage. Obviously, that was not the case with Jordan and Kelly Adams.

He was a handsome man, a polished businessman with his well-trimmed hair and his fancy suit. He carried off the look of success with flair. Kelly, however, looked as if she'd just hopped off a horse and grabbed a ride into town with him. They both had to be in their forties, but while Jordan had a touch of gray in his hair and a few lines on his tanned face, Kelly was as vibrant and lovely as a girl. No one would have taken a quick look at them and guessed them to be a match. But judging from the way Jordan gazed at her, he adored her. And Kelly couldn't seem to keep her own gaze from straying to her husband every few seconds.

If only she could have fallen in love like that, Trish thought with a sigh. Instead, she'd fallen for a playboy with about as much substance as whipped cream.

Well, never again. Even if she stayed in the area for a few days or even a couple of weeks, she would do her best to avoid Hardy Jones. Rather than intriguing her, Lizzy's recitation of Hardy's attributes had solidified her determination to stay the heck away from him. And all of the hints that Harlan Adams might try to throw the two of them together were enough to make her skin crawl.

Realistically she couldn't take off in the next day or two, but she wouldn't hang around much longer than that. These people could plot and scheme and matchmake to their heart's content, but she was immune.

More important, in no time at all she and Laura would be far away. Hardy Jones wouldn't even be an issue once she'd found a new place to settle down. She'd been thinking New Mexico or Arizona, but Alaska was beginning to seem attractive. Or Maine. Any place that would put a few thousand miles between her and the growing number of people who seemed to think they knew just what she needed to make her life complete.

Hardy was constantly amazed at just how hot and sweaty a man could get when the temperature was barely above freezing. He and Harlan Patrick had been riding hard for most of the day, checking on the cattle to see how they'd done during the storm, making sure there was feed available, since most of the grazing land was still covered with a blanket of snow. All he wanted was a hot shower, a decent meal and sleep.

Instead, as he walked through the bunkhouse door, he was greeted by Harlan Adams.

"Hey, there, son, you're just the man I've been looking for."

In all the years he'd worked at White Pines, the owner had never sought him out before. Hardy regarded him warily. "Oh? Why is that?"

"Just wanted to add my congratulations to everybody else's. You did a fine thing the other night, helping out a stranger. Couldn't have been easy circumstances, but you kept your head and pulled through for her."

"Thank you, sir. I appreciate it, but the truth is, I just did what anyone would have done. I'm hardly anybody's idea of a hero."

"I doubt you'd get the new mama to agree to that."

"Oh, she's just grateful, that's all." He noticed that the old man showed no inclination to be on his way. "Is there something else?"

"Well, you could do me a favor, if you have the time."

"Now?" Hardy asked, trying not to let his dismay show.

"Not right this second, but tonight. Like I said, only if you have the time. I know what a busy social life you have."

Hardy searched for a hint of censure in his tone, but couldn't find any. "The truth is I thought I'd skip going into town tonight. It's been a long day."

Harlan Adams beamed, clearly ignoring Hardy's hint that he was exhausted. "Terrific. Then you have some time on your hands."

"I suppose. What can I do for you?"

"I'd like you to take a ride over to my son's and have a look at one of the horses." His expression turned regretful. "I declare, Jordan might have grown up on this ranch, but what he knows about animals wouldn't fill a thimble."

"Wouldn't Slade be better for the job? He's the expert with horses."

The old man was undeterred by his logic. "He's tied up tonight or I'd have asked him. Since you're free, would you mind? Kelly's been real worried about a little filly she's got over there."

Hardy sensed a trap, but for the life of him he couldn't figure out what it might be. "Let me clean up, have supper, and I'll ride on over."

"Take a shower, if you want, but forget supper. Kelly will have something for you over there. She's quite a cook. Better than Sweeney any day of the week. She said it's the least she can do to thank you for taking the trouble to stop by."

Nothing about this added up. There were a dozen or more men around White Pines who were every bit as qualified to look at that horse as Hardy was, some more so. To top it off, Kelly and Jordan's daughter, Dani, was a vet. Granted, she dealt primarily with small animals, but she surely could have examined the horse if her mother was so worked up about it. Add in the offer of dinner and Hardy was all but convinced there was something odd going on. He just couldn't figure out what.

Well, it hardly mattered now. He was committed. He'd find out soon enough.

"If you speak to Kelly, tell her I'll be by in fortyfive minutes or so," he advised Harlan Adams.

"Will do, son. Thanks. It will put her mind at ease, I'm sure."

He turned and walked off, whistling something that sounded suspiciously upbeat. Harlan Patrick arrived just in time to see him go.

"What was Grandpa Harlan doing here?"

"Beats me," Hardy said. "Something about a sick horse at your uncle's. He wants me to take a look at it."

"And you agreed?"

"Why not? I couldn't see how I could say no."

To his astonishment, Harlan Patrick burst out laughing.

Hardy's gaze narrowed. "Okay, what's going on? What do you know that I don't?"

His friend held up his hands and backed off. "Oh, no, I'm not getting in the middle of this."

"In the middle of what?"

"Nothing. Not a thing." He winked. "You have yourself a fine evening, Hardy. Something tells me it's going to be downright fascinating. I might just drop on over to my uncle's myself. Haven't seen Jordan and Kelly in ages."

Harlan Patrick's gleeful response nagged at Hardy the whole time he was showering and changing into something halfway presentable. When he was ready, he hopped into his pickup and made the short drive to the ranch that had belonged to Kelly's family for years. She had saved it singlehandedly after her folks died, and even though she and Jordan could have built something far more lavish on the property, they had kept the small, original house and simply added a few luxurious amenities to it. Hardy had been inside on a few occasions and admired the lack of pretension. This was a home, not a showplace.

When he pulled to a stop in front, he debated whether he should just go around to the corral, but finally decided on trying the front door first. As he stood on the porch waiting for someone to answer his knock, he thought he heard crying. Something about the sound reminded him of the wails of another baby, a baby he had held in his arms just the day before.

"Why that sneaky old coot," he muttered under his breath just as the door opened.

"Hardy, you're here," Kelly said just a shade too

cheerfully. "I can't tell you how grateful I am that you had time to stop by tonight. Come on in."

He stayed right where he was, still stunned by the baby's cries. "Why don't I just go on around back and take a look at the horse. No need to go tromping through the house. Sounds as if you have enough commotion in there."

Kelly sighed. "I was afraid you'd hear that. Laura doesn't waste any time letting us know when she's ready for a meal."

"Laura," he echoed, his worst suspicions confirmed. "Trish's baby?"

Guilty patches of color flared in Kelly's cheeks. Then her chin went up a defiant notch. She might be an Adams by marriage, but she was as brazen as the rest of them. "Yes. They're staying with us for a bit."

"Funny, no one mentioned that to me."

The color in her cheeks faded, and she actually managed to look totally innocent as she said, "Really? It was hardly a secret."

"Just tell me one thing."

"What's that?"

"Do you really have a sick horse?"

"Well, of course I do," she declared with a touch of indignation. "Surely you don't think I'd lie about a thing like that."

"Lie? Maybe not. Shade the truth a little? Now that's a whole different kettle of fish. As for your father-in-law, it seems to me he might flat-out fib if it suited his purposes."

"Yes, Harlan does have a way of shaping the world around him to his own ends," she admitted. "The rest of us prefer subtlety."

She met his gaze directly, "Are you coming in? Or are you going to go away mad?"

He wanted very badly to turn around and stalk away in a huff, but listening to Laura bellowing had reminded him of just how many times he'd thought of her in the past 24 hours. As for her mama, she'd been on his mind a lot, too. What could it hurt to stop in and make sure the two of them were doing okay? A quick little visit didn't mean anything.

"I'll stay," he said finally. "Just long enough to say hello to Trish and take a look at that horse. No dinner, okay?"

"Whatever you say," she agreed with a beaming smile. "Whatever makes you comfortable. Can I get you something to drink? Some coffee maybe? It's downright frigid out there and I know you've been outside all day."

"Coffee would be fine."

Kelly nodded. "Go on in the living room and say hello, then. I'll bring that coffee right in." She gave him a little shove as if she weren't entirely certain that he'd go in on his own.

Hardy stood just outside the living room and watched as Trish tried to soothe the baby, whose howls were showing no signs of letting up. Trish's hair was a tangled mess, as if she'd been combing her fingers frantically through it. Her complexion was pale. He wondered just how long she'd been pacing with the irritable baby.

"Sweetie, I don't know what else to do," she whispered, her voice filled with frustration. She looked as if she might burst into tears. "You've had your dinner. Your diaper's been changed."

"Mind if I give it a try?" Hardy asked, taking pity on her. He wasn't much of an expert, but at least he could give Trish a break so she could get herself together before she fainted from pure exhaustion.

She shot a startled gaze in his direction. "Hardy! I had no idea you were here."

"Then we're even," he said dryly. "What?"

"Never mind." He held out his arms. "Hand her over."

She hesitated for an instant, then placed Laura in his outstretched hands. "I can't imagine what's wrong with her."

He held the baby in front his face for an instant. "Hey, there, missy. What's all the fuss about?" he inquired. "You're giving your mama a tough time." The cries died down. The baby's gaze wandered as if trying to search out the source of this unfamiliar voice.

"Better," he soothed. "But let's try to stop altogether, okay, sweet thing?"

He put the baby on his shoulder and rubbed her back. Before long, a huge belch filled the air. He grinned.

"Oh, my," Trish murmured. "That's all it was? She needed to be burped?"

"Could be."

Trish sank into a chair and stared at him miserably. "I'm lousy at this. What on earth ever made me think I could be a mother?"

"For starters, you're a female," Hardy reminded her. "Even though you got yourself into a pickle the other night out on that road, you strike me as being smart enough. You've only been at this a couple of days now. Give it a month. If mothering is still eluding you then, we'll talk again."

"What will you do? Take over?"

He chuckled. "You never know. I might have a knack for it."

"Look at her," Trish said. "She's sound asleep. I'd say you definitely have a knack for it. Come on, I'll take her and put her down."

"Oh, no, you don't," Hardy said, reluctant to give up the baby. She felt right in his arms, as if she were something he'd been missing without even knowing it. "I did the hard work. Now I get the payoff."

She regarded him with amazement. "You want to hold her."

"Why not?"

"I don't know. I just figured you might want to get on with whatever you came here to do."

Hardy remembered the horse. He also remembered the coffee that Kelly had never brought. He had a hunch he was already doing exactly what he'd been lured here to do.

"How did you end up here, anyway?" he asked Trish.

"I think Lizzy had a hand in it. I'm pretty sure she talked to Kelly and Jordan. He and my father are business associates. I think they're pretty uncomfortable with the fact that I don't want my father to know I'm here, but they invited me to stay a while anyway. It'll just be for a few days."

He settled into a chair with the baby, then asked, "And then what?"

"I'll move on."

"To?"

"I'm not sure."

"But you won't be going home?"

"No, that's one thing I know for sure. I won't be going home."

"Why not?"

"If you knew my father, you wouldn't have to ask that.

He's the ultimate control freak. Add in my mother, who is horrified by my decision to have the baby on my own, and it seems like home is the last place for me to be."

Hardy thought over what she'd said, then recalled something he'd heard on the news earlier about some Dallas bigwig's missing daughter. "Delacourt? Your father wouldn't be Bryce Delacourt, would he? The oilman?"

She returned his gaze ruefully. "Afraid so."

"Oh, boy."

She immediately looked alarmed. "What?"

"He's got the whole blasted country looking for you. This may be a tiny place, but you've made a big impression. It won't be long before word leaks out that you're here. Don't you think it would be better to call him, so he knows you're okay? He might call off his dogs then. It also might be easier on Kelly and Jordan. I suspect he won't like the fact that his friends kept your whereabouts from him."

"No, he won't," she admitted with a sigh. Then she regarded him intently. "But I can't tell him. You can't, either. Promise me, please."

"Look, darlin', I'm not in the habit of ratting out my friends, but not everybody's going to feel that way, especially if that reward he's offering gets much bigger."

Trish looked horrified. "He's offering a reward? As if I'm a common criminal or something?"

"More like he's a desperate father," he replied reasonably.

"Oh, no. You don't know Bryce Delacourt. This isn't about desperation. This is about him being ticked off because I slipped out and he can't find me. It's about him not being able to control me."

She took four agitated strides across the room and grabbed up the phone. She punched in the numbers with enough force to have the phone bouncing on the table.

"Miriam, it's me. Is my father around?" Her foot tapped impatiently as she waited. Her eyes flashed sparks of pure fury.

Even from halfway across the room, Hardy could hear a man he assumed to be her father bellowing out a string of questions. Trish waited until he fell silent.

"Are you through?" she asked quietly. "Good. Because I am only going to say this once. Call off the detectives. Tell the media that I've been found and that I am perfectly fine, that it was all a huge misunderstanding and that you're terribly sorry for having sent everyone on such a wild-goose chase." She listened for a moment, then shook her head. "No, I am not coming home. No, I am not going to tell you where I am. I am fine. So is your granddaughter, in case you're interested. We're both doing just great. If you ever hope to see either of us again, you will give me some space now. Are we clear?"

Whatever her father said to that was too softly spoken for Hardy to hear, but her expression softened finally. She sighed.

"Yes, Daddy, I love you, too," she whispered. "I'll be in touch. I promise."

When she turned around, there were tears streaming down her cheeks. Hardy stood up, put the baby into the nearby carrier, then went to her. He touched a finger to her cheek, brushed away the dampness.

"You okay?"

She managed a watery smile. "Better now," she said.

"Remind me not to tick you off."

She gave him a full-fledged grin. "Oh, that. Sometimes yelling is the only way to get through to him. Delacourts tend to be stubborn."

He laughed. "Yeah, I got that part."

"Thank you for warning me about what was going on, so I could stop him from turning Los Piños into a circus."

"Do you honestly think he'll give up the search?"

"If he wants to see his granddaughter he will. And he knows I meant that, too. He may be difficult, but he's not stupid. Now that he's certain I'm okay, he'll give me some space."

"For how long?"

"Until he thinks it's time to come charging after me," she admitted. "I figure I've got a month tops to find a place to settle down and get my new life on track. I have to have every little piece in place or he'll run roughshod over me until he gets his way."

"What exactly does he want?"

"He wants me to come home and marry Laura's father."

Hardy was surprised by just how deeply he detested that idea himself. "And you disagree?"

"Oh, yes," she said fervently. "It won't happen. Not now. Not ever."

Because relief flooded through him at her response, Hardy knew it was time to go.

"You going to be okay?" he asked, grabbing his jacket off a chair.

"Sure."

He nodded. "Keep your chin up, darlin'. Something tells me everything is going to work out just the way you want it to."

"Do you carry a crystal ball around in your pocket?"

"Nope, but anybody hearing you stand up for yourself just now would put their money on you."

She seemed startled by the comment, but a smile began tugging at her lips. "Thanks, I think."

"Oh, it was a compliment, sweetheart. Make no mistake about that." He winked at her. "Tell Kelly if she checks, I suspect that horse of hers is just fine now."

Trish stared at him blankly. "What horse?"

"Just tell her. She'll understand."

He took off then, before the yearning to stay became so powerful that he forgot all the million and one reasons he had for getting out before he landed squarely in the middle of emotional quicksand.

Five

Hardy had actually paid her a compliment, Trish thought, staring after him with what was probably a ridiculously silly grin. She'd finally been exposed to a sampling of that famed charm of his, albeit little more than a couple of softly spoken endearments. She could see how it might be totally devastating if fully unleashed.

There were the dimples, for one thing. For another, his eyes shot off sparks like a live wire, turning the amber color to something closer to an unusual glittering bronze. And there were the occasional glimpses of his wit. She could see how the combination could be wickedly seductive.

Of course, she was immune to all of it. She'd been down that path all too recently. She'd sworn off men with good looks and glib tongues. Since that was the case, why did she feel as if she'd finally passed some sort of a test?

She was still standing where he'd left her when Kelly walked in, a cup of coffee in hand.

"Where's Hardy?" she asked.

She glanced around as if expecting to find him still

lurking in the shadows. Her behavior might have been more believable if her timing hadn't been so obvious. She'd shooed him into the room nearly an hour before, promising coffee as she'd breezed off into the kitchen. Even if she'd had to grind the beans and brew enough for an army, it would have been ready before now. She'd deliberately waited to give Trish plenty of time alone with him.

"He had to go," Trish explained, playing along with whatever game her hostess was up to. "He said to tell you he thought the horse was fine."

Kelly looked vaguely guilty. "Great. Did he go out to check her?"

"Actually, no. I thought that was a little odd myself." She peered intently at Kelly. "Any idea what he meant?"

"Just a mix-up," Kelly said blithely. "Crossed signals. You know, one of those things."

Trish's gaze narrowed. She might not know Kelly all that well, but she recognized a schemer when she saw one. She'd lived with the type most of her life. She'd been warned about Harlan Adams. She'd even guessed that Lizzy came from the same matchmaking gene pool. Now it appeared she was going to have to stay on her toes around Kelly Adams, too.

"One of what things?" she inquired in a silky tone that belied her agitation. "Something tells me you'd better explain."

Kelly patted her hand. "Never mind. It's not important. Did you two have a good visit?"

"After he managed to do what I couldn't, calm Laura down," she conceded. "Apparently his skills with the ladies even extends to those only a couple of days old."

"That's Hardy, all right. The kids around here tend to

gravitate toward him. He's extraordinarily patient with them," she enthused. "Underneath that devil-may-care attitude, he's a good, solid man."

Trish smiled at her. "You don't have to sell him to me. He saved my life, more than likely, and brought Laura safely into the world. I'll always be in his debt." Her expression sobered. "But that's all."

"Oh, of course," Kelly said hurriedly, but without real conviction. "You just met. What more could there be?"

"Exactly."

"So," she began with obviously undeterred fascination, "what else did you two talk about?"

Trish sighed as she recalled the primary topic of conversation. "He told me my father's reported me missing."

Kelly's eyes widened. "Oh, dear. I hadn't heard that."

"Hardy said he heard it on the news. Don't worry. I called my father and warned him to call off the bloodhounds. I'm pretty sure he will."

"Did you tell him where you were?"

"And have him come charging over here tonight? Not a chance."

"Trish…"

"Don't even try. It has to be this way, at least for now. If that's going to be a problem for you or Jordan, I can move on," she said, reiterating her earlier offer to go, rather than involve them in a sticky situation. "I don't want to put you in the middle of my battle."

"Believe me, we're used to being caught up in squabbles around here. We can take it," Kelly reassured her. "But we also believe, in the end, that family counts more than anything."

"I know. I doubt there's anyone in Texas who doesn't know just how tight-knit the Adamses are. My brothers and I are extremely close, too. I'd contact them if it wouldn't just put them in the position of having to lie to our parents. I'm not going to get into everything, but I will say that the senior Delacourts are cut from very different cloth."

Kelly regarded her somberly. "If that's true, then it's a pity."

"Oh, it's true enough."

"Then for the time being, just think of us as family. We'll be right here for you until you're completely back on your feet again."

"Thank you," Trish said. "I can't tell you how much that means to me."

"It's our privilege to have you here," Kelly assured her with absolute sincerity, then grinned. "It doesn't mean I'll stop nagging you about opening the lines of communication with your own family, though."

Trish laughed at the openly declared warning. "Fair enough."

When Kelly had gone off to finish getting dinner ready, Trish settled back against the chair's soft cushions and let her eyes drift shut. She had to think about the future, had to plan her next move, but just for now she felt more at home and at ease than she had in months.

"So, how was dinner last night?" Harlan Patrick asked when Hardy joined him to ride out in the morning.

"I picked up a couple of burgers in town," Hardy replied, keeping his gaze averted. He could just imagine the shocked expression on his friend's face.

"I thought you were going to eat over at Kelly's," he said, clearly puzzled.

"Plans changed," Hardy said succinctly.

"Why is that?"

"It seems the whole thing was a bit of a mix-up. The horse was fine. I took off. End of subject." He climbed into the saddle and spurred his horse to a canter.

Harlan Patrick scrambled to catch up. "What about...?" His voice trailed off.

Hardy turned and regarded him with exaggerated curiosity. "What about what?"

Harlan Patrick scowled. "You know perfectly well what I'm asking about."

"Do I?"

"Trish and the baby, blast it. Did you see them?"

"Hard to miss them. Little Laura was howling like a banshee when I got there. Funny how nobody thought to mention before I went over there that she and her mama were staying at your uncle's."

"I figured you knew," Harlan Patrick said defensively, then grinned. "Seeing how tight you two are."

"We are not tight," Hardy said. "I barely even know the woman."

He just knew that her skin was soft, that her eyes flooded with tears at the drop of a hat, that she smelled like something exotic and spicy. He also knew that she rattled him more than any woman he'd ever met. Under the circumstances, those were more than enough reasons to give her a wide berth. "Any plans to see her again?" Harlan Patrick inquired innocently.

"Not on your life."

Harlan Patrick chuckled at the fierce response. "Oh, really?" he said doubtfully. "I've never known you to protest so loudly about spending time with a beautiful woman."

"A beautiful woman with a brand-new baby," Hardy

reminded him. "I'm not in the market for a ready-made family. I'm the love 'em and leave 'em type, remember?"

"Funny thing about types," Harlan Patrick mused. "Love comes along, and things change faster than lightning."

Hardy scowled at him. "You don't know what you're talking about. You were a lousy bachelor. You never had eyes for anyone except Laurie. Even when she dumped you, it was like pulling teeth to get you to go out with another woman."

"True enough, but I've seen enough confirmed bachelors bite the dust to know that all it takes is the right woman, the right timing and a little nudge."

"Well, you can keep any ideas you have about nudging to yourself," Hardy declared, then added, "You might pass that along to anyone else who might be getting ideas, including your grandfather. Last night had to be his sneaky idea, though your aunt Kelly was clearly in on it, too. I'd hate to have to flee to Montana just to get away from all the scheming that goes on around here."

Harlan Patrick shook his head. "Oh, brother, are you in trouble. Any time a man has to skip town just to steer clear of a woman he claims to have absolutely no interest in, he's in so deep, it'd take a tow truck to extricate him."

Hardy faced him squarely. "I am not interested in Trish Delacourt. I am not interested in a serious, long-term relationship with any woman. I don't know how I can say it any plainer than that."

He rode off, leaving Harlan Patrick howling with laughter. The sound followed him, setting his nerves on edge and stiffening his resolve. No one was going to trap him into marriage. No one was going to turn him into a daddy for a kid who wasn't his own. No one was going to...

An image of Trish flashed in his head, as if to stubbornly remind him that he might be able to control his actions, but not his thoughts. Obviously, she was going to plague him whether he liked it or not. "Terrific," he muttered, digging his spurs into his horse until they were flying and all he could think about was staying in the saddle.

That night when his temper had cooled and his nerves had calmed, he concluded that what he desperately needed was a hot date, someone who could get his mind off of a smart-mouthed, blond beauty with vulnerable eyes.

He dug out his little black book, settled beside the phone in the bunkhouse and began leafing through pages. Normally the process didn't take more than a minute. He could decide on which female suited his mood faster than most men selected a steak from the menu.

Not tonight, though. He seemed stuck on finding faults. Fran's laugh was a little too loud. Paula hadn't had a real thought in all of her twenty-five years. Renata painted her fingernails blue, for Pete's sake. Ursula—now there was a beauty, he thought appreciatively—unfortunately chattered incessantly. Mindy annoyingly hung on his every word. Jan argued over everything.

He sighed heavily and snapped the book shut. Funny how none of those traits had ever bothered him before. Maybe what he needed was a new woman. Of course, single females he didn't already know were in short supply in Los Piños. The selection wasn't much better if he expanded the search to Garden City. Flying to Dallas just to find a date that would banish thoughts of Trish

Delacourt from his head seemed a little extreme. Some might view it as a sign that he was in over his head with the pretty new mama in town.

Finally he settled for taking a drive back to the End of the Road Saloon in Garden City, the last place he'd spent a peaceful, albeit lonely, evening. Maybe Rita would be around and would have another indecent suggestion that would get his juices flowing.

Of course, on the way he would have to drive past Jordan and Kelly's without giving in to the sudden temptation to stop by and check on Trish and Laura. He might have made it, too, if he hadn't spotted Trish, all bundled up for the cold weather, at the end of the lane looking as if she were about to collapse. She was clinging to the gate just to stay upright. He swerved into the driveway and leaped from the truck.

"What are you doing out here?" he demanded irritably. "Trying to get yourself killed the other night wasn't enough? You had to try it again."

"I just went for a walk," she said. "I'll catch my breath and be fine in a minute. Then I'll walk back. No need to trouble yourself on my behalf."

"You will not walk back," he argued. "Get in the truck."

"I will not get in the truck," she said, that stubborn little chin of hers shooting into the air.

Hardy scowled at her. "Would you rather collapse out here than accept a ride back with me?"

"Yes," she insisted.

He regarded her with bemusement. "Why?"

"Because it is too humiliating. Because you will throw it in my face. Shall I go on?"

"Try a reason that makes sense," he suggested, swallowing the urge to smile. She was clearly in no mood to discover that she was providing him with the best entertainment he'd had all day.

"Okay," he said at last. "We'll compromise. Are you familiar with the concept?"

She frowned at his teasing.

He nodded as if she'd actually responded. "Good. Then here's the plan. I will walk back to the house with you. That way if you collapse en route, I will be there to catch you. Deal?"

"It will still be humiliating," she grumbled. "You will still throw it in my face."

"Probably," he agreed. "But it's the best deal you're going to get. I walk with you or I toss you over my shoulder and put you in the truck. What's it going to be?"

She set off on foot without bothering to respond. Hardy couldn't control the laughter that bubbled up this time. Her scowl deepened and she kept her gaze averted as she plodded along. He had a tough time slowing his pace to her hobbling gait. He had to control the urge to save her from her stubborn pride and toss her over his shoulder. He figured she might protest that so loudly that half the Adamses would come flying. The resulting explanations would only complicate his life. He could just imagine the twist Kelly and the others would put on his concern.

They walked in silence for a hundred yards or so before he asked, "Have you always had such an independent streak?"

"Always."

"Get you in much trouble?"

She finally slid a glance his way and grinned. "More than you can imagine. The other night pretty much tops the list, though. I guess you've been unlucky enough to catch me at my worst."

If this was her worst, he had a feeling he was extremely fortunate not to have been around to sample her best. He would probably have found her irresistible. As it was, he found her pluck annoying and ill-advised, but admirable just the same. And that was without adding in the hormonal punch she packed.

"What exactly do you do when you're not running away from home, having babies by the side of the road and taking a hike when you should be in bed?" he asked. He had a feeling she could command a small army, if she was of a mind to.

"Nothing right now," she admitted. "I sold my business before I left Houston."

"What sort of business?"

"A dinosaur, really. A small, independent bookstore. I specialized in mysteries mostly, which gave me a niche and a loyal customer base. I even had a mail-order catalogue and Internet Web page that were doing really well."

"I thought all the independent bookstores were being forced into bankruptcy by the big chains," he said. "That Meg Ryan movie that made a fortune a while back was about that."

"Which is why everyone told me I was nuts," she agreed. "But with good customer service, the right niche, the right location and some innovative marketing, it's possible to survive."

"Why not do that here?" he asked. He almost groaned aloud the instant the words were out of his mouth. Was he nuts? He'd spoken before he considered the implication. As soon as he'd said it, he regretted the suggestion. Hadn't he just lectured himself about the dangers of doing anything at all to keep Trish around town? He was usually a whole lot more careful about the words he uttered around any female.

She stopped so fast, he almost charged right into her. "Here?" she echoed as if he'd suggested setting up shop on Mars.

"Probably not a good idea," he said hurriedly. "It's a small town. You'd go broke in a month."

As if she hadn't even heard him, her expression turned thoughtful. She began to move again, albeit at an even slower pace. "There's no bookstore in town?"

He sighed, then reluctantly admitted what she could discover in ten seconds on her own anyway. "No."

"What about Garden City?"

"I think there's one at the mall, but no superstore, if that's what you're asking."

"Hmm."

He could practically see the wheels turning as she toyed with the idea. As for him, his palms started turning sweaty, and his stomach began churning as he realized she'd taken him seriously and was actually considering settling down in Los Piños. Heaven help him!

"Property downtown probably has very low overhead," she mused. "I could create a new catalogue and a jazzy new Web page. Legally I'd probably have to expand beyond mysteries and be a fullservice bookstore, so I wouldn't be competing directly with the business I sold. Maybe I could add in a lot of Westerns. That might do really well on a Web page. I've heard stores in other parts of the country don't stock that many beyond Louis L'Amour and Zane Grey." She gazed at him with sparkling eyes. "What do you think?"

"It sounds like a possibility," he said neutrally, regretting his lack of nerve to tell her it was insane so she'd forget all about it.

"Maybe I'll drive into town tomorrow and take a look at what's available."

"You shouldn't be driving," he scolded, seizing on any excuse he could think of to delay her putting this impetuous plan into action. Maybe if he could stall her long enough, she'd forget all about it.

"Thank you, Dr. Jones," she retorted.

He snatched another excuse out of thin air. "Besides, your car's still in a ditch."

"No, it isn't. Jordan arranged to have it towed, checked out and brought over here this morning."

"You still shouldn't be driving," Hardy insisted. "Surely that's just good common sense. After all, you just had a baby."

"In some parts of the world, women have babies out in the field and get right back to work," she pointed out.

Having just seen firsthand how difficult giving birth was, Hardy shuddered. "It can't be good for them."

"I'm not saying it is. I'm just saying that giving birth is natural. It doesn't turn you into an invalid."

"Whatever you say. If you're getting a little stircrazy sitting around, I'm sure Kelly can find some chores for you to do. Scrubbing floors and washing windows, maybe. Or maybe you'd like to ride out and round up some cattle with me?"

He'd been teasing, but her expression immediately brightened. "Oh, could I? I've always wanted to do that."

He stared at her incredulously. "You actually want to bounce around in a saddle?"

She winced. "Well, maybe not today, but soon. You won't forget, will you?"

Hardy had a hunch she wouldn't allow him to. Since she didn't seem to have a lick of common sense, he said, "Look, if you can wait till tomorrow evening to go into town, I'll take you. We can grab some dinner and then cruise up and down Main Street to see if any property is available. I doubt there's much. Most of the businesses have been there since the town was first settled."

"Then it's time a new one came along to shake things up," she said, undaunted by his deliberately discouraging assessment.

They had reached the porch. Hardy stood at the foot of the steps, determined not to set foot inside that house where all manner of schemers lurked. Where Laura might be around needing to be held, he conceded; that was the real threat.

"The baby's doing okay?" he inquired, forcing himself to act as if the question were no more than idle curiosity.

"She's fine," Trish said, beaming. "The best thing I've ever done. Want to come in and see her?"

"Not tonight," he said a little too hurriedly.

She gave him an oddly knowing look, then shrugged. "Whatever. I'll see you tomorrow then. What time?"

"Six o'clock okay?"

"Perfect. I can get Laura fed and she'll stay down for a few hours. I'll make sure it's okay with Kelly if I leave her here."

"Oh, I doubt she'll object," Hardy said dryly. In fact, if he had to put money on it, he'd bet that Kelly would do a little jig in the street when she discovered that Trish was thinking of staying and that it had been his idea.

Obviously, he'd lost his mind.

Six

Maybe he could still talk her out of staying in Los Piños, Hardy consoled himself as he drove over to pick up Trish the next night. After all, the decision hadn't been carved in granite.

He had told absolutely no one about his impulsive, ill-considered idea. He just prayed that it would come to nothing and no one would ever find out about it. He was taking enough ribbing about Trish and the baby as it was. If people found out he'd all but asked her to stick around town, they would make way too much of it.

"Come on in," Kelly said, greeting him at the door with a beaming smile.

Hardy took one look at her expression and concluded he was already out of luck. She knew. Either Trish had already blabbed about the reason for this excursion or Kelly had drawn her own conclusions. Either way, his goose was cooked.

"I can wait out here," he said, hoping to forestall a cross-examination. "Unless it's going to be a while."

"No, she'll be right down. She's just checking on the baby one last time." She gave him a knowing look. "You aren't afraid I'm going to subject you to some sort of inquisition if you come inside, are you?"

"Of course not," he lied.

"Well then, I don't see any need for the two of us to stand out here freezing. Jordan's away on business, so you're safe on that front, too."

He forced a smile. "Not to be disrespectful, but you really are a handful, aren't you?"

She grinned. "I certainly try to be. It keeps marriage from getting stale."

Hardy stepped inside, then stood there, warily eyeing Kelly Adams. She was all but popping with curiosity. He figured her promise not to subject him to a string of nosy questions was likely to be as short-lived as his resolve to steer clear of Trish. She didn't disappoint him.

"I hear you suggested Trish open a bookstore right here in Los Piños," she said conversationally.

"It didn't happen exactly like that, but yes, I suppose I'm the one who planted the idea."

"I think it's a brilliant idea. It would be wonderful not to have to drive all the way over to Garden City just to pick up a paperback."

"Sharon Lynn stocks paperbacks at Dolan's," he pointed out. "Maybe she's thinking of expanding. How's she going to feel about a bookstore going in?"

"She only carries a few bestsellers," Kelly said dismissively. "Not nearly enough for an avid reader. Besides, she thinks they're a nuisance."

He twisted his hat in his hands. "Yeah, well, it probably won't work out. I doubt there's any property available on Main Street."

"Actually, there is," Kelly said, clearly enjoying his discomfort. "I checked it out today. That little tailor shop right next door to Dolan's is closing. I think it's the perfect size for a bookstore, don't you? With a little work, it would be wonderfully cozy. And the rent is reasonable. More than reasonable, really. Trish couldn't believe it."

Hardy bit back a groan. "Harlan Adams wouldn't by any chance own that property, would he?" he asked suspiciously. If the man hadn't owned it this morning, he probably did by now.

Kelly beamed. "Why, as a matter of fact, he does."

"I don't suppose it was his idea to boot the tailor shop out of there?"

"Of course not. Willetta's eyes aren't what they used to be. Can't thread a needle if you can't see, you know. She's been wanting to retire for a long time. She finally made the decision to join her sister in Arizona."

It wouldn't surprise Hardy to discover that Harlan Adams was paying her moving expenses and giving her some sort of payoff to get her out of there.

"Funny, I hadn't heard a thing about that," he said, watching Kelly's face for any sign of a telltale blush. She didn't so much as blink.

"It was a recent decision," she told him, then glanced upstairs. "Oh, here's Trish now. Doesn't she look wonderful?"

Hardy didn't need any coaching to agree. She looked fabulous. She was wearing a dark-blue wool skirt that fell to midcalf, boots, and a pale-blue sweater that looked so soft he had to stop himself from reaching out to brush his fingers over it. She'd worn her hair down, so that it skimmed her shoulders in soft waves. Suddenly he felt just as he had in high school when he'd picked up his date for the senior prom. He was flustered and tongue-tied.

Why was it this woman could reduce him to a jumble of nerves, when no other woman on earth could?

"Ready to go?" he asked, his tone brusque.

"Absolutely."

He turned to Kelly. "We won't be long," he said, as if she'd just reminded him of some curfew.

"Stay as long as you like," she retorted, her eyes glittering with amusement. "I don't have any plans for this evening. Laura and I will be just fine."

After they were settled in his truck and on the way, Trish turned in the seat to face him. "It's very nice of you to do this," she said.

"No problem."

"It's great to be able to start thinking about the future, making plans. For a long time all I thought about was getting away from Houston, away from my father, away from...well, everything."

"Including Laura's father?"

"Him most of all, I suppose."

"Have you told him about her?"

"No, but I'm sure my father has. They're very tight."

Hardy gritted his teeth. "Is that so?"

"Jack works for him. He's been envisioning a vice presidency ever since he and I started dating. I'm sure it must be a huge disappointment to him to think he might actually have to earn it."

Hardy shot a look at her. "You don't think much of the man, do you?"

"I did for a while. He was handsome and charming. He courted me with fancy dinners and thoughtful little gifts. I got caught up in the romance."

"Doesn't sound so bad to me. What happened?"

"It turned out I was only one of the women being

treated to such attention." She made a face. "I've never been fond of being part of a crowd, especially when I'm the one wearing an engagement ring. I made a rather public scene and broke it off the same day I found out I was pregnant."

"Lousy timing," he observed.

"I don't suppose there's any good time to make a discovery like that, but in a way I'm glad it happened when it did. What if I'd actually married the jerk and then found out? Bottom line, Laura and I are both better off without him."

"But your folks don't see it that way?"

"Oh, no. They had visions of us being one big happy family. Still do. The more distance I keep between us until they accept my decision, the better. My father tends to bulldoze over any decision he finds inconvenient. He found my decision to dump Jack extremely inconvenient. It's left him with a gap in his executive staff. He can't very well make Jack a vice president when all of Houston society knows what happened between him and me. The whole country club witnessed me dropping my engagement ring down the overexposed cleavage of one of his girlfriends."

Hardy laughed, which earned him a scowl. "It wasn't funny," she chided.

"I'm sure it wasn't at the time, but you have to admit it made quite a statement. I'm impressed."

Her lips twitched ever so slightly. "Yes, I suppose it did. I always wondered, though, which of them retrieved it. Jack, probably. The diamond was worth a fortune, and she didn't strike me as a keeper."

"So you packed up and took off?"

"Not right away. I had to plan for it. I had to sell my

business, close up my apartment and do it all without my father getting suspicious. He would have locked me in my room at the family mansion if he'd guessed what my intentions were."

"Being cut off from your family must be difficult. Obviously he loves you or he wouldn't have stirred up such a ruckus when he realized you were missing."

She shrugged. "He does love me, in his way. So does my mother. But they're both more concerned about how what I do reflects on them than whether or not I'm happy. They hated my bookstore. It wasn't in the right neighborhood. It didn't cater to the right clientele. My father referred to it as my little hobby. It drove him crazy that it operated in the black and I didn't have to keep running to him for money to prop it up. He'd be shocked to find out what I got for it when I sold it."

Hardy saw an opportunity to slow down her rush to open a bookstore in Los Piños. "Then you don't have to go back to work right away? You could stay home with Laura for a while?"

"Not immediately, no, but I can't live off the money forever. I have to use it to start over."

They finally hit the outskirts of town and her gaze was promptly drawn to the main street of Los Piños. Hardy tried to see it through her eyes. Compared to the high-rise splendor of Houston, it must seem like a shabby distant cousin. Not that the storefronts were dilapidated. In fact, most of them had been spruced up, but they were small, family-owned restaurants and practical businesses designed for the local residents. There wasn't an expensive boutique or a fancy café among them.

"Oh, it's charming," she declared, her eyes shining. "I feel as if I've stepped into the middle of *Our Town*.

It's like something from another era. Which shop is the one Kelly said is available? She said it was next to someplace called Dolan's."

Hardy pointed out the drugstore. "Dolan's is owned by Kelly's niece, Sharon Lynn. Her mother used to run the lunch counter inside and then Sharon Lynn followed in her footsteps. When old man Dolan decided to retire, Sharon Lynn bought him out. She's modernized it some, but it's still basically the same way it's been since back in the thirties, a real old-fashioned drugstore and soda fountain."

"And there's the tailor shop," Trish said, studying it intently. "Can we park here? I'd like a closer look. I see a light inside. Maybe we can get in so I can look around."

Hardy had a feeling Willetta was counting on it. She'd probably been asked to linger after hours in anticipation of just such an impromptu visit. Resigned, he pulled into a parking space out front. Trish was out of the car before he could turn off the engine.

"Are you coming?" she called back impatiently.

"I didn't realize it was urgent," he muttered.

"I heard that." She grabbed his hand and tugged him toward the door. "Shall I try it or knock?" she wondered aloud, then settled the matter, by doing both simultaneously. "Hello. Is anyone here?"

Willetta came in from the back, reading glasses perched on the end of her nose. She gave Hardy a sour look. "Oh, it's you."

"Hey, Willetta," he said, ignoring her brusque manner. He'd brought his mending by a time or two and they'd always gotten along well enough. She was just naturally cranky.

She turned to Trish and looked her up and down. Apparently the survey didn't satisfy her curiosity. "Who are you?" she demanded. "I don't recall seeing you around town before."

"Willetta, this is Trish Delacourt," Hardy explained. "She's interested in renting this space."

"Somebody told me about that," she said distractedly, moving to a desk and searching through the pile of papers scattered over it. "I wrote it down." She finally picked up a scrap of yellow paper. "Here it is. Trish Delacourt. Yes, that's what it says, all right."

Trish appeared startled. "Who told you I might be by?"

"Harlan, who else? The old coot's anxious to get a new tenant in here before the last one's even out the door. For all of his money, he's still a greedy old man."

"Harlan?" Trish echoed. "Harlan Adams?"

"Isn't that what I said? Are you deaf, girl?"

"No, I'm just surprised, that's all. I had no idea he was even involved."

"Owns the place," Hardy informed her, enjoying her startled reaction.

"I see."

"I doubt it," Hardy said grimly.

"Well, are you going to look around or waste time gabbing?" Willetta demanded. "I don't have all night. I've got to get home and get my dinner or I'll be up all night with indigestion."

Clearly taken aback by her abrupt demeanor, Trish hesitated. Hardy could have encouraged a quick departure right then, but he figured she'd only insist on coming back at a more convenient time. He tucked a hand under Trish's elbow.

"We'll look around," he told Willetta. "Won't take but a minute."

"Yes, thank you," Trish said. "I really appreciate you letting us interrupt your evening."

As near as Hardy could tell, there wasn't much to see. The tailor shop was one long, narrow room with a fireplace on one wall that looked as if it might still work, though it was doubtful it had been used in years. Halfway back, Willetta had hung a drape across a rod to close off a room where she kept material, took measurements and did her sewing. In front a few old mannequins displayed out-of-date dresses she had apparently designed. He tried to envision it with the clutter gone, the fireplace blazing and books lining the walls. His imagination didn't stretch that far.

Apparently, however, Trish's did. Her eyes were alight with excitement as she spun in a slow circle. "It's wonderful," she declared. "Could I see in the back?"

"Don't see why not," Willetta said. "Everybody else in town traipses back there."

Hardy followed as Trish opened the curtain and stepped into the back room. Only then did he realize just how deep the shop was. There was at least twice as much room in the back as in the front, plenty of room for a small bookstore.

"There's a storeroom that goes with it," Willetta grudgingly told them. "Runs behind the office next door." She pointed to a door. "Through there. There's a bathroom, too."

Trish eagerly opened the door and wandered through. "Oh, my, it's huge," she announced. "More than enough room for stock and the mailorder operation." She turned her gaze on him. "It's perfect. And I can't believe the rent. Compared to Houston, it's a steal."

Hardy could see that the whole plan was spinning wildly out of his control. She was going to land smack in the middle of his life, and there was almost nothing he could see to do about it.

"You're in the middle of nowhere," he reminded her, trying to keep a desperate note out of his voice. "That's why it's so cheap."

"Internet. Mail order," she countered. "For those, location doesn't matter."

Giving up, he shrugged. "If you say so."

She spun around, then grabbed Willetta and hugged her, to the old woman's obvious astonishment. "Thank you. It's wonderful."

Willetta gathered her composure, then actually smiled. Hardy was surprised her face didn't crack under the strain.

"It's been a long time since I've seen that kind of optimism. Hope you don't live to regret this."

"I won't," Trish declared firmly. "When were you planning on closing your shop?"

"Eager to run me off, are you?"

"Absolutely not," Trish said, looking horrified. "I'm just trying to predict my own timetable."

"End of next week," Willetta said. "Will that suit you?"

"If you're sure it's not rushing you too much."

"Tell you the truth I'll be glad to get to Arizona," Willetta admitted. "I've just been hanging around here out of habit."

The two women actually beamed at each other. It

had turned into a blasted lovefest. Hardy had to swallow back panic.

"We'd better be going so Willetta can get home," he said, interrupting Trish's chatter.

"Oh, of course," she apologized. "Unless you'd like to join us for dinner."

Willetta looked tempted for an instant, which would have suited Hardy just fine. She could have served as a buffer between him and Trish. For the last half hour, watching excitement put color in her cheeks and sparks in her eyes, he'd wanted desperately to kiss her. He figured it was going to take a natural disaster or the intercession of someone like Willetta to keep him from following through on the inclination before the night was over.

Instead, though, the seamstress patted Trish's hand. "No, indeed. I wouldn't dream of barging in on your date with your young man." She tugged Trish aside. "Keep your eye on him, though. I've heard stories."

Trish glanced his way. "Is that so?"

"Okay, that's enough," Hardy said. "Willetta, you're just jealous because I've never asked you out. You've forgotten all about the ice cream sundae I bought you at Dolan's last summer."

"Indeed, I haven't. It was butterscotch, as I recall."

He grinned. "That it was. Now don't you go telling tales about me to Trish."

"Young man, it will take more than one butterscotch sundae to buy my silence."

He winked at her. "I'll tell Sharon Lynn to make you a banana split tomorrow, on me."

Willetta grinned. "Now you're talking," she enthused. "Now go on, you two. Get out of here."

When they were outside, Hardy suggested walking up the street to the Italian restaurant. "You'll need the walk after you eat. They serve enough to feed an army."

"Perfect. I'm starving." She glanced up at him. "You really are a shameless womanizer, aren't you?"

"Me?"

"Willetta's not the first person to suggest it."

"You shouldn't listen to gossip."

"Is it all lies?" she persisted.

Uncomfortable with the fact that the better part of it was actually pure fact, Hardy tried to think of an evasion. Then he recalled what had happened with her ex-fiancé. Maybe this was the answer. Maybe if she lumped him in with Jack the jerk, she'd keep him at arm's length. That would take the decision out of his hands. It was the perfect solution to the attraction that was beginning to drive him just a little crazy. He was beginning to think he wouldn't even make it through this evening without succumbing to temptation.

But for some reason, he didn't want Trish to think of him that way. It was important that she not classify him as a jerk.

"You're avoiding the question," she pointed out when his silence dragged on.

"I date a lot," he conceded finally. "But I'm not like your ex-fiancé. I don't have long-term relationships, and I don't cheat. I just enjoy playing the field."

"An interesting distinction."

"Look, I think what he did to you was lousy. He'd made a commitment. He should have honored it."

"So you think it's okay to play the field, as you put it, as long as everything's out in the open."

"Exactly. That way nobody has any illusions and nobody gets hurt."

"Bull," she declared.

He stopped and stared at her, shocked by her curt dismissal of his philosophy. "What?"

"You heard me. That's just a cop-out and you know it. I suppose you end every date by promising to call, because it's expected, and then never bothering to do it."

"I never do that," he retorted indignantly. "I never make promises of any kind that I don't intend to keep. Never."

"If you say so."

Hardy didn't like the disdain he heard in her voice. "Just how am I supposed to prove to you that I'm telling the truth?"

"Why should it matter to me one way or the other?"

"Maybe it doesn't, but it matters to me."

"Why?"

"Because…" His words faltered. "Just because."

"Just because you can't bear to have one single woman think you're anything other than a sexy, charming hunk?"

"No, of course not," he said, jerking open the door of the restaurant and standing back to allow her to precede him. The entire conversation was ruining his appetite. Not even the aroma of garlic and spices was enough to overcome the sudden churning of his stomach.

"Come on, admit it, Hardy. You like being the playboy of this part of the western world."

"I never said I didn't like that," he grumbled. "You just don't want to be labeled as a bad guy."

"Right."

"Well, I say if the shoe fits…" She allowed her words

to trail off as she sashayed on ahead and settled into a booth.

Hardy followed and slid in across from her. "You're a very annoying woman."

"So I've been told." She grinned at him. "And I am way out of your league."

He blinked and stared. "Excuse me? When did this turn personal? Have you heard me ask you out on a date?"

She peered at him over the top of the menu that had been handed to her by an overtly curious waitress. "What do you call this?"

"I brought you into town to look at property. That's it. End of story. I'm doing you a favor," he said. "This is definitely not a date."

"Feels like one to me," she said. "But, of course, you're the expert."

The waitress tried unsuccessfully to choke back a laugh. At Hardy's fierce look, she swallowed hard and asked, "Can I get you two something to drink? Maybe cool things off?"

"I'll have a beer," Hardy said. "What about you, Trish?"

"Herb tea, if you have it."

"Sorry," the waitress apologized. "Anything nonalcoholic or decaf?"

"Orange soda."

Trish nodded. "Fine. I'll have that."

When the waitress had gone off to fetch their drinks— and probably tell everyone in the place about the very provocative conversation she'd overheard—Hardy stared hard at Trish. "Back to our discussion. You can ask any woman I've ever been out with if I misled her in any way. There's not a one who can say I did."

"That doesn't mean you didn't stir up hopes and then leave them unfulfilled," she said. She made it sound like an accusation of attempted armed robbery or worse.

"Darlin', I made it my business to fulfill their every little desire."

She made a face. "I am not talking about sex."

"Well, I am."

"Of course you are."

Hardy hadn't been struck by so many verbal blows in such a short period of time in all his years of going out with women. Of course, that was probably because he avoided the smart-mouthed variety like Trish as if they carried the plague. He had to concede, though, that the exchange was invigorating. It was also stirring up a whole lot of fascinating images of how explosive Trish would be in bed. If she was that passionate in conversation, it followed that she'd be a regular vixen in bed.

Too bad he would never find out.

Why not? his charged-up and thoroughly frustrated hormones screamed.

Because Trish was also about permanence and happily ever after. Any fool could see that. That made the two of them as incompatible as oil and water, fire and ice. He would just have to keep reminding himself of that before he started something they'd both regret, something that proved to her that he deserved his reputation as a low-down scoundrel.

Seven

"The space was absolutely perfect," Trish enthused as she and Kelly curled up at opposite ends of the sofa and sipped on cups of chamomile tea later that night. Despite the difference in their ages, Trish felt as comfortable with the older woman as she would have with one of her friends from home.

She certainly felt more comfortable than she would have with her own mother.

"Then you think you might actually stay?" Kelly asked, her expression neutral, as if for once she didn't want to influence Trish's decision.

"I'm definitely considering it," Trish said. "I love the town. I think it would be a great place to raise Laura. I am a little worried about chasing Willetta off, but she swears she's ready for the move to Arizona."

"And Hardy? What did he have to say about this?"

Trish's exuberance faded. "He didn't say a whole lot, at least not about the store. I doubt we'll be seeing all that much of each other." She couldn't hide the note of regret that crept into her voice, but it perplexed her. How could she regret not seeing a man who embodied everything she despised? What sort of perversity had her wishing that things could have been different, that he could have been different?

"Why on earth not?" Kelly demanded. "You two didn't have a fight, did you?"

Trish shook her head. "Let's just say tonight was an eye-opening experience."

"In what way?"

"Well, I'd heard bits and pieces of the gossip, of course," she began.

Kelly cut her off. "You can't believe everything you hear. You ought to know that," she scolded.

"Oh, he all but admitted that he was a total scoundrel where women are concerned. And seeing him in action tonight—he even flirted with Willetta, for heaven's sakes—listening to him talk about how he feels about women and relationships, I realized he's just not for me, that's all," she declared defensively. "I've been there, done that."

"Oh, for heaven's sakes," Kelly said impatiently. "He's exactly like Jordan was, searching for something without even realizing it. It's because he's never met the right woman. The minute he does, he'll settle right down."

"What's the saying? You can't expect a leopard to change his spots? I think that applies," Trish said, ignoring the comparison Kelly was making to her own husband. "His attitude seems pretty entrenched to me. Besides, if I decide to open this store, I'll be too busy to even think about dating for a long, long time, much less about getting involved with anyone."

"But you do like him, don't you?" Kelly persisted. "The sparks were flying when he picked you up tonight."

"You can't trust chemistry," Trish said. "Sometimes

it just blows up in a big puff of smoke and there's nothing left afterward."

"Don't you at least want to find out?" Kelly asked. "Do you want to spend the rest of your life wondering if you made a mistake, if you judged him too harshly?"

Trish regarded her curiously. "Why are you pushing this so hard?"

"No reason," Kelly said hurriedly. "I just like you. I like Hardy. I think you'd be good together. You already have an unbreakable bond."

"We're not back to the fact that he delivered Laura again, are we?"

"Well, you have to admit there's very little that's more intimate than that."

"It was an accident of fate, nothing more. I'm grateful. End of subject."

Kelly sighed. "If you say so."

"I do," Trish said very firmly. Her expression brightened. "Now let's talk about something I do want. Do you think it's too late to call your father-in-law and tell him I'm interested in the property?"

Kelly grinned. "For news like this, it's never too late to call Harlan. He'll want to rush right over and get you to sign the papers."

"Well, maybe that part can wait till morning, but let's at least tell him not to rent it out from under me."

"Oh, believe me, I doubt there is any chance that would happen," Kelly said wryly. "He has his heart set on having you stay right here."

Trish hesitated, feeling that renewed sense of walking into a trap that she'd experienced earlier when she'd discovered that Harlan owned the property. "Why would he feel so strongly about that? We've barely even met."

"Oh, for a man known for his business acumen, Harlan makes totally impulsive decisions when it comes to people. He's taken an interest in you, and that's that."

She handed Trish the portable phone and recited the number.

Harlan Adams answered with a booming greeting, despite the late hour.

"Sir, it's Trish Delacourt. I hope I'm not disturbing you."

"No, indeed. I was hoping you'd call. What did you think of the store? Does it suit you?"

"It's wonderful. And the rent—"

"We can negotiate, if you think it's too high."

Trish laughed. "No, it's fine. If you'll have the papers drawn up, I'll sign them in the morning. I'd like a year's lease, if that's okay."

"Make it five," he countered. "We'll lock in the rent. Takes that long to see if a business will thrive. Can't be opening and closing after a few months, just when folks are discovering you're there."

A five-year commitment, Trish thought warily. Could she do that? Should she? An image of Hardy popped up. He was already invading her thoughts entirely too frequently, despite all those firm declarations she'd just made to Kelly. What if she couldn't keep him at bay? What if she let her hormones overrule her head and got another nasty taste of reality as she had with Jack? Would she want to stay in a town like Los Piños where she was bound to keep right on bumping into him?

"I'll give you a release clause," Harlan offered, as if sensing her uncertainty and very likely guessing the reason for it. "Something important comes up and you need to take off, you send me a letter and that will be that. Deal?"

She'd never get a better one, she realized. And a five-year lease at the terms he'd offered ensured that her overhead would remain stable until the store was on a sound financial footing.

"Deal," she agreed.

"Then you come on up to the house in the morning and we'll lock it in," he said. "Bring the baby, if you like. Nothing makes my day like cuddling a little one for a bit. Come for breakfast. Only way I get anything decent is if we're having company. Otherwise, my wife feeds me bran flakes and a banana every single day. You can help me sneak a cup of real coffee, too."

Trish grinned at the thought of a powerful man like Harlan Adams having to sneak around behind his wife's back to get anything. She suspected he enjoyed the grumbling as much as he savored the occasional victory.

"I'll be there," she agreed. "Eight o'clock too early?"

"Perfect."

"I'll see you then, young lady. I'll be looking forward to it."

Done, she thought with a little sigh of satisfaction as she hung up. By this time tomorrow she would be on her way to being back in business and settling in Los Piños for the foreseeable future. It seemed that fate had known what it was up to when she'd been stranded nearby.

"Daddy wants you to stop by the house this morning," Cody told Hardy when he found him in the bunkhouse dining room at seven-thirty, taking a break between chores.

"Why?" Hardy asked, genuinely perplexed. It wasn't

as if he and Harlan Adams were buddies. And if it had something to do with ranch business, Cody would be passing along the orders.

"Far be it from me to question my father's motives," Cody said. "He works in mysterious ways, but he is still the boss around here. If he wants to see you, that's all that matters to me."

Hardy had a sinking sensation in the pit of his stomach that the command performance had nothing to do with the ranch and everything to do with his personal life. He also knew there wasn't a snowball's chance in hell he could wriggle out of going. "What time?" he asked with a resigned sigh.

"Eight," Cody said. "You might as well take off and head up to the main house now. The sooner you get it over with, the sooner you can get back to work."

"If you need me—"

Cody chuckled. "Oh, no. I'm not taking the blame for you not showing up. Obviously Daddy has some bee in his bonnet that concerns you."

Hardy heaved an even deeper sigh and headed for his pickup. When he reached the main house, Janet Adams answered his knock.

Harlan's wife was a handsome woman. With her high cheekbones and black hair streaked now with gray, there was no mistaking her Native American heritage. She carried herself as regally as a queen. One look at him, though, had her shaking her head, her expression amused. "I should have known," she murmured.

"Known what?" Hardy demanded, perplexed.

"You'll find out soon enough. He's expecting you. He's in the dining room having breakfast."

"I can wait till he's finished."

"Heavens, no. He wants you to come right on in and join the party, I'm sure," she said, that twinkle back in her dark brown eyes.

She led the way to the dining room, then gestured for him to go in. "If you need rescuing, give me a call," she said in an exaggerated whisper as she turned and walked away.

Only then did Hardy hear the voices, one deep and masculine, the other feminine and familiar. A baby's whimpers counterpointed the other two. So, he thought, that's what this was about. Harlan had set him up...again.

Before he could beat a hasty retreat, the sneaky old man caught sight of him.

"There you are," he boomed. "Come on in, son. Grab yourself some breakfast."

"I wouldn't want to intrude," Hardy said, his gaze locked on Trish and the baby even as he spoke to Harlan. Patches of color blossomed in her cheeks, proving that she, too, had been caught by surprise.

"I invited you, didn't I? Now get some food before it gets cold and have a seat. We have some planning to do."

"We do?" Hardy and Trish said in unison.

"Of course we do," the old man said, undaunted by their reaction. "If Trish here expects to get her store up and running soon, there's a lot of work to be done."

Trish's gaze shot from Hardy to Harlan Adams. "Sir, with all due respect, any work that's to be done is my responsibility."

"I'm the landlord," Harlan countered. "I can't have you moving in when the place is a mess, can I? Now I've been thinking. You'll want it painted, of course, maybe some bookshelves built in, a counter for your cash register. What else?"

Trish looked stunned. She also looked as if she were about to blow a gasket. Apparently Harlan Adams was unaware that she'd left Houston because another domineering man—her father—had been intent on taking over her life and making all of her decisions for her.

"Mr. Adams," she began, her chin lifting defiantly.

"Harlan, young lady. I thought we'd settled that."

"Mr. Adams," she repeated just as firmly. "After Willetta moves out and I have a chance to go over the space more thoroughly, I will decide what needs to be done. Then I will make arrangements for the workmen. And I will pay for it."

Rather than being incensed by her declaration, Harlan let out a whoop of laughter. "Oh, you're a fiery one, aren't you? That's good." He went right on as if she hadn't just made her wishes perfectly clear. "Hardy, you're handy with a hammer and a saw, aren't you?"

"I suppose," he said, finally getting the full picture. "But I'm working for Cody with the cattle, sir. I can't just pick up and take off for however long it takes to get the store ready."

"You can if I say you can," Harlan Adams countered. "Old age still has some privileges around here." He frowned at Trish. "You got any objections to Hardy doing the work?"

Hardy could see her struggling with her reply. She was obviously torn between diplomacy and indignation, between practicality and a desire to keep Hardy at arm's length.

"None," she finally said with evident frustration.

"Good. That's settled then. Willetta will be out by the end of the week. I'll speak to Cody. You can start work down at the store on Monday, Hardy. Does that suit you, Trish?"

Looking as if she were surprised to be consulted, Trish responded tightly, "That will be fine."

"You just tell Hardy whatever you need, and he'll take care of it," Harlan said. "The bills will come to me."

"Absolutely not," Trish said forcefully. "These are my renovations."

"To my property," Harlan countered evenly.

Their gazes clashed, though Hardy was pretty sure he detected more humor than fire in the old man's. Hardy grinned at Trish.

"Give in gracefully," he advised. "You can't win."

"I most certainly can," she said, frowning at him. She turned back to Harlan. "If you insist on having your way on everything, I'm afraid this won't work out."

Harlan looked vaguely startled by the declaration, then held up the paper she'd just sighed. "We have a contract."

Her gaze met his evenly. "With an escape clause," she reminded him. "All it takes is a letter from me and the deal's off." She reached for pen and paper. "I can write it right now, if need be."

Harlan chuckled. "Okay, you can have it your way. You pay the bills."

Trish looked pleased with the victory, but Hardy had the distinct impression Harlan would have the last laugh. He suspected the bills would come in, just as she'd asked, but that not a one of them would reflect the market value of the purchases. He could hardly wait to see the fireworks when Trish received the first one.

Harlan stood up, walked over to the sideboard and

picked up the pot of coffee sitting there. He had barely poured himself a cup, when Janet walked into the room.

"I saw that," she said, sliding the cup out of his reach.

"Woman, don't you have someplace to be?"

"Not since you made me give up my law practice so we could share our golden years," she replied sweetly.

"What's golden about 'em when a man can't even get a decent cup of coffee?" he grumbled, but his gaze was warm as it rested on her face. Something in Hardy's chest tightened just watching the two of them.

"I'd best be on my way," Hardy said, suddenly needing to be out of the room and away from Trish, away from Laura and away from the kind of glowing, unconditional love he knew he'd never experience.

"Wait," Trish said, drawing his gaze. "I'll come with you, so we can make some arrangements for next week."

"Whatever."

As they left, Hardy thought he heard Janet ask, "Satisfied?"

Something told him she wasn't referring to breakfast. He suspected she wanted to know if her husband thought his scheming had paid off.

"I'd say it's looking promising," he told her, confirming Hardy's guess. "Now come on over here beside me and make me forget about that coffee you're denying me."

Hardy chuckled. He turned and caught Trish's grin. Obviously she had caught the exchange as well.

"He's something, isn't he?" she asked.

"He's a sneaky meddler," Hardy contradicted, but without any real rancor.

"That's certainly true enough. I'm sorry about you getting roped into this. If I could have thought of a way out, I would have. I'm sure there are plenty of contractors I could have hired to do whatever work is needed at the store."

Her eagerness to rid herself of his company annoyed him, especially under the guise of consideration for his feelings. "I'll survive. I imagine you will, too. In the end, you'll have your bookstore. Isn't that what matters?"

"I suppose." She peered at him intently. "Hardy, do you regret ever suggesting that I stay here? I know you said it impulsively and then I ran with the idea. I've always been like that. If something sounds right to me, I do it. I don't always stop to consider all the ramifications. Just look at how I ended up here in the first place."

He shrugged. "What I think doesn't matter now, does it? You're staying."

"But you'd rather I go," she persisted.

"Why?" He had thought that was obvious.

"Because of what just happened, for one thing. Harlan's not the kind to let go once he's gotten an idea into his head. He's settled on getting us together, and he won't rest until he's accomplished that."

"We don't have to go along with it," she pointed out as if she genuinely believed it was a simple choice. "We're adults. We both know what we want and what we don't."

What Hardy wanted right this minute, more than anything, was to kiss the woman who was staring at him so earnestly, the woman who actually believed they were in control of their own destiny. He wanted to wipe that certainty off her face. He wanted her to tremble in his arms with sensations she couldn't simply wish away because they were inconvenient. And because he usually took what he wanted, he stepped closer. Before she could begin to guess what he had on his mind, he dipped his head low and brushed his lips over hers. It wasn't enough, not nearly enough, he thought, startled by the depth of his sudden need for more. He cupped a hand behind her head and kissed her again, ignoring her startled gasp, savoring the fact that it enabled him to dip his tongue into the sweetness of her mouth.

With the baby clutched tightly in her arms and trapped awkwardly between them, she swayed toward him. Hardy was pretty sure the earth tilted on its axis, that heaven opened up and welcomed him, when he'd been counting on hell.

It was Laura's whimpers that finally cut through the sensations rocketing through him. Clasping Trish's shoulders to keep her steady, he took a step back and fought for control. She stared up at him, her expression dazed and dreamy. Two red patches appeared in her cheeks.

Then, in the blink of an eye, fury replaced bemusement. "You have one heck of a nerve," she declared furiously. "Just because you're doing me a favor, don't start thinking—"

Hardy cut her off before she could travel too far down that particular path. "I am not doing you a favor," he reminded her. "I am doing a job that my boss has requested that I do. That's it."

"All the more reason not to take advantage of the situation," she countered. "This is a business relationship. It's not personal."

"You call it whatever you like," he taunted. "Personally, I'm beginning to think the benefits outweigh the salary."

"I am not part of the deal," she insisted. "If I have to, I will tell Harlan that it's not working out and that

I don't want you anywhere near the store. Then he'll want to know what you did to offend me." She let the threat trail off.

"And you'll say I kissed you?" Hardy suggested. "Darlin', believe me, that will make his day."

As acceptance of the truth washed over her, she sighed heavily. "I suppose you're right."

"So do we try to make this work?"

"We don't seem to have any choice." She scowled at him. "No more kisses, though, and that's final."

Hardy kept his expression sober and nodded dutifully. "No more kisses," he echoed, then grinned, "unless you ask real nicely."

"I won't ask."

"We'll see."

There wasn't a woman on earth he couldn't make want him if he put his mind to it. A little charm, an innocent caress or two, a careless wink. He'd have her right where he wanted her in forty-eight hours. Maybe less.

Then what? he wondered as she went stalking off toward her car, her back ramrod straight, her shoulders squared with singed pride. Would a few more kisses satisfy him? Was that the goal? Or did he want her in his bed, just like all the others who'd come so easily? Thinking of Trish as nothing more than another notch on his bedpost turned his stomach sour. She didn't deserve that. Laura's mother deserved better.

There was just one trouble with that. He didn't have better to give.

Eight

Unable to control her exuberance, Trish twirled around in the middle of her new store, then clapped her hands in delight.

The property was hers as of this morning, and it was going to be fantastic. She could envision every bookcase, made of a warm wood that would give the room a cozy feel when the fireplace was lit. Two comfortable chairs for reading were arranged in front of it. The chairs would be covered in a bright chintz and deep enough to snuggle into. An antique table in the same wood as the shelves would sit between the chairs, with porcelain teacups and a silver teapot that was always filled. Maybe she'd even learn to bake scones. And there would be fresh flowers in a small crystal vase.

Of course, there would be books, jamming the shelves, invitingly displayed on more antique tables, stacked high near the cash register for impulse sales. And while the atmosphere would be deliberately old-fashioned, there would be a state-of-the-art computer for tracking everything, including all the special orders and catalogue and Internet sales she anticipated.

Right now, however, the space looked more like a nightmare than her dream store. Willetta apparently hadn't done a thorough cleaning since the fifties. Maybe longer. The last paint job had been haphazard at best, doing nothing to conceal patches or fine cracks in the plaster. The floors, which had been a lovely oak once, had been dulled to near-black by years of wax and dirt building up. It was even more decrepit than the building she'd rented in Houston, and that had been a dump.

If it hadn't been her nature to be optimistic, Trish might have been appalled by the work that faced her. Instead, she drew in a deep breath and headed to the store for cleaning supplies.

She had virtually the whole weekend ahead of her. Kelly was looking after Laura and had promised to do so again after church on Sunday. Trish planned to make a lot of progress over the weekend so that the real work could get under way the instant Hardy showed up on Monday. The sooner he was finished and out of her hair, the better. That kiss had told her quite clearly just how dangerous a mix it would be for the two of them to be in the same room for long. Therefore it was with no particular pleasure that she spotted Hardy leaning against the side of his pickup in front of her store as she returned from her shopping. Struggling with her bags, she frowned at him.

"What are you doing here?"

"I came to help."

"You're not scheduled to start work until Monday."

"You're here, aren't you? There's work to be done, right?" he said, taking the bags from her before she could utter a protest.

"But—"

He sighed and faced her. "Trish, I am not going to

throw you down on the floor and ravish you. Get that picture right out of your head."

Of course, as soon as he said it, that was all she could see. Heat stirred low in her belly as she imagined herself flat on the floor with Hardy's body on top of hers, with him buried inside her. Obviously her hormones didn't have the sense of a gnat.

"I was not worried about that," she insisted, unlocking the door and preceding him inside.

He surveyed her with a skeptical expression. "If you say so. Now what do you want done first?"

She wanted him to go.

But not nearly as much as she wanted him to stay, she concluded with regret. They could do the work together in half the time that it would take her alone. And having company always made work seem easier. It was just that his company promised to leave her feeling every bit as rattled and unsettled as that kiss they'd shared.

Just as she accepted that, she saw him heading for the door. "You're leaving?" she asked, fearing that her lack of a warm reception had finally daunted him.

He grinned. "No, darlin', Don't go getting your hopes up. I don't scare off that easily. I'm going to get my radio out of the truck. We can't work without music."

She stared at him. "We can't?"

"Well, I suppose we could, but this will be better. There's a six-pack of beer in there for me and some sodas for you. And a bag of chips, a couple of sandwiches, apples, brownies. I'm not entirely certain, but there may be a pig in there ready to go on the barbeque."

She was stunned. "Hardy, we're not having a party."

"Tell that to Kelly. She packed it all."

She stared at him blankly. "Kelly? When?"

"When I stopped by the house to see what you were up to. She told me you'd come into town. She sounded as if you'd gone off to work in a coal mine in some god-forsaken land where no human had ever gone before. Before I knew it, I was carting bags of provisions out to the truck. She seemed to think we'll perish from hunger."

Trish stared as he carted in a card table, two folding chairs and grocery bags every bit as bulging as he'd described.

"Maybe she was anticipating a blizzard," she joked weakly.

Or maybe she'd merely been hoping for one, a doozy of a storm that would leave Trish trapped here with Hardy for a day or two. She peered into the bags and caught a whiff of the just-baked brownies, clearly still warm from the oven. Unable to resist, she snatched one from the package, then offered them to Hardy.

"Not just yet," he said. "Why don't you have a seat, enjoy your brownie and start bossing me around?"

With regret, she put her brownie aside and wiped her fingers on a napkin. "No, no, I'll get started, too."

He clasped her shoulders, nudged her toward a chair, then handed the chocolate square back to her. "Come on, boss lady, bark out some orders. You know you want to. There's not a woman alive who doesn't get a thrill from having a man at her beck and call."

"You'll do anything I want you to?" she asked speculatively.

His eyes widened. "Now that certainly sounds promising. What did you have in mind?"

"Nothing like that," she protested, guessing the wicked direction his thoughts had taken.

"Too bad. For a minute there, my heart almost stopped."

She regarded him with resignation. "You can't really help it, can you?"

"What?"

"Flirting."

"Why would I want to stop?" he asked. "It keeps things interesting."

"But it's all a game to you. Are you ever serious about anything?"

"Not if I can help it. We only get one shot at living. I figure it ought to be fun." He regarded her curiously. "What about you?"

She tried to think back to the last time she'd had fun without giving a thought to the consequences. "Fun has its place, I suppose."

He studied her thoughtfully. "How many times have you laughed today?"

The question threw her. "I have no idea. Why?"

"Because sharing laughter is almost as good as sex." He moved closer and touched a finger to the corner of her eyes. "When you laugh, when your eyes light up, I think I can see into your soul."

She shuddered as if his touch had been far more intimate. But it was his words, his unexpectedly poetic turn of phrase, not his touch, that stirred her deep inside where she'd vowed never again to let any man reach, especially not a glib charmer like Hardy.

A smile tugged at his lips. "I surprised you, didn't I? You figured me for a rough-and-tumble cowboy with nothing on his mind besides a quick roll in the hay."

"Of course not," she denied heatedly, because he was too close to the truth.

"Liar."

She didn't even try to defend herself. She just picked up a broom and turned away. She felt his hands on her shoulders, felt herself being turned until she faced him. His gaze settled on her gently, seriously.

"Trish, I'm going to warn you one time and one time only, don't underestimate me. I flirt because I enjoy it. I laugh because it's better than the alternative. But just when you think you know me, I guarantee, I'll surprise you."

She met his gaze evenly, felt another stirring of the heat that scared her and said quietly, "You already have."

He gave a little nod of satisfaction, then reached for the broom she held. "Then I suppose that's enough surprises for one morning." He winked at her. "I have to parcel them out or you'll start taking them for granted."

No, Trish thought, as he went to work. She had a feeling that after today she would never take anything about Hardy Jones for granted ever again.

Hardy had done his share of odd jobs over the years. He'd worked for a wide variety of bosses, some downright mean, some kind and patient, some demanding. But he'd never before worked for one who smelled of exotic spices and worked alongside him with nonstop chatter.

It seemed Trish was finally accepting his presence. Her nervous conversation, which didn't seem to require any response from him, suggested she might not be entirely comfortable with him yet, but she was clearly determined to make the best of it. He kept trying to get her to take it easy, reminding her that she'd just had a baby, that she needed to rest, to eat a decent lunch. She sat only when he sat, ate only when he ate.

Which meant that not very much got done. Hardy took more breaks than the best union contract in the country called for. He skipped the beer and drank milk, just to set a good example. He snacked on apples when he wanted chips. He claimed exhaustion and sat, when every fiber of his being cried out to get the job done.

"What made you decide you wanted to run a bookstore?" he asked as they sat side by side on the floor, sipping milk and eating the last of the brownies, their backs pressed against the wall.

"I always loved to read," she said. "I could lose myself in a book, go anywhere I wanted to go, be somebody daring and adventurous."

He thought of her taking off and heading far from home when she was about to have a baby. That seemed pretty daring and adventurous to him. "You didn't think of yourself as adventurous?"

She laughed. "Hardly. My father and my brothers got to have all the adventures. From the moment I was born, as the youngest child, the only girl, I was put on a pedestal and pampered. I hated it. I wanted to do what my brothers did. No, not exactly what they did," she corrected. "I didn't especially want to play football or get my nose broken in a fistfight, but I wanted the freedom they had. Do you know that I never came home from a date *not* to find my father sitting up waiting for me when I came in?"

"A lot of fathers wait up for their daughters," Hardy said, not understanding the problem. He'd been caught in a compromising kiss more times than he cared to recall, but it hadn't been the humiliating end of the world she was making it out to be. "Isn't it some sort of tradition?"

"But I was in my twenties," she said ruefully. "It was

embarrassing. I tried to move out and get my own place, but he and my mother were so horrified I finally caved in and stayed home."

"How on earth did you ever manage to get—" He cut himself off before he could say it.

Trish slid a glance his way. "How did I get pregnant?" He nodded.

"With Jack it was different, because he was the man my father had chosen for me. The apron strings were loosened. Everybody assumed that no harm could possibly come to me when I was with Jack. I'm sure they were stunned when they realized just how wrong they were. Then again, the thinking went, what did it matter? After all, we were going to be married, weren't we? When I put an end to that fantasy, that's when the trouble started."

"Surely by now you've made your point," he suggested.

"I doubt it. The Delacourts are stubborn to a fault. My father more so than any of us. Even if I'm gone for years, he'll probably keep Jack dangling on a string just in case I change my mind."

Hardy studied her expression. She was serious. "What does that say about him?"

"That he's a weak man," she said readily. "That he wants what my father's holding just out of reach more than he cares about his self-respect."

"The man's a fool."

"Which one?"

"Both, now that you mention it. Your father for not trusting your instincts and Jack for not having any gumption. I'd have told your father what he could do a long time ago," he declared, then captured her gaze. "And I would never have let you get away."

He realized even as he said the words that a part of him didn't want to let her go even after knowing her so briefly, even without sleeping with her. At the same time he also knew that he would eventually let her go— would send her away, in fact—because that was what he did. He was every bit as much a fool as Jack Grainger.

Because he didn't like the direction his thoughts had taken, he stood up and grabbed sandpaper and spackle and went to work on smoothing and patching the walls. The country music station played songs that echoed his mood, love-gone-wrong tunes that seemed to mirror the way his future was laid out.

In the past he'd heard the sad words, sung along with them, in fact, but he hadn't related to them because he'd never lost a woman he loved. Now he was faced with the prospect of losing a woman he'd never even given himself a chance to love. Regrets, something he rarely indulged in, taunted him.

He glanced over and caught Trish trying to mimic his actions. She had climbed onto one of the folding chairs and was reaching high to sand a sloppy patch job. The movement lifted her breasts and pulled her sweater loose from her jeans, displaying a sliver of bare skin. His mouth went dry at the sight.

Then she rose on tiptoe, and the unstable chair wobbled beneath her, throwing her off balance. Barely in the nick of time he realized that she was about to topple off. Thankful for his lightning-quick reflexes, he caught her in midair and pulled her tight against his chest.

"Oh, dear," she murmured, as her gaze clashed with his.

He saw the precise second when fright gave way to an awareness that their bodies were pressed intimately together. He felt her skin heat, felt his own temperature soar. He could feel her breasts heaving with each startled gasp of breath she took.

Bad idea, he told himself firmly, but he couldn't seem to make himself release her. She felt too good, fit too perfectly against him. And he couldn't resist holding her just a little longer to see precisely what she would do after the initial shock of her near fall wore off.

He saw the muscle work in her throat, felt her pulse fluttering wildly beneath his touch, but she didn't jerk away, didn't struggle to get out of the compromising position. In fact, she was so still, her gaze so watchful, he gathered that she intended to leave the next move up to him. Anticipation simmered between them.

It would have been so easy, so natural to kiss the parted lips just inches from his own. For an instant he actually considered it, even ran his tongue over his own lips in readiness.

But then he saw the predictability of it, knew that that was precisely what she was expecting. Better, he concluded, to be disappointed himself at one missed opportunity and surprise her with his restraint.

Because he wasn't a saint, he allowed her body to slide slowly along his until her feet touched the floor. Every inch of him was aware of the contact, ached with it. Still, once he was assured she was steady enough, he released her and deliberately backed away.

"Are you okay?" he asked, jamming his hands in his pockets to keep from reaching for her again.

"Fine," she said unsteadily, her eyes filled with confusion, and maybe just a hint of relief.

It was the latter that reassured him he'd made the right choice. He knew he could get to her with a kiss, knew that the chemistry was explosive enough to lead to se-duction when the time was right. But not yet, not when it would only prove every single rotten opinion she already held about him. Having the reputation of a womanizer had never especially bothered him before, because his conscience was clear when it came to each of the women he'd dated. Having Trish think the worst bothered him for reasons he wasn't sure he really wanted to explore.

Slowly, and again with careful deliberation, he turned his back on her and retrieved his sandpaper and spackle. He went back to work as if the incident had never taken place, as if his nerves weren't jumbled and his pulse weren't racing.

"Hardy?"

"Hmm?"

"What just happened here?"

He bit back a grin at the irritation in her voice. "Nothing, why?"

"It didn't feel like nothing."

He glanced over his shoulder to see that she was sit-ting on the chair now, regarding him with a perplexed expression.

"Oh?" he said innocently. "What did it feel like?"

She peered at him intently. "You honestly didn't no-tice anything?"

"Darlin', you're going to have to be more precise than that. Notice what?"

She held up her hands in a vulnerable, helpless gesture that would have drawn another smile, if he hadn't fig-ured that was a sure way to get clobbered by a hammer.

"Never mind."

He shrugged. "Whatever." He forced his attention back to the job.

"Hardy?"

"Yes."

"Why didn't you kiss me just now?"

He swallowed a laugh at the plaintive note in her voice. Keeping his expression perfectly serious, he met her gaze. "You told me no more kisses. That was the deal, wasn't it? I never go back on my word. Haven't I told you that?" He studied her an instant. "What about you? Have you changed your mind?"

"No, of course not," she said impatiently, then sighed. "I suppose you think I'm totally perverse." He grinned.

"No, what I think is that you don't know your own mind. Let's face it, you've had a bad experience with a jerk. You don't trust your own judgment. I can wait."

She eyed him warily. "Wait? For what?"

"For you to admit you want me."

Her expression froze. "Want you?" she echoed as his very explicit response sank in. "Oh, no, you are definitely wrong about that. I absolutely, positively do not want you. No way. You can just get that idea right out of your head."

He shrugged as if it made no difference to him one way or the other. "Oh well, maybe I was wrong."

"You were. Absolutely."

"Whatever you say."

"Hardy, I am serious. Don't go getting any ideas. I don't do flings."

"Of course not. No ideas," he echoed. "I'm taking you at your word."

Her gaze narrowed as if she sensed a trick, but she finally gave a little nod of satisfaction. "Good."

"Besides, you're a blunt, straightforward woman. I'm

sure you'll let me know if you change your mind," he suggested.

"I won't change my mind."

"Okay, then. It's settled. Can I get back to work now?"

"Of course." She reached for the bag of chips and began munching them as if she hadn't eaten for a month. After a couple of minutes she stared at them as if she had no idea how they'd gotten into her hand. Scowling, she dropped the bag as though she'd just discovered it was filled with worms.

"Anything wrong?" he asked.

"Not a thing," she said firmly. "I think I'll go sweep out the storeroom."

He grinned as she backed out of the room, carrying the broom in front of her as if it was meant to ward off any unwanted advances.

Oh, she wanted him, all right. Hardy recognized the signs. Unfortunately he had no idea what he should—or dared—to do about it. He had a feeling that the longer he went on playing with fire, the greater the odds were that someone was going to get burned. He had an even stronger, even more troubling feeling that this time—for the first time in the history of his social life—it could be him.

Nine

Hardy headed straight for Garden City the minute he and Trish wrapped up work on Saturday. He needed a drink. He needed a heavy dose of uncomplicated flirting. He needed to go home with a woman who wouldn't wake up in the morning with expectations.

Of course, as usual lately, what he needed and what he got were two different things.

Harlan Patrick was seated at the bar, listening raptly as his wife performed her latest song in a test run before a very friendly audience. In this one, the romance had a happy ending and the tune was upbeat, reflecting the state of their marriage. Hardy was a whole lot more comfortable hearing about broken hearts. Those songs reaffirmed his cynical conviction that real love didn't exist.

Harlan Patrick gestured toward the vacant bar stool next to him. "Join me. I'll buy you a beer."

Hardy figured the beer would come with strings attached. Harlan Patrick would probably waste no time pumping him for information about Trish and the state of the romance everyone in the Adams clan was hoping for.

"Sure, why not?" he agreed, hiding his reluctance.

Hoping for at least a temporary distraction, he added, "Laurie sounds good."

Harlan Patrick's expression brightened. "She always does."

"The song's a little different from her usual."

"Yeah. She's worried about it, too," he admitted.

"She thinks happiness is boring and that she's losing her edge. I keep telling her she could sing the phone book and her fans would be ecstatic."

"I'm sure she finds that reassuring," Hardy commented.

"No, as a matter of fact, she gives me the same 'oh sure' look you're giving me."

"Does she have another concert tour coming up?"

As Hardy expected, Harlan Patrick's expression soured.

"Not for a few more months, but that's too soon for me. I'm hoping there's enough time for me to persuade her to do a television special instead."

"You really hate it when she's on the road, don't you?"

Harlan Patrick nodded. "And now with two kids, there's even more reason for her to stay put, but I learned my lesson a few years back. If touring makes her happy, I'll figure out a way to live with it."

Laurie wrapped up her set, strolled over and put her arms around Harlan Patrick's neck. "Hey, cowboy, buy a girl a drink?"

"You've got it," he said, brightening at once.

Laurie grinned at Hardy. "So how much work did you and Trish actually get done today?"

"I see the White Pines grapevine is alive and well," Hardy noted, ignoring the question.

"Indeed. Between Kelly, who packed the lunch, and

Sharon Lynn, who crept next door to peek in the windows, we pretty much know everything," Laurie said with unrepentant glee.

"Then why ask me?"

"Confirmation, of course. Plus spin. These second-hand reports lack all the juicy details."

"Too bad," Hardy grumbled. "Because I'm not talking."

Harlan Patrick regarded him speculatively. "Is that so? I wonder why?"

"I never kiss and tell," Hardy said.

"Of course you do," his friend contradicted. "Why do you think the guys in the bunkhouse wait up for you? They're living vicariously through you."

"So, spill it," Laurie said. "Do you like her?" Now there was a dangerous question.

Hardy considered his response carefully. "Of course I like her. She's a very nice woman."

"Nice?" Laurie made a face. "What a disgustingly lukewarm description. She's beautiful."

"You'll get no argument from me about that."

"Then you are attracted to her?" she gloated, putting her own spin on things.

"I never said—"

"Give it up," Harlan Patrick advised. "Once these women get an idea into their heads, you'll only make yourself crazy trying to convince them otherwise."

"I thought your grandfather was the one I needed to watch out for," Hardy said, unable to keep a plaintive note out of his voice. At the rate the number of matchmakers was multiplying, he might as well go out and buy the blasted engagement ring.

"Where do you think they get their inspiration?" Harlan Patrick retorted. "He won't live forever and he's making darn sure that others share his skill."

Hardy noticed the amorous Rita watching him from across the room, her expression hopeful. He knew that a simple nod of his head would bring her over, knew precisely where it would lead. That was what he had wanted when he'd walked through the door, simple, uncomplicated sex.

Unfortunately all this talk about Trish had cooled his desire. He knew he'd never get her image out of his head, no matter how wickedly clever some other woman might be. He sighed with regret and forced his gaze back to Laurie and Harlan Patrick. He noted that the man was regarding him with undisguised sympathy.

"You going back into town to help her tomorrow?" Harlan Patrick asked.

"I imagine," Hardy said reluctantly.

"Maybe we should go, too," Laurie suggested. "We can make a party of it. I'll call Val and the others first thing in the morning."

Terrific, Hardy thought. Not only would he have to contend with the frustration of being around Trish without doing anything about the attraction that was building between them, but he'd have avid witnesses to his resulting discomfort.

Maybe he just wouldn't go. After all, if she had all that willing help, why did she need him? He wasn't on her payroll until Monday. He could stay at the ranch and do something physical, something that would wear him out, something that would drive any and all thoughts of Trish Delacourt and her sexy little body and vulnerable eyes out of his head. Then he could take an icy shower for good measure. Maybe if he tamed every last trace of lust, he could get through the next week without losing his mind.

The store was crawling with people, so many that they were getting in each other's way, then laughing good-naturedly about the ensuing chaos. Trish stood back and watched the various members of the Adams clan scrubbing floors, washing down walls, patching plaster and teasing each other with an affection she envied. Only Kelly was missing. She'd stayed home with Laura once again.

And Hardy, of course. Trish's gaze shot to the door each time it swung open, but he hadn't shown up. She kept telling herself it didn't matter, that he wasn't obligated to be here today, but she missed him more than she wanted to admit.

"Looking for anyone in particular?" Laurie asked, sneaking up beside her.

"Of course not," Trish denied, fully aware of the heat that scalded her cheeks.

"Well, if you are looking for Hardy, I think I'm responsible for him not being here."

"Why on earth would you think that?"

"To tell you the truth, I might have scared him off," Laurie admitted. "He was in Garden City last night."

"Oh, really?" Trish said. "With a woman?"

The telling question popped out before she could stop herself.

Laurie grinned. "No, alone. Anyway, we got to talking after one of my sets. I suppose I was prying a little too much. It might have made him skittish."

"Prying? About what?"

"The two of you."

"There is no two of us," she said vehemently.

Laurie chuckled. "Funny. He denied it, too. Almost as emphatically as you just did. Makes me wonder, especially since you seem to be so fascinated by whether or not he was by himself."

"What exactly are you wondering about?" Trish asked warily.

"Why you're both protesting so hard. What would be wrong with the two of you getting together?"

"Hardy is not interested in a serious relationship," Trish said. "He likes chasing women, plural. I've just gotten out of one relationship with a man of similar inclinations. I don't intend to jump back into that particular frying pan."

Laurie nodded, her expression thoughtful. "Yes, I can see how that could be a problem. Then just be friends. Nothing wrong with that, is there?"

"I don't think a man like Hardy is capable of being just friends with a woman."

"Try it. He might surprise you."

Trish recalled that he had said much the same thing. "I'm at the point in my life where the fewer surprises I have, the better."

Laurie looked horrified. "Oh, don't say that. If there are no surprises, you're settling. You're not living. Trust me, you'll be bored to tears in no time."

"After the past few months, boredom sounds downright refreshing," Trish countered. She chuckled at Laurie's downcast expression. "Don't look so glum. My life is exactly the way I want it to be right now. I have a beautiful baby girl. I'm about to open a new business. What more could I possibly want?"

"Someone to share it all with," Laurie suggested, clearly undaunted.

"I have all of you," Trish said. "I feel as if I've found a whole slew of new friends."

"Well, of course, you have, but—"

"No buts," Trish insisted. "This is for the best." The door opened, and her gaze swung toward it.

Laurie chuckled at her obvious disappointment when it turned out to be Val and Slade.

"You're deluding yourself," Laurie told her with undisguised amusement. "But far be it from me to destroy the illusion. If you don't mind, though, I think I'll just sit back and see what develops. My money's on love."

Between the conversation with Laurie and a flurry of innuendoes from every other person who dropped by, Trish was downright cranky by the time she got back to Jordan and Kelly's. She was also convinced that she needed to put some distance between herself and the meddling Adamses.

She headed straight for the portable bassinet Kelly had set up in the living room and picked up her daughter. Thankfully there was at least one person she could count on who wouldn't be badgering her with questions about Hardy.

"How's mama's darling girl?" she asked the sleepy baby.

"She's been a little angel," Kelly assured her. "No fussing. Drank every last drop of her bottle and went right back to sleep. I kept hoping she'd wake up so I could play with her, but no such luck."

"Thanks for taking care of her."

"It was my pleasure. Besides, I had some help."

"Oh?"

"Hardy dropped by."

Trish stared. "He did?"

"Never really said what he wanted, but I assumed it was to see your precious little one. He fed her and rocked her as if he'd been doing it all his life. They had quite a chat. I tried eavesdropping, but he kept his voice too low for me to hear," she said, obviously disgruntled.

"Are you sure he didn't come by to see Jordan or something?" Trish asked.

"Nope. He seemed to know that Jordan was out of town and that you were at the store." She grinned. "I'll admit, Laura was wailing and I sort of shoved her into his arms while I fixed her bottle, but when I came back into the room, he was cooing at her like a proud papa. He settled her right down. You should have seen him with her. It would have melted your heart."

Trish didn't doubt it. She sank into a chair. What on earth had possessed him to drop by? she wondered. Apparently the fact that he'd delivered Laura had created a more powerful bond than she'd realized, not just with her, but with her daughter. Just as obvious was the fact that he didn't want her to know about it. He'd deliberately chosen to come by when he'd known she wouldn't be there, as if he feared her making too much out of whatever attention he paid to the baby.

She glanced away from the baby's face and realized Kelly was staring at her with a puzzled expression.

"You're not upset because he spent time with Laura, are you?"

"No, of course not. I'm just surprised."

"How did things go at the store? Did you get a lot of work done?"

"Yes." When everyone hadn't been busy prying into

her love life, she thought wryly. "Everyone was wonderful. But I can't go on depending on all of you for everything. I need to start making my own plans for living arrangements."

"Absolutely not," Kelly said. "There's plenty of room here, and we love having you. Once you get the store up and running, if you want to find your own place we'll help you. In the meantime, I'm right here to look after Laura while you work. It's winter, so there's less for me to do on the ranch. I always get a little antsy this time of year. I'm glad of the distraction. Besides, if you moved now, you'd have to find a sitter. You can't take Laura with you. She has no business being there while you're painting."

"I suppose you're right," Trish admitted. "Staying here for the time being does make sense."

"Of course it does. So, that's the end of that."

Kelly peered at her. "What brought that up out of the blue, anyway? Too many nosy people trying to run your life today?"

Trish grinned at the assessment. "Something like that."

"Ignore us. No one means any harm. We just can't help ourselves."

"One person I could ignore. Maybe even two," Trish argued. "But there are so many of you."

"And we're all right," Kelly teased. "Still doesn't mean you have to listen to us. Tune us out. Make your own decisions. Tell us to take a flying leap, if it suits you. We won't be insulted. In fact, we're used to it."

"Yes, I imagine you are," Trish said, thinking that however many insults had been hurled at them over the years, they remained steadfastly undaunted when it came to meddling.

"Can I ask one last nosy question before I quit for the night?"

Trish regarded her with amusement. "Could I stop you?"

"Probably not."

"Then go for it."

"Are you even the teeniest bit tempted by Hardy? I mean the man is seriously gorgeous. Even I'm not too old to recognize that."

Trish sighed heavily and admitted, "I'd have to be dead not to be."

Kelly grinned. "Then we're not wasting our time. Good."

Too late, Trish realized that she'd just offered encouragement to an entire clan of matchmakers. Now they'd never in a million years believe that their cause was hopeless.

Hardy finally discovered a serious flaw in Trish.

When it came to choosing the wood for her bookshelves, she couldn't make a decision to save her soul. Unfortunately he found her indecision more amusing than annoying.

She hadn't been satisfied with the selection at a local lumber company, so he'd suggested a trip to Garden City. Now they were surrounded by samples of maple, pine, oak, cherry and mahogany. She rubbed her fingers over the grain. She sniffed deeply, as if she might be swayed by the fragrance alone. She studied the prices, punched numbers into her little pocket calculator and noted them on the paper they'd brought with measurements. Then she sighed and went through the same routine all over again.

Hardy lounged against a pile of two-by-fours and watched her. When he could stand it no longer, he asked, "Mind if I make a suggestion?"

She blinked and stared at him as if she'd just realized he was along. "Sure."

"Buy the less expensive wood and stain it to get the effect you want. I'm assuming what you're going for is something warm. You keep gravitating toward the cherry. A few cans of stain and a little work and you'll have the next best thing."

Her expression brightened. Before he realized her intention, she threw her arms around him and gave him a smacking kiss on the cheek. "You're a genius! I want the cherry so badly I can taste it, but the cost would really eat into my budget. Do you really think the stain won't look cheap?"

Hardy couldn't think at all. That little kiss-and-run gesture of hers had left him reeling. All the hard work he'd done over the weekend to make himself believe that what he felt was nothing more than infatuation was wasted.

"Hardy?"

He swallowed hard. "It'll look fine," he assured her. "I'm sure there are samples over there with the stains, so you can get an idea of how it would look."

"Of course," she said, and darted off.

He drew in a deep breath and tried to reclaim his composure before he followed her to the next aisle. She was already holding up little blocks of wood and examining them this way and that. When she caught sight of him, she beamed, and his heart did another of those annoying little flips.

"Look," she enthused. "It will work, don't you think? You can't tell this isn't really cherry."

"That's the idea," he pointed out. "If it didn't work, no one would do it."

She frowned at him. "Okay, smarty. Just order the stain and the wood," she said, handing him the sheet with their measurements before bounding off.

"Where are you going?"

"To see about renting a sander and polisher to refinish those floors. They're going to gleam by the time we're done."

Hardy seriously doubted that anything short of sandblasting would clean the grime off those floors, but he shrugged and went to order the lumber. By the time he'd finished, Trish was at the checkout counter with her own purchases, which included two huge concrete flower planters.

"What are those for?" he asked.

"On either side of the front door. I'll fill them with different flowers, depending on the season. They're going to deliver the potting soil with the lumber."

Hardy had never been able to see the sense in planting and tending flowers that served no useful purpose. A garden was meant to be productive. All that work ought to result in tomatoes, peppers, corn and beans, at the very least. It was just one more difference between them. Practicality versus daydreams.

"Do you have a problem with flowers?" she asked, regarding him with amusement.

"Not on principle," he said. "Besides, you're the one who's going to have to take care of them."

"Exactly," she said, then wrote a check for the staggering total without even batting an eye.

Even after they were in his truck, Hardy couldn't shake his unease about the amount of money she was throwing around. "Don't think I haven't noticed that you're paying as you go, just so Harlan can't get at the bills. Are you sure you're not spending too much on fixing the place up?"

"Absolutely not. It has to have the right atmosphere from the very beginning. You can't make up for a poor first impression."

Hardy wondered about that. He and Trish hadn't exactly gotten off on the right foot, but he'd pretty much forgotten her snippy attitude, attributing it to temporary stress. Now he couldn't seem to shake the effect of all her good points.

Of course, the same couldn't be said for her. She'd been holding tight to her first impression of him, probably because it was getting reinforced at every turn.

"Obviously you know what you're doing," he said eventually. "What's next?"

"Are there any antique shops nearby?"

"Probably downtown. That's the historic district. I seem to recall passing a few in that area."

"Show me," she commanded as if he were a tour guide she'd hired for the day.

He scowled at her. "You know, darlin', you might not have liked being the pampered baby in the family, but you seem to have developed a real fondness for behaving like a princess."

She stopped dead in her tracks. "Excuse me?"

"The high-and-mighty tone," he explained. "You're the one who asked what I wanted to do next."

"So I did. Forget it."

"No. I think we should talk about this. Aren't you the one who insisted that this whole project was strictly business, that you were doing a job, not a favor?"

He didn't like where she was heading with this one little bit. "Yes. So?"

"So that makes you my employee for all intents and purposes."

"And you think that means you get to order me around like some loyal subject?" he demanded, ignoring the fact that he'd told her to do that very thing on Saturday.

"Of course not," she said, her complexion flushed. She heaved a sigh. "Hardy, sometimes I don't know what to make of you. I have no idea what you really want."

Hearing her confusion, it was his turn to sigh. "Sometimes I'm not sure myself."

He gazed into eyes the same shade of blue as the brilliant winter sky. "Except for this," he murmured, bending his head to capture her lips beneath his.

Oblivious to their surroundings, oblivious to everything except the feel of satin under his mouth, he threw himself into the kiss.

He didn't touch her, didn't put a hand on her, but the swirl of heat from the kiss alone was enough to melt steel. His blood roared through his veins. His heart pounded. The mysterious, exotic scent of her teased his senses. He sank into the kiss, dragging her with him until they were both unsteady, both all but gasping for breath.

Her eyes were wide with shock when he finally pulled back. Her lips were swollen with the look of a mouth that had just been thoroughly, devastatingly devoured.

"Oh, sweet heaven," she whispered, touching her

trembling fingers to her lips as if she couldn't quite believe how they had betrayed her.

"This isn't supposed to…it can't be…"

Hardy grinned at her incoherence. "Darlin', I know
you're quite a talker, but I don't think you can talk this
away. Words aren't going to change anything. And I don't
think *supposed to* has anything to do with it."

Her gaze narrowed. He caught the quick rise of temper.

"Are you pleased with yourself because you managed
to get a physical reaction out of me?" she demanded.

That was one way of putting how he felt, Hardy supposed, but he sensed that he'd be smarter to deny it. "I
enjoyed kissing you, there's no question about that," he
said carefully. "You going to deny you enjoyed it?"

She looked as if she wanted to, looked as if the denial
were on the tip of her tongue, but she was too innately
honest to pull off the lie.

"Okay, it was a great kiss."

"Just like the last one," he suggested.

She scowled. "Don't push it. The point is, a kiss is
just a momentary phenomenon. In our case it also rep-
resents a lapse in judgment."

Hardy couldn't help it. He chuckled. "You are so cute
when you get all prim and earnest."

Practically trembling with rage, she stared at him.
"This is not a game, Hardy Jones. I will not be another
notch on your bedpost. If that's what you've got in mind,
you can take your little innuendoes and your flirting
and your help and go straight to hell." She flounced off
before he could snap his mouth closed. She was two
blocks away before he caught up with her. He'd figured

it would take at least that long for her to cool down and listen to reason.

When he fell into step beside her, he noted that her color was still high, her mood still precarious. He opted for silence. Maybe after another block or two, he'd think of something to say to soothe her ruffled feathers.

"That's not what this is about," he finally said quietly.

She kept her gaze straight ahead and remained stoically silent.

"To tell you the honest truth, I'm not sure what it's about," he admitted. "I've broken every single one of my rules where you're concerned."

She finally stole a glance at him. "Oh?"

"You're vulnerable and innocent," he began.

"I'm an unwed mother," she pointed out.

"Hardly innocent."

"A technicality," he insisted. "In my book you're innocent. And you have a daughter, who could be hurt if we don't play by the rules."

She regarded him with confusion. "Whose rules are we talking about now? Yours?"

"No, society's."

"I had no idea you even knew what those were."

"Oh, I know. I just prefer to ignore most of them." He met her gaze. "I can't with you. You come from a good family. You have permanence and happily ever after written all over you. I'm a ranch hand who doesn't think much farther ahead than tomorrow. I'm all about living in the moment. We're not suited."

To his chagrin, she nodded. "I agree."

"Then why can't I keep my hands off you?" he asked, genuinely perplexed. "Why can't I get you out of my head? Usually I steer so far away from women like you, we're practically not even in the same state."

"Probably because you know we'd be a disaster, which makes me forbidden. People always want what they can't have, what's bad for them. It's just a totally irrational fascination, one we just have to try harder to nip in the bud."

"You think so?"

"I know so," she said with confidence. "So now that that's clear, we can just settle down and be friends. Deal?"

"Friends," Hardy echoed dutifully. He didn't even need the impact of that last kiss to tell him that they had a snowball's chance in hell of pulling that off.

Ten

Friendship should have suited Trish just fine. It was what she had asked for, wasn't it? And Hardy was throwing himself into the role with total dedication. He hadn't so much as glanced straight into her eyes, much less uttered a teasing remark to her for the past two weeks.

He also went to great lengths to avoid touching her. If he handed her something, he released it practically before she could get a grip on it, just to ensure that their fingers didn't brush. He was prompt, cheerful and helpful. She couldn't fault him for that. The store was taking shape a whole lot faster than she'd anticipated. In fact, she suspected he couldn't finish the job fast enough.

So why was she so disgruntled at the end of every day? Why did she feel as if she'd lost something precious?

Because she was a ninny, that's why. Friendship was what she'd asked for. Friendship was what she'd gotten. If she wasn't satisfied, then it was her own fault.

She glanced over at Hardy who'd stripped off his shirt to display a devastatingly muscular back and shoulders that a body builder would have envied. He was bent over a sawhorse, cutting through a piece of lumber for the last set of shelves. Staring at his gleaming flesh, at the bunching of his muscles, her mouth went dry. His tush wasn't bad, either, she concluded when she shifted her gaze in that direction.

Sweet heaven, what was happening to her? She was turning into some sort of sex-crazed female. Maybe it was all the hormonal ups and downs her body had been through lately. She seized on that explanation like a lifeline. That had to be it. It couldn't possibly be personal when they had decided, very clearly, very plainly, that friendship was all that was in the cards for the two of them.

"Trish?"

She snapped back to reality and met his gaze. Was she mistaken or was there a wicked, knowing twinkle in his eyes? Had he guessed what she was thinking?

"Yes," she snapped more tersely than he deserved. She was instantly riddled with guilt, but she bit back the urge to apologize. She'd been doing that too much the past few days, making excuses every time her temper flared, trying to dismiss with nonsense the erratic behavior that could only be explained honestly by admitting to pure sexual frustration. Which of course she had no intention of admitting to, ever.

"You okay?" he asked, studying her intently.

That was another thing that drove her crazy. He was so blasted thoughtful, so unrelentingly considerate. He always seemed to know when she was tired, when she needed a break, when something was on her mind. Just the way a friend would, she thought sourly.

"I'm fine," she said, trying for a more eventempered tone. "Just distracted."

"Let's take a break," he said at once, regarding her worriedly. "I could use a milkshake. How about you?"

"A milkshake sounds good." Anything that would get him out of the store for a few minutes so she could gather her wits.

"Come with me. You can visit with Sharon Lynn for a bit. She asks about you every time I go into Dolan's to get something. She's complaining that you're right next door and you never drop by."

There was a good reason for that, Trish thought. Sharon Lynn was a direct pipeline to the rest of the family. The less Trish saw of her, especially in Hardy's company, the better.

"Not this time," she said. "I have things to do."

"What things?" he asked, deliberately testing her.

"Things," she declared more emphatically.

He chuckled. "Darlin', you're going to have to be more specific than that or Sharon Lynn will think you don't like her."

"I like her just fine. And you don't have to tell her that I'm doing *things,* just that I'm busy."

Hardy's gaze narrowed. "I think I'm beginning to figure out the problem. You don't want her to see us together. Is that it?"

"Of course not."

"Oh, I think it is. Because if she sees us together, she'll draw all sorts of wild conclusions, report them straight back to Harlan or the others and, *bam,* we'll be right back where we started."

Trish sighed at his perceptiveness. "Bingo." Why did the man have to have so many admirable traits? Why did he have to be perceptive, of all things? Men were usually clueless. When she'd thought of him as nothing more than a handsome, sexy scoundrel, they'd both been better off.

He tucked a finger under her chin and forced her to meet his gaze. Her skin tingled, even from such a simple touch, and Hardy looked as if he'd been singed. Still, he gazed at her evenly, his expression serious.

"Surely we can behave for fifteen minutes," he teased. "I won't kiss you senseless in front of her, the way I do at least ten times a day in here, when we're all alone. I will keep my hands to myself. She won't suspect a thing."

Trish chuckled despite herself. "Okay, I suppose we don't have to give her anything to report back to the army of meddlers. In fact, it might be good if we're seen out in public doing absolutely nothing romantic or personal."

"I'll even let you pay for your own shake, so no one will think it's a date."

"Fine. I'll get my purse." She glanced at him worriedly. "You are going to put on your shirt, aren't you?"

He shot her a look of pure innocence. "Me being halfnaked doesn't bother you, does it?"

"Of course not," she lied, perfectly well aware that he'd deliberately chosen the word *naked* just to rattle her. She refused to let him see that she was suddenly awash in images of him without a stitch of clothing from head to toe. Keeping her voice cool, she said, "But you'll freeze if you step outside like that, and besides, I'm pretty sure Dolan's has a shirt-and-shoes policy."

Good, sound, rational reasoning, she thought.

Hardy laughed.

"Then by all means, let me grab my shirt," he said, his eyes twinkling with unabashed amusement. Five minutes later they strolled next door. At twothirty, the lunch counter was deserted. Sharon Lynn was scrubbing the grill. She brightened when she saw them.

"Oh, am I glad to see you," she said. "I can take a break. I hate this job. It's one of those necessary evils I can't seem to make myself foist off on the part-time help. Are you here for food, sundaes, what?"

"Milkshakes," Hardy told her. "Thick, chocolate for me."

"Make that two," Trish said.

"How's the work coming on the store?" Sharon Lynn asked as she put double scoops of chocolate ice cream and milk into the metal container and attached it to the machine that would stir it into an old-fashioned, thick, frothy shake.

"The shelves should be done this week. I'm expecting my book order on Monday. I figure I'll be open by the first of March," Trish told her. "I thought I'd have some sort of grand opening party."

"Let me do the food," Sharon Lynn volunteered. "I can fix things other than burgers and fries. I'd love to do it. There are days when I'd kill to be able to make pretty little hors d'oeuvres."

"Work up a menu and a price list and you're on," Trish said.

"No price list," Sharon Lynn said. "The Adams family will pitch in. It will be our grand-opening present."

"I can't let you do that," Trish argued.

Sharon Lynn exchanged a look with Hardy. "Tell her," she commanded.

"It won't do you any good to argue," he said. "They're a stubborn bunch."

Trish heaved a sigh. "So I've noticed."

Sharon Lynn beamed. "Good. That's settled. I will

let you okay the menu, though, in case there's anything you absolutely hate. Do you want TexMex? Something more formal?"

"I'll trust your judgment. Whatever will bring the most people out."

"This time of year, when winter boredom has set in, you could get them out for chips and dip," Hardy said.

"I think I can do better than that," Sharon Lynn said, grabbing a pad of paper, a pen and moving out from behind the counter to sit beside Trish. "Okay, let's decide on a theme. How about English tea? Doesn't that sound perfect for a bookstore? You could do it on a Sunday afternoon."

"I love it," Trish said, enchanted. "That's exactly the sort of atmosphere I want to create."

"Tea?" Hardy echoed disdainfully. "Itty-bitty sandwiches? We're talking cowboys here, ladies. Big appetites."

"He has a point," Sharon Lynn said.

"Then we'll have lots of itty-bitty sandwiches," Trish said. "And scones and cakes."

Hardy's expression brightened. "Cakes? Personally I like chocolate with fudge icing."

"Petits fours," Trish informed him, enjoying the way his expression fell. "Itty-bitty individual cakes," she added for emphasis.

"Girl food," he declared, dismissing it.

"Women buy more books than men," she pointed out. "Why shouldn't I cater to their tastes?"

"Yoo-hoo," Sharon Lynn said, waving a hand between them. "Remember me?"

They stared at her as if they'd forgotten her existence. Trish barely restrained a moan. This was exactly what she'd hoped to avoid. She and Hardy had been so busy arguing with each other, Sharon Lynn might as well have been on the moon. And Sharon Lynn knew it, too. The knowing sparkle in her eyes was proof of it.

"I think we can update the tea idea a bit to satisfy the male appetites," she told Trish. "I'll make a more substantial filling for some of the sandwiches, maybe some little ham biscuits or even miniature barbeque buns."

"Better," Hardy agreed.

Trish scowled at him. "I'm so delighted you approve."

"Regular cake, too," he said, ignoring her and appealing directly to Sharon Lynn. "Sliced thick, with lots of frosting."

"I hate to say it," Sharon Lynn said, "but knowing the men in my family, they'd go along with Hardy on this one."

Trish recognized when she was beat. "Okay, regular cake, then."

"What about beer?" Hardy asked.

"Not on your life," Trish declared. "Champagne, maybe. Sharon Lynn, what do you think?"

"Let's stick with tea. It will be Sunday afternoon. We'd better do both hot tea and iced, though. I can't see these clumsy men balancing little tea cups in their hands while they shovel cake into their mouths. The phrase *bull in a china shop* comes to mind."

"Hey," Hardy protested. "Men are not clumsy."

"I still think we'd better not risk Granddaddy Harlan's best porcelain, which I intend to borrow for the occasion. He's the only one who has enough for a huge crowd." She made another note on her paper, then turned back to Trish. "What about invitations?"

"Since you two seem to be caught up in party planning, I think I'll go back next door and get some work done," Hardy said.

To Trish's discomfort, he gave her shoulder a quick, friendly squeeze before he left. Naturally Sharon Lynn caught the affectionate gesture. No doubt her imagination would run wild.

"You two seem to be getting along well," she observed, her gaze fixed on Trish's face.

"Well enough," Trish said. "About the invitations—"

Sharon Lynn cut her off, her expression alight with curiosity. "What have you two been doing all day long over there?"

"Working," Trish said, not even trying to hide her impatience. "What else?"

"Besides that?"

"Nothing," Trish declared very firmly. "There's a lot of work to be done."

"Nothing?" Sharon Lynn regarded her with a mix of disbelief and disappointment. "I thought for sure by now..." Her voice trailed off.

Trish shrugged. "Sorry. Now about those invitations, how many do you think I should have printed?"

She finally managed to drag Sharon Lynn's attention back to the task at hand. By the time she left an hour later, they had worked out most of the details for the grand-opening party. She was also pretty sure she had managed to squelch any speculation that she and Hardy were a hot item.

As she opened the front door of her store, she heard voices from the storeroom. Male voices. One, of course, was Hardy's. The other was... She listened more intently, recognized the familiar lazy drawl and almost turned around and dashed right straight back out of the building. Before she could, Hardy came in, caught sight of her and called out.

"Hey, Trish, look who's here."

Her stomach knotted as her oldest brother followed Hardy into the room.

"Dylan, what are you doing here?" she demanded tightly. "How did you find me?"

A grin spread across his face, despite the lack of welcome. "I'm a private detective, Sis. Finding people is what I do."

"Well, go find somebody else. I don't want to be found," she said, stubbornly refusing to walk into his embrace.

Dylan was as close to a rebel as any male in the Delacourt family had been allowed to get. Disgustingly handsome and fully aware of it, he'd left a trail of broken hearts in his wake until he'd met his wife and she'd turned around and left *him* with one, taking their son right along with her. Dylan had balked at going into the oil business. After listening to his father rant and rave for months, he'd gone right ahead with his own plans for his life. He, of all of her brothers, should have understood why she'd needed to get out. Obviously he didn't because he was here, probably intent on dragging her home again.

His expression softened. "I haven't told Dad where you are," he said quietly. "This is just between us."

Hope spread through her. "You swear it?"

"Cross my heart."

Then she did fly into his embrace. "I've missed you, Dylan. I would have called you, but I didn't want you to get caught between Dad and me."

"When have I ever been scared to take a bunch of garbage from Dad?" he scoffed.

"I didn't want you to because of me." She turned to Hardy. "Have you met?"

"We've met," Hardy said.

"For a minute I thought he was going to take me on, until he realized I was your brother and not Jack the jerk." He gestured at the work they'd accomplished. "I like it. It's going to be even better than the store in Houston."

She nodded. "I think so, too."

"Look, why don't you two go on?" Hardy suggested. "I'm sure you have a lot of catching up to do. I'll finish and lock up here."

"Only if you'll join us for dinner," Dylan said. "Is there someplace close we can go?"

"I'm sure Hardy already has plans," Trish said hurriedly. She didn't want her big brother getting any ideas about her and Hardy. He could be as much of a nag as an Adams. "Besides, I want you to come out to the ranch and see your niece."

"Another time," Hardy said. "Once you get a look at little Laura, you won't want to leave her. I guarantee it."

"A real beauty like her mama, huh?" Dylan said.

"Pretty as a picture from the moment she was born," Hardy said. "I ought to know. I was there." Trish knew he had said that deliberately, that he was staking his claim on the two of them so her brother wouldn't mistake it. Not that Dylan was likely to go more than a minute without plaguing her with questions about Hardy, anyway.

"I'll explain on the way," she said, drawing Dylan toward the door, even as she shot a scowl over her shoulder at Hardy. Obviously unintimidated, he winked.

"Nice to meet you, Dylan. I hope to see you again before you go."

"Count on it," Dylan said, regarding him speculatively.

Trish dragged her brother out of the store. "Where's your car?"

"Across the street. Where's yours?"

"At the ranch. Hardy drove me in."

He waited until after they were in his sports utility vehicle before he glanced over at her and asked idly, "So what's going on between you and the cowboy?"

She seized on the label, rather than answering him directly. "How do you know he's a cowboy?"

"He told me. He said this work for you is just some temporary gig his boss set up."

"Exactly."

"Now that that's out of the way, why don't you tell me what's going on between the two of you?"

"Nothing," she said flatly.

"Look, Patricia Ann, you might be able to fool some people with the innocent act, but not me. There were enough sparks in that room just now to light up Houston."

"Don't be ridiculous."

"Okay, let's try this another way. Why did you decide to stay in a town like Los Piños?"

"I like it here," she said with a touch of defiance.

"What is it you like?" he persisted patiently.

The persistence and the patience were both traits that served him well as a private eye. As a brother, they made him damned annoying.

"The people," she said tightly. "Everyone here has been wonderful to me."

"Including this Hardy person."

"Yes, of course. He's been very helpful."

"How did you meet?"

She scowled at him. "Is this really necessary? I am not some criminal you're cross-examining."

"No, you're my sister, which makes this personal. How did you meet?"

She sighed. "I was stranded on the side of the road New Year's Eve. He came along."

"And?"

"I was in labor," she finally ground out. "He delivered Laura."

Dylan's eyes widened. "Well, well, well. Isn't that interesting? No wonder he's so attached to your daughter. I assume he's single."

"An inveterate playboy," she acknowledged, hoping the description would be enough to tell him why Hardy would never be a serious candidate for a husband.

Dylan didn't seem convinced. "You sure about that, sis? He struck me as a solid guy. He obviously cares about you and the baby."

"He's been very kind. And he's definitely a decent guy, which is why we have agreed that we will be friends and leave it at that."

Dylan turned and stared at her as if she'd calmly announced a decision to fly off to Mars. "You've agreed to be friends?"

"Yes."

A grin tugged at the corners of his mouth. The grin spread, displaying the devastating dimple that drove women crazy. "Oh, Sis, you are in such deep trouble."

"I beg your pardon?"

He regarded her patiently. "Men and women do not agree to be just friends, unless they're fighting the urge to be a whole lot more."

She frowned. "And you would know this because…? Is it your vast success rate with members of the opposite sex? Or the psychology degree you apparently received without me knowing about it?"

"Experience," he insisted, still chortling with glee at what he viewed as her self-deception. "I've reached a few of those agreements myself. Meant 'em at the time, too. Bottom line, though? They're not worth the time they take to spew the words out. In fact, the opposite is true. Once you've declared each other off-limits, the attraction escalates. Label something forbidden and everybody wants it. That's human nature."

"Thank you, Dr. Ruth." She was very much afraid he was right. She certainly hadn't been able to stop thinking about Hardy in a sexual way since she'd made the decision to keep things strictly platonic. In fact, the whole friendship thing was making her a little crazy.

"Just how bad do you have it for this guy?" Dylan asked.

"I don't. We're just friends," she said one more time as if repetition would make it true.

Her brother shrugged. "Fine by me, if that's the truth. Probably just as well, too."

Her gaze shot to his face. He was staring out the windshield, his gaze locked on the highway, his expression suddenly way too innocent. "What do you mean, it's probably just as well?"

"Dad would hate him."

"Why on earth would he hate him? He's a fine man, better than Jack the jerk, by a long shot."

"But he's not an oilman. He can't be heir apparent to a vice presidency in the family business."

"Neither are you, but he tolerates you."

"I'm blood. He can't wish me away."

Trish waved off the whole discussion as absurd. "It doesn't matter. They'll probably never even meet."

Dylan's expression sobered at last. "Then you don't intend to tell Dad where you are?"

She sighed. "Sooner or later I suppose I'll have to. I'm amazed his private detectives don't already know where I am. After all, you found me."

"I'm better than most of those goons he keeps on staff. They're better at white collar crime than chasing wayward daughters."

"How did you find me?"

"It was pathetically simple, really."

"How?"

"You transferred your money from your bank account in Houston to the bank here."

Trish groaned. "I'm obviously not career criminal material."

"Thank the Lord."

"You are going to keep this a secret, right? You promised."

"On two conditions."

"What?"

"You check in with me regularly."

"Done."

"And you keep an open mind about the cowboy."

So, they were back to that again. "Why are you pushing so hard to make something happen between us?" she asked, genuinely puzzled. Dylan had never been prone to counseling her on her love life before. "Because I saw the way he looked at you, Sis. It's not something you should ever take for granted."

She caught the shadows in his eyes and realized he

was thinking of Kit, the woman who'd stolen his heart and then shattered it. Or if not of his ex-wife, then definitely of his son. Dylan missed Shane terribly, but he refused to admit it.

"Kit was a witch," she declared fiercely.

"No," he said just as vehemently. "I took her for granted. I neglected her. It was my fault she walked out. It took me a long time to admit it, but that's the God's honest truth."

"Then go after her, Dylan. Get her back, if you still love her."

"Too late. She got married again last week. I let her and the new hubby get full custody of Shane."

Trish was shocked and filled with pity. She knew what a terrible sacrifice her brother was making. She even thought she could understand why he'd made it. Dylan wouldn't want his son torn between two fathers. "Oh, Dylan, I'm so sorry."

He shrugged. "Too bad these brilliant flashes of self-awareness come too late. Don't you sit around until it's too late, Trish. I'd give anything to have my baby back and somebody who looks at me the way your cowboy looks at you."

"You will," she promised him. Maybe she'd go about finding the perfect candidate herself.

No sooner had the thought occurred to her than she realized that she'd been around Adamses way too long. She had four bachelor brothers and she was in serious danger of catching the matchmaking fever that seemed to be contagious in Los Piños.

Eleven

Hardy couldn't sleep. He kept thinking about the unexpected arrival of Trish's brother. He wasn't sure which of them it had shaken more, him or Trish. For Trish there had been the fear of discovery. For him it had meant the possible end to having her to himself. It had meant Laura's father might be only hours or days away from finding her, as well.

Trish claimed to want nothing to do with Jack Grainger, but when she was face-to-face with her daughter's father, would she be able to resist? Especially with her own father pressuring her?

When the stranger had first walked into the store asking for Trish, Hardy's muscles had tensed. His stomach had knotted. He wasn't crazy about the idea of any man that good-looking having a claim on her.

For five minutes, maybe longer, the possibility that he'd been the father of her baby had eaten Hardy up inside until Dylan Delacourt had finally gotten around to introducing himself.

Once Trish had turned up, some sort of mental telepathy had been exchanged between brother and sister. After that Dylan's gaze had turned speculative. He seemed to be sizing up Hardy as if he guessed that Hardy might be more than the man who was helping her build the shelves for her store. Since Dylan had suggested dinner, Hardy figured he'd either passed muster or that further interrogation was required.

Hardy wasn't entirely sure how he felt about that. He figured he already had too many people passing judgment on how he and Trish matched up as a couple. They'd been under scrutiny and under pressure since day one. For two people who had vowed to avoid marriage like the plague, it amounted to a whole lot of unwanted interference.

After Trish and Dylan had left for the ranch, Hardy had spent the evening putting the finishing touches on the shelves. He hadn't much felt like going back to the bunkhouse and enduring the inevitable teasing about his recent lack of a social life and the taunting speculation about what it meant.

Nor had the prospect of going to any of his usual haunts appealed to him. Not one single name from his little black book popped into his head. The only woman he wanted to spend the evening with was otherwise occupied. Everyone else seemed like a poor substitute. It was pathetic. What the hell was happening to him?

With the last of the shelves built and ready for the books that would be arriving any day, he had turned his attention to the floor. He spent another hour with the sander, then polished the wood until the old planks gleamed.

When he was through, he'd stood by the front door and studied the bookstore. As a child he hadn't spent a lot of time reading books, and those he had read had been borrowed from a library. As an adult, he'd never found the time either. He could see, though, how a place like this would be appealing. There was an inviting warmth to it, a hominess, a personal charm that was all Trish.

In fact, he could imagine curling up in one of those big chairs Trish had found and recovered with bright chintz. He could practically feel her settled in his lap, a beer in his hand, a glass of wine in hers, as the fire flickered cheerfully. The image aroused him as none of his past conquests ever had.

He'd finally left the store after ten, exhausted and frustrated but pleased, as he anticipated Trish's reaction when they arrived in the morning and she discovered all that he'd accomplished in her absence. The work was all but over now. Soon he'd be back in the saddle and working at White Pines. His only contact with Trish would be by chance unless something changed.

Back at the bunkhouse, he'd crawled into bed, then tossed and turned for an hour before finally giving up and going outside. Maybe a walk would settle his nerves and wipe out the thoughts that kept churning no matter how hard he tried to shut them off.

He automatically gravitated toward the creek. Even in winter, he found solace in the fast-moving water and rustling of the wind. On a night like tonight, with a full moon and a sharp nip in the air, there was something almost magical about it.

As he neared the water, he thought he heard the soft whisper of crying. Slipping quietly through the shadows, he walked toward the sound, then halted at the sight of Trish, sitting on a boulder, her knees drawn up, her coat wrapped tightly around her. She looked so dejected, so completely lost and alone, it almost broke his heart.

He stood there forever debating what to do. Obviously she had come here to be by herself, to sort out whatever demons were troubling her after her visit with her brother. Maybe Dylan had tried to convince her to go home, Hardy thought, and mentally cursed the man. Hardy might not know exactly what he wanted from Trish, but he did know he didn't want her leaving. Even in such a brief time, she had become a part of his life. Little Laura had stolen his heart.

Whatever had brought Trish here tonight, though, he had the sense that she wouldn't welcome him catching her at such a vulnerable moment. He settled for remaining out of sight, watching over her until she decided finally to leave, then following at a discreet distance as she made the long walk back to Kelly and Jordan's. Only when she was safely inside, did he go back to his own bed, where he finally fell into a restless sleep.

In the morning Hardy felt as if he'd been on an all-night bender. It was a sensation he was familiar with but this time had done nothing to deserve. That made him irritable.

When he got to Jordan's ranch, he pounded on the front door as if that carved oak barrier had offended him.

"What on earth?" Kelly demanded, when she opened it. "Hardy, is something wrong?"

He winced, then shook his head. "Sorry."

"Come on in and have some coffee. You look as though you could use it."

"No, thanks," he said, well aware that he wasn't fit company. "I'll wait in the car."

"It could be a long wait. You might as well come in. Trish isn't quite ready. She had a rough night last night, and Laura's been fussing since way before dawn."

It was the mention of the baby that got to him. "Where is she?"

Kelly regarded him with amusement. "Laura? In the kitchen in her bassinet, squalling up a storm. She seems to be unhappy about everything today. Maybe she's catching on to her mother's mood. Trish has been distracted and sad ever since her brother left."

"Let me have a try at settling Laura down," he said, already heading in that direction. He could hear the pitiful wails before he was halfway down the hall. When he reached her, she was red-faced and waving her tiny fists in the air as if to protest being neglected.

"Come here, angel," he murmured, picking her up and settling her against his shoulder. The scent of baby powder and the feel of her soft flannel blanket wiped out the last traces of his lousy mood. He patted her back. "Are you having a tough day?"

As if she understood that she finally had a sympathetic audience, her cries trailed off. Hardy grinned as she hiccuped once, then again, then finally uttered what sounded like a tiny sigh.

Trish walked in just then, looking almost as frazzled as her daughter. Her eyes weren't red from crying, but they were shadowed with exhaustion.

"Aren't you a miracle worker?" she muttered, sounding more annoyed than grateful.

"Hey, I can't help it if she likes me."

"Maybe not, but I'm sure you're thrilled to have another female conquest you can claim."

He studied her intently, trying to guess where the hostility was coming from. "Bad night?" he inquired finally, as if he hadn't already witnessed part of it and heard about the rest.

She sighed heavily and looked vaguely contrite. "Bad enough," she admitted. "I don't think she slept for more than fifteen minutes at a time. She didn't want to be fed, didn't need to be changed. I was at my wit's end. Sorry if I was taking it out on you."

"I can handle the occasional short-tempered mood. I've had my share. Ask Kelly. I almost broke the front door this morning, before she wisely got it out of my way."

She studied him quizzically. "Why?"

"Not enough sleep, too many crazy thoughts running around in my head." He shrugged. "General contrariness."

"Aren't we a pair, then?" she said, finally mustering a halfhearted smile. "I guess Kelly will be thrilled to see the last of us."

Kelly appeared at precisely that moment. "Not until you've both had a proper breakfast. Something tells me neither one of you has eaten. That's probably why you're acting like a couple of grouchy old bears."

She added something under her breath that Hardy couldn't quite catch. "What was that?" he asked, all but certain he already knew. If he'd guessed right, Kelly Adams was a very intuitive woman.

Trish's cheeks turned bright pink. Kelly beamed at him. "Not a thing."

He looked at Trish. "What about you? You heard her."

"I never heard a thing," she insisted, avoiding his gaze.

He held Laura out in front of him. "What about you, sweetness? Did you hear her?"

The baby gurgled something he couldn't interpret. "Hmm, not talking. Must mean all the women intend to stick together. Guess it had something to do with sex." He gazed into the baby's eyes. "Was that it? Was she blaming our foul moods on sexual frustration?"

"Hardy!" Trish protested, as Kelly chuckled, pretty much confirming his guess.

"Sit," Kelly ordered, putting two plates piled high with pancakes in front of them. She reached for Laura. "I'll take her now. You eat."

Hardy knew better than to argue. Even if he hadn't been starving, he would have eaten every last bite of those light, fluffy pancakes. Sweeney's flapjacks were as tough and heavy as rubber. Trish, however, toyed with hers, taking no more than a bite or two before finally pushing the plate away. Kelly studied her worriedly, then cast a helpless look at Hardy.

"Trish, you want something else?" he asked. "Maybe a banana."

"No. I'm not really hungry."

"You have to eat. You've just had a baby."

She scowled at him. "Don't you think I know that?"

"Is this that post-partum blues stuff they talk about on TV?" he asked.

Trish stood up. "No, what it is is none of your business."

She bent down to give Laura a kiss. "I'll see you later, darling girl." She managed a smile for Kelly. "Thanks for breakfast."

"No problem. You two have a good day." Hardy added his thanks to Kelly, then followed Trish, who was already out the front door and halfway to his car. He waited until he had the car started and the heater going before he finally glanced over at her.

"Mind telling me what's really going on?" he asked

gently, determined to get to the bottom of her dark mood. Like Kelly, he was all but certain it had something to do with her brother's visit.

"It's my problem. I'll work it out," she said stiffly, huddled by the door.

Hardy decided to tackle it indirectly. "How did your visit go with your brother?"

"Great. It was wonderful to see him."

He thought she sounded more glum than happy. "You two seem close."

"We are." She actually managed a smile. "Dylan's the oldest, and I'm the baby, so he's always been outrageously protective of me. At the same time, he's the only one who ever seriously rebelled against our father. He's the only one who can completely understand why I left."

"And he's going to keep quiet about where you are?"

"He promised he would."

"Did he go back last night?" She nodded.

"Is that what's gotten to you? Are you regretting not going with him? Are you sorry you're cut off from your family?"

"No, absolutely not," she said at once. "I mean, I wish Dylan had stuck around longer. He was great with Laura. She must really like men, even at her tender age. She settled down for him, just the way she does for you."

The observation left Hardy feeling vaguely disgruntled without totally understanding why. Surely he couldn't be jealous of Laura's uncle. Did he want to be the only male she responded to, just the way he wanted to be the only male in her mama's life? Apparently.

Trish gazed at him with blatant curiosity. "Dylan seemed to like you. Believe me, that has to be a first. He hasn't had a lot of use for most of the men I know. What did you two talk about yesterday before I showed up?"

"This and that," Hardy said. He figured Trish would be mortified if she knew her big brother had subjected him to a cross-examination worthy of Perry Mason.

"I suppose he demanded details about our relationship," she said with a resigned sigh. "Dylan scared off almost every guy I ever wanted to date in high school with the macho big brother routine. Too bad it didn't work on Jack. It probably would have, if Jack hadn't been fully aware that he had my father in his corner."

"I wasn't scared off, either," Hardy assured her. "I just told him we were friends."

"So did I. He didn't believe me."

"That's his problem."

She slanted a look his way. "We are just friends, aren't we?"

It seemed to him she sounded a little plaintive, a little regretful. "That was our agreement," he acknowledged.

"And you always honor your word, right?"

"Absolutely." He glanced at her. She looked downright forlorn. "You aren't having second thoughts, are you?"

"About being friends? No, I suppose not."

Something in her tone alerted Hardy that she was not being entirely honest here. He decided it was worth pursuing. "Because if you were to change your mind, if you did want to go out sometime on a date, it would be okay with me," he said in what was probably the understatement of his lifetime.

He turned just in time to catch her frown.

"You don't have to sound so blasted thrilled about it," she muttered.

"Actually, I would be," he said. "Thrilled, that is."

Her gaze narrowed. "You would?"

He figured he was treading on thin ice here. She wasn't exactly doing cartwheels over the prospect of dating him. He couldn't afford to put his heart on the line, didn't even know if he wanted to. He just knew things weren't working out the way they'd been the past couple of weeks. There was too much sizzling tension in the air when they were together. The only way it was likely to die down was if they did something about it.

"Sure. Why not?" he said as if it were of no consequence.

She seemed to be struggling with indecision. "Okay, we could have dinner sometime," she said at last, then hurriedly amended, "If Laura can come along, of course."

Hardy fought a grin. "She's awfully small to be a respectable chaperone," he pointed out.

"That is not why…" she began, then let her voice trail off. "Okay, yes, I did think having another person along would keep things from getting, you know."

"Too intense? Too intimate?"

"All of that," she agreed.

"Darlin', something tells me things could get intense between the two of us in a room filled with half the town."

She regarded him glumly. "Yeah, I'm afraid of that, too."

Hardy would have chuckled, but something told him he ought to be satisfied to count his blessings. Trish finally trusted herself—and him—enough to go out with him. Now why did that make him so blasted nervous?

He had perfected the art of dating by the time he was fourteen. He couldn't even count high enough to calculate the number of dates he'd been on. Showing a woman a good time was as natural to him as breathing.

But Trish was different. A date with her actually mattered. He didn't want to blow it, didn't want to come on too strong. Didn't want to do anything from which there would be no turning back.

Oh, he was losing it, all right. He was staring straight into something every bit as frightening as the jaws of death and preparing to jump right in. In fact, he was damned eager to jump in, which just proved what happened when a man lost track of the rules that had kept him free. Obviously, before this big date of theirs, he was going to have to brush off that rule book and take a refresher course or he was going to be in the kind of emotional trouble he'd spent a lifetime avoiding.

Why was she behaving like a lovesick schoolgirl?

Trish asked herself for the thousandth time as she dressed for her date with Hardy. She didn't have his track record with dating, but she'd certainly been to dinner and the movies enough times that the thought shouldn't have her palms sweating. She was as jittery as a teenager getting ready for a blind date. If she could have, she would have backed out, pleading a headache or anything else she could dream up. Unfortunately she knew that Hardy would see straight through any excuse she offered. After tonight, though, she'd rarely have to see him again. The work on the store was all but done. Hardy must have worked like a demon the night before to get the shelves finished and the floor polished. She had been astounded when she'd walked in that morning and seen the full effect of all their hard work. Tears had stung her eyes and she'd had to fight the urge to throw her arms around him and give him the resounding kiss he deserved. Fortunately she'd learned that kissing Hardy was seldom an innocent act. Her body always wanted to turn it into something more. She'd settled for giving his hand a quick squeeze, then walking around to do a thorough survey of the all-but-finished store. He'd watched her intently, his expression worried, until she'd finally turned back and beamed at him.

"Oh, Hardy, isn't it the most beautiful bookstore you've ever seen?"

"I can honestly tell you yes," he said wryly. "Of course, I probably don't have nearly as much to compare it to as you do. To me it just feels real homey."

That was precisely the effect she'd been going for, so nothing he could have said would have pleased her more. A sudden vision of this being their home, with a cozy fire blazing, had her turning away as if he might read her thoughts.

If ideas like that were going to be popping into her head, it was a good thing that their time together was drawing to a close, she concluded. What little work was left she could do herself. Tonight was to be a much-deserved celebration of sorts.

And an ending, she added, feeling more depressed than she cared to admit.

She tugged on a pair of wool slacks that she could finally fasten around the middle, then pulled one of her favorite soft-blue sweaters over her head. She added an antique necklace with a scattering of tiny sapphires to dress the outfit up, then studied herself in the mirror. Casual enough, she concluded, and not bad for a woman just shedding the extra pounds she'd added with pregnancy. She was almost back to her old figure again, except for her breasts, which were fuller. She scooped her hair up into a loose arrangement of curls, held in place by little butterfly clips made of sparkling blue jewels.

Finally satisfied, she went downstairs just as the doorbell rang.

"I'll get it," she called out to Kelly.

She opened the door, then froze, mouth agape, her breath caught somewhere deep in her throat. Hardy was wearing a Western-style outfit, all in black. If she'd ever hoped for a pure rebel in her life, he personified it.

"You look…" they began in unison, then grinned.

"Gorgeous," he concluded. "Very handsome," she said.

And then they both seemed to run out of words, as if the importance of the evening ahead had finally sunk in.

"You two have a lovely evening," Kelly said, breaking the silence as she came into the foyer, holding Laura in her arms.

"It's just dinner and a movie," Trish insisted.

Hardy said, "We will." He glanced toward the baby. "Is Laura coming?"

Trish shook her head. "I decided she'd be better off right here. It's a cold night."

"Besides, one of these days Trish will move out and take this little darling with her. I want every second alone with her I can get," Kelly declared.

Trish caught Hardy's expression, watched it darken at Kelly's words. He said very little until they were in the truck and underway.

"You planning on moving on, after all?" he asked finally.

"No, of course not," she said, surprised not only because he'd misinterpreted Kelly's remark, but because it seemed to bother him. "But I will have to find my own place one of these days. I can't impose on Kelly and Jordan forever. We agreed I'd start looking as soon as the store is up and running."

It sounded to her as if Hardy breathed a sigh of relief.

"You might have to build," he said, his expression turning thoughtful. "There aren't a lot of houses available around here. Families tend to stick close. If you decide to buy some land, let me know. I'll drive you around. I've spotted a couple of pieces of property that might suit you."

"Why haven't you bought one of them for yourself?" she asked.

He shrugged. "Too much like settling down, I suppose. The bunkhouse suits me."

See, she told herself. There was absolutely nothing to fear from spending the evening with him. Hardy Jones was not a marrying man. How many times did she have to hear that before she got the message? And why did hearing it once more irritate her so?

"You don't need your own space?" she asked. "Not really. The place I grew up never felt much like a home, so I haven't missed having one of my own. You can't miss what you never knew. What about you?"

"I suppose I always assumed I'd have a house one day, complete with a white picket fence and a rose garden like the one Janet has at White Pines. I never wanted the sort of huge mansion my folks have. It's a showplace. In fact, I think the only reason they bought it was because they figured it would be photographed every time someone wrote about my father."

She sighed, then confessed, "The only place I ever felt really at home was at the little cottage they had at the beach near Galveston. My mother hated it, so she would send us kids off with the housekeeper for the summer. She and my father would pay us duty visits on weekends. They never arrived before dinnertime on Saturday and they were gone by noon on Sunday. I always laughed whenever she told a reporter about their weekend getaways as if they were some romantic little adventures she cherished."

"Do they still have that house?"

"Dylan has it now. He bought it from them, and he and my brothers go there every chance they get. I suppose it's their bachelor pad. They invite me once a year, and I'm sure it takes them a month to clean up before my visit."

He grinned. "If they're anything like the bachelors I know, it might take longer."

A few minutes later they arrived in Garden City. Hardy pulled up in front of an old hotel that had clearly been restored in recent years.

"I hope this is okay. There's a great little restaurant inside and there's a dance floor." He studied her uncertainly. "Sound all right?"

The mention of the dance floor set her pulse to pounding. The prospect of stepping into Hardy's embrace, of feeling his body pressed against hers rattled her so badly she could do little more than nod.

He grinned. "Good. I've heard the band does all the old-fashioned stuff. I can't promise you I can tell a waltz from a foxtrot, but I should be able to avoid stepping on your toes."

As they walked through the lobby, Trish's gaze shot to the registration desk. Of course there would be rooms upstairs. Was that why he had brought her here? Was he expecting something more out of tonight than dinner and dancing? And what about the movie they'd talked about? Maybe he'd been hoping she'd agree to watching one in bed. How many other women had he brought here and seduced? The rat! The louse! She was about to snap out some sarcastic observation when he grinned at her.

"You can forget about dragging me up to one of those rooms," he taunted.

"Me?" she all but sputtered, radiating indignation.

His grin broadened. "Oh, I know exactly what kind of ideas popped into that head of yours, but I'm not going along with it. I promised you a quiet evening, no pressure, no need for a chaperone. I stick to my word." He gazed deep into her eyes. "You can count on it."

Trish should have been relieved, should have rejoiced at the teasing declaration that she was safe with him. So why did she suddenly wish she could drag him straight into an elevator, up to a room and then strip his clothes off?

Because he had cleverly planted the idea in her head, she realized, frowning at him. No wonder he was so successful with women. Every one of them probably thought the seduction had been their idea. Well, she knew better, and now that she did, she would be on guard.

In fact, she had a few clever moves of her own. She knew how to drive a man crazy, and no one she knew deserved it more than Hardy. Dinner was going to be lovely, she was sure. But the dancing was going to be downright fascinating.

Twelve

Hardy knew he hadn't mistaken the panic in Trish's eyes when she'd spotted the registration desk and realized the implications of the fact that they were in a hotel. She'd jumped to an instantaneous conclusion that he'd brought her here to seduce her. That she thought so little of him irked him. At the same time, he'd thoroughly enjoyed teasing her about the wicked direction of her thoughts. She had been completely flustered when she realized that he'd read her mind and turned her conclusions topsy-turvy.

Of course, now she seemed dead set on making him pay. Every time he asked her to dance, she made darned sure that she fit herself so snugly against him that every muscle in his body went rigid.

Then she'd toss an innocent look over her shoulder and sashay back to the table as if she had nothing more on her mind than another bite of salad. Meantime, he was so aroused, he ached.

They'd just returned to the table after their third slow dance, when he deliberately captured her gaze and held it. The muscles in her throat worked, and she seemed to be having difficulty breathing.

"Having fun?" he inquired lightly.

"Sure," she said, her voice choked.

The music slowed again. He held out his hand. "Care for another dance?"

"Umm, not right now," she murmured. "The salad will get…" Her voice trailed off as if she realized the absurdity of what she'd been about to say.

"Cold?" he supplied. "Hot?"

"Soggy," she said emphatically.

"Nothing I hate more than a soggy salad," he agreed. "We'll wait till you're finished then."

She toyed with the lettuce for the better part of fifteen minutes before finally eating the last little bite with obvious reluctance. She finished just in time for another slow tune.

"Ah, perfect timing," Hardy enthused. He stood up before she could make another excuse.

This time, as if she'd sensed that his patience with her game had worn thin, she tried to remain a discreet distance away from him, but Hardy urged her in close, until their bodies were pressed intimately together once more. He was aroused before they took the second spin around the floor. In fact, there was so much heat being generated between them, the chef could have cooked their meals right there on the dance floor.

He gazed down into Trish's eyes and noted that her expression had shifted from alarm to something vaguely dreamy. Instinctively she snuggled a little closer.

Check and checkmate, he thought with a hint of desperation. If they weren't careful, this game was going to get wildly out of hand. And he was going to be cursing himself for that vow he'd made not to haul her upstairs to one of the rooms.

Back at the table, he glanced at his watch. If they rushed, they could still make that movie. A darkened movie theater suddenly seemed a whole lot safer and more sensible than a dance floor, unless he intended to spend the rest of the evening being physically tormented. A good action movie, that was what they needed. That way if their blood roared, if would be from the adrenaline pumping through them, not lust. "What do you say we get out of here?" he asked before the subject of dessert could come up.

Her startled blue eyes met his. "Now?"

"We've been here longer than I realized. If we're going to make that movie, we'd better hurry."

"We don't have to go to a movie."

"Yes, we do," he said urgently.

Suddenly a knowing grin spread across her face. "Oh, really? Why is that?"

"Just because."

"Because you're scared? Because you don't trust yourself with me, after all those assurances that nothing was going to get out of hand?"

He regarded her solemnly. "Okay, darlin', we have a choice here. We can stay here and tempt fate or we can go to a movie the way we planned, share some popcorn and drive home."

"Those are the only choices?"

"That's the way I see it."

"I vote we tempt fate."

He blinked and stared. "Excuse me."

"You heard me."

"Trish, do you have any idea what you're suggesting?"

"I'm not naive," she assured him. "But I also trust you not to do anything I don't want you to do."

Hardy all but groaned. He hated having a woman announce that she trusted him. It tossed all the responsibility for keeping a tight rein on their hormones back into his lap. He scowled at her.

"If you trust me, then believe this, we need to go to a movie. Right now," he added for emphasis. He beckoned for the waiter and started tossing bills on the table.

"No dessert?" the waiter asked.

"I guess not," Trish said with apparent regret.

"We have someplace we need to be," Hardy said, as if he owed the man an explanation.

He hustled Trish out of the restaurant, through the hotel lobby and into the car, before he forgot his good intentions.

Trish glanced over at him, eyes sparkling with mirth. "I guess this means you don't trust yourself."

"You've got that right."

She reached over and covered his hand on the steering wheel. "Hardy," she said softly.

He went absolutely still at her touch. "What?"

"I knew all along I could trust you."

He faced her and sighed. "Why? How?" he asked, perplexed by her conviction.

"Because I know the kind of man you are."

"I'm a womanizer," he reminded her emphatically. He was pretty sure there was a hint of desperation in his tone, as if he were trying to remind himself of that, as well as her.

"You're kind—"

"A playboy," he interrupted, since she obviously hadn't gotten the message.

"And decent," she continued.

"A rogue," he added for good measure.

"And thoughtful."

He tried again. "I'm like Jack the jerk."

She scowled at him. "You are nothing like Jack the jerk," she insisted. "Nothing!"

Puzzled by her vehemence, he stared. "You're the one who made the comparison, after hearing my romantic rap sheet from practically everybody in town."

"That was before I knew you," she said dismissively.

"What exactly are you saying here?"

"Just what I said earlier, I trust you. I trust you not to play games with me. I trust you not to toy with my feelings. I trust you to be honest with me." She was regarding him with such utter sincerity that Hardy had no choice but to believe her. On some level he was absolutely humbled by her declaration. On another level, it scared him spitless. It was the kind of fervent statement that a man had to live up to. He wasn't one bit sure he could.

How could he be honest, when he didn't understand his own feelings? How could he not play games, when playing games was all he'd ever done? He met Trish's gaze, saw the warmth in her eyes—the trust—and wondered what he'd ever done to deserve it. He also knew he would turn himself inside out before he would ever knowingly do anything to let her down.

Trish spent the rest of the week thinking about her date with Hardy. He had lived up to every one of her expectations. He had been thoughtful, sensitive and sexier than any man had a right to be. He had also been a perfect gentleman, giving her no more than a perfunctory, chaste kiss when he'd dropped her back at Kelly's after the movie. Every wildly rampant hormone in her body had protested the slight. She had anticipated another one of those mind-numbing, sizzling kisses. Apparently all that talk of trust had cooled his ardor.

Which was just as well, she assured herself, throwing herself into unpacking the boxes of books that had arrived at the store that morning. It was exactly what she had wanted, a pleasant evening with no pressure.

So why did she still feel thoroughly frustrated and cranky days later? Maybe it was because she hadn't caught so much as a glimpse of Hardy since that night. Maybe it was because despite all her claims to the contrary, she had enjoyed his attention, had basked in the flirting and the sexual tension that sizzled between them whenever they were in the same room.

She heard the bell over the front door ring and glanced up from the stack of books she'd been sorting. Harlan Adams filled the doorway.

"You and that boy turned this place into something real special," he declared approvingly. "Mind if I come in and take a peek around?"

She grinned because he was already inside and actively poking around when he asked.

"It is your building. I suppose you're entitled to a sneak peek," she told him.

She watched warily as he moved slowly around the store, taking in everything. He paused by a table of bestsellers, studied the jackets of several books, then nodded approvingly.

"Good selection."

"Thank you."

"You have anything in here by Louis L'Amour?"

"I've ordered everything I could. They're in one of these boxes I haven't unpacked yet."

"Good. There's nothing like a Western to relax a man at the end of a long day. Pick out a handful for me and send 'em on out to the ranch."

"What if I pick ones you've already read?"

"Probably will," he told her. "I think I've read most of them at one time or another. Still enjoy reading them. It's like visiting with old friends. You get together over the years, tell the same old tales, laugh at the same jokes, but there's something satisfying in the repetition and in the sharing."

Trish wished she had old friends to share things with. She'd lost touch with most of the women she'd known in Houston. Her brothers had been her best friends, and she was cut off from all of them except Dylan.

"You're a very wise man, Mr. Adams."

"Harlan, girl. I keep telling you nobody around here thinks of me as anything else."

"I feel I should be more respectful," she told him.

"That's because your folks raised you right. Okay, then, call me Grandpa Harlan, like the rest of your generation. Will that give me the respect you figure I should have?"

Trish was deeply touched by the offer. "If you're sure."

"I am. As far as I'm concerned, you're one of the family."

"Thank you."

He moved to one of the chairs in front of the fire and sank into it with an appreciative sigh. "You sure you knew what you were doing when you brought these chairs in here?" he asked. "Seems to me like folks might take such a liking to them, they'd just stay the day."

"That's fine with me. I like the company."

He regarded her intently. "I hear you and Hardy went out the other night," he said, broaching the subject so casually Trish almost missed the speculative glint in his eyes.

"Yes. Dinner and a movie."

"How did that go?"

"We had a lovely time. He's a very nice man."

"Poppycock!" Harlan declared. "The man's a rogue. Needs to settle down. You need a daddy for that little girl of yours and a man to look after you. Seems like a perfect match to me."

Trish's hackles rose. "I do not need a man to look after me," she said fiercely, then added, "sir."

He chuckled. "Guess that respect for your elders just about flew out the window for a second there, didn't it?"

"Well, with all due respect, I think you have it all wrong. Hardy and I are just friends."

"If that's the truth, then it's a pity," he said, studying her. "Can you swear to me it's the truth?"

"I don't see why I should have to."

He slapped his knee at that. "Whooee! That's just what I was hoping to hear. Means you can't say it with a straight face."

The last vestiges of Trish's determination to treat Harlan Adams with total respect flew out the window. Her gaze narrowed. "It's true what they say about you, Grandpa Harlan. You're a meddler."

"I am indeed. And proud of it. You look around Los Piños and you won't have a bit of trouble spotting some of my success stories. Haven't had a failure yet." He peered at her intently. "You smart enough to understand the implications of that?"

She chuckled, despite herself. "In other words, I should listen closely to what you say and take your advice, because you are very seldom wrong."

"Good girl. But you've got it just a little wrong. I am *never* wrong." He stood up. "Best be going now. I don't want to wear out my welcome."

Impulsively Trish crossed the room and gave him a peck on the cheek. "Thank you for caring, even if I have no intention of listening to a word you say."

He gave her a look of pure regret. "You'll learn. You're not the first to tell me to bug off, and undoubtedly, you won't be the last." He winked at her. "But in the end, I'm always right."

Trish was suddenly struck by the terrifying sensation that he very well might be right about her and Hardy, too. A part of her even wanted him to be.

But another part had lived through the disaster with Jack Grainger and couldn't help making the very comparisons that she'd denied so vehemently to Hardy just the other night. What if she was wrong? What if Hardy turned out to be exactly like the man who had betrayed her? Could she take that kind of a risk with her heart again?

Hardy tossed the fancy invitation down on his bunk without even opening it. He knew what it was for. Trish had invited him to the grand opening of her store, and he was pretty much duty bound to accept. Too many people would jump to all sorts of ridiculous conclusions if he failed to show up.

He supposed he could take a date and put all the matchmaking nonsense to rest once and for all. But he knew he couldn't do it. Not only wasn't there a single woman he even wanted to spend the afternoon with, but he knew it would hurt Trish if he showed up with a woman on his arm. It would be tantamount to admitting that her first impression of him had been the right one.

That was why when Sunday afternoon rolled around, he took a shower, dressed with extra care and drove into town for this shindig Trish and Sharon Lynn had planned. After all, how much trouble could he possibly get into at a bookstore opening? He doubted he'd have a single minute alone with the hostess, not so much as a second for stealing a kiss that might push him over the edge and shatter his New Year's resolution.

Hardy thought back to that night just a couple of months back when he'd been so confident that he could make it through another year as a bachelor. After all, he'd gone through most of the last thirty years on his own. He'd never once been tempted to change that.

Of course, he hadn't counted on delivering a baby, either. Who could have guessed that that simple act of rescuing a lady in distress would tumble his whole view of the world into disarray?

Before he could analyze the meaning of all that, he arrived at the store, only to realize that he'd instinctively arrived early. Maybe subconsciously he'd wanted that stolen moment alone with Trish, after all.

As long as he was the first one parked on the block, he couldn't very well hide out in the truck until the other guests started showing up. He might as well go inside and see what he could do to help.

He opened the door to chaos. Sharon Lynn and Trish were running around like crazy trying to get all the food arranged on folding tables they'd set up across the back of the store. Laura was in her carrier screaming at the top of her lungs, furious at being ignored. Trish took one look at him and latched on to his arm as if it were a lifeline.

She cast a look from him to her daughter and pleaded, "Do something. I thought she'd sleep through this, but she hasn't stopped crying. I don't have a second to pace the floor with her, not if everything's going to be ready when people get here."

"Leave her to me," he soothed. "Looks to me like you and Sharon Lynn have everything just about ready. Laura and I will take a little walk around the place, so she can get acquainted with the business."

"Bless you," she said fervently.

"No problem." He scooped his favorite miniature person out of her carrier and settled her against his chest. "Hey, sweet thing, let's you and me go check out the children's books. Maybe we can find you a bedtime story. How does that sound?"

To his amusement, Laura gurgled appreciatively.

Trish shot him a look of pure venom.

He winked. "Your mama can't stand it that you and I have a thing going," he advised the baby. "Personally, I think she's jealous."

"No, what she is, is frazzled," Trish declared, slapping a plate of fresh vegetables and dip onto the table so hard that the dip splattered. "Now look what you made me do."

"It's okay," Sharon Lynn soothed. "We just plop the plate on top of the stain and no one will notice a thing."

Hardy headed for the children's books to get out of the line of fire. He figured if he weren't careful, the next plate was likely to end up in his face.

Unlike the huge chairs in front of the fire, the only

chair in the children's section was meant for someone about a quarter of his size. He managed to scrunch down on it, while he selected a board book that looked as if it was about Laura's speed.

"Goodnight Moon," he said, reading the cover. "Sounds like a winner to me." He held it up for Laura's approval. He took her gurgles for a yes. He turned the thick pages slowly, reading to the baby and showing her the pictures. He was pretty much engrossed in the simple story when he heard the front door open and close, followed by a hoot of masculine laughter.

"Will you look at that?" Harlan Patrick said. "The world's most dedicated bachelor has taken to reading stories to the baby."

"Can this bachelorhood be saved?" Slade Sutton chimed in.

"Oh, stop it," Val ordered before Hardy could get up and silence both men with a punch. "I think it's wonderful."

"I agree," Laurie said.

Hardy felt his cheeks flame. "I was just helping Trish out. The baby was upset and she had things to do and—"

"It's okay," Val soothed. "Don't pay any attention to the two of them. They're cretins."

Slade bent down and kissed the tip of her nose. "That's not what you were saying last night."

"Last night I was deluded into thinking that you had a sensitive side," she countered.

More people flowed into the room, filling it to capacity with laughter and conversation. Slade's daughter joined them before her father's teasing could veer into dangerous territory. "Oh, she's darling," Annie cooed. "Can I hold her?"

Hardy hesitated.

"I'll be real careful," she promised.

"Over in the chair," Val instructed. "And you don't budge."

Hardy followed Annie to the chair and delivered Laura to her with some regret. "Just holler if you want me to come and get her."

"She'll be fine," Annie said, gazing at the baby with a rapt expression. She glanced up at Val. "When are you and Daddy—"

"Don't even go there," Slade said. "I'm just now getting the hang of being a father to you."

"That means you've had plenty of practice," Annie countered. "I need a baby brother or sister."

"It isn't about what you need," Val declared. "Your father and I will decide when the time is right to expand our family."

The look she gave her husband suggested to Hardy that the time was a whole lot closer than Slade suspected.

Suddenly feeling as if he were intruding, Hardy searched for Trish in the growing mob scene, then moved off in her direction. She was standing apart from the crowd, looking a little shell-shocked by the sheer number of people who'd turned out for the grand opening.

"Looks like you have a success," he observed, moving to her side.

"I never had this many people turn out for my year-end sale in Houston," she said, her expression dazed. "And I gave really good discounts. I owe this to the Adamses, I'm sure. Their approval counts for a lot around here."

"No," he corrected. "You owe it to all your hard work and planning. Don't sell yourself short."

"I wasn't. It's just that this is amazing. I had no idea so many people would come. What if we run out of food?"

"Sharon Lynn made more than enough. Besides, most of these people just like getting together. The food's a bonus."

"I wonder if I should have hired a cashier for today," she asked worriedly. "Several people have wanted to make purchases."

"They'll be back. I think it's better that the party is just to show the place off." He glanced around. "It makes a good impression, doesn't it? Did it turn out the way you envisioned?"

"You know it did," she said. "Thanks to you."

"They were your ideas. I was just the muscle."

"Still, I can't thank you enough."

Her gaze met his, and he felt his head spin. "Trish…"

Whatever he'd been about to say was lost, because she stood on tiptoe and kissed him. It was the same kind of chaste peck on the cheek he'd given her when he'd taken her home on their date. Suddenly, though, he hated the polite little charade, the mockery of the passion that a kiss between them could be.

Before she could move away, he turned his head and captured her mouth beneath his. He took full advantage of her startled gasp, tasting her, savoring the shock of sensations swirling through him, the slight trembling he could feel in her.

When he finally released her, she stared at him mutely, her lips swollen, her eyes bright.

"We need to talk about this," he said tersely, all too aware that the room had gone silent and that they were being watched with evident fascination. "Later. I'll come back when this is over."

Trish nodded.

Because he didn't want to explain to anyone what had just happened—wasn't even sure he could explain it—Hardy fled.

He figured he had an hour, two at most, to get a grip on the emotions churning inside him. Otherwise, when he came back here tonight, he was going to break every vow he'd ever made to himself and to Trish.

Thirteen

Trish sensed that she and Hardy were at a major turning point in their relationship. The barely restrained lust
simmering between them was about to sizzle out of control. She was no longer in control of her own reactions
to him and, she suspected, he was losing his tight rein
on his responses to her.

As the party swirled around her, she went through the
motions of being a proper hostess. She chatted innocu-
ously, skirted prying questions from the Adamses about
Hardy's sudden disappearance, and made sure everyone
ate their fill of scones and little sandwiches.

After a few minutes of forcing herself to play the
role, it began to come naturally. She finally remembered
the purpose of the party beyond simply showing off the
store. She asked people about their book preferences,
making mental notes for her next order. She queried them
about other items that they wished a local store would
carry and collected a whole list of ideas for a gift section.

All the while she kept track of the time, counting the
minutes until the afternoon tea was scheduled to end.
She knew Hardy would wait until the last guest was gone

before making an appearance. Her pulse zipped as she mentally skipped ahead by an hour or so.

What exactly did he want to talk about? The kisses? The barely leashed passion? Was that something someone could sit down and discuss as rationally and dispassionately as the weather? She doubted it. She knew she couldn't. She had never before felt the out-of-control spinning sensations that Hardy's touch set off in her. She had nothing to compare them to, no idea if they were the sort of responses that cooled once they'd been allowed to rush wickedly to a natural conclusion.

Maybe Hardy, with all of his practice, could put a name to what was going on between them. But as badly as she wanted to label and identify it, so she could deal with it as straightforwardly as she paid invoices or balanced a checkbook, it irked her that he might have answers that she herself did not.

"Everything okay?" Sharon Lynn asked, studying her worriedly. "You're not too tired, are you? After all, it's only been a couple of months since you had the baby. You've been pushing yourself to get ready for this."

"It's okay," Trish told her. "I'm fine. I just have a lot on my mind."

"A lot or one particular man?" Sharon Lynn asked.

"A lot," Trish insisted.

Sharon Lynn grinned, her expression filled with skepticism. "Whatever you say, but I saw that kiss. If it had been me on the receiving end of it, I'd still be weak-kneed."

Before Trish could respond to that, Sharon Lynn patted her hand. "Don't worry. People are starting to leave. I'll stick around and help you clean up."

"No," Trish said a little too emphatically.

Sharon Lynn's eyes widened. "Someone else coming back to help?"

"No, of course not. I just meant it can wait till morning. Since I'm not officially opening until next Friday, I'll have plenty of time to put things back in order."

"Cleaning up is part of the caterer's responsibility," Sharon Lynn countered.

"But you're not a real caterer, so it doesn't count," Trish said, trumping her argument. "Don't fight me on this. You and your family have done more than enough to help out today."

"Okay. Then I'll just go and try to shoo everyone else out of here, graciously, of course."

Trish wasn't about to argue with that plan. "Thank you," she said fervently.

She forced herself to say goodbye to the last of the well-wishers. As soon as Sharon Lynn was gone, Trish brought the still-sleeping baby into the front so she could keep an eye on her. Then she sank down in a chair in front of the fireplace and kicked off her shoes with a sigh of relief.

She closed her eyes and allowed herself to savor the sweet success of the event. If half the people who'd said they'd be back on Friday came, she would do a booming business on her first day. Her first catalogue for this new location would go into the mail tomorrow. And the next day she would get her Web page up and running so that Internet orders could start coming in. By this time next week, she would have the first indications of whether her decision to stay here had been a sound one, at least from a business perspective.

On a personal level the jury was still definitely out.

As if just thinking that had conjured him up, Hardy returned, pausing in the doorway.

"All clear?"

"The meddlers have pretty well vanished, content with their day's work," she said wryly.

He closed the door, then turned the lock, his gaze never once leaving her face. On his way across the room, he seemed to make himself look away, then paused by the food.

"Can I bring you something?"

"Any scones left?"

"A few. Orange, cinnamon-raisin and plain."

"One of each."

"With this fancy cream stuff?"

She grinned at his description of the very expensive clotted Devonshire cream that Sharon Lynn had somehow tracked down. "Of course. A little raspberry jam, too."

"You've got it."

He handed her a plate loaded down with the bitesize scones. His own plate had a half-dozen little ham and biscuit sandwiches and miniature barbeques. He'd even poured them each a glass of the still-cold punch.

"You look beat," he said, studying her worriedly.

"It's a good kind of beat," she said.

"Today was a triumph, wasn't it?"

"I don't know if I'd go that far, but it did surpass my wildest expectations."

He finished his sandwiches, then leaned forward, his elbows propped on his knees, and regarded her intently. "Now what, Trish? What's the game plan?"

"Game plan?"

He gestured toward her and then the baby. "Will you

stay at Kelly's so she can baby-sit? Find that house you talked about? Move on?"

He said the last as if he fully expected her to seize that option, despite today's success.

"Why would you think I'd be moving on? Especially after today? This is it, Hardy. The store's about to open. I intend to become a part of the community here. I'll probably start to look for my own place this week."

He nodded, again with that vaguely relieved expression that she'd caught once or twice before.

"Hardy, tell me about your family." She had the feeling that once she knew about his past, she could finally unravel the mystery of Hardy Jones.

His head snapped up. "My family? Why would you bring them up?"

"Because you never talk about them. I know you must have one. You reacted pretty violently when I brought up your mother. You mentioned your grandmother when we named Laura, but beyond that you've never said a word. Where's your father?"

"Dead," he said tersely and with no obvious sign of regret.

"And your mother?"

He shrugged indifferently. "No idea."

Trish stared at him. "You have no idea where your mother is?"

"She left when I was a kid. She took my sister with her. I haven't heard from either of them since. End of story. Can we talk about something else?"

With a sudden flash of insight Trish began to see the pattern that had been established in his life at a very early age. She wanted to talk about this, wanted to make him see that that early abandonment was probably the reason he never dated the same woman for more than a few weeks. He always wanted to be the one to go, rather than start to care and face another desertion. Suddenly she understood as she never had before why he kept asking if she intended to move on, despite all the evidence to the contrary. Her heart broke for him.

She sat forward and impulsively reached for his hand. Only when his gaze finally locked with hers did she say softly, "I'm not going anywhere, cowboy. I'm here to stay."

Rather than reassuring him, her words had him jerking away. "You can't make a promise like that," he retorted. "Things change." He struggled visibly until his temper cooled. "Life goes on."

Trish wanted to reassure him, almost pressed the point, but in the end she fell silent. Maybe she shouldn't make promises she had no way of knowing if she'd keep in the long run. She'd made a commitment to staying in Los Piños, but beyond that? Would she allow a full-blown relationship to develop with Hardy, a man who embodied all the traits she'd come to distrust in a man? Or would she, too, abandon him as too great a risk? She couldn't bear the thought of being one more in a string of women to hurt him so cruelly.

And so she stayed silent.

The only sound in the room was the crackling of the fire and the baby's soft whimpers as she finally stirred. Hardy reached for Laura before she was fully awake, settling her in his arms as naturally as if she belonged there. Only then did some of the tension in his face finally fade.

It was ironic, Trish thought, watching the two of them. Her daughter might well be the only female on the face of the earth that Hardy truly trusted, the only one he allowed himself to love. Seeing them together, some of Trish's reservations began to crack. How could she not fall a little bit in love with a man who was so obviously infatuated with her daughter, a man who'd put aside his own fears to bring her safely into this world?

"You're so wonderful with her," she said softly.

"Maybe it's because she's so beautiful, so completely innocent. It makes a man want to conquer the world just to make it safe for her. That must be what it feels like to be a real father, not the kind I had, but the kind a kid is supposed to grow up with." He met Trish's gaze. "Laura deserves a father like that."

"I know."

"Do you ever think about getting in touch with her biological father?"

"Absolutely not," she insisted fiercely. "I guess that means you'll just have to step into the role. You'll have to be her surrogate dad and do all the things that a real dad would do."

Stuck by a sudden inspiration, she added, "Her godfather. That's what you can be. Would you, Hardy? I should have her baptized soon, and nothing would please me more than to have you be her godfather. Please."

He looked tempted. His gaze, which was fastened on Laura's face, was filled with tenderness.

"I don't know," he said. "That's a big responsibility."

"No bigger than delivering her in the middle of nowhere," she reminded him.

"But this is something that lasts forever," he protested. "What if I mess it up?"

"All you have to do is love her, be there to guide her when she needs it. Please, Hardy. I'll ask Kelly to be her godmother, so you'll have back-up. And one of my brothers, too. You won't be in it alone." He nodded at last. "I'd be honored," he said finally. He grazed a knuckle lightly over Laura's cheek, a ghost of a smile on his lips. "You and me, kid. We're going to be a helluva team."

In that instant Trish realized that she didn't want Hardy merely as Laura's godfather, as important as that role was. She wanted him as the baby's father. She knew she would never find a better one.

And despite the nagging doubts about Hardy's frequent-dating miles, she had a feeling she'd never find a better husband for herself. Because once a man like Hardy— who'd been on the receiving end of too many broken promises—finally made one himself, she suspected he would never, ever break it.

Hardy wasn't sure when he finally admitted to himself that he might be falling in love with Trish.

It wasn't the first time he kissed her. He'd kissed a hundred women at least, and none of them had made him think about forever.

It wasn't when she stared at him so earnestly and apologized for the way people were throwing them together. In fact, at that precise moment he recalled being just a little insulted that she hadn't seemed interested in pursuing a relationship with him.

It surely wasn't when he found her sitting by the creek with the moonlight turning her hair gold and tears streaming down her face. She'd looked so lost and lonely it had almost ripped his heart out, but that wasn't love.

No, when he thought back really hard over the few months she'd been in Los Piños, he was pretty sure he could pinpoint the precise moment when he'd realized she was going to be the one woman he'd never forget. It had happened on a lonely stretch of Texas highway, when she'd been cursing a blue streak and having a baby with only him to help. She had trusted him with something incredibly precious. Without even recognizing the feelings, he'd been a goner from that moment on.

Since she was so darned set on staying single, on proving that she could be mother-of-the-year all alone, he figured it was going to be a while longer before he got around to sharing the news of his feelings with her.

When she'd asked him the night before to be Laura's godfather, he'd been taken aback. On the one hand, he'd been honored that she would consider him a fit role model for the baby. On the other, he'd cursed the fact that she didn't see him as actual daddy material. The realization that that was where his head was had stunned him. He'd never expected to want to have his own family, never anticipated that there would be a woman who would overcome all of his emotional roadblocks and sneak into his heart.

Trish had. That she was the one who'd done it a woman who had run out on another man, on an entire family— was equally startling. Funny how he had never blamed her for that, never held it against her but had assumed she'd had legitimate reasons for going, even before he'd heard the whole story.

Maybe he'd sold his own mother short all these years. Maybe she, too, had seen leaving as the only choice. He'd probably never know, but maybe it was time to forgive her, anyway.

He'd tried for a long time to tell himself his attraction to Trish was about nothing more than sex. She was off-limits, so naturally he wanted her. He'd lived his entire adult life making conquests, then moving on. With

Trish there had been no conquest. Honor and circumstances had forbidden it, so there had been no urgency to move on. Only now, when it was too late, did he realize he'd stuck around just a little too long, and the impossible—the inevitable, probably—had happened. He'd fallen for her.

Now what, though? None of his past experiences had prepared him for this. He had absolutely no idea how to catch and keep a woman who really mattered. Charm alone wouldn't do it. Trish had pretty well made that clear. She seemed to like seeing him with the baby, which suited him just fine since there was a powerful connection between him and the little munchkin. Was it possible that the way to Trish's heart was through her daughter?

Riding out to see how the cattle had weathered the latest storm gave him plenty of time to consider his options. Or it would have if Harlan Patrick had stopped pestering him for more than five minutes at a time.

"I still can't get over that kiss you gave Trish last night," he said, bringing it up for the second time in less than an hour. "Right there for all the world to see. What were you thinking?"

"I wasn't thinking."

"Instinct, huh? Fascinating."

"Drop it, Harlan Patrick."

"Not just yet."

Hardy sighed. The first time Harlan Patrick had mentioned the kiss, Hardy had brought a quick end to the conversation by telling him flatly that it was none of his damned business. Since the topic was back again, he doubted that he could silence Harlan Patrick with another sharp retort. Obviously his friend had something he needed to say.

"Is there something you want to get off your chest?" he asked, wanting the topic over with once and for all, even if it meant answering one or two sticky questions.

"Okay, here's the thing," Harlan Patrick said. "I know it's probably none of my business."

"Damn straight."

His friend scowled, but kept right on. "It's just that Grandpa Harlan has taken a real liking to Trish. And Aunt Kelly and Uncle Jordan have taken her under their wings. I'd hate to see her get hurt."

"She's not going to get hurt, not by me, anyway," Hardy declared.

"Then that'll be a first," Harlan Patrick said. "You're not exactly known around town for your staying power. Trish isn't the kind of woman a man plays games with. Even if half my family hadn't appointed themselves as her guardians, she's got a powerful father who might have a thing or two to say about anybody who does her wrong."

"I know that," he said calmly. "I'm not worried."

Harlan Patrick studied him intently. "What are you saying? Are you telling me you're serious about her?"

"I'm not telling you a blasted thing," Hardy said. "If I have something to say, I'll say it to Trish."

Harlan Patrick suddenly cracked a grin. "Then I can tell Grandpa Harlan that his scheming is paying off? He's going to love that. He'll probably wait at least twenty-four hours before asking about the wedding date."

"You tell your grandfather if he knows what's good for him, he'll leave the timetable to me. Otherwise there might not ever be a wedding. Trish is skittish. She's been hurt. She hasn't exactly announced her undying devotion to me. The situation is delicate. Your grandfather has the tact of a sledgehammer."

"And you're any better?" Harlan Patrick scoffed. "Subtlety has never been your strong suit."

Hardy regarded his friend ruefully. The remark had cut a little too close to the truth. "I'm learning, though. I am definitely learning."

In fact, he intended to start this evening by suggesting to Trish that they take a drive around to look at some property for a house. *Their* house. Of course, he had no intention of telling her that part of his plan just yet. No point in rushing things, when the outcome was still uncertain.

Fourteen

Trish glanced up from the mountain of paperwork that was rapidly piling up on her desk just in time to spot Hardy standing in the doorway. Her heart flipped, despite her many warnings to herself that expecting too much from him was a mistake.

"This is a surprise. What brings you by?" she asked.

"I thought you might want to go for a drive."

"A drive? With all this work to do? I really can't."

"You said you wanted to start looking for your own place," he reminded her. "I had some time this afternoon, so I can take you."

She had said that, and she really did need to get out of Jordan and Kelly's hair. The fact that it was a lovely day with just a hint of spring in the air decided her. She tossed aside her pen.

"Let's do it," she said, reaching for her jacket. "Where are we going? How many houses can we see? Have you talked to a real estate agent?"

Hardy chuckled. "Here and there, no houses and no, I have not talked to a real estate agent."

"What do you mean no houses?"

"We're looking at property."

"I see. What about the real estate agent, though? Wouldn't that be more efficient? I can tell them what I want so we don't waste our time."

"We don't need a Realtor for this. I'm going to show you a few things I already happen to know are on the market."

"Here in town?"

"No. They're out a ways, beyond White Pines."

"But that's so far," she protested. "It would be much more convenient for me to be right here in town."

He shook his head. "We can worry about convenience another time, if you decide against these places. Okay?"

Something told her that this meant more to him than he was letting on. She recalled him mentioning that he'd seen some property that he loved. If only to see what sort of place appealed to him, she relented. "I'm game. Let's go."

The drive, which realistically would probably have taken her about an hour, took forty-five minutes with Hardy behind the wheel. He was never reckless, but he definitely tested the speed limits.

She figured it was a good thing Jordan's son, Justin, was the sheriff. Maybe that was what Hardy was counting on.

Or maybe he was simply anxious to get her impression of this property he was being so mysterious about.

Expecting open land or some sort of ranch, she was startled when he turned into what appeared to be a forest of pines. In actuality it was little more than a grove of the trees for which the town had been named. As they bounced over the rutted dirt road carved through it, she felt as if she'd wandered into a completely different world of strong, fresh scents and deep shade.

When they emerged, she realized that the pine trees had been at the top of a rise. Spread out below was a sea of wildflowers just coming into bloom and the same sparkling creek that wandered through the White Pines ranch. It was a pristine piece of land, as perfect as anything her imagination could have conjured up.

She turned and found Hardy studying her with an anxious expression.

"Well," he demanded. "What do you think?"

"I think it's the most beautiful place I've ever seen," she told him honestly.

His expression brightened. "Really? You're not just saying that?"

"Of course not. I can just imagine a wonderful little house built right up there at the edge of the woods with lots of windows looking out on this gorgeous view."

"A log cabin?" he suggested. "Something that fits into the scenery as if it belonged there? With a wide front porch and maybe stained glass on the door so that when the sun shines in the living room is filled with color?"

She fell into his dream, absorbed it as if every detail were already real. It wasn't her home he was talking about, but his. He was envisioning something she now knew was a far cry from what he'd had as a child. As enchanted as she was with the setting, how could she even think of taking this place away from him?

"Oh, Hardy, I think you should do it. Build a house exactly like that, right here. It will be incredible."

"No," he protested. "This place should be yours. It would be a wonderful place for Laura to grow up. She could have horses and a tree house. She could swim in the creek."

"She would love it," Trish admitted wistfully, then shook her head. "But you found it. It should be yours. I know it's the place you talked about a few weeks ago. You said there were others you could show me. Let's look at those."

"You won't even consider buying this one?" he asked, looking vaguely let down.

"No. I'll look at whatever else you know about and then I'll check out what's available in town. That would be the sensible thing to do."

He nodded. "If that's what you want," he said, not fighting her nearly as hard as she'd expected him to... as she'd hoped he would.

But there was a mysterious little gleam in his eyes that she couldn't quite interpret. Since Hardy tended to be a man of many secrets, she finally dismissed it as just being one more.

As they drove away, she cast one last look back at the land he had shown her. Even though sacrificing it for Hardy's sake had been the right thing to do, she couldn't help feeling a twinge of regret that she wouldn't be the one to build a home here. She almost wished she'd never seen it. Nothing they looked at afterward was even a poor second. In fact, she doubted she would ever find anything to compare to it.

Just as she was rapidly coming to understand that she would never find another man quite like Hardy.

Hardy bought the property that same night. He rousted the real estate agent out of bed to do it, insisting on putting his deposit down and making the deal right then and there.

Two weeks later the bank closing went off without a hitch, because of the sizable down payment he'd been able to make with all those years of savings he'd had no reason to spend.

For the next few weeks he spent every spare minute building his house. Because he'd told no one, because he wanted to do every last lick of work himself, it was incredibly slow going. It also cut into time he should have been spending courting Trish, convincing her that they might have a future together.

When the nonstop thoughts of her eventually crowded out everything else, he finally took an afternoon off and drove into town. He stopped by Dolan's and picked up two thick chocolate shakes, then went next door.

There were several customers in the bookstore, all with armloads of paperbacks. Obviously Trish was fulfilling a need in Los Piños for new reading material. Everyone was chatting spiritedly with each other, except for Willetta who, to his astonishment, was sitting in a chair in front of the fire. Since Trish was busy. Hardy walked over to the seamstress.

"Hey, Willetta, I thought you'd be long gone by now."

"Went," she said succinctly. "And?"

"Didn't like it. I'm back to stay."

He grinned. "There's no place like home, right?"

"Seems that way to me." She gestured around the room. "You two did quite a job in here. Hardly recognized the place."

"You aren't thinking of trying to steal it out from under Trish, so you can go back into business, are you?"

"Heavens, no. Retirement suits me just fine. I do think

I might enjoy coming in here to visit with your girl on occasion. May even take up baby-sitting for little Laura if Trish moves to town."

"That sounds like a fine idea to me."

She studied the container in his hand. "What's that?"

"A chocolate milk shake. I brought it for Trish, but I'll bet she wouldn't mind if I gave it to you, instead."

She gave him a mock frown, even as she reached for the drink. "Can't bribe me, boy. I still intend to tell her you're a rascal every chance I get."

"I think she already knows," Hardy confessed. "But I'm hoping she doesn't mind."

Willetta nodded. "So, that's the way it is, is it? Nothing like a good woman to settle a man down. Have you asked her to marry you yet?"

The question had barely been uttered when Hardy heard a gasp. He turned to find Trish staring at Willetta in shock. Because Trish looked so thoroughly flustered, he winked at Willetta.

"Hush," he warned her. "She's listening."

Willetta touched a finger to her lips. "She won't hear a thing from me."

Of course, she already had. Try as he might, though, he couldn't get a real fix on her reaction. Was she merely surprised? Or dismayed?

Oh well, he thought. There was time enough for her to get used to the idea. He didn't intend to bring the subject up until he could show her the house he'd built for the three of them.

"Hey, darlin'," he greeted Trish as if his conversation with Willetta had been about no more than the weather. "I brought you a milk shake, but this customer of yours stole it away from me."

"Is that so? Guess I'll just have to take this one, then," Trish said as she nabbed his drink right out of his hand in a move so smooth the slickest pickpocket would have admired it. She regarded him triumphantly as she took a long, slow swallow.

Hardy shook his head with exaggerated regret. "I had no idea the women in this town were nothing but a bunch of sneak thieves."

Willetta stood up. "Guess I'll be going now. Looks like you two have things to talk about." She patted Trish's shoulder. "Thanks for the visit. You just let me know anytime you want me to baby-sit."

"Absolutely," Trish said, then fell silent as Willetta left them alone.

Hardy noticed that she seemed vaguely uneasy as she waited for him to say whatever was on his mind. Obviously she was expecting him to jump straight into a marriage proposal. She should have known he had more finesse than that. He'd also learned a whole lot about timing through his dating years. He knew when to make his move and—up until Trish, anyway—he'd always known when to make his exit. "Something on your mind?" he inquired, regarding her with lazy curiosity.

"Me?" She stared at him blankly. "No. I thought… I mean, Willetta…" Her voice trailed off.

"Eavesdropping?"

"Of course not!" She sighed heavily. "What brings you into town? You haven't been around for quite a while now."

"I've been busy."

"Really? Grandpa Harlan says he hasn't seen much of you at the ranch, either."

"The two of you spend much time talking about me behind my back?"

"Of course not."

He grinned at her vehemence. "Tell the truth, darlin'. Were you missing me?"

"No. I just wondered, that's all. I told him you probably had a new girlfriend."

Despite her oh-so-casual tone, she looked mad enough to spit at the prospect of him being with another woman. Maybe what they said about absence was true. Maybe it did make the heart grow fonder.

"Would it bother you if I did?" he asked innocently.

"Absolutely not," she said just a little too hurriedly. "You're free to do whatever you like."

"That's the way I see it," he agreed. Because she was beginning to look as if she might haul off and pummel him, he decided maybe he'd tormented her long enough. "There's no other woman, Trish."

"Did I say I cared?"

He chuckled. "You didn't have to. It was written all over your face."

"Well, you can hardly blame me for jumping to that conclusion, given your track record."

"I'm a reformed man. I thought you knew that."

He stood up and took a step toward her. She went absolutely still.

"Come here, darlin'," he coaxed softly.

Fire flashed in her eyes. "Why should I?"

"Because you know you want to."

She frowned at that. "I do not want to," she retorted emphatically.

"Once you're over here, you can decide then if you'd rather kiss me or smack me," he pointed out.

"Now that's an interesting suggestion," she admitted.

She crossed the few feet between them until she was so close that Hardy could feel her breath fanning across his cheek. He forced himself to wait, to let her make the choice.

Finally, after what seemed an eternity, she reached up and pressed her hand to his cheek. Hardly a smack, but not the kiss he wanted either.

"Trish?"

"Hmm?"

"I've missed you," he whispered, his voice ragged.

"I've been right here," she reminded him.

He touched her cheek, then ran his thumb over her lips. "You can't get the words out, can you?"

"What words?"

"That you missed me."

Eyes sparkling, she challenged, "Who said I did? Laura, however, is another story. She has definitely missed you."

"Has she said so?" he teased.

"No, but she fusses, and I can tell she's not happy that I'm the only one around to pick her up."

"Maybe I'll come see her tonight, if I'm invited."

Trish's gaze locked on his. "I don't know what to make of you, Hardy Jones," she said almost to herself.

"I'm a straightforward guy," he insisted.

"No," she contradicted. "You're the most complicated man I think I've ever known."

"Is that good or bad?"

Looking bemused, she admitted, "I'm still trying to figure that one out."

"Let me know when you do, okay?"

"Oh, you'll be the first to know," she assured him.

* * *

Hardy was deliberately driving her a little bit crazy, Trish concluded after his visit to the store and his brief stop to see Laura that same night. She didn't want to be falling in love with a man she couldn't figure out, but she was afraid it was too late to stop herself.

She also couldn't help wondering if that was why she'd put off finding a house in town. She'd made up a dozen excuses for not even looking. Kelly had aided her indecision by insisting that she loved having Laura with her all day, that Trish was doing her a favor by staying on and filling Kelly's "empty nest," as she put it.

But despite her inability to find a new home for herself, Trish was feeling good about her new life in Los Piños. She was surrounded by friends. Her business was already showing distinct signs that it would thrive. And Laura was getting bigger every day. At four months, she was already the delight of her mama's life, the bright spot in her days.

Satisfied that her life was on an even keel, and tired of Dylan's constant pestering, she finally decided she was strong enough to withstand her father's pressure and her mother's disappointment. She called her father at his office.

"Patricia Ann, where the devil have you been hiding out? I've had my men combing every major city in the country looking for you," Bryce Delacourt blustered when he recognized her voice.

"I thought you called them off," she chided. "Well, of course I did, for a time. Then I started to get worried when I didn't hear from you again. Thought maybe you'd gotten yourself in trouble in some strange city."

Trish grinned when she thought of how close she really was and how her unsuspecting father had never even considered looking in such a small town. She drew in a deep breath and admitted, "Actually I've been staying with some friends of yours."

"Who?" her father demanded indignantly. "They can't be friends of mine if they've kept your whereabouts a secret. Besides, I've called everyone I could think of to see if they've heard from you."

"I insisted that they keep quiet," she said. "I told them I would disappear if they told you. They've been doing you a favor by keeping my secret."

"What the hell kind of twisted logic is that?"

"Accept it, Daddy, or I will hang up this phone right now and you'll still be in the dark."

He sighed heavily. "Okay, okay, just tell me where you are and I'll come to get you."

"I'm in Los Piños, staying with Jordan and Kelly Adams," she confessed finally.

"Blast it all, I spoke to Jordan not three weeks ago. He never said a word."

"Because he's an honorable man and I had asked him not to. Don't blame him."

"Well, that's water under the bridge now. Get your things packed. I'll be over there to pick you up first thing tomorrow."

Trish sighed. He still wasn't listening to her. She tried again. "I am not leaving here, Daddy. Get that through your head right now. I would love it, though, if you and mother would like to come and meet your granddaughter. Her baptism will be in a few weeks. That would be the perfect time."

"I'll be damned if I'm waiting a few weeks. I'll be

there tomorrow," he repeated, then hung up before she could argue with him.

She carefully replaced the receiver in the cradle, then turned to find Kelly observing from the doorway.

"Everything okay?"

"I just spoke to my father. He says he'll be here tomorrow."

Kelly nodded. "It's good that you finally talked to him," she said. "And I'll make myself scarce in the morning, so you'll have some privacy. Just remember that you're an adult. He can't make you do anything you don't want to do. You have a life here now and plenty of people who love you."

Trish squeezed her hand. "Thank you."

"Maybe you should tell Hardy that your father's coming. I'm sure he'd be glad to stick around and prevent bloodshed. I doubt many men would want to tangle with him. He might be a more than even match for your father."

Trish wistfully considered the idea, then dismissed it. "It wouldn't be fair to drag him into the middle of this. It's not his battle."

"Oh, believe me, I suspect he'd be more than willing to make it his. He has a stake in what you decide, you know."

Trish wasn't entirely sure anymore that Hardy would care one way or another what she decided. He'd made himself scarce lately, which had left her wondering. The truth was, though, that the decision to stay had been made months ago, when her feelings for a certain cowboy had taken her down a path she'd sworn not to travel. She'd worry about his feelings another time.

"No, I have to handle this on my own, once and for all," she said firmly.

Then she went up to her room and spent a restless night waiting for the fireworks to begin.

Her father arrived on her doorstep at midmorning on Sunday. Jordan and Kelly had left for church with a promise not to return until late in the day.

"Call us over at White Pines, if you need us to come back sooner," Kelly had said, giving her a kiss on the cheek before they left. "Be strong."

Trish remembered that advice as she stared first at her father, then at the man beside him. Trish wished she'd asked the Adamses to stay, after all. She hadn't expected her father to drag Jack Grainger along, rather than her mother. Obviously he hadn't given up on his scheme to see them married. She was only surprised he hadn't brought a minister along.

"I want this settled right here and right now," her father declared as if he had a perfect right to take charge. He pushed past her into the living room without pausing to give her so much as a hug.

"We'll set a wedding date today," he announced. "It will have to be a small, quiet wedding, of course. As much as your mother and I had hoped for something lavish for our only daughter, we realize we can't have a huge blowout under the circumstances."

Trish clenched her fists and stiffened her resolve. Not once did she meet Jack's gaze. "No wedding, large or small. Not to Jack," she said quietly, but firmly. "I've made a life for myself here, and this is where I intend to stay."

"You're being emotional," her father said. "Let's look

at this reasonably. You and Jack have a child. You should be married and raising that child together."

"If that child is so important to you, why haven't you even asked to see her?" she shot back.

"There will be time enough after we get this settled," her father responded. He drew a pocket planner out of the briefcase he'd brought along as if this were a business meeting, rather than a reunion with his long-lost daughter. "I have a free Saturday coming up the second weekend in June. That ought to give you and your mother time enough to make the arrangements. She's already spoken to the florist and the caterer, so they're on standby."

"You're not hearing me," she said sharply. "I will not marry a man who was cheating on me when we were engaged." Her gaze clashed with her father's. "That is final."

Her father didn't seem any more surprised by the revelation than her mother had been months ago. To her fury he waved it off as if it were a minor inconvenience, no more important than a difference of opinion over how to squeeze toothpaste from the tube.

"Sowing his wild oats," he said, dismissing Jack's indiscretion as if the man weren't even in the room to speak in his own defense. "I'm sure he's sorry, aren't you, Jack?"

Without giving Jack time to reply, her father went right on trying to bulldoze over Trish's objections. Jack was beginning to look a little green around the gills, in Trish's opinion, which made her wonder what her father had done to get him here. Still, he never even tried to voice an objection. The truth was, Jack never took a stand for or against anything that mattered. Obviously he wanted that promised vice presidency too badly.

"No," Trish said again. "You're not listening to me, Daddy. This wedding is not going to happen."

Her father frowned, more at the interruption, no doubt, than her declaration.

"Forget it," she said, just to make her point one more time.

"Why are you stubbornly clinging to the past?" he demanded. "What's done is done."

"This isn't about the past," she retorted.

"Then what is it about?"

"Me," a familiar voice declared, startling all three of them. Hardy stood in the doorway, his eyes flashing sparks. He was dressed all in black, just the way she liked him best, but there was no question about him being the hero of the hour. "It's about me. Trish is going to marry me."

Trish's mouth gaped. Jack looked relieved. Bryce Delacourt stared.

"Who the hell are you?" her father demanded.

Trish rallied, grateful that once more Hardy was there when she needed him. She knew in her heart he was the kind of man who always would be.

"Daddy, this is Hardy Jones." She took Hardy's callused hand in her own and squeezed. "My fiancé."

Fifteen

Hardy could tell that Trish thought he was just putting on an act for her father's benefit, but he'd never been more serious in his life. Standing in the doorway, listening to Bryce Delacourt's commands and watching that sleazy Jack Grainger turn greener with every word his prospective father-in-law uttered had solidified his resolve.

He'd taken one look at Laura's wimpy father and seen red. That gussied-up stranger was not going to take his family away from him. He'd lost a lot of people he'd loved, but with a sudden flash of insight, he'd realized that he didn't need to lose Trish, that he *couldn't* lose her. He'd planned on waiting until the house was finished, until he had something to offer her, but Kelly's warning about the arrival of Trish's father had spurred him into action.

Heart pounding, he had raced all the way in from the pasture where she had found him working with Harlan Patrick. He hadn't even stopped to worry about the impression of pure desperation he was leaving with his friend and Kelly, a reaction that would no doubt be spread around White Pines by nightfall. The gossip was the least of his concern at this point.

Instead, he'd stood there trying to calm the frantic racing of his pulse, listening to Delacourt making plans for his daughter, riding roughshod over Trish's objections. All it had taken was a sign from Trish that she didn't want Jack Grainger, and Hardy had been more than eager to jump into the fray. He'd already heard her vehement protests from a hundred yards away, which made it all the more difficult to understand why her father couldn't grasp what she was saying when they were in the very same room. Hardy stepped forward and held out his hand to Delacourt. "Sir, I'm Hardy Jones. I'm pleased to meet you. I know how much Trish respects your opinion, so I'm hoping you'll give us your blessing."

The older man still appeared stunned by the sudden turn of events, but he was too much of a businessman to ignore an outstretched hand. He finally shook Hardy's hand. "Good to meet you."

Then he turned his gaze on Trish, regarding his daughter with a mix of disbelief and resignation. "You're sure this is what you want?"

"Absolutely."

She said it with such fervor that Hardy almost believed she really meant it. He took her hand again and gave it a reassuring squeeze.

Delacourt glanced at the once-prospective bridegroom, whose color had finally returned. "Sorry, Jack," he said gruffly. "I never meant to put you in an uncomfortable position. If I'd known what was going on in Trish's head, I wouldn't have insisted you come along."

Trish beamed at Jack, too. "I'm sure you agree that this is for the best," she told her former fiancé. "Now if you'll both excuse me. I need to go upstairs and check on Laura." She glanced at her father. "Would you like to meet your granddaughter?"

"Of course," he said, starting from the room after her.

Grainger cleared his throat. "Would you mind…could I see her, too?"

To Hardy he sounded as if it were a duty he dreaded, rather than a joy to be embraced. He dropped another notch in Hardy's estimation.

"Certainly," Trish said. "She is your daughter, Jack. Whether you play a role in her life is up to you."

"Before you go upstairs, there's one thing I'd like to say," Hardy said, needing to make his own intentions perfectly clear. He directed his gaze straight at Grainger. "Neither of you men know me, but I want you to know that I couldn't love Laura more if she were my own. I'll be the best father she could possibly have, so you can rest easy on that score." Delacourt nodded approvingly. Grainger flushed as if he guessed that Hardy was warning him away.

And Trish stared at him, looking surprised. Apparently she still believed that his sudden appearance, his sudden claim to being her fiancé was all a generous, impetuous charade just to get her father off her back. His sudden assertion that he intended to be a good father to Laura had taken things to another level. He clearly had shaken her.

"You all go ahead. I'll be here when you get back," he said. The thought of seeing Jack Grainger with the baby made his stomach turn over. Besides, he needed some time to figure out exactly how he was going to convince Trish to actually marry him. The three of them were gone for less than a half hour. Obviously Grainger hadn't been struck dumb by fatherly instincts at the sight of his daughter.

When they came back downstairs, Trish was carrying the baby. In a gesture that was probably meant to make a statement she promptly handed Laura to Hardy.

Grainger looked as if he couldn't wait to get away. He barely glanced at Laura before heading out the front door. Trish's father paused long enough to give Hardy a speculative look.

"I'll be in touch," he said to Hardy, then turned to give his daughter a hug. "Your mother will want to talk to you about those wedding plans."

Trish nodded, then stood in the doorway and watched him go.

As soon as Hardy and Trish were finally alone, she looked at him with that grateful expression he was coming to hate.

"Don't even say it," he muttered, beginning to pace.

"Say what?"

"Thank you."

"I wasn't going to," she swore. "I was just going to say that you don't have to go through with this. I'll figure out some way to get out of it. After things settle down, I'm sure I'll be able to come up with something. After all, it won't be the first engagement I've broken off."

Hardy swallowed back fury. Obviously she thought she had it all figured out. Well, she wasn't counting on him. He would hold her to their engagement if he had to conspire with her father and her mother to pull it off.

In the meantime, he thought he knew just how to show her that his intentions were honorable.

"We can talk about it later," he said. "I've got to get back to work."

"How did you know about my father being here, anyway?" she asked as she took Laura from him and followed him to the door. Before he could answer, she waved off the question. "Never mind. I'm sure Kelly told you. She couldn't wait to get out of here this morning. She said she had things to do before church."

"Don't blame Kelly."

"Of course not. She was trying to protect me, just like you were. I'm really—"

Hardy touched a finger to her lips. "I thought I told you not to say you were grateful. I don't want your thanks. I was here because I wanted to be, darlin', because I *needed* to be."

Let her think about that for a while, he thought as he bent down and brushed a kiss across her forehead.

"I'll pick you up tonight at six," he said. "Where will you be, here or in town?"

She stared at him blankly. "Tonight?"

"We need to talk about the engagement, remember?"

For a second a shadow moved across her eyes. Could it have been disappointment? Hardy wondered. Had she wanted to keep up the pretense just a little longer?

"Yes, of course," she said, looking vaguely unsettled. "Breaking it off. I suppose the sooner the better, so my mother doesn't have time to get too carried away with the plans."

"Definitely the sooner the better," Hardy agreed. Of course, he had an entirely different ending in mind than she obviously did.

"Six o'clock, then. I'll be here."

She sounded dismayed rather than pleased he was about to grant her a reprieve. He found that downright promising.

* * *

Apparently Hardy couldn't even bear the thought of a fake engagement, Trish thought bitterly as she watched him drive off, then chided herself for caring. After all, he had been there when she needed him. That was what mattered. The rest was simply a matter of coming up with a plan that would extricate them both from an awkward situation.

So why did she feel worse about a broken phony engagement with Hardy than she ever had about losing the real thing with Jack? Because she foolishly wanted it to be real, she admitted.

"What kind of fool does that make me?" she asked her daughter.

Laura stared back at her with solemn eyes, as if she knew just how much was at stake, as if she could guess that they were about to lose the most important man in both their lives.

Feeling as if she were about to face a firing squad, Trish still forced herself to dress with care that evening. Surely she could get some satisfaction from making Hardy regret walking out on her.

When she walked downstairs in a dress that dipped and clung in all the right places, Kelly shot her a knowing look.

"I gather you intend to render the man speechless," she said lightly.

Now there was a thought, Trish admitted wistfully. If Hardy couldn't gather his wits after getting a good look at her, he couldn't break the engagement.

"Something like that," she told Kelly.

When Hardy arrived a few minutes later, he was wearing a suit. Obviously he considered the end of their engagement to be a special occasion, too, she concluded sourly.

He also seemed nervous, which wasn't like him at all. He hadn't been this ill at ease since the night he'd been forced to deliver Laura in the front seat of his pickup, or the morning after when he'd faced her again.

Rather than head toward Garden City as she'd expected, he turned in the opposite direction.

"Where are we going?" she asked curiously. "Someplace new," he said.

Obviously he'd chosen a place where the memories of this awkward night wouldn't come back to haunt him later, she concluded.

When they neared the familiar sight of the pine woods, Trish's heart began to beat a little faster. When he turned onto that same rutted road, she shot a speculative look at him.

"This is an odd place for a restaurant," she said quietly, watching his face.

"No restaurant," he said. "I thought we ought to be someplace more private for this talk."

She supposed that was considerate, but why here? This was his special place, and now they were about to ruin it with a discussion about how to end something that had never really begun.

Just then they emerged from the woods. Trish's mouth gaped as she saw the beginnings of a house, the same beautiful log cabin that Hardy had described to her the last time they were here.

"You're building it," she whispered, delight spreading across her face. "Oh, Hardy, it's going to be wonderful. Is this what you've been up to these past few weeks?"

He nodded. "Do you really like it? It's still a long

way from being finished, because I'm doing it all myself." He gave her a surprisingly shy look. "Want to take a look around?"

"Of course," she said, already exiting the truck. He grinned at her enthusiasm.

"Wait for me. I'll show you around so you don't trip over something." When he reached her side, he took her hand and led her up the front steps onto the wide porch. The front door was in place, complete with the stainedglass window. The design was obviously a custom one, because right in the middle was a bouquet of flowers and—she leaned closer to be sure—an open book.

"Hardy?" she whispered.

"Don't say anything yet. Just stick with me."

He drew her into what would be the kitchen, then a formal dining room, then finally into a living room that faced the field of wildflowers, the creek and the setting sun.

"It's breathtaking," she said over the lump in her throat.

"Then you won't mind having dinner right here?" he asked.

"Here?"

He showed her out onto a back patio where a table had been set with the finest silver and china. Champagne was on ice in a bucket. Trish's heart skipped a beat. This was a far cry from the dismal way she'd expected the evening to go. Was it possible, could he have a different ending in mind? She wanted desperately to believe that it could be.

"You've really gone to a lot of trouble," she said, meeting his gaze, trying to read his expression.

"You like it?"

"Of course I do. The house, the dinner, everything. You even got the sun to set right on cue."

He grinned. "That took some planning."

"I'm touched," she said. "And grateful."

"Why?"

"I was dreading tonight."

He drew her close. "Darlin', there's nothing to dread."

"But I expected everything to end and now..." She studied him intently. "You're not going to end it, are you?"

He laughed suddenly. "You can read me like a book, can't you?"

"Not always," she admitted. "For instance, right now I can't figure out why you're keeping me in suspense."

"About?" he teased, eyes twinkling.

"Fine," she muttered. "Suit yourself. I think I'll pour myself a little champagne."

She walked over and picked up the bottle, then handed it to him to open. He popped the cork, picked up a glass and handed it to her. She heard something ping against the crystal wineglass and glanced inside. Her mouth dropped open, a lump formed in her throat.

When she could finally speak, she said, "It's a ring."

"Really? Let me see," he said, peering into the glass. "Why, so it is. A diamond, in fact. Now how do you suppose that got in there?"

She touched his cheek. "Hardy, don't," she pleaded. "Don't play games. Not about something this important."

He met her gaze, then silently plucked the ring from the glass and held it up so that the waning sunlight made sparks shoot from it. His gaze still clinging to hers, he said solemnly, "I know we got engaged this morning, and I know you assumed it was just an impulsive thing I did to get your father off your case, but it wasn't, darlin'. I love you. I want this engagement to be real. Brief," he added fervently, "but real."

Tears swam in her eyes. "How brief?"

"Oh, I'd say a few days ought to be long enough, but you can decide. That is, if you'll agree to marry me, if you'll let me be your husband and Laura's father."

A million things crowded into her mind at once. Joy spread through her heart. She couldn't seem to think of a thing to say.

"Trish?" Hardy prodded, his expression worried.

"I'm overwhelmed," she said finally. "I'm grateful."

"Dammit, I don't want your gratitude," he said impatiently.

She kissed him to silence him. "I am grateful," she repeated. "But I was also going to say that I love you, Hardy Jones. You are the most amazing, sensitive, incredible man I've ever known."

Hardy stopped and stared, clearly taken aback. Apparently he'd expected to have to put up more of a fight. "Say that again."

"I love you," she said, grinning.

"You do?"

She nodded. "Get used to it, cowboy. Your bachelor days are numbered."

Hardy whooped and gathered her into his arms. He twirled her around until they were both dizzy and giddy.

Laughing, Trish gazed into his eyes. "I take it you're not as upset by this as you would have been a few months ago?"

"Upset? No way." He peered at her intently. "You are saying you'll marry me, right? You are saying yes?"

"No need to say it," she informed him. "I've already

told the world—well, my father, anywaythat we're engaged. I wouldn't want to make a liar out of either one of us."

"No, indeed. We couldn't have that."

She regarded him seriously. "Hardy, I know you never planned on getting married or having a family. I heard all about your New Year's resolution when I first got to town."

Hardy grinned, seemingly unperturbed. "You ever know a New Year's resolution that hasn't been broken?"

"As long as you don't feel the same way about wedding vows, I'd say we're in business."

He kissed her until her head spun. "No, darlin'. Those words are the kind a man says just once, and they're meant to last forever."

Trish wanted him so badly she ached with it. "Does this house have a bedroom yet?"

Hardy swallowed hard. "Not yet. Why?"

"Because I desperately want to make love with my new fiancé."

"Is that so?" he asked, clearly intrigued. "I have a very thick, fluffy blanket in the truck and we're all alone in the middle of nowhere. How would you feel about making love right out here?"

She was already reaching for his tie. "Forget the blanket," she said at once.

"But—" The protest died on his lips, when she reached for the buckle of his belt.

His hands swept hers out of the way, then reached for her, sliding her dress over her head in one clever movement. "You never cease to amaze me," he told her.

"Think I can satisfy you after you being used to having a different woman every few days?"

"I think you can surprise me through eternity," he said, as he unclasped her bra and filled his hands with her breasts. "You are perfect."

"Not so perfect," she said, cataloging what she thought of as her many physical flaws. Hardy paid extra attention to each one she mentioned, moving from breasts to hips to thighs in a way meant to reassure her that what she saw as flaws, he viewed as sensuous, seductive parts of a whole woman, a woman he was desperately in love with.

He dragged a cushion from a chair before lowering her to the patio. No bed could have been as romantic as this impromptu one under a sky that was rapidly turning from orange to mauve to velvet.

"I have imagined being with you a thousand and one times," he told her as he entered her at last. "None of them were anything like this."

"You probably figured we'd be in a bed," she teased, rising to meet the thrust of his hips, awed by the sensations rippling through her. She had never felt so full, so complete, not just where he had entered her, but in her heart.

"I should have known," she said on a gasp of pure pleasure.

"Known what?"

"That it would be magic."

"We'll keep it that way," he promised as he began a rhythm that drove out all teasing, all thought. Wave after wave of wicked sensations washed over her, until she cried out his name, then felt him shudder with his own powerful release.

As the stars came out, they relaxed in each other's arms.

"I guess we're well and truly engaged now," Trish declared, turning to face him.

He grinned. "I guess we are."

"No backing out."

"I wouldn't think of it, especially since that entire box of condoms I bought in case tonight went the way I hoped is still out in the truck with the blanket. I'm sorry. We haven't even talked about having more kids."

"I want your babies, Hardy."

"Laura is mine, in every way that counts."

Her heart melted at the declaration. "I know you feel that way. It's one of the reasons I love you."

"Are there others?"

"Too many to name in a single night," she told him, meaning it.

"That's okay, darlin'. We have a whole lifetime for you to fill me in. Then we can spend eternity with me telling you all the ways I love you and how I'll never in a million years let you get away."

* * * * *

DYLAN AND THE BABY DOCTOR

Prologue

A half dozen yelling, laughing toddlers raced around the backyard of pediatrician Kelsey James. They were definitely on a sugar high after consuming enough birthday cake and ice cream for twice as many kids.

Maybe they hadn't actually consumed it, she concluded after a survey of the mess. An awful lot appeared to have been smeared over shirts, spilled on the dark green picnic table or dumped in the grass, along with trails of ribbon and shredded wrapping paper. Melting pools of vanilla ice cream were everywhere. Having the party outside had been a very smart decision.

"Obviously, the party is a success," Lizzy Adams-Robbins declared, conducting her own survey of the damage. "I can't imagine why you were so worried."

Finally, after days of ridiculous anxiety over throwing a kid's birthday party, Kelsey actually allowed herself to relax. She listened to the laughter and smiled for the first time in days, maybe longer. The tight knot in her stomach eased and something that felt a lot like contentment replaced it. It was such a fragile, unfamiliar sensation, she basked in it for just a moment before responding.

"It is wonderful, isn't it?" she said finally. "I know I was acting like a nutcase over this, but Bobby's been through so much these past few months—leaving his dad, moving to a new place, making new friends. I just wanted his birthday party to be special. The Western theme was his idea. Ever since we stayed out at your father's ranch, he's really taken with the idea of being a cowboy."

"Well, the new boots were definitely a big hit," Lizzy said.

"They ought to be. Custom boots for a three-year-old." Kelsey shook her head. "I must be overcompensating."

Lizzy, whom she had known since med school in Miami, squeezed her hand. "Kelsey, stop with the guilt this instant. You had no choice. You had to divorce Paul. He was a creep. And you were absolutely right to get out of Miami and come here. The clinic needed you. I needed you. And Bobby is fitting in just fine." She clasped Kelsey's shoulders and turned her to look at the chaos. "You can stop overcompensating. Does that look like a little boy who is unhappy?"

Kelsey found herself grinning again at the sight of her son, his chubby little legs pumping furiously to keep up with the older children, his face streaked with chocolate frosting and vanilla ice cream. He looked like a perfectly normal little boy who was having the time of his life.

"He is having a good time, isn't he? And the presents…" She shook her head in bemusement. "Your family really didn't have to go crazy with the presents. There are too many toys. He doesn't play with even half of the ones he has now."

Lizzy rolled her eyes. "Tell that to my father. He doesn't believe it's possible for a child to have too many toys. Nothing makes him happier than spoiling his babies, and as far as he's concerned you and Bobby became part of the family the minute you arrived in town."

Harlan Adams truly was remarkable. Kelsey had heard all about him from Lizzy, of course, but even all those old tales of a doting father hadn't prepared her for the incredible eighty-nine-year-old patriarch of the Adams clan. She had never known anyone as generous or as wise. Or as meddlesome, she thought fondly.

When he'd first heard about Kelsey's decision to leave Miami and the reasons for it, he'd called her himself and added his invitation to Lizzy's. Once she was in Los Piños, he'd welcomed her warmly, taking her and Bobby into his own home at White Pines until they could find a place of their own. He'd allowed the two of them to leave only when he'd checked out the new house for himself and concluded that it was suitable. He'd even insisted she raid his attic for furniture, since she'd taken very little from the Miami home she had shared with Paul.

Harlan Adams had also extracted a promise that they would go on joining the family for Sunday dinner at the ranch. He was as indulgent and attentive with Bobby as he was with all of his own grandchildren and great-grandchildren. Bobby had basked in the masculine attention, a commodity that had been all too rare in his young life. His own father had been too busy scoring business deals and pills to pay much attention to him.

With her own parents far away in Maine and not nearly as generous with their love or their time, Kelsey was more grateful for the Adamses than she could ever say. She owed them all, but especially Harlan, his wife, Janet, and of course Lizzy, the best friend any woman could ask for. Lizzy had made it all possible and acted as if Kelsey were the one doing her a favor, rather than the other way around.

"Have I told you how grateful I am?" she asked Lizzy.

"Only about a million times," Lizzy said. "I'm the one who's grateful. We needed a pediatrician here and I can't imagine anyone I'd rather work with than you. The timing couldn't have been better."

"Still—"

"Stop it," Lizzy said firmly. She studied Kelsey intently. "Are you really doing okay, though? No second thoughts? No regrets over divorcing Paul? Los Pinõs is a far cry from Miami and our little clinic would fit into one tiny corner of the trauma center back there."

"Definitely no regrets over Paul. And you were the one who was hell-bent on being a big trauma doctor. I just love kids. It doesn't matter where I treat them. I couldn't be happier right here," Kelsey reassured her, meaning every word.

The differences were all good ones. There was a sense of community here that was never possible in a bustling, urban environment like Miami. While she might have made a difference in Miami and while the medical challenges might have been greater, here the rewards came in the form of sticky hugs from her pint-sized patients and warm, grateful smiles from people she was getting to know as friends.

Most of all, Los Pinõs was far away from Paul James and the disaster he had almost made of both their lives. Hopefully, he would never discover her whereabouts. Hopefully, her ex-husband would forget her existence— and Bobby's. That was the deal they had made. She would forget his deceit, his illegal use of her prescription pads to get narcotics, and he would leave her and his son alone.

Forgetting hadn't been easy. At the end, Paul's behavior had been so erratic, so unpredictable, she hadn't been convinced he would stick to his word...or even remember he'd given it. It had been nearly a year now, and so far she hadn't heard so much as a peep from him. She was finally beginning to relax her guard a little. She'd stopped panicking whenever the phone rang or whenever a strange car drove past the house.

She glanced at Bobby, who was adding grape juice to the stains on his face and clothes, and smiled. He was all boy, a miniature version of her ex, with the same dimpled smile, the same light brown hair and dark brown eyes. But while her son's eyes were bright and clear and most often twinkling with laughter, Paul's had been shadowed or toobright with the drugs she hadn't guessed he was taking until way too late.

She felt Lizzy squeeze her hand, looked up and met her friend's concerned gaze.

"Don't go back there," Lizzy advised. "Not even for a minute. You couldn't have changed anything. It was Paul's problem, not yours. If he didn't care enough about himself or you to get off the pills, nothing you could have done would have helped." Kelsey was amazed by Lizzy's perceptiveness.

"How did you know what was on my mind?"

"Because it usually is. Besides, I always know what you're thinking, just the way you could read my mind back in med school. You knew how I felt about marrying Hank practically before I did."

Kelsey chuckled. "Not possible. You knew you were in love with Hank Robbins from the time you were a schoolgirl. From the moment we became roommates, all I ever heard about was Hank this or Hank that. It didn't require major deductive reasoning to figure out you were crazy about the guy."

"I knew I was in love with him, yes, but not that I was ready to marry him and juggle a baby, marriage and med school," Lizzy said. "I was scared silly when I found out I was pregnant. You helped me to see that I had to take that final leap of faith, that we could make it work."

Lizzy wasn't exaggerating her panic. Kelsey recalled exactly how upset Lizzy had been when she'd first realized she was pregnant with Hank's baby. There had never been a doubt in Kelsey's mind what the outcome would be, especially once Hank had found out about the pregnancy. Lizzy's handsome, totally smitten cowboy had pursued her with relentless determination, ignoring her doubts, finding solutions and compromises that Lizzy had claimed were impossible.

"It's worked out fine, hasn't it? No regrets?"

"Better than fine, smarty." Lizzy grinned, then leaned closer to confide in a whisper, "In fact, we're going to have another baby."

"Oh, my." Kelsey sighed, trying to hide any hint of envy. She had wanted a whole houseful of kids herself, but if Bobby was all she ever had, he would be enough. She gave Lizzy a fierce hug. "Congratulations! That's wonderful. Does Hank know yet?" Lizzy gave her a rueful look. "You may have found out before he did last time, but this time I thought Hank ought to be the first to know. I told him last night."

"And?"

"He's over the moon. He's wanted this for a long time. I was the holdout. While I was finishing my residency and getting the clinic started, I didn't think he should carry all the burden for child care, even though he seems to love it. I figured it was about time I pitched in, too. The clinic's hours are a whole lot more consistent than my hours at the hospital in Garden City. I might actually get to see this baby's first step and hear his or her first word. I missed so much of that with Jamey."

"I am so happy for you."

"Will you be a godmother to this one?"

Kelsey was enchanted with the idea of becoming an even more integral part of the extended Adams family. "Nothing would please me more," she said at once. "Of course, with the two of us to influence this baby, he or she won't have any choice but to be a doctor."

Lizzy shook her head. "Not a chance. Girl or boy, Hank wants a rancher. He says Jamey already spends too much time wanting to cut up frogs like his mama did in school."

Lizzy glanced around at the half dozen kids, most of whom were beginning to fade from all the partying. Her gaze sought out Jamey, who was tanned and had his daddy's rich brown, sun-streaked hair. He was five now and had a definite mind of his own. The stubborn streak was Lizzy's contribution, according to Hank, along with the fascination with cutting up dead critters.

"Well, I think it's time to get the troops home before they all wind up sound asleep in your backyard," Lizzy said.

"Thank you again for helping today," Kelsey said.

"Anytime. If you need any of us for anything ever, all you need to do is call. Day or night, okay?" It was something Lizzy never failed to remind her of, Kelsey thought, as her friend left with a carload of exhausted

Adams kids. Although she appreciated the gesture of support, too often it only served as an unnerving reminder to Kelsey that as unpredictable as Paul James was, there very well could come a time when she would desperately need their help.

One

Dylan Delacourt knew perfectly well why he'd been spending so much time visiting his baby sister lately. Oh, he claimed that he was just checking up on her for the rest of the family. He said he liked helping his new brother-in-law work on the house Hardy had built for Trish. But the truth was, he was in Los Pinõs because of his niece.

Baby Laura had stolen his heart. On his worst days, when he was so low everything looked black, Laura's smile was like sunshine. Seeing it was a bittersweet sensation, though. It reminded him just a little too much of another baby, another sweet smile.

The last time he'd held his son, Shane had been just about Laura's age, thirteen months. He'd just begun to toddle around on unsteady legs. He'd uttered his first word, *Mama,* and that had pretty much been the moment when Dylan had concluded that Shane belonged with Kit and her new husband fulltime.

Saying goodbye to his boy, doing what was best for him and letting him grow up with a "father," rather than a stepfather, had almost killed Dylan. He'd agonized over it for months, hated Kit for divorcing him and forcing him into making such an untenable decision.

But he had also known just how deep the bitterness between him and Kit ran, recognized that no matter how hard they tried, there would never be agreement or peace or cooperation between them. In the end, he hadn't been willing to subject his son to the inevitable battles, the simmering resentments. Giving up Shane was probably the single most unselfish act of his life. And not a day went by that he didn't regret it.

His own grief and pain had been lessened somewhat by the knowledge that Kit's new husband was a kind, decent man, who already had two boys of his own. Steve Davis kept regular hours, not the erratic, unpredictable schedule of a private eye. He would give Shane the time, the love and the whole family that the boy deserved.

Dylan tried never to look back, but there were too many days and twice as many nights when that was impossible. It had been more than four years now and he still ached for his boy. He wondered how tall he was, if he still had the same cowlick in his hair, if he was athletic, if he remembered his real daddy at all. That's when the regrets would start to add up and he'd turn up in Los Pinõs, his mood bleak, his soul weary.

Trish intuitively understood what brought him there and over time, Dylan had revealed some of it to Hardy. He withstood their pitying looks, accepted their love and their concern. But with little Laura, there was only the sunshine of her brilliant smile and the joy of her laughter. He could be a hero, instead of the dad who'd walked away.

"Unca Dyl," she squealed when she saw him climb out of his rugged sports utility vehicle on a dreary Friday night. Arms outstretched, she pumped her little legs so fast, she almost tripped over her own feet trying to get to him.

Dylan scooped her up and into the air above his head until she chortled with glee. He brought her down to peer into her laughing blue eyes that were so like her mama's. He'd been nine when Trish was born and he could still remember the way she, too, had looked up at him as if he were ten feet tall.

"Munchkin, I think you're destined to be a pilot or an astronaut," he declared. "You have absolutely no fear of heights."

Laura giggled and gestured until he lifted her high again, then swung her low in a stomach-sinking dip. "Still making career choices for her, I see," Trish said, stepping off the porch to join them. "For a man who refused to let anyone tell him what he should grow up to be, you seem intent on controlling your niece's destiny."

"Not controlling it," Dylan insisted. "Just listing a few of her options." He dropped a kiss on his sister's cheek. "Thanks for letting me come."

Instantly, sympathy filled her eyes. "I know it's a tough weekend. Shane will be six tomorrow, right?"

Dylan nodded. "I don't want to talk about it, though."

Trish sighed. "You never do. Dylan, don't you think—"

"I'm not going to get in touch with him," he said fiercely. "I made a deal with Kit and Steve. I intend to stick to it. If the time ever comes when Shane wants to know me, she'll help him find me. Until then, I have to forget about him."

"I don't know how you can live with that," she whispered, touching his cheek. "I know you think it was the right thing to do, but—"

"It was the only thing to do. Now can we drop it,

please? I could have stayed home and listened to Mother, if I'd wanted to go over this again. Goodness knows, she never lets me forget how I'd deprived her of getting to know her first grandchild." Trish looked as if she might argue, then sighed. "Done. I hope you're hungry, though. Hardy's out back making hamburgers on the grill. It's his night to cook and if it can't be done on a grill, we don't eat."

Over the weekend, Dylan fell into the easy rhythms of his sister's family, grateful to be able to push the memories away for a few days at least. When Sunday rolled around, he still wasn't ready to go back to Houston and face real life. None of the cases on his desk were challenging. Just routine skip-traces, a straying husband, an amateur attempt at insurance fraud. He could wrap any one of them up in less than a day, which was one of the reasons he'd been so desperate to get away. Tackling them wouldn't have crowded out his misery.

"Stay one more night," Trish begged.

He figured she'd sensed his reluctance to go. His baby sister had always been able to read him like a book, better than any of the younger brothers who'd come between them. Fiercely loyal and kindhearted, the male Delacourts taunted each other and banded together against the outside world. But as tight-knit as they were, none of his brothers dared to bulldoze through his defenses the way Trish did.

"Yeah," Hardy agreed, picking up on some unspoken signal from his wife. "Stick around. You can get the tile up in the second bathroom. Trish says I don't have the patience to do it right."

"And I do?" Dylan said, amused by their ploy to make him feel that his continued presence wasn't an intrusion.

Crediting him with more patience than anyone was a real stretch.

"Trust me," Trish said. "You're bound to have more than my husband. He keeps getting distracted."

Hardy grinned. "Because I happen to have a very sexy new wife."

Sometimes witnessing their happiness was more painful than going back to his lonely existence in Houston, but tonight there was no contest. Anything was better than going home.

Dylan held up his hands. "Okay, okay, no details, please. You two may be married, but she's still my baby sister. I'll stay."

"Good," Trish said, beaming, clearly pleased with herself.

That night, just as they were finishing supper, the phone rang. Because he was closest, Dylan grabbed it.

"Oh, Dylan, is that you?" a vaguely familiar voice demanded.

Dylan tensed, alerted by the tone to trouble. "Yes. Who is this?"

"It's Lizzy. Lizzy Adams. I'm the doctor who treated Trish after Laura was born. We met at Trish's wedding."

He recalled a slender, dark-haired woman who'd radiated confidence. She didn't sound so sure of herself now. "Of course. You want to talk to Trish. She's right here."

"No, no. It's you I need to speak to."

"Oh?"

"You're a private detective, right?"

"Yes." He slid into professional mode, finally grasping that what he was hearing in her voice was a thread of panic she was trying hard to hide. "What's going on?"

"My friend, the doctor who works with me at the clinic, Kelsey James…have you met her?"

Although he'd met dozens of people at the wedding and on subsequent visits, no image came to mind. "I don't think so."

"Well, it's about her little boy, Bobby. Something's happened."

Dylan's heart began to thud dully. Something told him he didn't want to know the rest, but he forced himself to ask anyway. "What about him?"

"He's disappeared. She thinks he's been kidnapped. Can you come, Dylan? Can you come right away?"

"Just tell me where," he said grimly, beckoning for paper and pencil. As soon as he had them, he jotted down the directions. "Have you talked to the police?"

"Justin's here now," she said, referring to her nephew who also happened to be the local sheriff. "He needs help, though. Kelsey wants this kept quiet. She won't let him call in the FBI or anyone else from outside."

The knee-jerk reaction of a panicked parent—or something more? "Why?" he asked.

"Let her explain. Just come. Please."

"I'm on my way."

"What?" Trish demanded, already standing as he reached for his jacket. "Why did Lizzy call you? What's happened?"

"It's about somebody named Kelsey. Her little boy's disappeared."

"Oh, no," Trish whispered, suddenly glancing at Laura as if to reassure herself that her daughter was right where she belonged. She regarded him worriedly. "Dylan, I don't know about this. Are you sure this is something you should get involved in? I know you're the best and I adore Kelsey and Bobby, but won't this be too hard?"

"I can't just turn my back," he said, wondering what the look Trish exchanged with Hardy was all about. "You obviously know this Kelsey person. Is there something more that I should know?"

"No," Trish insisted.

She said it without looking at him, which sure as anything meant she was covering up something. Trish had never been able to lie worth a hoot.

"Trish?"

"Just go."

He thought Hardy looked every bit as guilty as his sister, but he didn't have time to try to find out what they were hiding. If he didn't like the answers he got from Kelsey James, he'd come back here for the missing pieces.

"I'll try to call," he said, "but don't wait up for me."

"If you need people for a search, call me," Hardy said. "I can get all the men from White Pines to help out."

"Thanks. Let's see what's going on first."

If he had been anyplace other than Los Piños, Dylan would have called one of his buddies to take over right this second, because Trish was rightsearching for missing kids tore him up inside. But there weren't a lot of private detectives nearby and time was critical in a situation like this. He had no choice. All he could do was pray that this disappearance would have a happy ending.

Kelsey felt as if someone had ripped out her heart. Anyone who'd been through med school and worked in an emergency room was used to terrible stress and was able to think clearly in a crisis. Despite all that training, though, she hadn't been able to form a coherent thought since the moment when she'd realized that Bobby was no longer playing in the backyard where she'd left him.

She had simply stood staring blankly at the open gate, frozen, until adrenaline kicked in. Then she had raced to the street, pounded frantically on doors, trailed by bewildered, helpful neighbors as she'd searched futilely for her son. Although plenty of people were outside on such a sunny summer day, no one had seen him leave the yard. No one had seen him toddling down the street. A child Bobby's age, alone, would have drawn attention.

She had no idea how long it had been—minutes, an hour—before she concluded that Bobby hadn't simply wandered away. By then both Justin and Lizzy had arrived, alerted by the neighbors. Justin had taken charge automatically, asking crisp, concise questions, organizing a search and leaving Lizzy to sit with her and try to keep her calm, when she wanted to be out searching herself.

With neighbors crowded around wanting to help, talking in hushed voices, Kelsey didn't feel calm, not after three cups of chamomile tea, not after the mild tranquilizer her friend had insisted she take. She wasn't sure she would ever be calm again, not until she had her baby back in her arms. This was her worst nightmare coming true. It didn't matter that no one had seen a stranger on the street. She knew what had happened. She knew who had taken Bobby. And why.

"It's Paul," she whispered finally, forcing herself to say aloud what had been tormenting her from the mo-

ment she'd realized Bobby was gone. "He's taken him.
I know he has."

"You're probably right," Lizzy said, her tone soothing, as if she still feared that Kelsey would shatter at any
second. "And I know you hate the man's guts, but isn't
that better than a stranger? Paul won't hurt Bobby. Despite what a louse I think he is, I know he loved Bobby.
He just wants money or drugs and Bobby's his bargaining chip. I think you can count on him being in touch.
He's not going to run with him. He'll bring Bobby back
the minute he gets what he wants."

"If he's desperate, who knows what he'll do?" Kelsey
countered, shuddering.

This wasn't the old Paul, the one she'd fallen in love
with. That Paul had been brilliant and driven and passionate. He had loved her in a way she'd never expected
to be loved, charming her, convincing her in the end that
he couldn't live without her, that they shouldn't wait till
she finished med school or her residency to marry. It
was ironic, really, that she'd struggled with the thought
of marrying, just as Lizzy had, had finally rationalized
that if Lizzy and Hank could juggle everything and make
it work, so could she and Paul.

She couldn't exactly pinpoint when Paul had changed.
Maybe he hadn't, not really. Maybe the drive she'd so
admired in him at first had always been an obsessive
need to win, to get what he wanted when he wanted it.
He'd gotten her. He'd gotten the perfect job at the right
brokerage house, then slaved to be the top broker, the
quickest to earn a promotion. He'd convinced her to have
a baby, even when she'd been so sure it was too soon,
that their schedules were too demanding.

"We have the money. We can afford help," he'd reasoned. "I want a family, while we're still young."

Now, always now. But she had gone along, because he had wanted it so much and she had wanted to please him. When Bobby came, every doubt she had had vanished. He was perfect. Paul was ecstatic and more driven than ever. Their son was going to have the best of everything.

"We have enough," she had told him more than once. But it was never enough for Paul, not for a kid whose family had struggled while he was growing up. He told her again and again that he knew the real meaning of adversity and he was determined that his wife and son would never catch so much as a glimpse of it. "Not as long as I'm able to bring in the big bucks just by putting in some long hours." Then he had taken a nasty spill on a ski trip and fractured his wrist. It should have been little more than a minor inconvenience, but she knew now that that was when his addiction began. He'd taken the painkillers so he wouldn't have to slow down for so much as a second. He hadn't wanted to miss making a single commission. He'd never stopped.

She had cursed herself a thousand times for not realizing he was hooked. She was a doctor, for heaven's sake. She should have caught the signs, but she was too busy herself. In her own way, she was every bit as much of an overachiever as Paul.

Then there was a traffic accident. Paul's injuries were minor, the other driver's only slightly worse, but the routine bloodwork the police insisted on had revealed a high level of painkillers in his system. Confronted, he'd promised to stop taking them.

Shaken to the core, Kelsey had searched the house, found every last pill herself and flushed them all down the toilet. She had warned Paul to get help or lose her. She had wanted desperately to believe that he loved her and Bobby enough to quit.

A month later, she'd realized that her prescription pad was missing. Suspicious, she had made calls to half a dozen pharmacies, verified that her husband had gotten pills at every one of them and at who knew how many more. He had forged her signature on every prescription.

She had seen a lawyer that same day and had the divorce and custody papers drawn up. It was a drastic course of action, but she hadn't known what else to do. She had prayed that maybe the sight of the divorce papers would shock him into getting help. It hadn't. He'd simply taken more pills and blamed her for backing him into a corner.

She had known then that she couldn't let him ruin their lives, destroy her reputation. That night she had made a shaken and contrite Paul sign the papers. A week later, she'd moved to Texas, praying that he really would get the help he needed.

Now this. God help her, but she would kill him if he did anything to hurt her baby.

"We have to find him," she whispered.

"Which is why I called Dylan," Lizzy soothed. "He'll find him. Trish says he's the best private eye in Houston. Unlike Justin, he's probably handled cases like this a zillion times. He'll be fast and discreet."

"Where is he?" Kelsey whispered, her desperation mounting with every second that passed. Unless he'd spent it all on pills, Paul had plenty of money, enough to run to the ends of the earth. She might never find him or her baby.

"Shouldn't he be here by now?" she asked, edgy with impatience and ever-growing fear.

Lizzy glanced toward the doorway just then and smiled. "Here he is right now." She stood up, offering her seat opposite Kelsey at the kitchen table. "Dylan, this is Bobby's mom, Kelsey James. *Doctor* Kelsey James."

Kelsey felt her ice-cold hand being enveloped in a strong, reassuring grip. His size registered, too. He was a big man. Solid, with coal-black hair and a grim expression. She focused on his eyes, blue eyes that were clearly taking in everything. She had the feeling that his gaze missed nothing, that he could leave the room and describe every person, every item in it. At the same time there was a distance there, a cool detachment. Funny how she found that reassuring. He was a professional, she reminded herself, just what she needed. The best. He would find Bobby and bring him back. That was all that mattered.

"Tell me what happened," he suggested in a voice that was surprisingly gentle. He sounded almost as if he truly understood her pain. "Tell me exactly what you did, beginning with the moment you realized your boy was gone. Where was he? How long had he been out of your sight?"

"I've already told Justin everything," she said, not sure she could handle going over it again. It seemed surreal, as if she hadn't lived through it at all.

"Tell me," he said insistently. "I might catch something that Justin missed. Or you might remember something else. Every little detail is important." He listened intently as Kelsey described everything that had happened, but when she mentioned Paul, something in his attentive expression changed. That disturbing coolness she'd noticed before subtly shifted into what she could only describe as icy disdain. He gazed at her with such piercing intensity that she shivered.

"You have full custody of your son?" he asked, as if it were some sort of crime.

She nodded, unsure why that seemed to unsettle him so.

"When was the last time the father saw him?" he asked, an inexplicable edge in his voice.

"Before we left Miami, about ten months ago. That was our agreement," she said, not explaining about the other part of that agreement, about her promise not to turn Paul in to the authorities. No one except Lizzy knew about that and no one ever would.

"You believe this was an abduction by a noncustodial parent," he said, summing up what she'd told him.

"I'm sure of it."

"Has he threatened to take Bobby before?"

"No, but—"

"Then why are you so certain?"

"I just am. It's the only thing that makes sense. Bobby wouldn't go off with a stranger, not without raising a fuss. Besides, I don't have enemies. I don't make a lot of money, so a demand for ransom's hardly likely. If someone wanted money in this town, they'd take an Adams."

He nodded. He might be an outsider here, just as she was, but he obviously knew who had the power and the fortune.

"You haven't treated any kids who didn't make it, whose parents might blame you?" he asked.

"No. Not since Miami." There had been a few inconsolable parents back then who'd wanted to cast blame on someone, *anyone,* and she'd been the easiest target.

"People who lose a child aren't always thinking clearly, but there were no malpractice suits. I doubt any of them would pursue me to Texas."

"Okay, then, let's assume it's your ex. Have you got a picture of him? And I'll need one of Bobby, too. The most recent one you have."

Relief flooded through her at his concrete suggestions. At last, something she could do. She went for the photo albums she kept in the living room, took out the most recent picture of Paul, then another of Bobby from his birthday party just a few weeks earlier. Ironically, the latest one she had of Paul had been taken on that ill-fated ski trip that had started his downward spiral.

"You're going to help?" she asked as she handed the pictures to Dylan.

The question had been rhetorical, but for a moment she actually thought he might refuse. His expression was grim. He looked as if he wanted to say no. In fact, the word seemed to be on the tip of his tongue, but with Lizzy and others looking on expectantly, he finally sighed heavily.

"I'll help," he said at last.

After he'd gone, Kelsey kept telling herself that was a good thing, that she could count on this man, because Lizzy had said she could. But in her heart she kept wondering about that tiny hint of reluctance. It had something to do with her custody agreement with Paul. She was sure of it. Until she had mentioned that, Dylan Delacourt had been on her side. Now she couldn't help wondering if he was really on hers...or on Paul's.

Two

Dylan wasn't sure which had unsettled him more, gazing into Kelsey James's worried green eyes and feeling her fear, or discovering that she had sole custody of her son, that she had taken the boy away from his natural father. The former drew him to her, made him sympathetic. The latter made him want to withdraw from the case before he even got started. He couldn't help making possibly faulty and unfair comparisons to his own situation. He instinctively lumped Kelsey in with Kit, assuming she too had backed a man into a desperate corner that had cost him his son. All of his own bitterness and resentment came surging back with a new focus: a slim, frightened mother who probably deserved better from him.

In the end, reason—and obligation to the Adamses for their past kindnesses to his sister—won out. There was also the slim chance that Bobby could have been taken by someone other than his father. Until he knew for certain that Bobby was not in real danger, Dylan knew he had no choice. He had to take the case.

Of course, if he hadn't been persuaded by duty, there

was the picture of Bobby, a robust little boy with an endearing grin. He couldn't help comparing him to Shane, wondering if his son was as healthy and happy as Bobby appeared to be in the picture. No matter what, Dylan knew he couldn't risk any harm coming to the child because his own personal demons kept him from pitching in to find him. With any luck they would locate Bobby quickly, Dylan's duty would be done, and he wouldn't have to spend much time around Kelsey James.

Eager to get away from her and to get started, he muttered an inane reassurance that neither of them believed, then left the crowded kitchen and went off in search of Justin Adams.

Justin might be a small-town sheriff, but he was smart and dedicated. He would have covered all the necessary bases and Dylan saw no need for them to duplicate efforts. Hopefully Justin would feel the same way, rather than going territorial on him the way a lot of cops did when faced with a private eye on their turf.

He found Justin outside by his patrol car, talking to his dispatcher over the radio. He signaled a greeting to Dylan.

"I want every last man on this, okay? Forget the shift roster and call them all in."

"Got it," the dispatcher said. "Want me to start calling motels? It could save time."

"Do it, Becky," Justin agreed. "Start with the immediate county, then widen it county by county. And make sure I can read your damn notes for once, okay?"

"There is nothing wrong with my handwriting," she responded tartly. "At least I *take* notes, unlike some people I could name."

Dylan would have smiled at the obviously familiar

bickering if the circumstances had been different. Justin sighed as he signed off. "The blasted woman's known me too long. She thinks she's the boss, even though I'm the one with the badge." He studied Dylan. "Lizzy called you, right? I figured she would."

"I hope you don't mind."

"Absolutely not. I can use all the manpower around on this, especially if you've got experience. Except for old Mr. Elliott, who wanders away from home and gets lost since his Alzheimer's has gotten worse, and the occasional missing dog, this is not something I'm used to handling. I'd be a whole lot more comfortable calling in the FBI, but Kelsey got so upset when I mentioned it, I backed off."

"Any idea what she's afraid of?"

Justin shook his head. "I'd be willing to bet Lizzy knows, though. One year as roommates in med school, and the two of them have been thick as thieves ever since. If we don't catch a break soon, I'll pound it out of her, if I have to. Figuratively, of course."

Sensing his frustration and sharing it, Dylan grinned. "I'll help. Do you know anything about Paul James?"

"Only that Kelsey wanted to get away from him badly enough that she gave up a promising career in Miami to move here. It came up suddenly, despite Lizzy's pretense that they'd always talked about working together. One minute Lizzy was running the clinic by herself, the next Kelsey was here and living out at my grandfather's. Grandpa Harlan seemed real reluctant to let her and Bobby leave to move here in town, and I sensed it wasn't just because he'd grown attached to them. He had me check the security locks on this place top to bottom."

"Domestic violence?" Dylan speculated.

Justin shrugged. "Always a possibility, but my gut tells me no. A few years back when Patsy turned up here in town, she was running from an abusive husband. I don't see the same signs with Kelsey. She's at ease around men, for one thing."

"Patsy's your wife, right?" Dylan asked, trying to recall what he had heard about her situation. Just that she'd run from a husband who'd been a highprofile political candidate in another state, a man who had had a nasty temper. Bottom line, Justin would know better than most about how a victim of abuse would behave.

"Right. She had a little boy when we met and we have another one of our own now. She's at home with them, in a panic that something will happen to them if she turns her back for a second. Until we know for sure that Paul James is behind this, there will be a lot of other mothers who feel the same way. I'd like people to know as soon as we're sure that there's no need to lock the kids inside and bar their doors."

"Can't say I blame them, in the meantime," Dylan said. "How about I start running checks on Paul James? Maybe we can pick up a trail from credit card receipts, see if he's in the area."

"Go for it," Justin agreed. "If you need access to a computer, use the one down at the station. I'll deputize you here and now to make it all nice and legal."

That was more than Dylan had hoped for. Normally, he preferred to operate on his own, but in this instance he was far from his own computer and other resources. A little hand-in-hand cooperation with the local authorities could cut through a lot of red tape. Having access to that computer would be a godsend. Besides, Justin struck him as a good man to work with. The past few minutes

had established that he wasn't a hardliner with an attitude. He was the kind of sheriff Dylan admired, a man
who just wanted to get the job done, utilizing whatever
resources he could command.

"I'll let you know what I find out," he promised. "I'm
not worried about that," Justin told him. "Nothing gets
past my dispatcher. Becky will be all over you while
you're around. If you find so much as an itty-bitty clue,
I'll know about it."

Dylan chuckled, liking the man more and more. "I
should have known you weren't just trying to make my
life easy."

Justin's expression sobered. "Nope. Just trying to find
that little boy before any harm comes to him."

"Amen to that," Dylan said.

Unable to sit still a moment longer, Kelsey wandered
into the living room and stared out the window at the
two men talking on the sidewalk.

Over the last few months she had gotten to know Justin Adams. She trusted him, but she also knew that Bobby's disappearance was not the sort of thing he typically
had to handle. She'd seen how upset he'd been by her
refusal to call in the FBI. Maybe she was crazy, but she
thought the fewer police involved, the better the chances
of keeping Paul's secret and keeping Bobby safe. Watching Justin talk to Dylan, she could almost sense his relief at having someone with more expertise involved.
She wished she was as confident.

She studied the private investigator, trying to overcome this fear that kept nagging at her. Once again, she
was struck by his size. He was taller than Justin by a
good three inches, putting him at six three or so. He was

broader through the shoulders as well. An ex-football hero, she was willing to bet. He moved with the ease of an athlete. None of that mattered, though. All she cared about was whether he could find her son.

She sensed Lizzy coming to stand beside her. Her friend hadn't strayed far from her side since this nightmare had begun. "Looks like they're comparing notes," Kelsey said. "They're probably wondering how I let something like this happen."

"Don't be ridiculous. You didn't do anything wrong."

"I should have watched him more closely. He shouldn't have been outside alone."

"He's a little boy, not a prisoner. He was in your own backyard. Maybe he wandered out front," Lizzy consoled her. "It only takes a second and if someone is watching, waiting for that to happen, there's not a thing you could do to prevent it."

"I should have—"

"Should-haves will make you crazy," Lizzy advised. "You're a wonderful mother. I won't listen to anyone— including you—who says otherwise."

Kelsey mustered a faint smile at Lizzy's fiercely protective tone.

"Why aren't they *doing* something?" she asked plaintively. "They're just standing around talking."

"Planning, coordinating," Lizzy corrected. "In the long run, it will save time."

Kelsey sighed, her gaze once again settling on the private investigator. "I don't think Dylan liked me much. He was so, I don't know, cold, I guess. At first I thought he was being professional, just trying to calm me down by seeming competent and practical, but now I'm not sure."

"Dylan liked you just fine," Lizzy reassured her. "I was there. He was just trying to get a fix on things."

Before Kelsey could debate her assessment, the phone rang, startling them both. Kelsey all but dived for it. "Hello," she shouted, then forced herself to quiet down. "Who is this?"

"Mommy?" a tentative little voice whispered. Oh, sweet heaven, it was Bobby. She clutched the phone so tightly her knuckles turned white. "Sweetie, is that you?"

"Hi, Mommy."

"Oh, baby," she whispered. Her knees went weak and she sank into a chair. She was dimly aware of Lizzy racing to the front door and shouting for Justin and Dylan. "Where are you, Bobby?"

"He's with me, of course," Paul said, interrupting.

Hearing his voice confirmed every one of her fears. He sounded as if he were on the edge. Too many pills? she wondered. Or not enough?

"Paul, please, bring him home. We'll forget this happened."

"Not just yet."

"Tell me what you want. I'll do anything. Just bring Bobby back. I know you didn't do this just because you missed him and wanted to spend time with him. If that had been the case, you'd have called."

"And begged? Is that what you want, Kelsey?"

"No," she said honestly. She wanted him to stay away, but he was back in her life for the moment, for better or for worse. "Paul, what is this about? What do you want?"

The only response was the quiet click of a receiver being put back into place. Kelsey stared at the silent phone in shock. He had hung up on her. She didn't know any more than she had before.

No, she told herself staunchly, that wasn't true. She knew for sure now that Paul had their son. She knew that Bobby was okay, at least for the moment. *For the moment.* The phrase twisted and turned in her thoughts, terrifying her. What about a moment from now? Or an hour? Then, to her chagrin, she burst into tears, gulping sobs erupting from deep inside. All the pent-up emotion of the past couple of hours came pouring out.

As if from a great distance, she could hear Lizzy murmuring to her. She was dimly aware of Justin barking orders into the phone. And then of a dip in the sofa as someone's weight settled next to her. For the second time that day, her hand was enveloped in Dylan Delacourt's. She recognized his touch, clung to him, because he was solid and reassuring and he was here.

"Talk to me," he commanded.

He tipped her chin up until she was forced to face him, forced to choke back another sob that threatened. He dug a clean handkerchief out of his pocket and silently handed it to her, then waited a minute until she was calmer.

"That was your ex?" he asked then.

She managed to nod. "Bobby first, then Paul."

"Good. Then we know what we're dealing with, who we're looking for. We know it wasn't a random act by a dangerous stranger, just a dad wanting to see his child."

She blinked back a fresh batch of tears. "That is good, isn't it?" she echoed, desperate for hope. Then she considered the rest of what he'd said, the faint note of sympathy in his voice. She didn't dare tell him he was wrong, that this wasn't about Paul's love for Bobby at all.

"The best news we've had all evening," he confirmed, giving her hand a squeeze. "We can narrow the search down from the get-go. It's a good sign, too, that he's willing to communicate with you, rather than simply disappearing with his son. We'll get a tap on the phone. Justin's already got an expert on the way. We can trace the next call, if you can keep him on the line."

Kelsey recalled Paul's abrupt hang-up. She sensed it had been more than an attempt to keep her from asking more questions, from demanding to speak with Bobby again. "How long?" she asked. "I think he knows he can't stay on the line very long. That's probably why he hung up on me just now."

"You'll do the best you can," Dylan told her.

"Sooner or later, he'll make a mistake."

That's it? Kelsey wanted to shout. They were going to wait for Paul to make a mistake? Didn't they know that Paul didn't make mistakes? He was the champion of doing every last thing right.

Except for the pills, of course. She had caught him at that. She consoled herself with the memory. He was only human. He could slip up. She realized that Dylan was studying her intently with those deep blue eyes of his. They'd gone almost navy in the fading light and once more they were quietly assessing her, leaving her more shaken than she had been. She had a feeling he was doing it deliberately to unnerve her.

"What?" he asked eventually. "What aren't you telling us, Kelsey?"

"Nothing," she insisted, aware of the hint of defiance in her voice. "I've told you everything."

He shook his head. "I don't believe you."

She forced herself to meet his gaze, to not look away. "I can't help that."

"You want your son back, don't you?"

"Of course."

"Then you have to tell us the truth."

"I am, dammit."

"The whole truth," he added with emphasis.

"I am," she said again, but without the same vehemence.

Naturally Dylan didn't miss the difference. She could see it in his eyes. He knew she was lying.

What if she told him about the pills? She almost did, then caught herself. For if Paul found out she had broken her promise and told anyone, who knew what he would do? It wouldn't matter to him that he had broken their agreement first by coming after Bobby. No, she reassured herself again, she had to keep silent, for all their sakes.

Dylan wanted to shake the whole truth out of Kelsey James. She was obviously a bright woman. She had to know that forcing him and Justin to operate blindly just made everything twice as difficult as it needed to be.

The noise level in the living room climbed as neighbors discussed the call that had just come in. He saw Kelsey's gaze seek out Lizzy, probably for moral support, and realized he needed to get her alone, just the two of them. He had to find a way to gain her confidence, so that she would trust him with the whole truth.

"Let's go," he said.

"Where?" she demanded, balking.

He latched on to her hand and urged her back in the kitchen, then shooed everyone else out and shut the door. Kelsey looked as if she might protest, but then she sighed and sank onto a chair and accepted the cup of tea he handed her. She sipped automatically and stared warily at him over the rim of the cup, as if she sensed his displeasure. Dylan concluded that she was terrified enough without him coming down on her as hard as he wanted to. Tact wasn't his long suit, but maybe it was worth a try. He turned a chair around and straddled it, took out a notebook and pen. "Okay, let's try this another way. Tell me about your ex."

She blinked rapidly, then studied her cup of tea as if it were the most important thing in her universe.

Dylan's short supply of patience was dwindling. "Kelsey, help me out here. I need to get a fix on this guy, get into his head."

"I know. It's just…" She shook her head. "I don't know where to start."

He bought her confusion. He sensed she really was struggling to sort through the information and put some order to it. He didn't need order. He needed raw facts. Still, he kept his tone mild as he suggested, "How about the beginning? Where did you meet? How long did you know him before you got married?"

She closed her eyes for a minute, as if the memories were painful. "He was a stockbroker," she began finally.

"Which firm?"

She named one of the biggest.

"Still there?"

"As far as I know."

He made a note, then nodded. "Go on."

"One of Paul's clients was a doctor at the hospital where I was in med school. We were just finishing rounds when he came in for an appointment to go over the man's portfolio. The doctor got called away on an emergency so he asked me to take Paul to the cafeteria and keep him company until he could get there." She regarded him wearily. "How is this helping? It's ancient history."

"Trust me. It will. So, was it love at first sight?" Dylan asked.

"Hardly," she said with a touch of wry humor. "I thought he was way too full of himself. A lot like you, in fact."

Dylan shrugged off the jibe. It wasn't the only thing he and Paul James had in common. He wondered how she would feel if she knew the truth about that.

"And?" he prodded.

"I never thought he would look twice at me."

"Why?" Dylan asked, genuinely incredulous at the suggestion that she wouldn't catch a man's attention.

"Let's just say I was a very bookish student. I didn't spend a lot of time with my appearance. He was very slick, very handsome, the ultimate yuppie. When I was studying, I was lucky to remember to put on lipstick and matching socks before I went out the door."

Dylan tried to reconcile the image she was painting with the woman seated across from him. He couldn't. Even in her shorts and T-shirt, her feet in sandals, she radiated both inner beauty and confidence. Her hair framed her face with the sort of tousled curls a man's fingers just itched to untangle. She had a scattering of freckles across her nose, but otherwise her complexion was near perfect. And those eyes—a man could sink in their glittering seagreen depths and go down for the third time happy. A sudden rush of heat told him he needed to avoid spending too much time gazing into those eyes.

"If you two were such a mismatch, how did you wind up together?"

"I don't know," she said with apparent bemusement.

"Somehow we just clicked. Not overnight. It took a few weeks, but suddenly everything changed. Then things moved very quickly. We got married, moved into an old Coral Gables house that had great history and lousy plumbing and then Bobby came along. I was doing my residency in pediatrics by then."

"Sounds stressful. Was your husband a big help around the house?"

A smile tugged at the corners of her mouth. "Paul? You have to be kidding. The only thing he did was hire a nanny, then race off to the office. I don't know what you know about being a resident in a trauma center, but the hours are hell. Paul's were worse. Into the office before the market opened to get a jump on things, out with clients after Wall Street closed to celebrate the victories or solidify the relationship."

Dylan thought back to Kit's complaints about his work habits. More than once, she had accused him of being an absent husband and father. It sounded as if in the James marriage the two of them had shared the blame.

As if she sensed his disapproval, Kelsey said, "We did the best we could."

"Yeah, I'm sure you did," he said perfectly aware of the note of sarcasm that had crept into his voice.

Bright patches of color flamed in her cheeks. "You don't approve of me, do you, Mr. Delacourt?"

Dylan was surprised that she had called him on it. So the lady had a temper, after all. And good instincts. Maybe that could work to his advantage. He'd rather have her fighting mad than docile and defeated. He deliberately shrugged. "It's not my job to judge you," he said, careful to imply that he did just the same. "All I care about is finding Bobby." After an instant's hesitation, she nodded. "Good. Then we can agree on that, at least."

He bit back his amusement at the tart tone. "You don't approve of me, either, do you, Doctor?"

"Honestly?"

"Of course."

"I don't care what sort of foul-tempered beast you are. All I care about are results. You find my son and you will earn my undying devotion."

Dylan studied her thoughtfully. "Now there's a thought to make a man's heart go pitter-patter."

"Anything to motivate you," she retorted just as dryly.

For the first time in what had been a very grim couple of hours, Dylan actually found something to laugh about.

"You and I are going to make a helluva team, Doc."

Startled, she stared. "A team?"

He nodded. "From now on, you and I are going to stick together like glue."

It was the only way he could think of to be sure she didn't do something crazy to get her son back.

Three

Even as the words came out of his mouth, even as he mentally tried to justify them, Dylan cursed himself for the impulsive suggestion that he and Kelsey team up. Wasn't it enough that he was already operating cheek-by-jowl with a sheriff? Now he wanted to add an amateur into the mix. He was breaking every one of his long-standing, ironclad rules tonight.

Maybe it was because she'd purposely baited him, deliberately tried to establish boundaries. Hell, he liked boundaries. Loved them. And now he was pushing at them as if he couldn't wait to see them topple.

Oh, he recognized it for what it was. It was a male-female thing and this was definitely not a male-female situation. This was a job and he did not involve amateurs, especially clients, in his work. They lacked skill and objectivity, damned dangerous shortages. There went another hard-and-fast rule. Obviously, he'd lost it. He figured it had to be the eyes. He was a sucker for sad, sea-green eyes.

Truthfully, though, Kelsey didn't seem any more

pleased by the idea than he was. In fact, she looked shocked.

"What do you want me to do?" she asked, regarding him with justifiable wariness.

He decided to back off in a hurry, just for the moment, not as if he were running scared, but just to establish a few of his own boundaries. There were things she could do to help…just not in the same place he was heading.

"Right now I'm going to the police station to run some checks. I want you to sit tight here. Make a list of questions to ask your ex when he calls. If he puts Bobby on the line, even for a second, ask what he's had to eat. Maybe he'll say something about a burger place we can trace or maybe he'll mention a specific diner. Ask what the room looks like or what he can see. Kids notice more than we give them credit for. And in case your husband is listening, try to make it sound as if you're just interested in hearing how Bobby's getting along. Know what I mean?"

Chin up, she nodded. "I think so. Post-preschool conversation, right? The sort of thing we'd talk about over milk and cookies?"

"Bingo. You catch on quick."

"Believe me, I am highly motivated." For an instant she looked lost again and very, very frightened. "I can't mess this up. I just can't."

Dylan tried to steel himself against the sympathy he was feeling. Still, he couldn't seem to prevent himself from giving her hand a reassuring squeeze. "You won't. You're doing fine, Kelsey."

She was, too. He was impressed with her despite himself. She was bright and tough. Love for her son, concern for him, radiated from her, but she hadn't allowed herself to give in to hysterics except for that one brief moment after her ex-husband's call. Nor was she giving in to Dylan's pressure to reveal whatever secret she was determined to keep. He didn't like it, but he had to admire her tenacity in clinging to whatever misguided principle she felt was so important.

He figured, though, that he'd gotten everything from her he could for the moment. He needed some distance to sort through what he'd learned, put it into perspective, and maybe get some cold, hard facts about Paul James from the computer at the sheriff's office.

"Want me to clear out some of these people before I go?" he asked.

She shook her head. "They just want to help. Lizzy will get them out later."

Another woman who could manage a small nation if she put her mind to it, he thought wryly. Lizzy had the Adams strength, as well as the family's fierce loyalty and protectiveness. He was definitely leaving Kelsey in good hands.

He ripped a piece of paper from his notebook and jotted down his beeper number. "If anything turns up, if you get another call, if you think of something, or if you just need to talk, call me."

She took the paper, holding it as tightly as if it were a lifeline. "Thank you."

"Get busy on those questions," he reminded her. "Be ready, in case he calls back."

"I will."

Dylan found himself fighting an odd reluctance to go. He knew there were better uses for his time, but he wanted to stay right here, offer whatever comfort he could. But Kelsey didn't need comfort from him. She needed his help in finding her son.

"I'll be in touch," he said and headed for the door, tucking his notebook into his back pocket as he went.

At the small but well-equipped sheriff's office, he was greeted by the dispatcher, who'd clearly been expecting him.

"Justin said you could use anything you need," Becky told him. "The computer's in his office. We've got several lines, so you won't be tying things up if you need to make calls. Don't worry about charges since you're making 'em as part of a case we're handling. You need anything, holler. There's coffee in here by me. It's strong and there's plenty of it."

"Thanks. I think I will have a cup. It could be a long night."

She poured it into a mug and handed it to him, then grinned. "Part of the service this time. After this, you're on your own." She winced as the radio screeched static. "Whoops! Got to go. I swear Billy Ray does that just to shoot my nerves to hell."

Dylan went into Justin's office and settled into the chair in front of the computer. He flipped through his notebook until he found the instructions Justin had given him for logging on. For the next few hours, he searched for any trace of Paul James, any mention of him no matter how insignificant. Credit information showed a man who paid his bills, mostly on time. He had no police record. There were no mentions of him in the Miami press.

He got on the phone and called a contact who could trace any credit-card activity. He woke the man out of a sound sleep, but by dawn he had a callback. Paul James wasn't using his credit cards, at least not so far. His last charge had been made a week ago, in Miami. He'd bought three new suits on sale at an upscale department store.

"Anything?" Justin asked, coming in and dropping wearily into the chair opposite Dylan. He looked as bad as Dylan felt.

Dylan shook his head. "Nothing. The credit-card trace was a bust, though I have to wonder why a man who planned on kidnapping his son would go out and buy three expensive new suits."

"Maybe he figured his next shopping trip would be a long time coming," Justin suggested.

"Or the sale was just too good to pass up," Dylan said lightly.

Justin's expression turned thoughtful. "Almost sounds like a man who doesn't intend to be gone all that long, doesn't it?"

"He can't be planning to take his son back to Miami," Dylan protested. "He'd go straight to jail for violating the custody agreement."

"Right. So, either he is just trying to scare Kelsey, or he wants something from her, or we're dealing with a nutcase who has no intention of taking his son anywhere except away from his mother."

"To punish her," Dylan said, following Justin's logic with a sick feeling in his gut. "I hope to heaven you're wrong about that."

"So do I," Justin said. "So do I."

"Kelsey, you have to get some sleep," Lizzy said at dawn.

"I can't. As long as I don't know where Bobby is, I can't sleep. What if he calls again?"

"I'll wake you," Lizzy promised.

"No. I don't know how Paul will react if someone else answers the phone. He might hang up. He might get angry and hurt Bobby."

"I just don't see him hurting Bobby," Lizzy countered. "That hasn't been his pattern, Kelsey. It's the one thing I don't think you need to worry about."

"I can't help it. He sounded so edgy before. If he's been out of pills for a couple of days, he's probably in withdrawal. People do crazy things when they're coming down, things they otherwise might not do. Even the fact that he took Bobby in the first place is out of character. Paul never broke a law in his life until he got hooked on the painkillers. I never even saw him jaywalk. Heck, he'd dash two blocks just so his parking meter wouldn't run out. On the rare occasions when he got a parking ticket, he paid it the same day. Now he's violating a court order. That's the pills at work."

Already jittery from nerves and lack of sleep, she jumped when the phone rang. She snatched it up. "Bobby? Is that you?"

"Sorry," Dylan said. "It's just me. I wanted to check in."

"Oh," she said, sighing heavily. "Anything happening over there?"

"Nothing."

"Did you get any sleep?"

"Not a wink."

"Kelsey, you're not going to do Bobby any good if you collapse. If you don't want to go to bed, at least nap on the sofa for a bit."

"I can't," she said simply. "Have you found anything?"

"Not yet, but I will," he said with reassuring confidence. "You just hang tight. Is Lizzy still there?"

"Yes."

"Let me talk to her a second, okay?"

Kelsey handed the phone to Lizzy, then listened openly to her end of the conversation. Lizzy's gaze settled on her and she nodded several times, murmuring agreement to whatever Dylan said. Kelsey figured she was the primary topic of conversation.

"I'll try," Lizzy promised before hanging up. "I suppose you're to try to get me to get some sleep," Kelsey said.

"He has a point. I was saying the very same thing before he called."

"I can't sleep," Kelsey protested. "I could give you something."

"Absolutely not," Kelsey said, horrified. After all, it was pills that had gotten them where they were now. The tranquilizer she had agreed to take the night before was one thing, but sleeping pills were another. Add in something to wake her back up again and she'd be on a roller-coaster. Who knew where it would end up? She could be in worse shape than her ex.

"You're not going to get hooked like Paul," Lizzy said, as if she'd read her mind.

"How do you know?"

"Because you don't have the same kind of obsessive personality he has." Lizzy clasped her shoulders and gazed into her eyes. "Sweetie, you need some sleep. If and when Paul does call again, you have to be thinking clearly. You can't be all strung out with exhaustion."

"And I can't be groggy with sleep, either."

Lizzy uttered a sigh of resignation. "Okay, at least go take a nice, warm bath."

Kelsey didn't want to leave the phone for a second, but she could see the sense in Lizzy's suggestion. A bath might relax some of the tension. And she would feel better in some fresh clothes, more in control.

"Okay," she agreed. "But I'll take the portable phone up with me."

Once she got upstairs, she considered taking a nice, invigorating cold shower instead, but the lure of a bath was more than she could pass up. She filled the tub with bubbles and sank into it up to her chin. The scent of lilacs, a distant memory from childhood summers in Maine, surrounded her. The water felt wonderful lapping gently against her skin. Her eyes drifted closed.

A soft tap on the bathroom door snapped her awake. Glancing down, she had just noticed that the bubbles were also a distant memory now, when the door inched open and Dylan poked his head in.

"You okay in here?" he asked, his gaze settling on her face for an instant, then drifting down.

Kelsey felt her nipples pucker under the intensity of his stare. A gentleman would have turned away, but he seemed to be frozen in place. There was enough heat in his gaze to warm the now-chilly bathwater. She couldn't seem to muster up the required indignation. Finally, he swallowed hard and backed out.

"I'll be out here when you're dressed," he said, his voice sounding choked.

As if her brain had finally clicked into gear, it registered that he wouldn't be there unless something had happened. Kelsey scrambled from the tub. Without bothering to dry herself, she pulled on a heavy terry-cloth robe and belted it as she flung open the door. Dylan was standing guard just outside, leaning against the wall.

"Why are you here? What's happened?" she demanded, standing toe-to-toe with him.

He put his hands on her shoulders. "Shh," he soothed. "It's okay. Nothing's happened. I just came over to relieve Lizzy for a bit. She said she'd sent you up to take a bath. When you didn't come back down, I thought I'd better check on you."

"Are you sure that's all?" she asked, still shaky. "That's all. I swear it. If we find out something, I'll tell you," he promised, his gaze locked with hers. "I won't hide anything."

"Even if it's bad?" she insisted. He nodded. "Even if it's bad."

She believed him. There was something in his expression, something in the way he held her that made her believe that Dylan Delacourt would never lie to her. She had the feeling he was the kind of man who told the unvarnished truth, even when it was painful. She found that reassuring.

"Sorry I overreacted," she apologized.

"Sorry I intruded on your bath," he said, though the glimmer in his eyes suggested otherwise.

Disconcerted by the attraction that was totally inappropriate given the circumstances, Kelsey backed up a step. Dylan allowed his hands to fall away from her shoulders. She almost regretted that, but she faced him squarely.

"You look like hell," she observed. His cheeks were shadowed with the beginnings of a beard. He looked exhausted. "Give me a minute to get some clothes on and I'll fix breakfast. You can tell me what you did all night."

"Take your time. I'll cook," he said. "Have you got eggs and bacon? Scrambled okay?"

"Just toast for me."

"You need the protein," he said decisively and headed for the stairs.

Kelsey stared after him. She'd never had anyone around who showed the slightest inclination to take care of her. After all, she was a cool, competent doctor. Everyone knew she was the caregiver. Dylan apparently hadn't caught on to that yet. But he would, she thought with a sigh. For now, though, it was rather nice to take a few extra minutes dressing and know that when she got downstairs breakfast would be waiting.

Even if she wasn't hungry. Even if she had no intention of eating it.

Well, that was sweet, Delacourt, Dylan thought to himself as he marched back downstairs. Ogle the woman in her bath, why don't you? But he hadn't been able to tear his gaze away. Kelsey was an attractive woman and that baggy T-shirt and shorts he'd seen her wearing earlier had done nothing to enhance her natural beauty. Out of those, with all of her on display, so to speak, it was evident that she was a sensual, voluptuous woman. What man wouldn't look?

One who was concentrating on his job, he retorted mentally.

Kelsey James was a single mom whose boy was missing, not a potential pickup in some bar, he scolded himself as he went through her refrigerator, collecting eggs, bacon and butter. He found a pitcher of fresh orange juice and took that out, as well. By the time Kelsey joined him, he had breakfast on the table and his libido firmly in check.

That didn't mean he didn't cast a surreptitious gaze over her—just to make sure she was handling things okay, he assured himself. There were shadows under her eyes and her complexion was pale, but beyond that she appeared to be in control.

"Sorry about losing it for a minute upstairs," she said.

"Don't apologize. You're entitled to lose it every once in a while."

She glanced toward the phone, her expression forlorn. "Why doesn't he call back?"

"He will."

"The waiting is the worst. I'm used to being in charge, to being decisive. I make things better. I don't just sit around waiting."

"Always?" Dylan asked skeptically. "Aren't there times when even you can't control the rate at which a patient responds to treatment? Haven't you ever told a parent they just need to sit tight and wait?"

She frowned. "Okay, yes. I guess the difference is that I know how long it's likely to take for a medicine to kick in. I expect the delays. With this…" She shrugged, her expression helpless. "I don't know anything."

"What would you tell the parent of a sick child?"

"To be patient. To have faith. Pray."

"Don't you think maybe the same thing applies now?" he suggested.

Her expression brightened ever so slightly. "Yes. I suppose you're right. Patience and faith," she reiterated, as if he'd just given her a new mantra to recite. "Patience and faith."

She gazed at him then. "Thanks."

"Kelsey, let's establish a couple of ground rules. No more thanks. No more apologies. Deal?"

She nodded, started to say something, then cut herself off. "Sorry. Force of habit."

He grinned. "Caught yourself, huh? That's a start."

"How do you stand it?" she asked then.

Dylan wasn't sure what she was asking. "What?"

"Searching for a missing kid?"

He hesitated. He didn't want to lie to her, but for some reason he also didn't want her to lose confidence in him. Funny, when a few hours ago he would have given anything not to be involved in this case.

"I don't do it often," he said, choosing his words with care. "I usually prefer to turn this sort of case over to another private investigator."

"Why?"

"It's not my area of specialty, that's all."

She seemed shaken by that, just as he'd feared. "Then why did you agree to help?"

"Because I was here and it's best to get started immediately in a situation like this. There wasn't time to get another private eye in here." He leveled a look straight into her eyes, regretting the doubts that he had put there. "I won't let you down, Kelsey."

She kept her eyes locked with his, then nodded. "I know. Is that why you seemed so—I don't know—*reluctant* last night?"

So she had noticed that, had she? He'd have to remember that she was good at reading people. She probably had to do that a lot with kids who couldn't—or wouldn't—describe what was going on with them. He realized now that he wouldn't be able to hide anything from her.

Because he didn't want to get into the other reason for his reluctance, he took the easy way out and said, "Yes, that's exactly why." He rocked back in his chair. "But I'm in this now, Kelsey. We're going to find Bobby and bring him home."

"You sound so confident. I wish I felt that way."

"Patience and faith," he reminded her. "And a few of those prayers you like to recommend wouldn't be out of order, either."

Paul couldn't seem to sit still. He'd paced the motel room from one end to the other most of the night. That was the pills at work. They kept him on edge. If he'd been back in Miami, he'd have given up on sleep and gone back to the office, but he had Bobby with him now. He couldn't go running off and leave the boy all alone in a strange place.

He glanced over at the big double bed. Bobby looked lost in the middle of it. He was sprawled out, arms and legs going every which way, just the way he'd slept as a baby. To Paul's regret, there were still signs of tears staining his cheeks. The kid was confused and Paul couldn't blame him. He'd been all but snatched from his own backyard, hadn't been allowed to say goodbye to his mother.

There hadn't been any way around that, of course. Paul couldn't exactly walk into the house and announce that he'd come for his son. Kelsey would have driven him off with that high-and-mighty attitude she'd developed. He wasn't sure when she'd become such a stickler for the rules. If she'd been a little more flexible, things would never have turned out like this. She could have written a few prescriptions for him and he wouldn't have had to steal her prescription pads, then forge her signature to get what he needed. It wasn't as if he were some sort of streetwise drug addict. He was in real pain. His broken wrist had hurt like anything. Just because it had healed didn't mean the pain had gone away. Rainy days made it ache and in Miami, especially during spring and summer's tropical cloudbursts, there were plenty of those.

Besides, he had missed his son. He hadn't expected to, but he had. Bobby had looked up at him as if he were the greatest guy in the universe. He was probably the only person who'd ever looked at Paul that way. Not even Kelsey had thought he was infallible.

He'd gone to Texas on impulse. He'd planned on begging Kelsey for more pills. He'd figured she would balk at first, but eventually she would give them to him just to get rid of him.

Then he had seen his son and everything had changed. He'd wanted Bobby, too. He'd wanted to feel ten feet tall again.

It had been easy enough to get Bobby to come with him. The kid had been so excited by the prospect of going for ice cream with his daddy, he hadn't even hesitated. Only later, when he'd started missing his mom, had things gotten dicey. Bobby had cried so hard, Paul had finally relented and called the house, even though he figured Kelsey had probably brought in the police and accused him of kidnapping. It had been a risk, but he'd watched the second hand on his watch to be sure he didn't stay on the line long enough for the call to be traced.

Even that hadn't been enough for the kid. He'd wanted to go home. When Paul said no, Bobby had curled into a ball and eventually cried himself to sleep. Paul had felt about three inches tall, then, but it was too late to turn back. He needed those pills and he needed Bobby to get them.

Another day or two and Kelsey would be frantic enough that she'd give him anything he wanted.

Four

When Dylan left Kelsey in Lizzy's capable hands again at midmorning, he made a quick trip out to Trish's for a shower and a change of clothes. Laura's sunshine smile and eager greeting did as much to restore his spirits as the cool water and clean clothes.

"Unca Dyl, I swing?" she asked, trying to tug him toward the play area in the backyard. "Pweeze."

"Not now, angel. Uncle Dylan's got work to do." He scooped her up and planted a couple of noisy kisses on her cheeks until she giggled. Then he handed her to Trish, who was studying him with sisterly concern.

"Are you really okay?" she asked as she walked with him toward his car.

"Hanging in there."

"Dylan, everyone would understand if you wanted to back off. I'm sure we could get someone else in here."

"Sorry, kiddo. I always finish what I start." He skimmed a knuckle along Laura's cheek, even as he thought of a little boy over in Houston he prayed was safe at home. "You keep a close eye on this precious little girl of yours. I don't think I could bear it if anything happened to either of you. It's times like this that remind us what's really important in life."

"Nothing's going to happen to us, Dylan. And nothing is going to happen to Bobby. He's with his father."

"Wouldn't be the first time a kid was mistreated by a father," he pointed out. "Maybe that's why Kelsey left him, because he was abusing Bobby."

"Not Paul," Trish said with conviction. "Everyone says he was an okay guy, just not right for Kelsey."

He paused for a minute, intrigued by such a consensus of opinion from people who'd apparently never even met the guy. "Is that what everyone says? Who's everyone?"

Trish seemed surprised by the question. Her expression turned thoughtful. "Lizzy, I suppose," she said slowly. "Several others out at White Pines. When Kelsey came here, that was what we were all told, that her marriage hadn't worked out and she needed a change. No hint of anything other than a friendly divorce over irreconcilable differences."

Instinct kicked in and had Dylan wondering.

"Does that sound right to you? Lots of people get divorced and don't move halfway across the country, especially if they're established in a profession."

"And lots of people want to put plenty of distance between themselves and the past. There's nothing wrong with wanting a fresh start."

"Okay, yes," he agreed. Although he was instinctively sympathetic with Paul James and wanted badly to buy Trish's conclusion, he still couldn't shake the feeling that something wasn't right. "Think about this—Kelsey got full custody of her boy, not shared custody. Something had to be wrong for a court to do that, especially in this day and age, when a father's rights are taken into consideration more than they used to be."

Trish didn't look as if she'd been persuaded by his theory. "I suppose," she conceded halfheartedly. "Maybe it wasn't the court's decision, though."

"Meaning?"

"Maybe she and Paul worked it out between them. After all, they were both intelligent people. Maybe they just decided to keep the lawyers out of it and keep the hard feelings to a minimum. Then all the court had to do was sign off on their agreement, right?"

He nodded. "I suppose," he conceded as halfheartedly as she had a moment earlier. "It just doesn't feel right to me, though."

"Face it, Dylan. It would never feel right to you if the mother got sole custody. That's like waving a red flag in front of a bull. It'll get you going every time. Even though in the end it was your decision to give up custody of Shane, not Kit's, you blame her for it."

"Okay, okay, I'm biased on the subject. I admit it."

She regarded him curiously. "Have you told Kelsey about this particular bias?"

He shrugged off a nagging sense of guilt. "It hasn't come up."

"Dylan, you're my brother and I love you. I think you're an incredible, skilled, caring investigator, but don't you think she has a right to know? She might conclude you don't have the objectivity to handle this case."

"She probably would," he agreed. "Which is why I'm not telling her. I'm all she's got right now. She needs to believe I'm doing my best for her. She's shaky enough without adding a whole lot of doubts about me into the mix."

Before his sister could respond to that, his beeper went off. He checked it, saw Kelsey's number and used his cell phone to call her back. Lizzy answered on the first ring.

"It's Dylan. What's up?"

"Paul called again."

"Is Kelsey okay?"

"She's hanging in there."

"I'll be right there." He gave Laura another peck on the cheek, then added one for his sister. "I'll check in when I can."

"'Bye. Love you."

"I love you, too."

Checking his rearview mirror, he saw that Trish stood watching him until his car curved into the pine forest that separated the house from the highway.

Maybe Trish was right. Maybe he should be telling Kelsey the whole story about Shane, letting her decide if she wanted him to stay on the job.

Not just yet, though. There was time enough for that after he found out what had happened when her ex-husband called. Maybe luck was finally on their side.

Kelsey was still shaking. She couldn't seem to stop. The trembling started inside, in the pit of her stomach. She had to get a grip. Falling apart wouldn't help anyone, least of all Bobby.

He was still okay. Paul had given her a whole thirty seconds to make sure of that. Bobby had barely said, "Hi, Mommy," when the phone was snatched away.

"Paul, please. I want to talk to him," she had begged.

"Another time."

Every one of the questions she had prepared so diligently at Dylan's direction flew right out of her head. She asked the first thing that popped into her mind. "Is he eating properly?"

"We're on vacation, Kelsey. He's getting all the junk food he wants." His tone was a mix of amused tolerance and familiar sarcasm.

Kelsey was about to protest, when she saw the absurdity of worrying about whether Bobby was getting enough carrots and broccoli.

"No argument? I'm amazed," Paul said. "You were always such a stickler for the four basic food groups."

She let that pass. "What about clothes? Are you sure he's warm enough?"

"Kelsey, it's summer in Texas. He's plenty warm. If he needs clothes, I can afford to buy him some things."

"Of course you can. That's not the point." Tears welled up and she batted at them impatiently. "Paul, this is not a vacation and you know it. You've kidnapped him."

"Now that is not a word I like to hear," he said, suddenly tense. "You haven't called the police, have you?"

She hesitated, then saw no point in lying. Obviously he'd already guessed that she had. "What else was I supposed to do when my son vanished from the backyard? Just let it pass and pray you were the one who had him?"

"He's *our* son, Kelsey. You might have custody, but he's still my boy, too."

"Is that what this is about? Some belated sense of possessiveness?"

"We'll discuss it another time," he said tersely and hung up before she could think of some way to stop him.

"It wasn't long enough," she muttered, hearing the frantic note in her voice, the catch of a sob, and guessing that she was about to lose it again. She drew in a deep breath, fought for control, then met Lizzy's worried gaze. "Call Dylan, will you? He needs to know about this. I need to get out of here for a second."

She had gone outside and walked around the block, then circled it again at an even faster clip. She wasn't sure if she was running from something or just blocking out the pain. Either way, she was breathless by the time she got back home again and Dylan was waiting for her on the front lawn.

Seeing him there, his expression solemn, his gaze penetrating, she sighed with relief. She didn't know exactly what it was about him, but as long as she could see him, she had the feeling that everything would turn out okay. Was that something a good private investigator learned how to do, to reassure the victims of crimes, to instill confidence, to radiate a rock-solid strength? Or was it unique to this man? "You okay?" he asked, his study of her face never wavering.

"Just peachy," she responded acerbically. "Okay, dumb question. Let's get to the point," he said briskly. "Tell me what Paul said when he called."

His quick reversion to strict professionalism calmed her. But then she thought back to the brief conversation and felt tears of frustration build again. "Nothing, dammit. I forgot all the questions I had planned, but he was so careful. He wouldn't give me so much as a hint about where they are. He barely let Bobby say hello."

"Did Bobby sound okay?"

Thinking of that sweet whisper of a greeting, she choked up and settled for nodding.

Dylan tucked a finger under her chin and forced her gaze up. "He didn't sound frightened, did he?" She thought about it. He'd only said a word or two, so it was hard to tell, but no, he hadn't sounded scared. "Actually, no," she admitted.

He smiled. "See? He's doing okay. He probably thinks this is just a big adventure with his dad. It's the grown-ups back here who are scared, not your son."

"That's good, isn't it?" she said, clinging to it. As furious as she was with Paul, this could be so much worse. Bobby was fine. He just wasn't where he belonged—with her.

She met Dylan's gaze. "Thank you for making me see that. I won't stop worrying until he's back here, but I'm not as panicked as I was."

Dylan nodded, then glanced toward the house where neighbors were still gathered in small groups on the lawn and on the porch. "Feel like another walk around the block?"

"Why?"

"Fewer people. There are a few more questions I need to ask you."

"I've already told you everything," she protested. "Paul was only on the line a minute."

Dylan grinned. "You just think you've told me everything." He gestured toward the sidewalk. "You game?"

Uncertain what more she could possibly add, she still set off around the block again, albeit at a slower pace. Suddenly she was aware of just how hot it was. The late morning heat rose from the cement in waves. The sun beat down, making her clothes cling and her hair damp. It was hardly the time for a stroll, but then this wasn't about getting a little exercise or even settling her nerves. It was about Dylan grilling her, she realized as he began to bombard her with questions.

"First thing you heard when you picked up the phone?" he asked.

"Bobby's voice," she said at once.

"Right away? There wasn't a pause. Kids don't usually speak right off. It takes them a second to realize there's somebody on the line."

She thought back. Had she heard Paul coaching him? Telling him to say hi to Mommy? "Paul," she said with a sense of amazement. "I heard him telling Bobby to say something."

Dylan nodded his approval. "Good. Anything else? Cars? Dishes being set down on a counter? Music? A clock striking the hour? A church bell?" Kelsey slowed her pace, then stopped and closed her eyes, listening to the silence, listening with everything in her for some clue. Finally she sighed with frustration. "Nothing," she said, staring at Dylan in disappointment.

"No TV in the background?"

"No. I told you, I didn't hear anything except Bobby's voice, then Paul's."

"What about road noise? Could he have been on a cell phone?"

"He has a cell phone. No broker can live without one. They might miss the big deal," she said sarcastically. "But it didn't sound like that. It was just..." She shrugged. "I'm sorry. It was just a regular call from some everyday phone. They could have been anywhere."

He turned her to face him, kept his hands on her shoulders. "It's okay. You'll listen differently next time. Pay less attention to what's said and more to the background."

"But you told me to ask questions," she retorted with mounting frustration. "How can I ask questions and listen to the background all at once? God, I can't do this. I'm no good at it."

"You're not supposed to be good at it. No one should ever have to be good at it," Dylan said heatedly. "But you'll do the best you can."

She gazed up at him, feeling that unfamiliar wave of helplessness roll over her again. "I hate this," she said vehemently. "I'm his mother. I should have been able to protect him. I'm a doctor. I make other people's kids well and I can't even keep my own safe."

"You're a doctor and a mother, not God," Dylan reminded her with surprising gentleness. "Nobody expects perfection."

"I do," she said. "My whole life has been about getting it right. My parents were overachievers, who expected me to excel, and I did. Full scholarship to the University of Miami med school. Straight A's. Top of my class. I had my pick of internships and residencies. Kelsey Donnelly James was one of the best and brightest," she said with self-derision. "What does it matter when my son is snatched right out from under my nose?"

Dylan's grasp of her shoulders tightened just enough to snap her out of her bout with self-pity. "Did you teach him not to go anywhere with strangers?"

"Of course."

"So if some stranger had come up to him in your backyard, what would he have done?"

"Screamed for me. Run to the house. That's what I always told him, make a lot of noise and never, ever go with somebody he didn't know."

"Right. So you prepared him for that threat." She nodded, beginning to see his point.

"You didn't think you needed to tell him not to go with his own father, did you?"

"No," she conceded, exhaling a tiny sigh. But she should have. Wasn't Paul the bigger threat, maybe not more dangerous than a stranger, but certainly the most likely candidate to come after Bobby? In the back of her mind wasn't that precisely why she had insisted on sole custody, why she had moved so far from Miami? She said none of that to Dylan.

"Bobby had no idea that going with his dad was wrong," Dylan consoled her. "This is about Paul violating a court order, not anything you did or didn't do to protect your son."

"Still, if I'd been watching more closely, Paul couldn't have gotten to him."

"You plan on never working at the clinic again?" She regarded him indignantly. "Of course not."

"You going to take Bobby inside and lock the doors and windows until he's old enough for college?"

"No," she said, even though the idea was so preposterous that it didn't even deserve a response.

"Kelsey, there are risks, especially in the world we live in today. Los Piños is a great little community. It probably has fewer crimes than most places. You can prevent a lot of bad things, you can prepare for some, but just when you think you have every angle covered, something unexpected can come along. Unless you want to stop living, you can't protect Bobby from every single one of them." His gaze locked on hers and he spoke with added emphasis. "You did not do anything wrong. I can't say that strongly enough."

She wanted to believe that, almost did because Dylan said it so forcefully, but until her dying day she knew there would always be a nagging doubt that she could have done something more.

What, though? Would she really have warned Bobby about his dad, turned a little boy against his own father? Would she have gone that far? A more vindictive woman certainly would have, maybe even one with a stronger sense of self-preservation. She'd believed the court-approved custody agreement and distance were enough. Paul had desperately wanted her silence, because anything else would have destroyed his career. He'd wanted that agreement as badly as she had. So she'd trusted him to honor it. And for reasons that definitely escaped her now, she hadn't wanted to take away Bobby's good memories of his dad. She'd wanted those to be salvaged for some future date when Paul got his act together and could be trusted to be with his son again.

"It doesn't matter now," she said wearily. "He's gone. I just have to concentrate on getting him back."

"Exactly. Let's stay focused on that." He studied her intently. "Just a couple more questions about the call, okay?"

She started to protest that it was a waste of time, then stopped. "Fine. Anything."

"What was the first thing you asked Paul?"

"About what Bobby was eating. He said junk food."

Dylan nodded. "Nothing specific, though?"

"No, just junk food."

"And then?"

"About his clothes. If he was warm enough."

"And what did he tell you?"

"That it was summer in Texas," she repeated, then stopped as she realized what she'd said. "He said Texas." She felt a grin starting to spread across her face. "They're still in Texas." It was such a small clue, but she felt like jumping up and down.

Dylan grinned back. "See? I told you there was more locked away in your memory than you realized. That's a start. We don't have the whole country to worry about right now, just the state. He's sticking close, Kelsey. I can feel it. And if he's nearby, we'll find him." His gaze settled on her. "Will you be all right? I want to get back to work." She nodded. "I'll be fine. Where are you going? What will you do now?"

"I'll stop by the sheriff's office. I want to touch base with Justin, see if they've come up with anything. I've got some calls out for information. I need to check to see what's turned up." He glanced toward the house. "Lizzy waiting inside?"

Kelsey nodded. "Yes. I don't know what I'd do without her, but she can't stay forever. Somebody needs to be at the clinic. We have patients scheduled." She thought of a whole slew of kids who were due in this week for their preschool checkups, all her responsibility. "I should—"

Dylan cut her off. "You should be right here. Everything else can wait. I'm sure if someone needs a doctor for an emergency, they'll know to reach Lizzy here. She can have the clinic's calls forwarded."

"But there are shots," she protested. "The kids need them for school."

"And they'll get them. We'll have Bobby home soon and you'll get right back to work. A few days won't make that much difference."

She supposed he was right, but it just seemed so irresponsible to be putting her own crisis ahead of duty. Her uptight mother would be appalled. A Donnelly always took care of obligations, no matter what. How many times had she heard that? How many disappointments had she endured as a child because duty called, keeping one or both of her parents away from some triumph that mattered to Kelsey, but no one else, at least not enough for them to be there? She halted that line of thinking, because it was counterproductive. It was in the past. Everyone had history they'd had to overcome. Her life was no different.

In the here and now, she could admit that a few delayed shots wouldn't be the end of the world. The kids would no doubt relish the reprieve and the parents would understand. So would the school system, if it came to that. This was a town where people mattered more than schedules and rules. And if some poor bureaucrat didn't believe that, Harlan Adams would be more than willing to explain it to him.

"I'll bet we could search the whole town and not find a single kid who's upset at not getting a shot," Dylan teased gently, as if he'd read her mind.

"You're probably right about that, though the word is that I am very slick with a needle. In and out before they even know what hit them. And I have some very good lollipops for the brave."

He looked taken aback by her evident pride in that particular skill. "I'll keep that in mind next time I decide to get a flu shot," he said. "Probably won't be any time this century, though, so don't keep an appointment open for me."

She laughed at the thought of this tough guy being scared of shots. "Why, Dylan Delacourt, don't tell me you're afraid of needles."

"Afraid?" he retorted indignantly. "No way. Just of the people who go poking around with them and especially of those who so obviously enjoy it." He gave her a disconcerting once-over. "Though I'll bet if anyone could give me a shot and make me like it, it would be you, Doc."

With that and a wink, he was gone before she could fully absorb the compliment. What was wrong with her? Her son was missing and she was getting all warm and mushy inside because a private investigator was acting mildly flirtatious. He probably hadn't even meant anything by it. He'd just been trying to lighten the mood, to lift up her spirits.

And it had worked, too. She went back inside feeling a whole lot better than she had when she'd hung up after Paul's last call.

"Is that pink in your cheeks from the sun or from a certain detective?" Lizzy demanded when Kelsey found her in the kitchen.

"It's hot out," Kelsey declared, but she kept her gaze averted because Lizzy had always been able to see right through her.

"Whatever it is," Lizzy replied, "it's good to see some color back in your face. You've been too pale. I've been worried. You were starting to look defeated. Now you look as if your fighting spirit is coming back."

"Oh, yes," Kelsey declared. "If I ever get close enough to Paul to get my hands around his neck, he's a dead man."

Lizzy beamed. "Now there's a thought." She held out a glass of iced tea. "Shall we toast to it?" Kelsey took the tea, rubbed the icy glass against her cheek, then took a long swallow, savoring it as it soothed her parched throat. She felt better than she had in more than twenty-four hours. Her emotions were no longer on such a wild roller-coaster. She knew now exactly what she was dealing with. Paul had Bobby somewhere in Texas. It was a big state, but not impossible to search, not with the people and resources committed to helping her.

There was comfort in that, she realized. Dylan had made the illusion of control possible by putting everything into clear focus, by giving her concrete things to do when Paul called, by ferreting out the one clue that had slipped past her. She would be listening even closer next time. Not so much as a whisper of background noise would escape her. If getting Bobby back depended on it, she would listen like a hawk.

And with Dylan's help, she would sort through the most innocuous of clues until she had her precious son back home.

Five

Dylan had never been so thoroughly frustrated in his entire career. They couldn't seem to catch a break. Paul James wasn't making mistakes. He wasn't leaving a trail. Even Kelsey's discovery that he was apparently holding Bobby someplace in Texas wasn't going anywhere.

And with every hour that passed, there was a very real likelihood that he would slip out of their grasp for good, if that was his intention. He was that clever.

"Damn," Dylan muttered, looking over the list Becky had compiled of the motels within a hundredmile radius. "Not a sign of him. I was so sure he was close by."

"I've moved on to the next counties," the dispatcher told him, her own frustration evident.

"Where can he be staying? Surely he wouldn't take that boy to some cheap, fleabag place. Do you think he's left the area? If he's gone to Dallas or Fort Worth or any other big city, there are too many hotels and motels for me to check between handling other calls. We'd have to have more help."

Dylan didn't even want to consider that just yet, but it was a real possibility he couldn't ignore. A father traveling with his son wouldn't stand out in a metropolitan area the way he would in some small town where people were attuned to the comings and goings of strangers.

Worse, despite what he'd said to Kelsey in this morning's call, by now Paul could have left Texas entirely. He could have hopped a plane and fled the country, for that matter. That's what Dylan would have done, if he'd gotten a notion to take Shane. He would have gone as far away from Texas as he possibly could to stay out of the law's reach.

Of course, as far as he knew, the two situations were entirely different. He'd voluntarily given up custody of Shane for his son's own good. He'd made a solemn vow—not just to Kit, but to himself—that he wouldn't intrude in the boy's life again.

For the most part, he'd stuck to that promise. Except for one person, no one knew about the lapses and he prayed to God no one else ever would.

He'd made three trips to see Shane, only from a distance, of course. Just to reassure himself that the boy was getting along okay. He believed with all his heart that he'd done the right thing in giving up custody, but he'd needed to see the evidence of it with his own eyes.

It hadn't been hard to track Kit and her new husband down. They were living in a fancy suburb of Houston on the opposite side of town from Dylan's own place. It wasn't like they'd made a secret of it. He hadn't had to go digging through confidential records to find them. They were in the phone book for anyone to find. That was how much Kit had trusted him to keep his word.

And he had—more or less. He'd just driven through the neighborhood a couple of times during the first few months after she'd remarried. Okay, once he'd lingered down the block from the house, waited until he'd seen Shane playing in the yard with his new brothers.

Even now his throat tightened as he recalled how happy the boy had seemed. Shane had dogged the footsteps of his new big brothers, trying to keep up with them, and they had been oh-so-patient with a toddler tagging after them. Watching them with a mix of amusement, nostalgia and sorrow, he knew he hadn't been half that patient with his own kid brothers. In the end, he had driven away reassured. It had been over a year before he'd paid another visit. He'd realized one day in October that Shane would probably be in preschool. The fact that he'd missed his boy's first day of school had overwhelmed him. Another cursory check of the phone book had led him to the school closest to Kit's. He'd parked a block away from the playground, then kept his eyes peeled for some sign of his dark-haired son. He'd spotted Kit first, waiting on the sidewalk as Shane ran out, a red lunch box in one hand and a brightly colored finger painting in the other. He'd been chattering a mile a minute even before he reached his mother. Dylan had longed to hear the sound of his voice, but he'd been too far away. Thankfully, Kit hadn't seen him...or so he'd thought at the time.

A week later the finger painting had turned up in his mail. The picture had been a childish rendering of a mother, a father and three boys. Even though no note had been attached, the message was unmistakable—this was Shane's family now.

That picture and a few photos that he'd taken from Shane's baby album were all he had of his son. He kept them tucked away in a dresser drawer, so no one else

would know that he hadn't completely forgotten the little boy he'd given up.

He needed his family to believe he was okay with his
decision, that he never looked back. He couldn't take
having to defend the choice over and over again. Though
his father and brothers avoided the topic, it was always
there, albeit unspoken, especially around holidays.

Only Trish and his mother dared to broach the subject aloud—Trish out of love and concern, his mother for
her own selfish reasons. In fact, his mother never let up
with her pestering. She had complained bitterly about
giving up all rights to see her first grandchild, at least
until Trish had had Laura. Now the grumbling had died
down, but there were still enough barbs directed his way
that Dylan knew she hadn't entirely forgiven him. He
suspected his father also resented his decision to give
up the first male heir to the Delacourt oil dynasty, but
after Dylan's rebellious defection from the family business, Bryce Delacourt had learned his lesson. He knew
better than to bring it up.

So they all lived with Dylan's decision in relative
silence. Dylan couldn't help wondering if Paul James
had made the same kind of commitment to Kelsey for
all the right reasons, then spent months of hell second-
guessing himself before finally breaking and following
her to Texas. Dylan wanted to believe he was a better
man because he'd never put Kit through the kind of pain
Kelsey was enduring now, but who knew how close he'd
come to breaking his vow without realizing it? Those
surreptitious visits had certainly crossed the line, albeit
not as dramatically as what Paul had done.

Then came another nagging doubt. What if Kelsey
deserved what was happening? What if he'd completely

misread the kind of person she was? What if she had forced Paul into relinquishing custody? Had she been holding something over his head? Was that the secret she was guarding so tenaciously? Maybe she'd even blackmailed him into giving up his son.

Sweet heaven, he was losing it. He'd been around Kelsey enough in the past forty-eight hours to know better. That wasn't the kind of woman she was. His gut instincts about people were rarely wrong. He hadn't even been wrong about Kit. She was a good woman, just all wrong for marriage to a man like him. As much as he'd wanted to blame her, even hate her, for the way things had turned out, he'd known the fault for their failed marriage was as much his as hers. Reason just wasn't always enough to counteract bitterness.

He glanced up and realized he'd been staring blankly at Becky's report for some time. The dispatcher was regarding him with blatant curiosity.

"You okay?" she asked.

"I'd be a whole lot better if we could pick up a trail. Where's Justin? Has he called in?"

"Right before you got here. He'll be back in five minutes. He wants you to wait."

"I'm not going anywhere," Dylan said and poured himself another cup of coffee before sitting down to go over Becky's list of motels one more time.

Justin came in moments later, looking frazzled and frustrated. "Nothing," he muttered with disgust. "I've had men questioning everybody in the whole town and nobody saw anything yesterday. I've checked the flights from Miami coming into Dallas-Fort Worth yesterday. If Paul James was on one of them, he was using a pseudonym and paid cash. The rental-car people weren't any help, either. He would have had to use his driver's license to get a car and he didn't."

"Phony papers?" Dylan suggested. "Or he drove from Miami."

"On the off chance you're right, let's call the DMV in Florida and get his car registration," Dylan said. "It'll give us something to look for. I have a man in Tallahassee I've used before. I can call him. Then we can get Miami P.D. to take a look around Paul's place there to see if the car's still in the vicinity. You call the police and make the request official."

Justin nodded, his expression brightening. "I'd give just about anything for an honest-to-God lead about now. Lizzy says Kelsey's holding up okay, but the longer this drags on the more likely I'm going to have Grandpa Harlan down here busting my chops for not getting it resolved. Believe me, I do not need my grandfather getting a notion in his head to play cop."

Dylan grinned. He could totally understand Justin's concern. A powerful, strong-willed man like Harlan Adams, who wasn't used to sitting on the sidelines and waiting, could make a policeman's or a private investigator's life miserable. It would be worse if they were related.

"Then let's make those calls," Dylan said, already reaching for the phone. While he waited for his contact to call back, he and Justin went over Becky's list one more time to see if there was anything about any of the hotels and the guests they'd acknowledged that bore further checking.

A few minutes later, Dylan's man in Tallahassee called back with the car description and tag number.

Dylan passed the information to Justin, who called Miami police and requested assistance.

Dylan paced while they awaited a return call. It took a whole helluva lot longer than he would have liked, but when the news came back, it was good. There was no sign of Paul James's car at his home or in the lot by his office. The police promised to check the airport lots within the next few hours and get back to them about that.

"For now we can work on the assumption that he drove that car here," Justin said triumphantly, then bellowed, "Becky!"

"I'm right here, not in the next county," she retorted from just outside the door.

"Call those hotels back and check to see if this tag number is on any car in their lots." He added a description of the car, as well. "For all we know he could have put stolen plates on it by now."

"Or stopped off and registered it in another state, if he's planning on settling someplace new with Bobby," Dylan said thoughtfully. "Damn. Have you called his employer in Miami?"

Justin nodded. "First thing this morning after we knew for sure he had Bobby. As far as his boss knew, Paul is just on a two-week vacation."

Dylan couldn't hide his surprise. "What did you make of that?"

"Either he was covering his tracks or he fully intends to return home in a couple of weeks."

"He can't go back with Bobby," Dylan protested. "Does that mean he intends to give him back to Kelsey before he goes home?" He shoved away from the desk

and started to pace again. "Is this some sort of temporary game with him?"

"I'd give anything to be able to get inside this guy's
head," Justin said. "I can't figure out if he's got a screw
loose, if he's desperate, or if he's just plain mean."

"Or if he's just a dad who misses his son," Dylan
said quietly.

Justin's gaze narrowed. "You sound sympathetic.
Whose side are you on here?"

"Kelsey's, of course," he said, but he couldn't hide
the defensive note in his voice.

"You sure of that? Because if you're not, I'll see to it
you're off the case and out of town before you know it."

"Look, I'll admit to having a custody issue of my
own, but it's not influencing how I handle this case. I'm
on Kelsey's side."

"I sure as hell hope so," Justin said, his tone and his
steady gaze a warning.

"If that changes, you'll be the second to know," Dylan
promised. "The first person I'll tell is Kelsey."

People kept coming and going. It was driving Kelsey
just a little bit crazy. They all meant well. They all
wanted to help, some by offering to join the search, some
by bringing food for all the other people dropping by,
some just by expressing their concern.

The one person she wanted to see, Dylan, hadn't been
by in hours. Nor had he called with any news. Lizzy had
kept her from calling him by reminding her that he and
Justin were doing their jobs.

"Leave them alone and let them work," Lizzy said.
"Now I am going to shoo everybody out of here and
you're going to get some rest."

Before Kelsey could protest, Lizzy pointed her toward the stairs. "There's a phone by the bed. If it rings, you'll be able to grab it. If you can't sleep, fine. At least close your eyes and rest. Otherwise, you're going to collapse. The clinic's going to be a madhouse when we open it again. I can't afford to have the pediatrician out sick."

Kelsey had finally started toward the stairs, but her head snapped back. "You closed the clinic?"

"Who was going to treat anybody? You and I are both here. People will just go to Garden City if there's an emergency. That's what they did before the clinic opened. Besides, I'm pretty sure my father has forbidden anyone to have a medical emergency while we're in the midst of this crisis. You know how people around here listen to Harlan Adams."

Kelsey chuckled. He very well might have. He would have been affronted if anyone dared to defy him, too. When her chuckle threatened to turn into hysteria, she knew Lizzy was right. She needed sleep.

Still, she went upstairs reluctantly. One of the reasons she'd avoided going to her room was because to get there she had to pass Bobby's. She hadn't been sure she could bear to walk by it, knowing it was empty, that he might never see it again. Now, she dragged in a deep breath and paused in the doorway.

The room was exactly the way it had been when he'd disappeared, a mess. She smiled at the clutter, something she didn't always do. She had bought a huge old trunk at a garage sale and painted it bright colors. It was meant to be a toy chest, but as far as she could tell nothing was in it.

Bobby's favorite toys—and he had almost none that weren't favorites to hear him tell it—were all over the floor, scattered under the bed, and piled on the colorful desk that had been one of his birthday gifts from Harlan Adams. Stuffed animals Bobby claimed to be getting too big for still seemed to find their way onto his bed. She went in and picked up his Pooh bear.

Well-worn from all the loving a little boy could give it, Pooh smelled of grass stains and orange juice and Bobby. The mixture of scents brought tears to her eyes and she sank down on the edge of the bed feeling lost. Had Bobby been able to sleep without his beloved bear? Had he asked for it? How had Paul consoled him? By buying him a replacement? Or just ordering him to be a big boy and forget Pooh? That sounded more like Paul.

Suddenly she was sobbing, hot, scalding tears of fury and betrayal this time. Clutching the fragile bear, she rocked back and forth, letting her tears roll down her cheeks until they soaked her blouse and eventually Pooh himself. He'd seen his share of tears before, she knew, and her own mixed with Bobby's.

"Hey, hey, what's this?"

She didn't have to look up to know it was Dylan. His voice was becoming as familiar to her as her son's. She felt the bed sink under his weight and the next thing she knew he had gathered her close, Pooh smushed between them. His murmured words of comfort were mostly nonsensical, but it was the sound of his voice that soothed, the strength of his embrace that gave comfort. She gave herself over to it, letting the tears flow.

"Oh, God, Dylan, what if I never see him again?" she whispered, her voice muffled against his chest.

"You will," he vowed.

She blinked back tears and drew back to gaze at him. "You sound so sure. Has something happened?"

"We found out Paul's car isn't at his house or his office. Justin and I agree it could mean he drove here. We also found out he's only taken a two-week vacation at work. He hasn't quit."

Kelsey stared at him mutely, trying to grasp the implications.

"Kelsey, did you hear what I said?"

She nodded. "I just don't know what it means."

"It means we not only have Bobby and Paul to look for, but a specific car. We have police all over the state checking hotel and motel parking lots and registration books. We also think it could mean that Paul doesn't intend to go on the run with Bobby, maybe not even to keep him."

She felt the tight knot in her stomach ease ever so slightly. "He'll bring him back, then," she said, half to herself. Hadn't she believed from the beginning that Paul had only done this to frighten her, to back her into a corner so she would help him get more pills? It all fit. She just had to wait him out, wait for his demand.

And then what? Would she give him a supply of narcotics? How could she do that in good conscience? And if she did it this time, would he simply come back again and again, using Bobby for leverage each time? No, she had to put a stop to it now, but how?

She looked at Dylan, noted how intently he was watching her, and realized just how certain he already was that there was more to this than she had told him. Could she tell him the rest? Did she dare? Would he help her keep the secret or feel compelled to turn Paul in to the authorities?

She was struck by a sudden thought. Paul was already in trouble with the police. He'd violated a court order when he took Bobby. That alone should be enough to put him in jail and keep him from coming after her for more pills. All they had to do was catch him and her problems would be over, for however long such a sentence lasted. Maybe jail would be the best for him. He'd have to get over his addiction in there. Still, the thought of Paul in jail sent a chill down her spine.

"Kelsey?"

She glanced at Dylan. "What?"

"What is going on in that head of yours? I can practically see the wheels turning."

"I was just thinking about the future," she said, which was honest as far as it went.

"Oh?"

"Will Paul go to jail?"

"Most likely."

"For how long?"

Dylan shook his head. "I'm not certain. If he brings Bobby back on his own, it would probably help."

"What if I didn't press charges?"

Dylan stared at her, clearly shocked. "Why the hell would you not press charges?"

"Because…" She searched for an explanation that made sense. She wasn't sure there was one. Paul had to pay. She knew that, but the thought of Bobby's dad being in jail made her physically ill. What would Bobby think when he grew up and realized his mother was responsible for putting his father in prison? "I guess I'm just thinking of how Bobby would feel."

"When he's older, he'll understand," Dylan said. "Besides, there's no choice. He violated a court order. You won't really have a say in whether he's prosecuted."

"Not even if I say he had my permission?" she asked,

grasping at straws. She knew she was being irrational, that she ought to want him punished, but she just wanted Bobby back. She wanted things to be normal again. It was what she had desperately wanted when she'd moved to Texas, a normal life with her son. She had known then she was taking a risk by making her deal with a man hooked on pills, but it had seemed worth it. Getting out with Bobby had been all that mattered.

Dylan's unflinching gaze remained on her face. "What's really going on, Kelsey? What are you afraid of?"

"I told you, I'm afraid for Bobby, how he'll react to all of this."

Dylan shifted away from her then, his expression blank. Kelsey realized that once more he didn't believe her. She also thought she detected something else in his reaction: hurt. He was hurt, probably disappointed, too, that she didn't trust him with the whole truth.

She hadn't thought she could be any more miserable than she had been ever since Bobby had disappeared, but she was. She felt as if she had let down yet another person in her life. Dylan had been a stranger just a few short days ago, but she already knew that under different circumstances he was someone she would like, someone who deserved better than what she was giving him.

She reached out and laid a hand on his arm, felt the muscle bunch beneath her fingers. "I'm sorry," she said.

"For?"

She shook her head. "Just sorry."

He caught her gaze, held it, then sighed. "Yeah, whatever."

A moment later, he was gone. Kelsey shuddered, feeling a sudden chill in the air that had nothing to do with the air-conditioning. When she'd left Paul, she had made a solemn oath to herself to live without regrets. Now they were piling up faster than she could count them.

Six

More than ready to be doing something useful, Dylan got as far as the kitchen after walking out on Kelsey. He fully intended to hit the road and join the door-to-door search of hotels and motels, but Lizzy stopped him.

"What's going on? You look mad enough to chew nails."

He jerked his head toward the stairs. "Your friend up there is keeping things from us."

He noticed that Lizzy looked vaguely guilty and seized on it. "You know what she's hiding, don't you? Justin figured you would."

Her chin shot up with a typical touch of Adams defiance. "I have no idea what you're talking about."

"I'm not a fool, Lizzy. Don't you go making the same mistake that Kelsey's making."

"Dylan, of course I don't think you're a fool." She plunged her hands deep into a batch of bread dough, concentrating fully on the task for a moment before she met his gaze again. "Look, this isn't my story to tell."

"Not even to save Bobby?" he asked quietly. "That's what this comes down to, you know. That little boy's life could depend on one of you coming clean with me or with Justin."

That said, he walked out and let the back door slam behind him. Maybe the message would sink in, maybe it wouldn't. Maybe she'd pass it on to Kelsey, maybe she wouldn't. Either way, he'd delivered the warning. It was all he could do, he concluded with frustration. He couldn't beat the rest of the story out of either one of them. He felt his lips curve in a grim smile. He'd leave that to Justin.

Almost an entire day had passed without a single word from Paul and Bobby. Back in the kitchen again after a few hours of restless sleep, Kelsey stared at the phone until her eyes hurt from the strain.

"Eat," Lizzy commanded, putting a loaf of warm bread on the table along with freshly churned butter from the housekeeper at White Pines and a pot of blackberry jam. "I'll have some scrambled eggs for you in a sec."

Kelsey regarded her bleakly. "I'm not hungry."

"Tell someone who cares. Eat, anyway. You have to keep your strength up."

Kelsey stared at Lizzy, shocked by her cool tone. "What's wrong, Lizzy?"

"Oh, not much. A few hours ago I was reamed out by the man we brought in to find Bobby. He all but accused me of standing in the way of Bobby's safe return."

Kelsey stared, openmouthed. "Dylan blamed you?"

"Not for the kidnapping, but for keeping something from him. I wonder where he got the idea there was some big, dark secret?" she asked, staring pointedly at Kelsey.

"Well, I certainly didn't tell him," she retorted, then sighed. "It's just that the man can read me like a book.

It's uncanny. Either he's a terrific private eye or…" She stumbled over what she'd been about to say.

"Or there's a connection between the two of you," Lizzy suggested lightly. "I vote for that. I think he's as upset because you don't trust him as he is because there might be something that could help in the search."

Kelsey sighed. "Yes, that was the impression I got, too." She met Lizzy's gaze. "Am I wrong? Would it help to tell him why I think Paul really took Bobby?"

"I honestly don't know," Lizzy said. "But we're not the experts. Only Justin and Dylan know for sure if it would help. Maybe it's time to break your promise to Paul. After all, he hasn't exactly lived up to his end of the bargain."

"I know. I just keep thinking he'll freak if he finds out. Then what?"

"There's no reason for him to find out you've told them. It's not like they're going to announce, hey, buddy, we hear you've been popping too many painkillers and getting them illegally, to boot."

"But they could file charges," Kelsey said.

"He didn't write the forged prescriptions in Texas," Lizzy pointed out. "The crime occurred in another jurisdiction."

"I suppose." She buried her face in her hands. "This is so awful. I never in a million years thought things would come to this when I left Paul. I thought it was over, that he would see that the agreement was in his best interests. He's a brilliant man. His whole career, everything he's worked so hard for, all of it's on the line. How could he be so dumb?"

"Because his brain is clouded by narcotics," Lizzy

said flatly. "That's what makes the whole situation so dangerous. He can't possibly be thinking clearly."

She sat down next to Kelsey and grasped her hands. "I think you need to tell Dylan or Justin the whole truth. Now, Kelsey, before something happens and you live to regret it."

She drew in a deep breath, then nodded. "Okay. As soon as Dylan comes back, I'll tell him," she promised.

"You don't want to call him, get him back here?"

"No. He's out looking for Bobby. Maybe he'll find him and all this will become moot."

Lizzy looked as if she was about to argue, but her father's arrival silenced her. "Hey, Daddy," she said, when Harlan Adams rapped on the back door. "Come on in."

He came straight to Kelsey and held out his arms. "How are you, darlin' girl? This must be making you crazy."

"I've had better days," she agreed. "Thanks for stopping by."

"Just wanted to see for myself how you're holding up. Janet says if you need her, just give a shout and she'll come in. She's in the car, but thought you might be getting sick of people hovering."

"Not the two of you," Kelsey said.

"Is my grandson doing right by you?" he asked. "Justin's been wonderful."

"To tell you the truth, I thought he'd have that boy back by now. Maybe I ought to start making a few calls. I've got some friends around this state who can shake things up."

"Daddy, leave this to Justin," Lizzy said. "He doesn't need you interfering in his work."

Harlan regarded Lizzy indignantly. "Who's interfering? I'm just trying to see that the job gets done." He turned his gaze back to Kelsey. "What about this Delacourt fellow? Is he any good?"

"He seems to be," Kelsey said. "He and Justin have come up with some solid leads. They're checking them out now."

"Tell him to come by the house. I want to meet him, see for myself whether he's up to the job."

"Daddy," Lizzy protested. "You can't crossexamine Dylan. He'll tell you to mind your own damned business."

"If he does, he does. At least I'll have had a look at him. I like that sister of his a lot. She's settled Hardy down, turned him into a regular family man.

Didn't get to see too much of her brothers at the wedding, except to notice that they're a handsome lot. Dark-haired, blue-eyed scoundrels from the look of them. And of course, I know they're from a fine family. Jordan says the Delacourts are honorable people."

"Well, you would certainly know all about scoundrels, wouldn't you?" Lizzy teased. "Just look at the men in this family."

"Watch your tongue, young lady. I raised fine, honorable sons and a couple of rambunctious daughters. My grandbabies are living up to the same tradition. I won't listen to anyone who says otherwise."

"Because you're prejudiced," she accused. Kelsey listened to the banter, then chuckled despite the gravity of her own circumstances. "You two are so wonderful," she said. "You might bicker and tease, but there's so much love there. It's the way with your whole family. I want Bobby to grow up feeling that kind of love."

As suddenly as she'd laughed, her voice caught on a sob and the tears flowed again.

Harlan Adams took her hand in his. "He will, darlin' girl. You can count on it. If there's a God in heaven, Bobby will be back here before you know it. Just have faith."

Kelsey wanted desperately to believe him, but right this second her faith was in short supply.

When Justin was parceling out search assignments, Dylan opted for going to scour the Dallas-Fort Worth area. He needed to put some space between himself and Kelsey James. He was too irritated with her. He was also undeniably attracted to her. It was a lousy mix for a situation that required cool, calm objectivity.

Besides, he was itching for action. Some private investigators could spend all day just doing computer research. Not him. He needed to be on the move, especially when he had so many reasons for wanting to succeed.

A part of him wanted to find Paul and Bobby, so he could be the one to reunite mother and son. Another less attractive part of him wanted to put a fist in the other man's face. It was a toss-up which part would win when the moment of truth came.

And there was still a tiny, albeit rapidly fading, part that hoped the dad made a clean getaway with his boy. That part made him work all the harder to find the two of them and get them home.

Armed with pictures of Bobby and Paul, along with the tag number and description of Paul's car, plus the Yellow Pages' listings of hotels and motels, he began making his way around town.

He started with the fancier places first, guessing that

even in a situation like this Paul would want his creature comforts. From everything he'd learned from Kelsey, the man was seriously into status. Besides, exclusive, luxury hotels were famed for their discretion. They might be inclined to ask fewer questions of their guests as long as their credit cards had very high limits.

He strode into the lobby of the fifth hotel just as a man and a boy exited the coffee shop off the lobby. His pulse leapt. He crossed the lobby in quick strides, almost panicking when the elevator doors opened before he got there. But the elevator was going down, not up, and the pair waited for the next car.

Dylan edged closer, then took a good hard look. The boy had Bobby's sun-streaked hair, but that's where the similarities ended. The eye color didn't match, the freckles that should have stood out across his nose weren't there. The man regarded Dylan with an open, friendly smile, then turned away as the elevator came.

"You going up?" he asked, holding the door. Dylan shook his head. "No, sorry. There's something I need to do first."

He headed back to the desk. Here, as at the other hotels, the clerks shook their heads after looking over the pictures.

"Nope. Haven't seen them," the supervisor said. "If you want to wait a minute, I'll compare the tag number to those on file."

"How about letting me do that?" Dylan suggested, offering the man a fifty-dollar bill.

The man pushed it back with obvious regret. "Sorry. It's all on computer, and I can't let you back here."

Dylan nodded. "I'll grab a cup of coffee and come back."

He ate a sandwich while he was at it, though five minutes later he couldn't have said what it was. He kept thinking about the last few minutes he'd spent with Kelsey, about her refusal to trust him. He wasn't sure why that had cut straight through him. He'd tried telling himself it was just because her silence could be keeping him and Justin from finding her kid, but it was more than that. It was personal.

After all, he thought, still vaguely disgruntled, he'd put aside his reservations about her and the whole sole-custody thing. He'd respected her feelings, listened to her, but when push came to shove, she wasn't willing to return that same level of trust. Why? he wondered. Just because he was a man and her ex-husband had turned her off men? Or was it about him, some innate distrust of him specifically?

Or was it as simple as fear? Was whatever she was hiding so devastating that she felt she didn't dare reveal it? What could be that bad?

He went over it and over it and couldn't come up with a thing. What could a woman like Kelsey James, a brilliant doctor from all reports, have to hide? Or was it her ex's secrets?

Damn, this was getting him nowhere. He went back to the desk where the supervisor told him he hadn't been able to find a match for the tag number. Dylan gave him his card. "Call me if anything turns up, okay?"

"Absolutely. I have kids of my own. I can't imagine what that mother must be feeling."

"She's terrified," Dylan said succinctly.

"Well, I'll keep my eyes open. You can count on that."

Dylan nodded and set off for the next hotel on his list. He was running out of big, impersonal hotels. A few more and he'd be down to the moderately priced chains. There were a lot of them, scattered from one end of Dallas to the other with more in Fort Worth. Maybe he should just take a page out of Becky's book, find a room for himself and settle down with a phone. He could call faster than he could visit. It was a less time-consuming form of legwork, even if it was less likely to put a dent in his restless energy.

He booked a room near the airport, ordered up a pot of coffee, then settled down at the desk. The first call he made wasn't to a hotel on the list, but to Kelsey. Most clients didn't get frequent updates, didn't expect them, but this case was different and not just because she was a terror-stricken mom, either. It was because he had the un-mistakable feeling that she was the kind of woman who could matter to him, a disconcerting discovery in the middle of a kidnapping investigation, especially when there was so much distrust between them.

"Hey, Kelsey," he said when she snatched up the phone on the first ring.

"Dylan? Where are you?"

He tried not to sigh at the eagerness in her voice. It wasn't for him. It was for news of Bobby. There was no point in lying to himself about that. "In Dallas, check-ing out the hotels."

"Anything?"

"No. Sorry, darlin'. Anything turn up back there? Any calls from Paul?"

The question was greeted by silence. "Kelsey?"

"Oh, sorry. No. I was shaking my head, but I guess you couldn't know that," she said wryly. "I'm not think-ing very clearly."

"You're excused." He fell silent himself, aware that

he had nothing more to say that she really wanted to hear and that they were tying up the line as well. "Listen, I'll check in with you every so often. You hang in there, okay?"

"I'm doing the best I can. And, Dylan…"

"Yes?"

"When you get back, we need to talk."

"About?"

"We'll discuss it when you get here," she said. "Face-to-face."

So, he thought, staring at the phone after they'd hung up, she was going to share her secret, after all. He couldn't help wondering if it was worth dropping everything to go straight home to hear.

Then again, maybe he could get through with these calls in record time and be back in Los Pinõs before daybreak. His spirits brightened at the prospect. He figured the reasons for *that* didn't bear close examination.

"Daddy, I want to play outside," Bobby pleaded for the tenth time in as many minutes.

"No," Paul said, clinging to his patience by a thread.

"I don't like it in here. It smells funny."

The room did have the musty smell of smoke and old furniture that had absorbed the scents of too many guests. Paul doubted it had had a good cleaning in months, if not years. Normally he wouldn't have set foot in a dive like this, but he figured the police would be looking for him in the big, fancy hotels he tended to favor. Besides, he'd discovered that there were a lot of small, out-of-the-way motels in Texas where a man could buy silence. He only needed a few more days. By then, he was pretty sure Kelsey would agree to anything he asked.

"Why can't we go out?" Bobby asked.

"Because I said so," Paul snapped. "Watch TV."

"No," Bobby said with a stubborn tilt to his chin. "It's all fuzzy. Want to play catch."

"Not now."

"When?"

"Later."

"When is later?"

Paul sighed. This was harder than he'd anticipated. Entertaining a three-year-old was timeconsuming work. He'd forgotten that. It wasn't like he didn't have other things on his mind, either.

"Look, son, I'll get you some books next time I go out. You can look at the pictures, okay?"

"I like *my* books. Call Mommy. She knows which books I like."

"We are not calling your mother."

"Why?" Bobby's eyes filled with tears. "I miss Mommy. Why can't she come with us?"

"Because she's a very busy doctor and this is just a guy trip. You and me, buddy. Okay?"

Bobby heaved a sigh, then curled into a ball on the bed, looking miserable. Paul regarded him with real regret and heaved a sigh of his own.

Then he reached for the bottle containing his last few pills.

Seven

He must have made a hundred phone calls, all without picking up so much as a whiff of Paul James and Bobby, Dylan thought, slamming the motel phone down in disgust. He was wasting time. He might as well head back to Los Pinõs, which he'd wanted to do the night before. Kelsey finally appeared to be in a talkative mood. Maybe he'd get something out of a heart-to-heart with her. He could be there in a few hours, longer if he stopped to check the guest registers of any motels he passed along the way.

He punched in the number for the Los Pinõs sheriff's office and got Becky on the line. "Any news?"

"Nothing," she said, sounding as exhausted as he felt.

"There's nothing here, either. I'm coming back. Let Justin know, okay?"

"Will do. Gotta run. There's another call coming in."

"Thanks, Becky. See you soon."

He made one last call, this time to Trish. "Hey, sis."

"Dylan, where on earth have you been? I've been worried sick."

"Why?" he asked, not used to anyone worrying about

him. It had been a long time. After a couple of years, Kit had given up asking about his schedule. She'd said she was tired of his insensitivity. He'd accused her of nagging. In fact, that had been the beginning of the end of their marriage.

"I thought you'd at least check in last night," Trish scolded.

"Sorry. As soon as I was assigned to do a quick search in the Dallas-Fort Worth area, I took off. It never even occurred to me to call you."

"I think I'm beginning to see why Kit complained so bitterly," his sister said mildly. "You get so caught up in the hunt, you forget all about the people who love you."

"Okay, Trish. I get it. I'm sorry."

"Good. Now, tell me, did you find anything?
When are you coming back?"

"Nothing," he said for the second time that morning. "And I should be back in a few hours. Do me a favor."

"Anything," she said at once.

"Call Jeb and see what he's got going on at work. Tell him I could use him on this, if he can get away."

"You want me to get our brother to come to Los Pinõs and help you on a case? Won't Father have a cow?"

Dylan chuckled. "I certainly hope so. I try to stick it to him whenever I can. Jeb's a better P.I. than he is an oilman and everyone except Dad knows it."

"You're kidding," Trish said, clearly amazed. "He's worked with you before?"

"Every chance he gets," Dylan told her. "What about Michael and Tyler?"

"No, I am very much afraid that neither of them will leave the family business, though Tyler is showing evidence that he'd like to slip out of a suit and tie and go work the rigs. Dad hasn't quite decided how he feels about that one yet."

"How come I didn't know about any of this?"

"Because you were too busy with your own rebellion."

"Yes," she agreed thoughtfully. "I suppose I was. Okay, I'll call Jeb. Anything else?"

"Nope. Just pray that today's the day we get a break. I don't like the way this is dragging on. I want that boy back home, where he belongs."

He heard Trish's quiet intake of breath.

"Dylan, does that mean you're really okay with the fact that she's got full custody? There's not a part of you hoping that Paul will get away with Bobby?"

"Not anymore," he said, praying he was being truthful.

"You're sure?" she persisted.

"I have to accept that Bobby's with her for a reason. I just wish to hell someone would come clean and tell me what it is. See you later, sis. I will check in. I promise."

"You'd better, or I'll tell Laura that her favorite uncle is a perfect example of the kind of man she should steer clear of."

"That might be good advice under any circumstances," he admitted. "Just don't lay it on her now."

"Don't give me any reason to," she countered. "Love you."

Dylan smiled as he hung up. He really needed to spend more time counting his blessings. Trish and Laura would be at the top of the list, sharing first place. His brothers—especially Jeb—ranked a close second. They were the people he'd always known he could count on. Just like the Adamses, they were fiercely loyal, strong-willed and honorable.

And Dr. Kelsey James? The thought popped into his head, startling him. Where had that come from? His libido, no doubt. He'd have to find some way to deal with that when this was all over. For now, though, he definitely needed to table it.

That was easier said than done, he concluded when he walked into her house just after noon and found her on her hands and knees scrubbing the kitchen floor, her sexy little butt poked in the air, and a pair of shorts exposing way too many inches of her legs. Her sleeveless T-shirt had crawled up her back, leaving her midriff bare. He sucked in a deep breath and tried to tame his wildly errant thoughts.

"It's a little late in the year for spring-cleaning, isn't it?" he suggested. He spoke quietly, but startled her just the same.

She jumped, knocking over the pail of sudsy water beside her. Her gaze shot up. "You," she exclaimed as if he'd been an unwelcome thief. "Look what you made me do."

"Tell me where to look and I'll get a mop."

"Never mind. I'll clean it up as I go."

Dylan let it pass. He circled the spreading puddle of water, grabbed a chair and sat down to watch. He could see that the scrubbing and regaining her composure were giving her an equally difficult time.

"Don't mind me," she said eventually. "Sitting around waiting was driving me nuts. When I'm upset, I clean. If this drags on much longer, the house will be spotless."

"Paul hasn't called today?"

She shook her head, then rocked back on her haunches to meet his gaze. "He's doing it deliberately," she said bitterly. "He wants me to suffer."

"Why? Because you divorced him?"

"Maybe."

Dylan had a hunch that was only part of the story. "Why did you leave him?"

"It wasn't working out."

"Kelsey," he chided. "I thought you were going to talk to me when I got back. I'm here now. Let's have the whole story."

A wave of something that might have been shame washed over her face. "It's just so ugly," she began, then stopped when the phone rang. Clearly relieved at the interruption, she grabbed for the portable phone sitting on a nearby chair.

"Yes?"

Dylan couldn't hear what was said, but something in her expression told him all he needed to know.

"Paul?" he mouthed.

She nodded. "Let me talk to Bobby," she said, as Dylan slipped into the living room to pick up the extension there.

"Mommy?"

The tentative little voice tugged at Dylan's heart. Did every little kid sound like that on the phone? Would Shane if he could hear him?

"Hi, baby," Kelsey said, the upbeat note in her voice clearly forced. "How're you doing?"

"I wanna come home, Mommy. I miss you."

"I miss you, too, sweetie. You'll be home soon. Are you having fun with Daddy?"

"Uh-uh," Bobby complained. "He won't let me go outside. He bringed me hamburgers and French fries for lunch and dinner every day. Don't want hamburgers anymore."

"I thought you loved hamburgers," Kelsey said to him, responding to the petulance with a teasing tone. "You always grumble that I never buy you hamburgers."

"No more," he said adamantly. "Want pizza and ice cream."

"Well, maybe Daddy will get that for you tonight. Let me talk to him again, okay?"

Dylan heard the exchange between Bobby and his father, then Paul snapped, "Yes?"

"Bring him back, Paul."

"Just like that? I don't think so."

"When?"

"You'll be hearing from me," he said and hung up.

Dylan slowly replaced the receiver, still struck by the tension and anger in Paul's voice. If he'd ever doubted that this was about something besides a dad wanting to be with his son, he had his proof now. Paul wasn't making the most of this chance to be with Bobby. They weren't bonding, making up for lost time. Paul was all but holding his son captive for reasons that weren't yet clear to Dylan.

No, this was definitely about something between Paul and Kelsey. It was a power play, Dylan concluded.

He walked slowly back into the kitchen and found Kelsey sitting right where he'd left her, holding the phone and staring at it dejectedly.

She glanced up. "You heard?"

"Most of it." He hunkered down beside her, took the phone and set it back on the chair. "You okay?"

She gazed at him, fire flaring in her eyes, just as he'd hoped it would.

"Of course I'm not okay. My ex-husband has my son and is using him to play some kind of sick game with me. How could I possibly be okay?" she demanded in a voice that shook with fury.

Dylan reached for her just as the sobs started. Like a child seeking the comfort of a parent's embrace, she came willingly into his arms. Dylan held her and rocked her, feeling the tight knot of blame and resentment that had been inside him from the beginning of this case slowly ease. This was Kelsey, not Kit, and despite the odds against it, she was growing dear to him. So was a little boy he'd never even met. Hearing Bobby's voice had made him more real than ever.

Dylan knew he was still missing critical pieces of the puzzle, but it didn't seem to matter so much anymore. Beyond the tension and anger, he hadn't liked what he'd heard in Paul's voice. The man was a bully.

Plus, seeing that haunted look in Kelsey's eyes, hearing her little boy beg to come home were enough to convince him that Bobby belonged here, and the sooner he was back, the better. If there were legal issues to be resolved, they could be sorted out later.

He tipped Kelsey's chin up, until their gazes clashed. "We will get Bobby back," he told her firmly. "Soon."

"I'm so afraid," she whispered, tears still spilling down her cheeks.

"Don't be," he whispered, pressing a kiss to her forehead. She trembled. Lost in the shimmering, expressive depths of her eyes, Dylan shuddered as well. Wanting only to give comfort, he touched his lips to her cheek in another kiss, tasted salty tears, then without thinking he moved on to her mouth.

Her lips parted beneath his, welcomed him, but with a desperation born of circumstances, not passion for him. He doubted she was even aware of who held her, conscious only of the need to be held, the yearning to feel alive instead of dead inside. He knew because in the first weeks after Shane was gone for good, he had tried losing himself in a succession of meaningless encounters. It hadn't worked for him. It surely wouldn't for Kelsey.

Finally he pulled back, rested his forehead against hers, and let his breathing slow to normal. And then he carefully withdrew, the act both physical and emotional. He retreated, praying he could hang on to his professional objectivity just a little longer, just until Bobby was safely home again.

Kelsey obviously didn't understand what was going on. She stared at him in confusion. "Why?"

"Not now, Kelsey. It's not the time."

A shudder washed over her, as if she had suddenly become aware of what she'd been about to do. "Oh, God, what was I thinking?"

"You weren't," he said dryly. "Neither was I. We were feeling." He forced her gaze to his. "And that's okay, Kelsey. In fact, it's more than okay. I promise you, we'll get back to it, when the time is right."

A blush stained her cheeks and she gave him a smile that wobbled. "You think?"

"Oh, yes, darlin'. I can all but guarantee it," he said fervently. "Now let me get Lizzy or somebody else over here to stay with you, so I can get back on the job."

"I'll be fine by myself. I don't need somebody hovering."

"I think you do," he said, just as firmly.

But in the end, he couldn't track Lizzy down, so he called Trish. "Can you come over and spend some time with Kelsey?"

"Of course," she said at once. "I'll be right there." She

hesitated. "Dylan, what about Laura? Should I bring her or find a sitter?"

He knew exactly what she meant. Having a baby around right now might be more than Kelsey could bear. "A sitter, I think."

"No," Kelsey said at once, obviously guessing the topic. "Tell her to bring Laura. Seeing that precious girl will do me a world of good. It'll remind me of what I'm fighting to get back."

Dylan regarded her worriedly. "Are you sure?"

"Absolutely."

He nodded. "Trish, bring the munchkin. Kelsey wants her here."

"Will do. By the way, I spoke to Jeb. He's on his way. You were right. He was downright eager to get out from under Dad's thumb."

Dylan laughed. "At this rate, dear old Dad is going to have to come to Los Pinõs, if he expects to see his kids again."

"Does that mean you're thinking of sticking around?" Trish asked.

Dylan's gaze sought out Kelsey, who was busying herself putting the sponges and bucket away. "We'll see, sis. You know me. I take life the same way I build a case, one step at a time."

"Not that you asked, but nothing would make me happier than to have those steps lead you here."

"We'll see," he said, as Kelsey turned and met his gaze. He hung up the phone, then repeated the words for Kelsey's benefit. "We'll see."

He gave her a wink and headed for the door. "Trish will be here soon. If a rogue who looks a lot like me turns up here, don't let him in. Send him straight to the sheriff's office."

She regarded him quizzically. "Is that because he belongs in jail?"

"A few days in lockup probably wouldn't hurt him," he said. "But actually, it'll be my brother Jeb looking for me. I asked him to come and help out."

"One more thing to thank you for," she murmured. "How will I ever repay you?"

"Oh, I'm sure, when the time comes, we'll think of something. Meantime, keep that chin up."

Kelsey couldn't believe how much Dylan had become a part of her life. He was rapidly becoming her linchpin, her tower of strength. Despite those early misgivings, she was sure that he was fully and completely on her side now.

Under other circumstances, she might have joked with Lizzy about what a hunk he was, but now she hated herself for even noticing. And, of course, there had been that kiss. She wasn't entirely sure how it had started, but, holy kamoley, there was no mistaking how it could have ended. How she had wanted it to end.

What on earth was wrong with her? How could she be attracted to Dylan—to anyone—when her boy was missing? How could she have considered, even for a second, just giving in to passion and letting it wipe out the pain, even temporarily?

Normally he wasn't the sort of man who'd even notice her, but she could tell that he did. But just when she thought she detected a male-female sort of heat in his gaze, he withdrew to that distant place where she couldn't reach him. He'd done it after that kiss, despite his reassurances that they'd get back to it another time.

Her skin was still burning, just as it had to his touch, when Trish knocked at the back door. "Okay to come in?"

"Absolutely," Kelsey told her, relieved to have the distraction. She caught sight of Laura clinging to her mother's hand and knelt down. "Hey, you. How about a cookie?"

Laura's eyes brightened. "Cookie?" she said at once, her head bobbing eagerly. Then she cast a cautious glance at her mother. "'Kay, Mama?"

"Yes, it's okay. But just one," Trish said. "Then you have to lie down on the sofa and take a nap."

"Nap," Laura echoed dutifully, already reaching for the oatmeal-raisin cookie Kelsey was holding out.

"Want to bet she forgets all about that nap when the time comes?" Trish said. She touched Kelsey's cheek. "How are you holding up?"

"By a thread," Kelsey said honestly. "Your brother has been amazing. He's been working on this nonstop."

Trish seemed about to say something, then caught herself.

"What?" Kelsey prodded.

"Nothing."

"I thought we knew each other well enough to speak our minds," Kelsey scolded. "You don't have to censor yourself with me."

Trish still seemed hesitant. "I just don't think I should get into this. Dylan wouldn't want me saying anything."

"About?" Kelsey asked, then waited.

"It's just that this has been incredibly hard on him," Trish said finally.

Puzzled, Kelsey stared. "Why? I'm sure he's a caring man who'd be upset to see anyone suffering, but you make it sound as if something more is going on."

Trish hesitated.

"You're making me nervous, Trish. What don't I know?"

"Did you know he has a little boy of his own?"

Kelsey was stunned. Dylan had never mentioned him. "No. He hasn't said a word."

"He doesn't talk much about Shane."

He certainly hadn't said anything to her, she thought, hurt by the omission. How could he not share something so personal with her, especially in the past day or two when they'd been getting closer?

"Why?" she asked Trish.

"Because he gave up custody. Shane is with Dylan's ex and her new husband. He pretty much tries to pretend his son doesn't exist, but it tears him up inside that Kit has the boy and he never sees him." In that instant Kelsey realized why Dylan had kept his distance, why disdain had once crept in just when she thought they were getting closer.

"I see," she said, fighting the feeling that she'd been had, that he had betrayed her. It wasn't an entirely rational reaction, given how hard he'd been working for her and the secret she had deliberately kept from him, but that didn't seem to matter. She had to wonder just how hard he really had been working. Had he only been going through the motions, because it was expected of him by people who *did* matter to him?

Trish studied her worriedly. "I've made it worse, haven't I? I knew I should keep my mouth shut. Now you don't trust him. This is exactly what Dylan was worried about."

"I do have to wonder whose side he's really on."

"Yours," Trish said adamantly. "He would never let his personal feelings interfere in a case."

"I should have known about this, just the same."

"I agree," Trish said. "I told him to tell you."

"Then why didn't he?"

"He said he needed you to trust him, if he was going to help you."

"He was right about that," Kelsey said coolly. "I need to trust him."

Trish squeezed her hand. "You can, you know."

Kelsey shook her head. "I don't think so."

Numb, she fell silent. A short time later, she made an excuse that she had a raging headache and sent Trish away. Then she called Dylan at the sheriff's office.

"I want to see you," she said, when he came on the line.

"Can it wait?"

"I don't think so."

"Has Paul called again?"

"No. Just come, Dylan. Now."

Something in her voice must have alerted him that she was in no mood for excuses, because he said quietly, "I'll be right there."

When he came in, she studied his face, trying to read the truth. What were his real motivations in taking this case? Had he already betrayed her? Had he deliberately let Paul slip away? Was he eager to see another dad succeed where he had failed?

"What's wrong?" he asked.

She put it bluntly. "Are you really on my side or Paul's?"

He looked wounded by the question. "Where did that come from?"

"Trish told me about your little boy."

He went absolutely still, then stood up and began to pace.

"Well, was she lying?"

"No, of course not, but she had no right to tell you about that."

Kelsey steeled herself against the pain in his eyes. "I'm glad she did. It was about time somebody filled me in. I had a right to know that you might have divided loyalties. Now answer me. Whose side are you on?"

He hesitated for no more than an instant, but it was long enough to infuriate her, long enough to condemn him in her eyes.

"You're fired," she told him. "I don't want you working on this anymore."

"Kelsey—"

She cut off the protest. "No. You've probably helped him get away."

"Why would I do that?" he asked reasonably. "I'm working for you. My professional reputation wouldn't be worth spit if I let my own feelings interfere in a case I'd accepted. Believe me, if I felt that strongly about your situation, I would never have taken the case in the first place."

"You were under a lot of pressure to take it," she pointed out. "Lizzy asked. Trish lives here in town. You probably felt you owed it to them."

He ran his fingers through his hair. "Okay, yes. I did feel I owed them, but there was never a time when I couldn't have called in another investigator if I'd thought it would be for the best."

"But isn't that just the point?" she demanded. "Best for whom? Me or Paul?" Even as she said it, she knew she was beyond reason. She'd been wanting somebody to blame for days now and Dylan was right here. He was an easier target than Paul.

"Okay, I'll ask you again," he said with exaggerated patience. "Why would I do that?"

His mild tone which suggested he was merely tolerating her outburst incensed her. She lashed out again. "Because your ex-wife has sole custody of your son and you haven't forgiven her for it. You're getting even with her through me."

"She has sole custody because I made the decision that it was for the best."

"So you say."

Dylan flinched under the bitter assault, but he didn't argue with her. He let it drop, accepting her judgment, obviously because she'd hit on the truth. He *was* on Paul's side. And for that, Kelsey was certain she would never be able to forgive him.

Later, when her temper had cooled and she could think back on the conversation rationally, she realized that at that moment, it looked as if a light in Dylan's eyes had gone out. She ached for the unfair accusations she had hurled at him, but it was too late to take them back.

By then he was gone and she was all alone. Completely alone. The silence was deafening.

Only then did she hear the tiny, nagging voice in her head all but shouting that she had just made the worst mistake of her life.

Eight

Dylan dropped into a chair in Trish's living room without even bothering to turn on the light. He was too exhausted to move, too drained to even drag himself off to bed. Kelsey's charge that he'd let her down because of sympathy for her ex hadn't been nearly as unfounded as he would have liked.

Oh, he had done his best to find Bobby. He'd left no stone unturned, no lead ignored, but he couldn't honestly say he'd done it with enthusiasm. Not in the beginning. True, he had wanted Bobby reunited with his mother, a woman he'd come to care about more than he wanted to admit. But at the father's expense? Even now, when he knew in his gut it was the right thing to do, the idea still brought up more bitter memories than he'd ever wanted to revisit. That was why he hadn't been able to argue with the damning conclusions Kelsey had obviously jumped to.

He was still sitting there when Trish came downstairs at dawn to fix breakfast for Hardy, who was splitting his days between duties at the ranch and search parties that continued to comb half of West Texas looking for some trace of Paul James and Bobby.

"Dylan, what are you doing sitting down here in the dark?" She stepped into the room and took a closer look. "You look like hell."

"Feel like it, too."

"What time did you get in last night? I never heard you."

He shrugged. He hadn't looked at his watch. After he'd left Kelsey's, he'd driven around for hours, then instinctively stopped in at the sheriff's office to check in with Justin. There had been no news, no leads.

Trish sat down opposite him. "Okay, big brother, spill it. What's wrong?"

"Aside from the fact that here's no sign of Bobby and the fact that I've been fired? Aside from those two things, I'd say life is just about perfect."

Trish stared at him with undisguised astonishment. "Fired? Why?"

"Your friend seems to think I might have a conflict of interest. I don't suppose you're the one who mentioned Shane to her."

His sister flushed guiltily. "Yes, and I could see she was overreacting, but I thought I'd calmed her down. I had no idea she'd go off the deep end. You've worked your tail off on this case. How dare she fire you?" she asked indignantly. "Don't worry, Dylan. I'll talk to her."

"No need. I'm not going to stop working, just because of a little technicality like being fired. I wasn't planning on getting paid anyway. Are you going over there today?"

She nodded. "Right after breakfast."

"Do something for me."

"Anything."

"See if you can find out what she's holding back. There's something she hasn't told me. She almost let it out yesterday, but then Paul called and we got sidetracked. Before that she clammed up whenever I asked. I know she won't tell me now, but I have a feeling it's crucial."

"Maybe Lizzy knows. Have you talked to her?"

"I tried. She was as evasive as hell, too."

"I'll do what I can."

"Thanks. I'm going to go up and grab a shower. Think you can have some lethally strong coffee ready when I get back down?"

"You got it, big brother." She gave him a hug. "Don't let what Kelsey did get you down. She appreciates your help and she cares about you. I know she does."

"Sure," he said grimly, thinking of the way she'd kissed him, the way she'd melted in his arms. She cared, all right. "She just doesn't trust me."

When he came back down, feeling marginally better after an icy shower, he found not only Hardy at the kitchen table with Trish, but Jeb. His brother, who was only a year younger, frowned at him.

"For a man in such a big hurry to get me over here, you might have stuck around last night to tell me what you need me to do," Jeb noted without any real venom, spooning cereal into his mouth as if he hadn't had a meal in a month.

Dylan winced. "Sorry. I got sidetracked."

Jeb stared, clearly incredulous. "You? In the middle of a case?" He turned his gaze on Trish. "Did I miss the sky falling?"

"Very funny," Dylan retorted. "Now if you're finished

trying to eat Trish and Hardy out of house and home, we can hit the road."

"Oh, no, you don't," Trish said, motioning toward a chair. "Sit. You're not leaving here until you've had coffee and breakfast. I'll make you an omelet."

Dylan knew better than to argue. Trish could nag worse than their mother, if she put her mind to it. Besides, he knew she wanted badly to make up for spilling the beans to Kelsey about Shane.

"I'll take the coffee and some toast. That's enough."

"You'll eat eggs and be grateful for them," she countered, whipping the eggs with a whisk. She poured them into a pan sizzling with melted butter. "Jeb might be able to run all day on a sugar high, but you need protein."

Hardy grinned at the display of bossiness. "You're the ones who spoiled her. Thanks to you, she thinks she's queen of the universe," he reminded them. "Now it's time for payback. I think I'll just be running along while all her attention is focused on the two of you."

Trish frowned at her husband with mock severity. "You'll pay for that remark later."

He gave her a hard kiss. "I'll be looking forward to it, darlin'." He winked at Dylan and Jeb. "See. Marriage has its rewards. You might want to consider it."

"The man has all the fervor of a recent convert," Dylan noted to no one in particular.

Jeb shuddered. "Marriage is definitely not for me. Women change once they get a ring on their finger. I've seen it too often not to believe in the phenomenon."

Dylan didn't really want to get drawn into that particular discussion. He concentrated all of his attention on the food Trish had put in front of him. He couldn't help noting, though, that an image of Kelsey popped into his head at the mere mention of marriage.

"Hey, Dylan, I don't hear you swearing off marriage," Jeb said, studying him curiously. "Is something going on over here I don't know about?"

"Nothing," he said tersely, fully aware of the long, speculative look that his brother exchanged with Trish. He threw down his fork. "That's it. Let's get out of here."

Jeb grinned at Trish as he dutifully stood up. "Guess I touched a nerve."

"And if you've got a grain of sense in that hard head of yours, you'll leave it be," Dylan snapped back.

Jeb's hoot of laughter trailed him to the car. He was inside with the motor running before his brother cracked open the door. "Is it safe?"

"As safe as it's going to get."

Jeb climbed in, snapped on his seat belt, then slid down in the seat before glancing over to gauge Dylan's mood. "Does this pleasant frame of mind have something to do with the case or with the beautiful mother?"

Dylan's frown deepened. "How do you know she's beautiful?"

"Where you're concerned, they always are."

"Meaning?" Dylan asked darkly.

"Nothing. Absolutely nothing."

Dylan wasn't buying the denial. "Are you suggesting I'm shallow?"

His brother heaved a sigh. "Okay, you asked for this. Under normal circumstances, no, you are not shallow. But ever since Kit divorced you, you've been more interested in beauty than brains. You haven't exactly been looking for anybody with real staying power. Now that may be okay for me. I'm not the happily-ever-after type.

But you're different. You want a home and a family. That's what you deserve. Unfortunately, Kit did a real number on you and threw you off your stride. But this love-'em-and-leave-'em stuff is not you, Dylan. Your middle name should have been dependable."

Dylan had had enough. "How the hell did we get off on this tangent, anyway?" he asked moodily. "I didn't have you come over here to discuss my love life."

"Hitting a little too close to home, am I?" Jeb countered. His expression turned thoughtful. "Maybe I guessed wrong about what's going on here. This Kelsey is a pediatrician, isn't she? Must be smart. Probably has some real substance to her. Am I right?"

"What you are is a pain in the neck."

"Ah, brains and beauty," Jeb concluded triumphantly. "Now we're talking."

"Do I need to remind you that the woman's child is missing? We haven't exactly been taking time out for a hot romance."

Jeb studied him. "But you have kissed her, haven't you?"

Dylan felt heat climbing into his cheeks. Jeb hooted. "I knew it."

"I am calling Dad first chance I get and telling him you're just itching to have more responsibility at the oil company," Dylan vowed. "I might even recommend he make you vice president of something that will require oodles and oodles of paperwork, something with lots and lots of numbers."

Unfortunately, his brother didn't seem the least bit daunted by the threat.

"Dad knows perfectly well I can't add without a calculator. He still has the accountant go over my checkbook because it's such a mess. He's not about to leave the company finances in my hands."

Dylan sighed. "You have a point. Okay, enough sparring. Let's talk about Paul James and where he could be hiding with his son."

Jeb promptly straightened in his seat. "Tell me what you know," he said with an eagerness he never displayed when talking about his work for the family oil business.

Dylan laid out the case point by point. For all of his carefree ways, Jeb had a quick mind. They were a good match. Dylan relished the details, the assembling of clues. Jeb could lay them out and see the big picture. When Dylan was finished, Jeb nodded. "He wants something from Kelsey," he concluded. "And he's stringing her along until he figures she'll be desperate enough to give it to him."

"But what?" Dylan asked. "Obviously not Bobby. He has him and he hasn't made a run for it. I heard him on the phone. I don't even think it's a play to get shared custody. It's something else."

"Money?" Jeb suggested.

Dylan considered it, then shook his head. "Kelsey's not rich. She's a small-town doctor. She probably has medical school bills left to pay. Besides, from what I gathered, Paul is a hotshot stockbroker. He's the one with the bucks."

"Maybe he played fast and loose with his ethics and got himself fired."

"So he stole his kid to get back his credibility?" Dylan asked doubtfully. "I don't think so. Besides, Justin talked to his boss. He's expecting him back after his two-week vacation ends."

"Maybe he's just trying to jerk Kelsey's chain. Maybe

this is payback for her leaving him." Dylan had certainly heard enough taunting animosity in Paul's voice to believe him capable of that kind of cruelty, but it still didn't ring true. He couldn't quite put his finger on why he felt that so strongly. "No," he said eventually. "It's something else. And my gut tells me that Kelsey knows exactly what it is."

"Then let's go see the beautiful pediatrician," Jeb suggested. "We can play good cop, bad cop with her. I'll be the bad guy, since you want to have a future with her when this is all over."

"I never said—"

"You didn't have to, big brother. It's written all over your face. You're the transparent one, remember? That's why Mom always knew you were the one who stole the cookies."

"No, she knew that because the rest of you blabbed," Dylan countered. "But you're right about going to see Kelsey. It's time to put an end to the evasiveness."

"Don't forget, though, I get to be the bad cop," Jeb said.

If the situation hadn't been so deadly serious, Dylan would have laughed at his brother's eagerness. Jeb had obviously spent far to many hours watching shows like *NYPD Blue*. He had the typical amateur's illusions about the glamour of police and detective work. And because he only popped in and out of Dylan's cases at the most critical junctures, he had no idea how much nitty-gritty, boring legwork was required to get to that point.

Dylan approached Kelsey's house with mounting trepidation. After all, she had fired him the night before. He doubted she was going to be overjoyed to find him still at work. Maybe the way around that would be to explain he had brought Jeb in as his replacement. Maybe she wouldn't recall that Jeb had already been on his way to town before Dylan had been fired.

Women tended to accept his brother at face value. Jeb was a charmer with the kind of friendly, open demeanor that drew them in droves. They also tended to take advantage of his good nature, which Dylan believed was the reason Jeb refused to take any relationship seriously. He'd been burned so many times that he now made it a point to be the first to walk away.

"Why is it you look as though we're about to stroll innocently into the lion's den?" Jeb asked as they exited the car. "I thought you liked this woman."

"I'm not exactly at the top of her hit parade at the moment," Dylan admitted, surprised that Trish hadn't explained the situation. "The truth is, she fired me last night."

"She fired you," Jeb echoed, shaking his head. "Now's a fine time to mention that. Maybe you'd better be the bad cop, after all."

Dylan chuckled. "Nah. You do it so well."

He rang the bell and waited. When Lizzy opened the door, she regarded him with shock. "I thought you'd been—"

"Fired?" Dylan supplied. She nodded.

"I was," he replied cheerfully. "So I hired him." He gestured over his shoulder. "You remember my brother Jeb."

Lizzy stared. "Jeb. Of course. I thought you were in the oil business."

"I'm a man of many talents," he said. "Dylan likes to call on me when he's in over his head."

"Very funny," Dylan muttered. He stepped past Lizzy. "Where's Kelsey?"

"In the kitchen. I'll get her."

"Never mind," Jeb said. "Well go in there."

"Don't mind him," Dylan said. "He's hoping there will be leftovers from breakfast. He's a bottomless pit."

"Then he's in luck. I've been baking again. Cinnamon rolls this time. It keeps my mind off of things and I keep hoping the aroma of all that sugar and cinnamon will get to Kelsey so she'll eat something."

"She's still not eating?" Dylan asked.

"Not so you'd notice. And she can't afford to lose any weight," Lizzy said.

Dylan thoroughly surveyed Kelsey when he walked into the kitchen and spotted her bent over, scrubbing out the refrigerator. Obviously, she was on another cleaning binge. He found himself agreeing with Lizzy. Even after a few days, her clothes were looser. More important, when she glanced up, her face looked drawn and pale.

Seeing him, though, put bright patches of color on her cheeks, right along with a frown. Dylan badly wanted to kiss her to heighten that color even more, but decided against it. To many fascinated onlookers. Instead, he opted for going on the offensive before she got any brilliant ideas about tossing him right back out the door. He pulled out a chair, then gestured toward it.

"Have a seat," he suggested.

Kelsey didn't budge. In fact, her chin lifted a defiant notch. She pinned his brother with a look. "Who is he?"

"This is my brother. Jeb, this is Dr. Kelsey James."

"I'm sorry about your little boy," Jeb said.

"Thank you." Her gaze shifted back to Dylan. "I

thought I'd made myself clear last night. I don't want you on this case."

"Which is why Jeb is stepping in."

"He's a private investigator, too?"

"Part-time," Jeb said, before Dylan could respond. "I ask the tough questions that Dylan's too nice to ask."

She blinked rapidly at that. "Oh?" she said, visibly nervous.

Jeb nodded, his expression still deceptively cheerful. "Such as, what is your ex-husband really after?"

"Excuse me?" Kelsey's voice faltered. She sank onto the chair Dylan was holding. "I'm not sure I understand."

"Sure you do," Jeb corrected. "You're a smart woman. It's bound to have occurred to you that your ex-husband hasn't taken Bobby so he can bond with the boy or go off on some grand adventure."

"I suppose," she admitted grudgingly. "Well, then, why has he taken him?"

"Because he's not a very nice man," Kelsey snapped.

"I think we can all agree to that," Dylan said. He rested a hand on Kelsey's shoulder. The muscles were tight with tension. His touch didn't seem to be helping. If anything, she stiffened more.

"Does he want money?" Jeb persisted. "After all, you're a doctor. You're friends with the most important family in town. He's got to figure you'd be good for some cash."

"This isn't about money," Kelsey said tersely.

The quick negative responses proved to Dylan that she knew exactly what Paul *did* want.

"But you do have something he wants, don't you?" Jeb prodded.

His gaze met hers with the kind of direct, penetrating stare that few people could ignore. Kelsey was no exception. Dylan felt her tremble, even though she held her own gaze defiantly steady.

"Don't mistake me for my brother, Kelsey," Jeb said, his gaze hardening. "I'm not going to let you off the hook. I'm going to come at this from a hundred different directions, if that's what it takes to get you to open up. We'll try the direct approach one more time. What does Paul James want from you in return for giving back your son?"

A tear spilled from Kelsey's eyes and rolled down her cheek. Lizzy jumped up. "That's enough," she said. "Leave her alone. She's not on trial here. Can't you see you're just upsetting her more? Hasn't she already been through enough?"

Dylan felt some of the tension drain out of Kelsey as she finally shook her head, evidently resigned to the inevitable. She touched a restraining hand to Lizzy's arm. "It's okay. I'll tell him. I should have told someone when this first started."

Lizzy stared at her. "Are you sure?"

"What difference does it make now?" But instead of looking at Jeb, she eased around in the chair until she could meet Dylan's gaze. "Paul wants drugs, prescription painkillers," she blurted in a rush. "He's addicted to them. He has been for a couple of years now."

"And that's why you left him?" Dylan guessed, more relieved than shocked by the admission. Finally, they had something to work with.

"I left him because of that and because he was forging my name on prescriptions to get them. I agreed not to turn him in, if he would give me full custody of Bobby and stay out of our lives. I know that was wrong and probably stupid, but it was all I could think of to do at the time."

"And now his supply of pills has run out and he's desperate," Dylan concluded.

She nodded. "I'm sure that's it, even though he hasn't said as much. He wants me half-crazy, so I'll do whatever he says, give him whatever he wants."

Jeb whistled. "So we've got a guy who's hooked on drugs and not thinking rationally out there with your son."

"Jeb!" Dylan protested, seeing Kelsey's face turn a ghastly shade of gray at the harsh assessment.

"Sorry. My mouth runs ahead of my brain at times."

She waved off the apology. "I'm terrified of what he will do if he finds out I've told you all this. I promised to keep the secret."

"And he promised to stay away," Dylan said. "I'd say you're even." He hunkered down in front of her. "This helps, sweetheart. We have to assume he won't go far, because he's going to want to make a quick exchange for Bobby when the time comes. He may be moving from motel to motel, but I'll bet he's within a hundred miles or less."

"But you've checked all the motels over and over," Kelsey said. "He's not there."

"What about campgrounds?" Jeb suggested. "Are there any close by?"

"No," Lizzy said. "But there are acres and acres of open land. He could have pitched a tent anyplace."

Dylan exchanged a look with his brother. "Feel like taking a drive?"

Jeb nodded. "I've been dying to get a better look at this part of the country."

"I want to come with you," Kelsey said, half rising. Then her expression registered dismay and she sank back down. "But I can't, can I?"

"No," Dylan agreed. "You need to stay here in case he calls again. If he does, see if we're on track with this camping idea. Maybe you can get Bobby to say something about sleeping outdoors."

"Bobby hates bugs," she murmured. "If that's what they're doing, it's no wonder he was so cranky the last time we talked."

"I hate to burst your bubble, but I just remembered something. I thought Bobby said something about Paul not letting him leave the room," Lizzy said. "Doesn't that mean they have to be in a motel?"

"He did," Kelsey agreed. "Was that last time? Or the time before? I'm getting it all mixed up."

"It's okay," Dylan reassured her. "We'll take a look around anyway. Call me on the cell phone if anything comes up."

She nodded, then opened her mouth to say something, but fell silent, her expression guilty.

Dylan had a pretty good idea what she'd been about to say, though. He gave her a grin. "It's okay, darlin'. I know I'm fired. This one's on the house."

Nine

Dylan and Jeb were almost out the door when the phone rang. Everyone froze. Kelsey's heart began to thud dully as it had every time a call came in. She reached for the receiver with fingers that trembled so badly she could barely grasp it.

"Hello."

"Mommy?"

Bobby's voice sounded scratchy and hoarse. "Baby, are you okay? What's wrong?"

"Don't feel good, Mommy."

Kelsey had never felt so thoroughly helpless in her entire life. Maternal instinct as much as her professional training kicked in. Thank heaven Bobby was now old enough to answer a few simple questions. "Where does it hurt, sweetie? Your tummy? Your head?"

"All over. I'm hot, Mommy."

Her fury and frustration boiled over. "Put your daddy on the phone, baby. Okay?"

Paul came on the line. "He's fine," he said before she could get a word out. "It's just a little fever. It's no big deal, so don't go making a federal case out of it."

"I want him home, Paul. I'm the doctor. I'll be the judge of whether or not he's seriously ill."

"Kids get fevers. It's nothing," he insisted. "Does he have a cold? Is that it? Have you been taking him in and out of air-conditioning?"

"Tsk-tsk," he chided. "You know I'm not going to answer something like that. Gotta run, Kelsey. Bobby wants some orange juice. I'll be in touch."

"Paul!" she shouted, but she could hear the click of his receiver being put back into place. "Dammit, Paul." This time the words came out as a frustrated whisper.

Her gaze sought out Lizzy, then automatically shifted to Dylan. It didn't seem to matter that she was furious at him for deceiving her about his own custody situation. She still looked to him for strength. How had that happened in such a short time? How did she know that despite everything, despite the angry accusations she had hurled at him, she could still trust him? With just a glance from her, he crossed the kitchen in three long strides. He pulled a chair up close beside her.

"Bobby's sick?" he asked.

"Paul says it's just a fever. Maybe he's right. He's probably right," she said more emphatically. "But I hate not being there, not knowing for sure."

"Of course you do," Lizzy said. "But stop a minute. Bobby's never had more than the sniffles. He's the healthiest little boy I've ever seen. There's no reason to imagine that this is anything more than that."

"Maybe he's overdue," Kelsey whispered, wishing she shared Lizzy's certainty. "Who knows where he's been the past few days or what he's been exposed to. He said he hurt all over."

"Could be the flu, then," Lizzy suggested, still maintaining a positive outlook. "It'll be over and done with in a day or so."

"Or it could be measles or chicken pox," Kelsey retorted, her imagination whirling into overdrive. She was suddenly thinking like a panic-stricken mom, rather than a cool, rational doctor. "We don't know. That's the problem."

Dylan gave a nod to Lizzy and Jeb, who vanished on cue. "Come here," he said, reaching for her.

Kelsey instinctively gravitated into his embrace, the previous night's argument forgotten. Dylan might not be able to cure whatever ailed Bobby, but she found comfort and reassurance in his touch. It was a reaction she didn't care to examine too closely.

"You heard what Lizzy said," he soothed. "Bobby's as healthy as a kid can be. This is probably nothing."

"But what if it's not?" she whispered.

"Then Paul will get medical attention for him." She backed away. "Why on earth would you think that? He's not going to give up this game just to help Bobby, not until he gets what he wants from me."

"Then he'll make a demand. You'll give him the pills. And we'll get Bobby back. He won't risk that little boy's life. No father could do that, even if he's not thinking clearly."

"I wish I shared your faith," she said.

"You married the man, Kelsey. He can't be all bad. Wasn't there a time when you trusted him, when you had faith he would do the right thing?"

She thought back to the early days of their courtship, when Paul had been tender and funny and attentive. He had actually taken time off from work once to nurse her through a bad cold. So, Dylan was probably right. The man she had fallen in love with wouldn't let his son suffer.

"Thank you for reminding me of that," she said at last. "It's just that he changed so much after the pills."

"You hang on to the fact that he was a decent guy when you met him, okay?" He cupped her cheek in his hand. "A few prayers wouldn't hurt, either."

"I've prayed so often the last few days, I'm sure God is sick of hearing from me."

Dylan chuckled. "I don't think it works that way. I think He expects us to check in regularly with updates in circumstances like this."

Kelsey sighed and rested her forehead against Dylan's chest. She could feel the steady beating of his heart. "I was so nasty to you last night. Can you forgive me? I know you've been doing your best on this case. I had no right to accuse you of doing anything less."

Dylan sighed. "Yes, you did. The truth is I did come into this case with enough baggage to keep a shrink busy for a year. I never let it interfere, but it was there. And you had every right to know about it, to make a choice about whether you could trust me. I suppose I didn't want you to know for fear you'd dump me right at the beginning when time was critical. I knew right then that I was all you had to count on and that I'm damned good at what I do. My ego got in the way."

He tipped her chin up, then gazed directly into her eyes. "I'm with you a hundred percent on this, Kelsey. Okay?"

She nodded, unable to speak because she knew how terribly difficult it must be for him to side against a father who'd been cut off from his son, even under these extenuating circumstances.

"Dylan, will you talk to me about Shane?" She felt his muscles tense at the mention of his son's name. "Please? I'd like to hear about him."

"After this is all over, you and I will talk," he promised eventually. "About Shane and a good many other things, I imagine. Will that do?"

She was disappointed by the delay, but she nodded. "Yes. That will do."

"Then it's a date, darlin'. Now let me get out of here and catch up with Jeb. I'm not doing you a bit of good standing around here in your kitchen."

"Yes, you are," she said, but she stepped back just the same. "You're just not finding Bobby. And that's the only thing that matters now."

He bent down and pressed a hard kiss to her lips, then took off without another word. Kelsey watched him go, then sat down at the table and rested her head on her arms.

"Dear God," she whispered. "Make this the day that my son comes home to me. And in the meantime, please keep him and all the people looking for him safe."

"Amen," Lizzy said, adding her voice to Kelsey's.

Either her timing was impeccable or she had never strayed far from the kitchen and had heard Dylan leave. Kelsey looked up at her friend. "I am so incredibly lucky," she told her. "I have you and your family and this community to lean on."

"And Dylan," Lizzy reminded her.

A half smile formed. "And Dylan," she agreed. "He's an amazing man, isn't he?"

"Definitely one of the good guys." Lizzy searched her face intently. "Have you fallen for him, Kelsey?"

"I can't even think about something like that right

now," she insisted, but in her heart she suspected that she was indeed falling in love with Dylan Delacourt. Finding out for sure was something that would have to wait until her son was safely home again.

Dylan drove himself to exhaustion that day and the next. He kept thinking of that little boy, his body flushed with fever, missing his mommy.

"I could wring the man's neck," he told Jeb. "Which is why I'm here, to keep you from doing something stupid. We're going to find Bobby, take him home to Kelsey, and leave his daddy in one piece for the authorities to deal with."

Dylan regarded his brother ruefully. "Don't make me regret bringing you over here."

Jeb laughed. "You know I'm right. That's exactly why you brought me over here, to temper your hot head. I'm the cool, rational thinker, remember?"

"Since when?"

"Okay, compared to you, I am," Jeb amended. "And you don't have the slightest urge to pummel Paul James's face to a bloody pulp?" Dylan asked.

Jeb drew himself up and returned Dylan's skeptical look evenly. "Absolutely not. Do I look like a thug?"

"No, you look like a man who's having the time of his life. When are you going to tell dear old Dad that you want to come to work with me full-time?" Jeb's expression fell. "On his deathbed, probably. The news will probably revive him just so he can make sure it doesn't happen."

"Life's too short to waste it doing something you hate," Dylan said.

"I did talk to him about doing some corporate investigative work for him," Jeb revealed. "He looked at me as if I'd suggested there were cockroaches in the pantry and I wanted to play at being an exterminator."

"Is there something going on at the company that needs investigating?" Dylan asked, startled by the suggestion that there might be. "He hasn't mentioned anything."

"Because he's in denial. You know Dad. He thinks he's in total control of his universe. You were his first slipup. Then Trish's defection shook him badly. He's got the rest of us under tighter rein than ever. As for anyone stealing from him, to hear him tell it, it's impossible."

"But you don't think so?"

"There are too many coincidences for my liking. Twice now, just when we were about to close a deal for a new site, another company has come in and snatched it out from under us."

Dylan was stunned. He didn't believe in coincidences of that magnitude, either. He was surprised that his father did. "Why isn't Dad acting on this?"

"Either he's in denial or he doesn't want to admit the obvious, that his new geologist is on the take."

"Beautiful Brianna is selling corporate secrets?" He thought he heard something else in his brother's voice, too. "You're unhappy about more than the soured deals, aren't you? Is it Brianna?"

Jeb sighed. "She's a terrific woman. I don't want to believe she's involved, but everything points to it."

"Then forget Dad. Investigate on your own. Find out if she can be trusted."

"What if my judgment's clouded by my hormones?"

"Believe me, Jeb, you won't be the first one. Look at me. Kelsey's got me tied up in knots. Besides, even though I know she was justified in going after full custody of Bobby, a part of me is still sympathetic to her ex. Of course, I've been getting over that in a hurry the last few days. I've finally concluded the man is pond scum and doesn't deserve so much as a glimpse of his son ever again." He spotted a diner up ahead and pulled into the lot. "I don't know about you, but I need coffee and some food. The last decent meal we had was that breakfast Trish cooked yesterday."

"And the cinnamon rolls Lizzy sent along," Jeb said.

"Cinnamon rolls? I never saw any cinnamon rolls."

"Oops. Sorry. I think what we both need is a good night's sleep," Jeb countered, quickly changing the subject. "We must have covered a thousand miles today, going in circles. I never knew so many sleazy motels existed."

"After we eat, if you want to go back to Trish's I'll drop you off. I want to check in at Kelsey's anyway."

"Sounds like a plan."

Dylan drank three cups of lousy coffee with his burger and fries. He figured that was enough caffeine to carry him through the night. Once he'd seen Kelsey, he was going out again. There was a better chance of spotting Paul's car at night. The man might stay on the run during the day, but surely he would stop to sleep.

He dropped Jeb off with a promise to pick him up again at daybreak, then headed for Kelsey's. It was already late, but the lights were still blazing and there were cars in the driveway, including the sheriff's. Dylan rang the bell. It was Justin who answered.

"Hey, Dylan, come on in. I was just filling Kelsey in on what we learned today."

"Which is?"

"We found Paul's car abandoned at the Dallas-Fort Worth airport."

Dylan muttered a harsh expletive. "He's taken off, then?"

Justin shook his head. "We don't think so. I put every man on it. They've checked every flight roster, every ticket counter in the airport. If Paul and Bobby were there, they were well disguised and traveling under assumed names."

Relief spread through Dylan. "Thank God. You figure they just dumped the car because he'd concluded by now that we might be trying to trace it?" Justin nodded, then smiled. "And here's the best part. Either he's right there at the airport, in one of the hotels nearby, or he's managed to get his hands on a rental with a phony ID. We're getting close, pal. I can feel it."

"How's Kelsey taking it?"

"Like a trouper. She's mad enough to spit nails. If she didn't have to stay here in case Paul calls, I think she'd tear that airport area apart on her own."

"No need," Dylan said. "I'll do it for her. As soon as I talk to her, I'm on my way." He started for the living room, then turned back. "What if Paul bought an electronic ticket? Or bought the tickets in town? No one at a ticket counter would have seen him. Did you cover the people who work the gates?"

Justin muttered a curse. "We'll get on it now. I'll call the lead guy I have over there. I sent about ten volunteers to scour the place, along with one deputy. It was the best I could do without bringing in the Dallas area authorities. Kelsey's still opposed to that. Any idea why yet?"

Dylan nodded and explained about Paul and the pills. "She made him a promise not to involve the police in the whole incident with the stolen prescription pads and forged prescriptions. She's been trying to stick to it, even though Paul has broken his part of their agreement."

Justin muttered a curse. "If his supply's running out, he could be increasingly unstable."

"That's what I'm afraid of, too," Dylan agreed.

That said, he went on into the living room where a number of Adams wives had gathered to lend moral support. Most of their husbands were either involved in the search or were doing double duty at various ranches to cover for those who were out looking for Bobby.

Kelsey's gaze immediately shot to Dylan. "You heard?"

Lizzy moved aside to make room for Dylan next to Kelsey on the sofa. He sat in the spot she'd vacated. "Justin filled me in. I'm going to head for Dallas again in a little while."

"Then you agree he's close to the airport?" Dylan nodded.

"So he can leave in a hurry," she whispered, a catch in her voice as she searched for his expression for confirmation.

"Maybe just because it's a busy place with lots of strangers," he soothed. "No one would notice him and Bobby there."

"Bobby loves airplanes," she told him. "He's only flown a couple of times, but he stops whatever he's doing when one flies overhead and points to it. He'd be crazy about being at an airport or getting on a plane. He wouldn't think twice about it."

"Darlin', hold on a second. There's no reason to think hc's gotten on a plane. Justin's been keeping a close eye on all the flight rosters. If Paul is near the airport now, it's happened very recently."

She stared at him, clearly surprised. "What makes you say that?"

"You've been listening for background noise whenever you talked to them, right? You didn't hear any planes when you talked to Bobby the other day, did you? Or any other time?"

"No," she said. Her expression slowly brightened as understanding dawned. "And if he'd been near the airport, I wouldn't have been able to miss the noise, would I?"

"I don't think so. Not as busy as DFW is." He studied her face, saw the deepening shadows under her eyes, the unmistakable exhaustion. "Why don't you try to catch a few hours of sleep?"

"We've all been telling her the same thing," Lizzy said. "She won't budge."

Dylan gave her a speculative look. "Is that so? I think I have a solution." He stood and scooped her up before she had a chance to react, then headed for the stairs. Their progress was greeted by amused looks from all the women.

"Dylan, put me down right this second," she demanded in a hushed tone. "You have no right. I am perfectly capable of deciding when I need to go to sleep."

"Then do it," he said tersely, climbing the steps. He met her furious, indignant gaze. "Say it, Kelsey. You're the doctor. Admit you're beat and that you need some rest."

"I will not."

"Stubborn woman."

"Arrogant man."

He chuckled. "Now that we've established that, how about pointing out which room is yours?"

She frowned. "Why should I help you?"

He shrugged, shifted her more tightly against him, and poked his head in the room where he'd seen her the other night just to be sure it was Bobby's. "Must be the one down the hall," he concluded. He nudged open the door with his knee and stepped inside.

The room was the antithesis of what he'd expected. Kelsey was a coolly competent physician. Her home was neat as a pin, the furniture more practical than stylish. But the bedroom...oh, brother. There was no mistaking it was the room of a woman, a very sensuous woman. Dylan felt as out of place as he would have amid the lacy lingerie at Victoria's Secret. He also started getting a whole lot of ideas that had nothing to do with sleep.

The bed was king-sized and inviting. It was covered with a thick, floral-printed comforter in shades of rose and green, and piled high with pillows, some in satin cases, others trimmed with lace and velvet. A vase of white and pink roses in full bloom sat beside the bed, filling the air with their sweet scent. A slinky nightgown, made of some incredibly silky fabric that promised to reveal all sorts of fascinating secrets about the wearer, had been tossed on the bed. On the dresser, there were at least a dozen fancy antique perfume bottles. Lipstick and other feminine secret weapons were scattered among them.

And on a table beside the bed, a radio had been left on and forgotten. It was tuned to a station that played ballads and love songs all day long.

Dylan was so taken with everything, so intrigued by what it revealed of the woman in his arms that he didn't move for fully a minute. For just as long he completely forgot about Bobby, the people downstairs and everything else.

"Dylan?" Kelsey finally whispered, a catch in her voice.

"Uh-huh?" He snapped back to reality, then moved to the bed and lowered Kelsey onto it. His gaze locked with hers.

"You know I want to stay right here with you," he said, his voice thick with longing. His body ached with arousal.

Eyes wide, she nodded. "I wish you could," she admitted, then covered her face. "Oh, God, what kind of woman does that make me? How can I even think such a thing while my son is missing?"

"You're just human, darlin'. So am I." He touched her cheek. "Rain check?"

"Yes," she said so softly he almost didn't hear her.

He shook off the feeling of being caught up in something that didn't make sense, something that was pulling at him and clouding his brain.

"Darlin', you sure do know how to motivate a man." He winked at her. "If there's a God in heaven, I'll have Bobby back here before morning."

"As desperately as I want that," she said. "It's enough just to know that you're trying. I know you'll find him for me, Dylan, however long it takes."

Ten

Once he hit Dallas, Dylan knew he was racing against the clock. Paul wouldn't wait forever before making his demands. If this really was about pills and not about Bobby's custody, then sooner or later his need for the narcotics was going to outweigh whatever satisfaction he was getting from torturing Kelsey.

He took Jeb with him and together they scoured the airport, looking for anyone who might have caught a glimpse of Paul. Even though it was turf Justin's men had covered, Dylan wanted no stone left unturned.

He finally left Jeb sweet-talking ticket agents into checking their computers for reservations for a father and son, under any name at all. It was peak travel time and the airport was a madhouse, but if anyone could wheedle the information out of an employee, it was Jeb. He had the charm and the patience for it. Dylan was running out of both.

He went back to his car, which was stifling in the summer heat, turned the air-conditioning on full blast, then used his cell phone and called one of his contacts to do another check of Paul's credit-card records. Surely by now he was running low on cash. Maybe he'd finally slipped up and used plastic for something, *anything,* that would give them a lead. His using it to book a hotel room or a flight would, no doubt, be asking too much, but maybe he would have seen no harm in using it to pay for a meal or buy some T-shirts for Bobby.

While he waited for a call back, he studied the locator map he'd picked up in the airport. Hotels for the surrounding area were highlighted. He'd checked most of them just days ago, but with Paul's car turning up in the airport parking garage, maybe he'd taken a room in one of them since then.

"Dammit, where is he?" he muttered. He hated failing under any circumstances, but this was Kelsey's son they were talking about. Dylan would never forgive himself if the boy slipped through their fingers due to some oversight of his. He was as driven to succeed as he would have been if it had been Shane's fate at stake.

When his cell phone finally rang, he grabbed it. "We've got a break," Frank Lane told him. "He used the credit card this morning."

"Where?"

"Don't get too excited. I'm not sure it'll help."

"Anything will help at this point."

"He used it at an airport gift shop."

"What for?"

"Coloring books and children's Tylenol."

Which meant that Bobby still had his fever, Dylan concluded. That wasn't good news. The toys were probably meant to distract a cranky child.

"Is there any way to tell which shop?"

"It took some doing," Frank said, "but the woman at

the credit-card company was able to track it to the one closest to the Trans-National ticket counter."

"Thanks, pal. I owe you." He hung up, then called Jeb inside the terminal and relayed the information.

"Got it," Jeb said. "I'm on my way."

If Paul was buying tickets, toys and medicine inside the airport, he had to be staying close by. Dylan set off to recheck each of the hotels he'd visited a few days earlier.

He hit pay dirt at the fifth hotel. The desk clerk recognized Paul and Bobby from the pictures Dylan showed him.

"But you're out of luck," he said. "They checked out about an hour ago."

Dylan bit back a groan. "How'd the boy look? I heard he's been sick."

"A little pale and quiet, maybe, but he looked okay to me."

"The man didn't say where they were going?"

"No, just that he had a business meeting scheduled not far from here."

In Los Piños, no doubt, Dylan thought wearily.

Would he head straight there? Probably not. But he might pick a new hotel between here and there.

Working on the assumption that the shortest distance between two points was a straight line, Dylan went back to his car and headed southwest without waiting to hear from Jeb. He doubted his brother would learn anything critical from the gift shop and, if he did, he could reach him on his cell phone. It was more important that he start hitting every single hotel or motel along the highway. He figured he had twenty-four hours, maybe less, before this whole case was going to blow wide-open.

* * *

It was midmorning when Kelsey's cell phone rang. She was so startled by the sound coming from her purse that it took her a minute to make sense of it.

Suddenly the knot in her stomach tightened. Her gut told her it was Paul and that this time he intended to make all of his demands. He was using the cell phone for the first time because he'd assumed that by now her regular line would be tapped. She hadn't even thought to tell the police about this phone. Paul knew she kept it primarily for emergency use on the road or when the hospital needed to reach her. How could he be thinking so rationally, so diabolically, when she was all but incoherent from the stress?

Maybe it was for the best that she was alone for the first time in days, except for the sheriff's deputy outside. Maybe she could walk a verbal tightrope and reach an agreement with Paul knowing that there were no eavesdroppers to challenge her decision. She took a deep breath and answered the phone.

"Hiya, sweetheart," Paul greeted her, sounding as if they'd just parted days ago on friendly terms, as if they hadn't argued two endless days ago about Bobby's spiking fever.

"Paul, where the hell are you?" she asked, even though she knew better than to expect an answer. "How is Bobby? How's his fever?"

"Bobby's just fine. I told you he would be. He and I are having a blast, aren't we, little buddy?" he said with forced joviality.

Kelsey couldn't hear Bobby's response. "Let me talk to him," she demanded.

"I don't think so. Not this time."

"Now, Paul," she insisted. A terrible sensation of panic washed over her. What if Bobby couldn't talk? What if he was terribly ill and Paul was keeping it from her? "I want to hear for myself that his cold or whatever it was is better."

"Not until we get a few things straight," he countered.

Kelsey fought the longing to scream at him, to rant and rave until he gave in. Because, of course, he wouldn't give in, no matter how desperately she pleaded or how loudly she shouted. He would only hang up on her. She sensed that he was at the end of his rope. She had to make herself go along with him a little longer.

"Such as?" she asked finally. "I need a supply of pills."

Hearing at long last what she had suspected from the beginning made her see red. "Is that what this is about, Paul? Is it really only about your addiction?"

"I'm not addicted. I'm in pain."

"Then see a doctor."

"Isn't that what I'm doing, doll?"

Frustration and fury brought stinging tears to her eyes. "How can you use Bobby this way?" she whispered. "He's your son. We made an agreement."

"And I wound up with nothing," he said bitterly. "You stayed out of jail," she reminded him.

"That should have been enough."

"It wasn't. I want more, Kelsey. I need those pills. It's not like I'm asking for an illegal substance."

"You might as well be," she countered.

"You're a doctor. You can prescribe them."

"Dammit, Paul, I can't do it. What you're asking, the quantities you want me to give you, it's illegal. I could lose my license."

"Not with all those powerful friends of yours. They'll

see that you keep your practice. This is a one-time deal, Kelsey. Get me enough pills now and I'll never bother you again."

"Why should I believe that? When we signed our agreement, you said it was over, that you'd go into treatment. Yet here you are. And when this supply runs out, you'll be back again. Face it, there aren't enough pills in the world for a man who's addicted to them. You need help."

"And I'll get it. I promise," he said, a coaxing note in his voice. "Please, Kelsey. One last time." She knew she would break eventually, that she had to for Bobby's sake, but she forced herself to say no once more, steeling herself for another explosion.

"Not even for Bobby?" he asked, his voice suddenly cold. "Do this or you'll never see him again. I'm a whole lot better at running and hiding than you are. I have the resources. And I have less to lose."

"You'll never be able to work for a brokerage firm again," she reminded him, trying to keep a note of desperation out of her voice.

"With my investments, I won't have to."

Dear God, she knew it was true. He'd made a fortune for his clients and, in the process, for himself. He would take her boy just for spite and she would never see him again. She would be dooming her son to a life on the run with a father who cared more for his next fix than for him. She had tried to prepare herself for this moment, tried to accept that he'd left her no choice, but it still made her feel sick.

"What do you want?" she said, resigned. "Pills, pain-killers to be precise, and lots of them."

"They're regulated. I can't just write a prescription for hundreds of them at once."

"You figure out how to do it, sweetheart. Just have them for me by this time tomorrow or Bobby and I will disappear."

"Where should I bring them?"

"I'll be in touch."

He hung up before she could ask anything more, before she could demand one more time to hear her baby's voice. Trembling violently, she forced herself to walk outside. She found the deputy on the porch. "My husband called," she said in an emotionless voice. "He wants pills and he wants me to have them ready by tomorrow."

He regarded her sympathetically. "Yes, ma'am. Are you okay?"

"I'll be fine," she said, but her knees buckled and she sank into a rocker, still clutching the cell phone. "I'll call Sheriff Adams right away, Dr. James. It won't take a minute for him to get here."

She nodded, then realized Justin wasn't the person she desperately needed right now. She needed Dylan. With shaking fingers she managed to punch in the number she'd memorized, then waited for him to answer his cell phone.

"Delacourt."

"Dylan…" Her voice trailed off. "Kelsey, what's happened?"

"Paul called. He wants me to have a lot of pills ready for him tomorrow. He said he'd call back about a meeting place. I have to do it. I don't have a choice."

"Does Justin know?"

"The deputy just went to radio him. He should be here in a few minutes."

"Good," he said. "Okay, here's what I think you should do. Can you come up with placebos that look enough like whatever he wants?"

Her spirits lifted at the obvious solution. "Of course," she said, suddenly feeling confident that she could handle this without just turning over a satchel full of narcotics to her ex-husband.

"Then that's what you'll do. Call Sharon Lynn to see if Dolan's has what you need. Otherwise, call the Garden City Hospital pharmacy. Justin can go and pick up the supply so we'll be ready whenever Paul calls back. He can make it all nice and legal so you won't have problems later."

"What are you going to do? Will you come back?"

"Not just yet. I'm heading that way, but I want to finish checking the hotels and motels between the Dallas airport and Los Pinõs. He's got to be close enough to get to you and then get out of here in a hurry. I'd like to find him before he sets up the meeting, but if not we'll get him then, Kelsey. Just hang on a little longer and you'll have your son back."

She was suddenly struck by a terrible thought. "Dylan, what if…?" She couldn't even bring herself to voice her greatest fear.

"What if…?" he prodded. "What's worrying you?"

"That he'll come without Bobby."

"I don't think he'll try that. There won't be any incentive for you to give him what he wants, if he doesn't have Bobby with him."

"He'll just take the pills. He's a strong man. He keeps himself in shape. I might not have a choice."

"It will be fine. You'll have backup, if it comes to that."

"What do you mean, 'if it comes to that'?"

"I intend to find him first," he said tersely.

"Thank you," she whispered. "I know I need to let you get back to work, but I feel stronger just hearing the sound of your voice. Thank you for sticking with this even after I fired you."

He chuckled lightly. "Did you fire me? I don't seem to remember that."

"When this is over, I'm going to make it up to you," she promised.

"I'll hold you to that, Doc."

A few minutes later, when Justin arrived, Kelsey was feeling calmer. She'd already made a note of the type of placebos that she thought would fool Paul, at least long enough that she would be able to grab Bobby away from him. She'd checked with Sharon Lynn. Dolan's had some in stock and Sharon Lynn was already making arrangements with the hospital pharmacy in Garden City for more.

"I want to make the exchange," she told Justin. "I want Bobby in my arms before Paul gets these pills and has time to find out they're fakes. Otherwise, if he figures out I've tricked him, he'll take Bobby and vanish."

"I think you should leave it to a professional," Justin argued.

"He's not going to deal with a professional," Kelsey countered. "He's only going to want to deal with me, anyway, and you know it. I have to be ready, Justin. You might as well help me figure out what to do."

Justin looked as if he wanted to argue, but wisely he didn't. "Why don't we just wait and hear what his demands for the meeting are?"

"Fine," Kelsey said, gathering strength and resolve. "But I have a few demands of my own this time and, by God, he'd better be ready to agree to them."

The next few hours were endless. Justin kept the neighbors and his family away, except for Lizzy, but not even her best friend could keep Kelsey from growing more frantic with every second that passed. Sharon Lynn brought the pills by in a duffel bag.

"Do you think that's enough?" she asked worriedly. "It's not exactly like stuffing a bag with cash. Even though there are a lot of them, they don't take up much space."

Kelsey glanced in the bag and saw at least two dozen large, unlabeled prescription bottles, each of which probably held two hundred tablets. Had these been the real thing, anyone using them as a legitimate doctor prescribed could go for years on what was in the bag. For someone addicted like Paul, it was impossible to say what his reaction would be.

"It will have to be enough," Kelsey said grimly. "I'll tell him it was all I could get on short notice. It's not like a town this size has a major drug company around the corner. I'll tell him if he wants more, he'll have to wait until you can get another shipment in. He won't want to do that."

Sharon Lynn wrapped her in a tight hug. "I'm so sorry you're going through this. I look at my own two kids and try to imagine how I'd feel..." She shuddered. "It was awful enough when I thought I was going to lose my daughter to that horrible biological grandmother of hers. I can't even think about something like this."

"Hopefully, you'll never have to face anything like it,"

Kelsey said. She patted the bag. "Thank you for these. I'll pay you for them after all this is over."

"You'll do nothing of the kind," Sharon Lynn said fiercely. "We look out for our own around here and you're one of us. Besides, if the police take Paul into custody, these won't be gone long."

"But they'll be evidence. You won't be able to put them back in stock," Kelsey protested.

"It doesn't matter," Sharon Lynn insisted.

Tears stung Kelsey's eyes. She tried to blink them back, but couldn't. Instead, she turned and walked away. Lizzy moved beside her and silently handed her a tissue.

"Tell Sharon Lynn I'm sorry," she whispered, her voice choked. "It's just that everyone is being so kind."

"There's no need to be sorry, not with any of us," Lizzy said. "Why don't you just have a good cry and get it out of your system?"

"I can't fall apart now," Kelsey said, drawing in a deep breath and trying to pull herself together as Sharon Lynn came to join them. "This is it. I have to be ready."

"I think you're the strongest woman I've ever met," Lizzy told her.

"Not me. I'm just trying to survive a nightmare."

"Sometimes surviving takes more strength than anything else," Sharon Lynn chimed in softly. "After Kyle died in that accident on our wedding night, I thought I wouldn't make it, but I did. Then Cord and my baby came into my life and everything changed. I'm living proof that you can survive anything."

Kelsey clung to that as the hours dragged on. There was no word from Dylan either. Kelsey had resigned herself to the fact that there would be no last-minute rescue. By the time the cell phone finally rang after midnight, she knew she was going to have to deal with Paul directly.

"Have you got them?" he asked without preamble.

"Yes," she said. "They're right here."

"Then we'll meet in the morning just after daybreak, six o'clock."

"Where?"

He described a place in the middle of nowhere, about halfway between Los Piños and Garden City. "There won't be anywhere for the cops to hide behind the bushes, so tell them to stay away," he warned.

"You're bringing Bobby, though, right?"

"No, but I'll tell you where to find him afterward."

"Forget it," she said vehemently. "I want to see Bobby. I want him with me before you get your hands on the pills."

"Don't you trust me, sweetheart?" he asked, sounding amused.

"Not as far as I could throw you."

"Well, that's too bad, because you're going to have to."

"Then you can forget all about your pills, Paul. I won't even bother showing up. Your decision."

She braced herself for an explosion. Her words hung in the air, leaving them stalemated. Silence fell. It went on for so long that she feared she'd overplayed her hand. But desperation for the pills finally won out.

"Okay, I'll bring him," he said at last. "But if you betray me, Kelsey, if the cops show up, I'll shoot you both and then I'll kill myself. No one will be able to save either one of you."

A chill ran down her spine at his words, not just because of the threat itself, but because of the I-have-nothing-to-lose way in which he said it. She knew then with a terrible sense of dread that any remnants of the decent man she'd once loved and married were gone, lost to the drugs that now tragically ruled his life.

Eleven

Dylan finally caught a break just before dawn at a sleazy motel on the northern outskirts of Garden City. The grizzled proprietor of the place looked like something out of an old Western. He wasn't especially pleased to have someone banging on his door in the middle of the night, which probably explained his cantankerous attitude.

Dylan noticed he didn't seem to have much interest in upkeep or in attracting business. He valued his guests' privacy so much, he didn't bother with a register or credit cards, either. But for the fifty bucks Dylan waved in front of him, he was eager enough to talk about the guests in room eight.

"Been here since late yesterday afternoon," he told Dylan. "Cute kid. Keeps crying for his mama, though. That father of his doesn't have much patience for it, either. I've heard him yelling at the boy to shut up."

Dylan saw red. "You didn't go down and check it out?"

The man shrugged. "None of my business."

Dylan bit back an angry retort. "Are they there now?"

"What do you think? It's early. I suppose they're asleep like everyone ought to be, if you catch my meaning."

Dylan ignored the sarcasm. "But you don't know for sure?"

"Do I look like the nosy type?" the old man retorted. "People come and go. It's none of my concern, as long as the room's paid up."

"If anything has happened to that boy, if there's so much as a bruise on him, it'll become your concern in a hurry," Dylan told him tightly. "Now give me a key."

"Can't do that," the man replied.

Dylan reached across the counter and grabbed a fistful of the man's hastily donned and still unbuttoned shirt. "Give me a key or I'll knock down the damned door." He got the key. "What kind of a car was the man driving?" he asked.

"Something flashy. Surprised me that a man with a car like that would stay in a dump like this."

Dylan walked to room eight, surveying the parking lot as he went. There were only a handful of cars parked outside the rooms and none could be described as flashy.

Outside room eight, Dylan listened at the door. He thought he heard the sounds of the television and maybe something else, possibly a child's whimpers. Just as he was about to open the door, a dark green sports car skidded into the spot in front of the room and a man he recognized at once as Paul James leapt out.

"Who the hell are you?" he demanded.

"A friend of Kelsey's," Dylan said, keeping his voice down. "I've come for Bobby."

"Like hell," Paul said, taking a swing at him. "Kelsey and I have a deal."

"I just changed it," Dylan countered.

To emphasize the point, Dylan's fist landed in Paul's pretty face. To his disappointment, the man sank to the ground like a stone. He'd been hoping to get in a few more punches. He stepped over him, opened the door and went inside. Bobby was huddled on the floor in front of the TV, clutching a stuffed bear, tears streaming down his flushed cheeks.

Dylan forced himself to stay calm and quiet, when he wanted badly to grab the boy up and hug him. He hunkered down. "Hey, Bobby."

"Who're you?" Bobby asked, regarding him suspiciously. "I heard you. You were fighting with my daddy. Where is he?"

"He's right outside. He'll be here in a few minutes." He was tempted to touch Bobby's forehead to see if he was as feverish as he looked, but he didn't dare. The boy was upset enough. Dylan wondered how long he'd been left here alone.

"How are you feeling?" he asked instead.

Bobby shrugged.

"Got a fever, maybe?"

"I guess," he said and inched backward.

"It's okay," Dylan soothed. "I'm not here to hurt you. Your mom sent me."

The boy's eyes went wide. "You know Mommy?"

"I sure do."

He uttered a tiny sigh and looked nervously toward the door. "Don't tell my daddy, but I miss Mommy."

Dylan grinned. "Want to talk to her? She'll tell you it's okay to come with me, all right?"

Bobby nodded eagerly.

Dylan took out his cell phone and placed the call to Kelsey.

"Paul?" she demanded, after snatching it up on the first ring.

"No, it's me, darlin'. I have someone here who'd like to speak to you." He handed the phone to Bobby.

"Mommy?" the boy said tentatively. At the sound of his mother's voice, his little face brightened. "Mommy!"

Dylan heard Kelsey's voice catch on a sob, then more of Bobby's excited chatter. He found himself blinking back tears. He gave the two of them another minute to talk, then said, "Hey, sport, let me talk to her, okay?"

Bobby reluctantly handed him the phone. "Kelsey?"

"Oh, Dylan, where are you? Is he really okay? I was supposed to meet them in an hour on that old road west of Los Piños. When the phone rang, I thought it was Paul calling to cancel or change the meeting place. Where is he? Had he left Bobby behind?"

"No. He's right outside the room. I decked him on the way in."

"Oh, God," she murmured, suddenly sounding panic-stricken. "Dylan, did you check for a gun?"

"A gun?"

"He told me if I showed up with the police he would shoot me, Bobby and then himself. He has to have a gun."

"Well hell," Dylan cursed, just in time to look up and straight into the barrel of the very gun in question.

"I'll take the phone now," Paul said with surprising calm for a man on drugs who'd just been leveled by a punch. His glass jaw didn't seem to be affecting his ability to aim straight.

Keeping one eye on Bobby, Dylan gave Paul the

phone. He couldn't risk a confrontation with an armed man as long as Bobby was in range, not after the threat Paul had already made to kill Kelsey, his boy and himself if the police interfered.

"So, Kelsey, I guess you've heard there's been a new wrinkle," Paul said with what almost sounded like good cheer.

Dylan stared at him. Paul was enjoying this, which could only mean he was in a drug-induced fantasyland.

"This means we'll have a little change in plans. I think I'll bring your friend along with me, instead of Bobby. What's he worth to you?"

"Nothing," Dylan said, interrupting. "I barely even know your ex-wife. I'm just an investigator on the case. Nothing more."

Paul looked skeptical. "He says you don't give a damn about him, which could mean he'd be a lousy bargaining chip. What do you say?"

Dylan couldn't hear what Kelsey replied, but Paul's expression turned grim. "I'm not bringing them both. You choose, Kelsey. Your pal here or Bobby."

"She'll take Bobby," Dylan insisted, not giving her time to answer. "Take her son back to her."

Paul displayed a chilling smile. "Why, aren't you the gallant gentleman? Just her type. Okay, Bobby goes. But what do I do with you?" he wondered aloud. Then he raised his gun toward the ceiling and pulled the trigger.

Dylan heard Kelsey's scream just before Paul disconnected the phone.

"That ought to keep her focused on what's important," Paul said.

He motioned Dylan into the bathroom, removed his belt, then used it to bind Dylan's wrists and tie them securely to the shower rod. Satisfied that Dylan was immobilized, Paul went back into the room long enough to grab a tie, then added that to the belt to further restrain him.

"That ought to keep you out of action long enough for me to settle things with Kelsey and be on my way," Paul said. "It ought to give her a few bad moments wondering if you're dead or not, too."

"You really are a heartless son of a bitch," Dylan declared.

Paul didn't seem particularly distraught by the characterization. It did, however, serve to remind him that once he was gone there was nothing to prevent Dylan from screaming for help. He found a handkerchief, stuffed it in Dylan's mouth, then used another tie to keep it in place.

"Daddy?" Bobby asked hesitantly, his eyes wide with fear. "Why are you hurting him? He's Mommy's friend."

"He's not hurt," Paul assured him. "Just out of commission for a bit."

Dylan winked at Bobby, hoping to relieve the boy's concern. Bobby had already been through enough. Besides, if he accepted that Dylan was okay, maybe he could pass the word on that along to Kelsey, who was already frantic enough without worrying about what had happened to him because he hadn't used his brain when he'd taken Paul down outside.

"Come on, son. Let's go see your mother." Casting one last worried look over his shoulder, Bobby eventually followed his dad.

And Dylan got to work on freeing himself.

Kelsey stood holding the phone in her hand, aware that the blood had probably drained from her face.

"Oh, God, oh, God, oh, God." She kept murmuring it over and over.

Justin's firm grip on her shoulders finally caught her attention. She stared at him blankly. His mouth was moving, but she couldn't seem to grasp what he was saying.

"What, Kelsey? What happened?" He shook her gently. "Tell me."

"He shot Dylan. I was talking to Dylan and then Paul came in and took the phone and then he shot him." She stared at Justin guiltily. "It's all my fault. If he's dead, it's because of me."

"We don't know he's dead," Justin insisted. "Stop thinking like that."

"But he shot him," she repeated, not just sick to her stomach, but sick at heart.

"Dylan can take care of himself," Justin assured her. "Let's try to concentrate, okay? Can you do that? Is the meeting still on?"

Kelsey nodded. Her baby. She had to focus on getting her baby back. If she thought about Dylan, she would go crazy.

"Then let's go."

"No," she retorted fiercely. "Just me. I have to go alone. If he sees you there, he'll kill me and Bobby." She shuddered as she heard the terrible sound of that gun echoing in her head. She wondered if she would ever be able to shut it off. "He'll use the gun again. I know it."

"All the more reason for us to be there," Justin insisted. "I can have a sharpshooter standing by. Paul won't get a chance to use the gun, Kelsey. It has to be that way. He's out of control."

She knew Justin was right. Going to meet Paul alone was foolhardy. Her best chance to get Bobby back and to live was to have professional backup, but she was so scared that Paul would see them, that he would panic.

"I need your promise that you won't let him spot you," she said, knowing how futile extracting such a promise was.

"We'll do our best," he vowed. "Nobody wants everybody to walk away from this safely more than I do. The last thing I want is Grandpa Harlan on my back if there's a screwup."

The mention of his grandfather's reaction had the desired result. Kelsey found she could still smile. A moment ago she'd been so certain she would never smile or laugh again.

She drew in a deep breath and squeezed Justin's hand. "Then, by all means, let's not screw up," she said staunchly.

Paul's restraints were downright pitiful. All it took was a couple of quick, sharp tugs for Dylan to bring the shower rod crashing down. He slid belt and tie over the end and off. That loosened them enough for him to work his hands completely free. He was already racing from the room as he slipped the second tie over his head and jerked the waddedup handkerchief from his mouth.

The sound of the gunshot and the shower rod crashing had stirred enough of the other guests to bring a small crowd into the parking lot.

"Which way did they go?" Dylan shouted. "The man and the little boy? Which way did they turn?"

The proprietor ignored him and rushed toward the room. He gasped when he spotted the bullet hole. "Somebody's going to have to pay for the damage."

"Take it out of the fifty I already gave you," Dylan

snapped. He turned to one of the guests who looked wide-awake, but not especially terrified. "Did you see which way they turned?"

"West," the man said. "Should we call the police?"

"I'll do it," Dylan said. Of course, it wouldn't be the local police he'd be calling, but Justin. He punched in the number of his cell phone as he turned onto the highway.

"Sheriff's Department," Becky responded. "Becky, it's Dylan. Can you get Justin for me?"

"He's on the road. I can't patch you through, but I can get him on the radio and relay messages," she said.

Dylan was impressed with the fact that she wasted no time. Clearly she grasped that Dylan wasn't calling just to chat. When she added, "I heard you were shot," he understood why.

"Not me," he corrected, "but the ceiling took a hit."

"Bad aim?"

"Nope, deliberate torture for Kelsey."

"What a creep!" she murmured, then said, "Okay, Dylan, I've got Justin. What do you want me to tell him?"

Dylan described his location and the car Paul was driving. "He's headed west toward the meeting place. He has Bobby and he has a gun. I'm maybe ten minutes behind him. Depending on how fast he's driving, I may catch up."

"Ten-four," Becky said briskly, then repeated the information to Justin. "Dylan, he wants you to stay clear. He has plenty of men to handle it. They're already in place. Back off. Do you read me?"

Dylan read her loud and clear, but he created the sound of static on the line, then deliberately hung up. There was no way in hell he was staying out of this now. It had gotten personal back there in that motel room.

Besides, he'd promised Kelsey that he would deliver Bobby safe and sound and he intended to do just that. This maverick streak of his had kept him from becoming a cop. But he also had sense enough to know what he could handle and what he couldn't. He could handle Paul James, especially now that he'd learned the hard way not turn his back on him. He accelerated and kept his gaze fixed intently on the highway ahead of him.

There was a turnoff about eight miles ahead that would head toward Los Piños. He guessed from Kelsey's earlier remark that the meeting point was about five miles beyond the turn. That gave him thirteen miles— or about ten minutes at seventy miles an hour—to catch Paul. After that, Kelsey was going to have to face her ex-husband. Dylan wanted to prevent that from happening if he possibly could.

He kept hearing her scream when she'd thought Paul had shot him. She had sounded genuinely anguished. That meant she'd be going into the meeting terrified or angry or both, when what was needed was a clear, cool head.

He pushed the car's speed up to eighty. Not ten seconds later he spotted the taillights of the flashy green car up ahead. At the same time, he saw a sheriff's car slide onto the highway from its hiding place behind a stand of trees. The cop didn't use lights or his siren, but there was no mistaking his intention to get Dylan off the road.

If Paul spotted that police car in his rearview mirror, there was no telling what he would do. It wouldn't matter that the deputy was after Dylan, not him. He could panic just the same, and that would increase the danger to Bobby and Kelsey.

Dylan knew he had no choice. Slamming his palm

against the steering wheel in frustration, he muttered a curse and pulled to the side of the road. The deputy coasted to the shoulder right behind him, then exited his car slowly and strolled up to Dylan.

"You're in a mighty big hurry for this early in the morning," he noted.

Dylan flipped open his investigator's license. "I was tailing a suspect. Thanks to you, he's getting away."

The deputy didn't seem particularly distressed by the predicament he'd caused. "Is that so?" He studied Dylan intently. "That wouldn't be the same suspect that half the cops in West Texas are waiting for just up the road, now would it?"

Dylan grimaced. This little speed trap had been Justin's doing. He could feel it. The man was sneakier than Dylan had imagined. "It would indeed," he conceded.

The man nodded, then handed him back his wallet. "It's damned frustrating sitting around and letting somebody else take down the bad guys, isn't it?" he asked sympathetically.

"If you understand that, why'd you stop me?"

"Because *you* were the bad guy I was assigned to take down," the deputy said. "Want some coffee?"

Dylan gave a sigh of resignation. "Might as well."

The man gestured toward his cruiser. "I've got a whole Thermos full right back there. Join me and we'll wait for news."

"You go ahead," Dylan suggested. "I'll be right there."

The man raised his sunglasses and peered intently into Dylan's eyes. "Son, what kind of fool do you take me for? The second I walk away, you'll take off like a bat out of hell." He gestured. "Out of the car. And hand over your keys while you're at it."

As badly as he wanted to do otherwise, Dylan got out of the car and gave the deputy his keys. He'd never catch Paul before he reached the meeting spot, anyway. It looked as if he was going to have to trust Justin to keep Kelsey and Bobby safe. Given how he'd sidelined Dylan, Justin was clever enough to handle the job.

And if he failed, Dylan would wring his neck. Though the prospect of doing bodily harm to the sheriff cheered him considerably, he found himself praying that there would be no reason for it. He'd rather find Kelsey and Bobby all in one piece when this was over.

The deputy regarded him sympathetically as he handed him a cup of coffee strong enough to wake the dead.

"Waiting's a bitch, isn't it?"

Dylan nodded. "You got that right."

Paul had spotted the car racing up behind him on the highway and knew in his gut it had to be the man he'd left tied up back at the motel. Dylan. That was his name. A friend of Kelsey's.

How had he gotten loose so quickly? Obviously Paul wasn't exactly equipped for a life of crime. Despite what they all thought, he didn't have a killer's instincts. Thankfully, today would be the end of it. Kelsey would give him the pills he needed and he would go back to Miami, where he belonged. He'd be back at work next week and this whole thing would be a distant memory.

"Daddy?"

He glanced down at Bobby and saw the fear in the boy's eyes. Guilt crept through him. He hadn't meant to scare his son. There'd been a time when Bobby had been his pride and joy, ranking right up there with Kelsey as two of the best things to ever happen to him.

He blamed the doctors for destroying all that. They were the ones who'd put him on such powerful narcotics after his skiing accident. Why couldn't Kelsey see it wasn't his fault he'd gotten hooked? Why had she blamed him when he hadn't been able to give them up? What kind of wife walked away from her husband when he was in trouble?

Once again the familiar anger swelled in his chest, crowding out the guilt. Still, he kept his tone even when he answered Bobby.

"Isn't this a blast, little buddy?"

Bobby's chin rose with a touch of defiance. He looked so much like Kelsey then, it was scary. "No, Daddy. You're driving too fast. I don't like it. Driving fast is wrong."

"Not out here in the country," Paul told him. "Out here it's okay to drive like the wind."

"No, it's not. Mommy said."

"Well, your mom's wrong about this one. Now, be quiet so Daddy can concentrate."

He glanced once again into his rearview mirror and saw that the car was gaining on him. It was no longer a distant dot on the horizon. He could see the front end well enough to tell the color and make. It was definitely the same one he'd seen in the motel parking lot, close to the office.

Suddenly a sheriff's cruiser slid onto the highway in hot pursuit. Paul felt a momentary flash of panic, then amusement as he realized the deputy was after the other man. He laughed when he saw the two cars pulling onto the shoulder of the highway, then fading into the distance as his own speed steadily accelerated.

Damn, he was good. It was about time he caught a break. Another hour, two at the outside, and he would be on his way home. This miserable Texas wasteland would be nothing but a distant memory.

Twelve

The air was hot and dry even though the sun was barely up. Kelsey sat in the car with the windows open just the same, listening desperately for the sound of an approaching vehicle. This road wasn't well traveled, which was precisely why Paul had chosen it. If she'd heard anything, more than likely it would be her ex-husband.

Would he have Bobby with him as he'd promised? Or had everything changed back at the motel? Had he actually shot Dylan and left him to die? She couldn't imagine Paul being that desperate and out of control, but there had been no mistaking the sound of that gunshot, the sudden silence as the phone had gone dead in her hand. Her stomach rolled over just thinking about it.

For the thousandth time, she prayed that Dylan was still alive, that they would have a chance to explore the feelings that had begun to grow between them in the midst of this ordeal.

Later, she told herself firmly. She would think of that later. Right now, all that mattered was getting Bobby back. She tried to recall everything Justin had told her to do. She nearly panicked when the details wouldn't come, then simply prayed that any second now she would see her son again, that the nightmare would end.

She glanced surreptitiously toward the distant grove of trees where one of Justin's men waited, a sharpshooter designated to take Paul out, but only if something went awry. She'd had to beg for that much. She hadn't wanted Bobby to live with the horror of seeing his father shot, not if there was any other way to bring Paul into custody. If she'd had her choice, Paul wouldn't even be arrested where Bobby could witness it. Justin, however, had only been willing to bend his rules so far.

There were more men posted along the highway in both directions, wherever the slightest cover allowed them to remain hidden from view. They would not prevent Paul from coming in, but they were there to set up instantaneous roadblocks that would keep him from getting away.

Concentrate, she told herself. Stay calm. She glanced at the picture of Bobby she had clutched in her hand. That precious smile. Those laughing eyes. Just remember what's important, she instructed herself. She had to keep reminding herself that rescuing Bobby was paramount. There were others who could deal with Paul. Her time to lash out at him would come later, once her son was safe.

Straining her ears, she thought she detected the distant sound of an engine. Squinting into the sun, which had just crept above the horizon in a blaze of orange, she kept her gaze pinned on the highway, looking for the first flash of sun on chrome or a swirl of dust that would prove her ears hadn't deceived her.

"Come on. Come on," she murmured. "Kelsey?"

The sound of Justin's voice crackling from the radio on the seat beside her made her pulse leap wildly. She grabbed it and whispered, "Yes," as if whoever was coming might hear her if she spoke any louder.

"This is it. We've spotted him. You doing okay?"

"I'm fine," she said with a certainty she was far from feeling. She *would* be fine, too, as soon as she saw her son, as soon as she held him.

She glanced toward the duffel bag filled with pills to reassure herself that her bargaining chip was in place.

"Don't do anything crazy," Justin warned her. "Remember, we're right here. Get Bobby. Give Paul the pills. Leave the heroics to us, okay?"

"Yes," she said, disgusted with herself because her voice squeaked instead of remaining steady.

"You'll do just fine," he reassured her. "Kelsey, one last thing."

Something more to remember? She wasn't sure she could. "What?" she asked as she finally spotted the first glimpse of the car in the distance.

"Dylan's fine. I've talked to him and he's fine. Okay? I just thought you ought to know that before this goes down."

A terrible knot of tension in her stomach dissolved at the news. She knew why he'd told her, too. He hadn't wanted Paul to be able to use Dylan's so-called death to rattle her. He could have, too. If Paul had taunted her with the fact that Dylan was dead, she very well might have lost it and done something stupid.

"Thank God," she murmured.

"Okay, angel, let's do this," Justin said with the absolute calm of a professional. "You with me?"

Her nerves steadied, along with her resolve. "You bet," she said firmly.

"Everybody else?" Justin asked.

Kelsey was dimly aware of other deputies responding, then Justin's call for radio silence from here on out.

She sucked in a deep breath, then stepped from the
car to wait for her ex-husband.

Dylan was chafing at the restrictions he was under.
He'd listened to Justin's radio contact with Kelsey, heard
the thread of fear in her voice, then the determination.
She had to be the bravest woman he'd ever known.

He'd been relieved when Justin had told her that Paul
hadn't left him for dead. He didn't want her thinking
about anything except Bobby. He knew all too well how
many things could go wrong when a person was even
the tiniest bit distracted. That was how he'd ended up at
Paul's mercy back at the motel.

The deputy glanced over at him. "She'll be fine. She
sounds like a woman who can handle herself in a crisis."

"Give her a sick kid and she can, but this?" Dylan
shrugged. "Can any parent ever be prepared to deal with
something like this?"

Sitting here, waiting, was giving him way too much
time to think—about Kelsey, about Bobby, about Kit, and
about Shane. The first thing he intended to do when this
ended was to see his son. To hell with the noble, decent
decision he'd made. He wanted his boy to know he had
a father who loved him. He didn't intend to disrupt their
lives. He just wanted a chance to spend a few hours with
Shane from time to time. He and Kit could work it out.
He'd matured since the divorce. In the last few days, he'd
learned he wasn't too old to learn to compromise when
it really mattered.

An image of Bobby popped into his head. He couldn't

help thinking about the future, making the inevitable comparison between any relationship he might have with Kelsey's son and the bond Kit's husband had formed with Shane. How would he feel if Paul James fought to remain a part of Bobby's life? Of course, he thought wryly, under the circumstances, it could be a very long time before Paul had any contact whatsoever with his son again.

Dammit, what was happening? The radio silence was setting his nerves on edge. Unconsciously, he leaned forward to listen, hoping for some clue about what was taking place just a few miles down the road.

"Do the right thing," he muttered as if Paul might somehow hear him.

"Now there's a prayer worth repeating," the deputy observed.

Dylan glanced at him and saw that his expression was tense, his frustration just as evident. Dylan's own resentment at being kept out of the heart of the action eased a little. He had a hunch with very little encouragement the deputy might be persuaded to creep a little closer.

He was even more certain that it was absolutely the wrong thing to do. So much as a whisper of activity might spook Paul. Dylan had seen for himself the shape the other man was in. It wouldn't take much for him to spin out of control.

"You figure Justin has things under control up there?" Dylan asked, half looking for an excuse to change his mind.

"As much as any man could under the circumstances," the deputy responded.

"Then I guess we'll do what he intended us to do. Sit tight."

"Got to say it's not in my nature," the man said.

"Mine, either," Dylan said with heartfelt agreement. Even so, they sat and waited.

Paul's car eased to a stop about ten feet behind Kelsey's. The passenger door opened at once and Bobby emerged with a whoop of excitement.

"Mommy!" he called and ran toward her, even as Paul was shouting at him to stop.

Kelsey and Bobby both ignored him. She knelt down and opened her arms, tears streaking down her cheeks. At the feel of his warm, solid little body next to hers, she trembled violently. A relief unlike anything she had ever felt before washed over her. It was several minutes later, with Bobby squirming to get free, before she released him, then rocked back on her heels to study him.

Bobby stared at her, his expression puzzled. "Mommy, why are you crying?"

"I'm just glad to see you, that's all. I've missed you."

"I missed you, too."

She ran a hand over his cheek, then touched his forehead to reassure herself that his fever was truly gone.

"Mommy," Bobby protested, wriggling away from the touch.

"I guess you don't need any of Mommy's kisses to make you better, after all," she said.

"I told you he was fine," Paul said.

The sound of his voice startled her. How had she forgotten about him? He was the reason they were out here. Controlling the surge of anger that rushed through her, she stood slowly and met his gaze.

She forced herself not to flinch when she saw the wild look in his eyes. "Thank you for bringing him back to me," she said, knowing that it could easily have gone another way.

"I told you I would. Now you need to keep your end of the bargain."

"The pills are in the car."

"You get them for me."

She didn't bother arguing. But as she moved toward the car, she took Bobby's hand. "Come on, sweetie. Help me get the bag I brought for Daddy."

"No," Paul said sharply. "He stays right here with me."

Kelsey wanted desperately to argue, but she released Bobby's hand. Just go along with him, she reminded herself. Give him the pills and let him leave. That's what Justin had told her to do.

Even so, giving in to his demands went against everything she believed in. She couldn't bear the thought of him taking Bobby out of her reach again. The only thing that made her comply was the knowledge that he could still take Bobby *and* the pills. This wasn't over yet. Not by a long shot.

She retrieved the duffel bag, then set it on the ground between them. Paul grabbed for it, took a quick look inside, then nodded with satisfaction.

"See, Kelsey, that wasn't so hard. We both end up with what we want." He glanced at Bobby and for just a second there was a hint of the old Paul in his expression, the faintest suggestion of real regret. "See you, son."

Bobby regarded his father with surprise. "You're going away again, Daddy?"

Paul nodded. "I've got to go back to Miami," he said, then briskly turned and headed for his car as if the past few days had been no more than a minor blip in his life.

Whatever had gone on the preceding few days, however frightened Bobby might have been at times, seemed to be forgotten. His face clouded over. "No, Daddy. Don't go."

Paul hesitated, then turned back. He knelt down and Bobby ran to him. Paul gathered him in a tight hug that brought the salty sting of tears to Kelsey's eyes. Whatever else she thought of her ex-husband, she knew his emotions now were genuine.

"'Bye, little buddy," Paul whispered, his voice breaking. "Remember that Daddy loves you, okay?"

Then he all but pushed Bobby in Kelsey's direction and sprinted to his car. Bobby began crying in earnest then and nothing Kelsey could do seemed to console him as they stood on the dusty, lonely road and watched Paul drive away.

"Oh, baby, it's going to be okay," she whispered, even as she heard sirens in the distance and knew that Justin's men were closing in on her ex-husband. She would do everything in her power to right Bobby's word, but she doubted Paul's would ever be the same again.

In that moment, she was able to recall with absolute clarity the man she had once loved so deeply, and all of the anger from the past few days died and gave way to regret.

"He's rolling, We're good to go." Justin's voice cut through the interminable silence as the radio crackled to life once more.

The deputy glanced toward Dylan. "You want in on this?"

Dylan thought of just how badly he wanted a piece of the arrest, but then he imagined Kelsey and Bobby just up the road and what they must be feeling.

"No, but thanks," he said. He stepped from the car and held out his hand for his keys. The deputy returned them.

According to the last transmission Dylan had heard, Paul was still heading west, probably intending to loop around at some point and make his way back to the Dallas airport where he thought he could pick up his car. By now, that car was in some police impound lot, and if Justin had his way, Paul would get nowhere near the airport anyway.

Dylan hit the highway only a few car lengths behind the deputy who'd detained him. He pushed his speed to eighty, confident that there wasn't a cop in the vicinity who was interested in handing out a ticket at the moment.

He covered the few miles to the meeting point in less than ten minutes. He spotted Kelsey at the side of the road, Bobby in her arms. Both of them were crying. He pulled to a stop behind her car, then waited a minute to give them some privacy before getting out.

"Hey, darlin'," he called with forced cheer as he made his way to them.

Kelsey's gaze shot to his and he could see the relief in her eyes. Without relaxing her grip on her son, she reached out a hand to touch his face.

"You're okay?" she whispered. "Really?"

He winked at Bobby, who was staring at him wide-eyed, no doubt recalling the last time they'd met. "Not a scratch on me," he assured them both.

His gaze caught Kelsey's and held. "You did real good."

She almost faltered then, as if the last of her strength had finally deserted her. Dylan took Bobby from her, then circled her waist with his other arm. "It's over, Kelsey. It's over and everything is going to be just fine."

"I want to believe that," she said as fresh tears spilled down her cheeks.

He gave her a squeeze. "Then believe it."

She sighed against him, then met his gaze. "I want to go home, Dylan. I just want to take my son and go home."

He nodded. "You still have that radio in the car?"

"On the seat."

"Let me okay it with Justin and we'll get out of here. Meantime, you hop on in the back with Bobby. I'll drive."

"What about your car?"

"I'll come back for it later." He picked up the transmitter and called Justin. "Mind if I take Kelsey on home? Can you catch up with us there?"

"Ten-four," Justin said.

"Everything okay on your end?" he asked, avoiding any direct mention of Paul or an arrest for Bobby's sake.

"Yep. We're on our way in now."

"Anybody get hurt?"

"Just their feelings," Justin said wryly. "He thought he was in the clear."

"Nice work. By the way, we'll talk about that clever little stunt you pulled with me later."

Justin laughed. "I thought you might have something to say about that. Over and out, pal."

Dylan glanced into the back seat and caught Kelsey's puzzled expression. An exhausted Bobby was sound asleep in her lap. Her hand rested protectively against his cheek as if she needed the contact to prove to herself he was with her again.

"What stunt?" she asked quietly.

"Your buddy the sheriff had me pulled over about ten miles from here so I'd stay out of the way," he responded with a touch of indignation. "I've got to admit it was a slick maneuver, though at the time I had a few choice words to say to him. Still, I wouldn't mind working for a man that devious."

Kelsey laughed, her expression finally relaxing. "Justin? Devious? Dylan, you've got to be kidding. He's a total straight-arrow."

"That's what he wants you to think, but believe me, darlin', I know a sneaky scoundrel when I meet one."

"It takes one to know one, I imagine."

Dylan turned and pinned her with a look. "You've got that right." He nodded toward Bobby. "Think he'll be okay?"

"Time will tell. So far, it seems he genuinely believes he was just on a big adventure with his daddy and he's not completely happy about it being over. We'll have to wait and see if he starts having nightmares."

"For what it's worth, I don't think Paul mistreated him," Dylan said. "When I found him in that motel, he was more scared of me busting in there than he was of his dad. He even stood up to him, when Paul was tying me up. He told him I was Mommy's friend and he shouldn't do that."

"That's my boy," she said with evident pride. "Quite a tough guy."

"Like his mama," Dylan noted, then asked sympathetically, "Reality setting in yet?"

"My knees haven't stopped knocking for the past ten minutes," she admitted.

"Then let's get home and get you something to eat and drink," he said as he started the car. "You'll need something to fortify you for all Justin's questions. This may be over, but there will be a ton of paperwork."

She chuckled lightly. "You're talking to a doctor, remember? The concept of paperwork is not alien to me. I can spend an hour pulling a kid through a medical crisis and another six hours filling out all the forms to justify the treatment. Does that make any sense?"

"It probably does if you're an insurance company, but to me, no. Paperwork is just one of the things that kept me out of the Houston police department."

"And the others?" she asked, studying him curiously.

"Rules," he said at once. "And more rules."

"I think I get the picture."

She fell silent and for a moment Dylan thought she, too, might have fallen asleep. A glance in the rearview mirror told him otherwise. She was staring at the passing scenery, though he doubted she was actually seeing it.

"Kelsey? What's up?"

"I was thinking," she said. "About?"

"You, actually. We've just been through the most traumatic days of my life together. I feel closer to you than almost anyone else I can think of, and I don't really know you at all."

Dylan recognized the feeling. It had swept over him from time to time in the last few days. "How do you feel about changing that? Starting from scratch?"

"I don't think that's possible. We can't go back and pretend this didn't happen."

"No," he agreed. "But we can move on, fill in the blanks." He hesitated, then asked, "Or will I just be a reminder of everything that's gone on?"

"Absolutely not," she said fiercely. "How could I blame you for any of this?"

"I wasn't suggesting you'd blame me, just that you'd always link me to a bad time in your life, a time you'd rather not relive."

She shook her head. "No. Something good has to come out of all this. Maybe it's you and me."

Dylan felt something in his chest tighten at her words. He wanted to believe that just as badly as she did.

"Is that okay with you?" she asked, sounding suddenly hesitant. "I mean this hasn't exactly been a picnic for you, either. I know it's stirred up all sorts of old memories."

"No, it hasn't been a picnic, but it's opened my eyes to a lot of stuff. It's put me in touch with some feelings I'd tried to pretend didn't exist."

"Feelings about your son?"

"Yes."

"What will you do about them?"

Dylan reached a decision he'd been toying with for the past few days. "As soon as everything is wrapped up here, I'm going to see Kit."

"And?"

"I'm going to ask her to modify the custody arrangement."

Kelsey reached over the seat and squeezed his shoulder. "Oh, Dylan, I hope it works out for you."

"It will," he said fiercely. His gaze caught hers in the rearview mirror. "Because then I have to get back here and attend to some unfinished business."

Thirteen

The day had dragged on endlessly and Kelsey was clearly exhausted. Dylan could see it in her eyes and in the pallor of her complexion. She never took her gaze off Bobby, as if she feared letting him out of her sight, even though Paul was now in custody.

By the time the authorities had sorted out everything at the jail, then come by to take Kelsey's statement, it was pushing dinnertime. Her house was still crowded with visitors, most of whom had come bearing food they clearly had every intention of sticking around to share.

To Dylan's frustration, there was nothing he could do about any of it. It would take time to ease her fears. And at the rate the evening was progressing, it was going to take almost as long to get everyone out from underfoot. His occasional attempts to shoo a few well-wishers toward the door had been met with resistence, so he'd finally given up and retreated to the kitchen to grab a beer.

"What are you growling under your breath about?" Trish asked him, cornering him before he could even get the refrigerator door open.

He frowned at her. "Don't these people know when to go home?"

"They just want Kelsey to know they care."

"They can tell her that tomorrow. She's beat." His sister studied him knowingly. "You're awfully protective of her. Do I detect more than a casual interest in her well-being?"

"The man's a goner," Jeb chimed in, joining them. "I doubt he's known which way was up since he met her."

Dylan glowered at his brother. "Watch it. I can have you on an oil rig in some very distant ocean with just one little hint to Dad."

"First you want to chain me to a desk, then you want to risk my neck on a rig. Make up your mind, big brother. I'm getting conflicting messages here."

"Bottom line, I'm looking for revenge," Dylan warned him. "Watch your step."

"It's not me you want revenge against," Jeb protested. He winked at their sister. "He'd like to wring Paul James's scrawny neck and he can't. It's got him frustrated." He cast an innocent look at Dylan. "Tell me again about how the man got the jump on you and tied you to a shower rod back in that motel."

"Okay, that's it," Dylan said. "It's the oil rig."

He deliberately glanced around the kitchen. "Where's my cell phone? I'm calling Dad."

Before he could place the call, Kelsey stepped into the kitchen and Dylan's pulse leapt into overdrive and all thoughts of revenge against either her ex-husband or his brother fled. He wanted very badly to haul her into his arms, but he didn't have the right. Not yet. And not in front of his nosy sister and meddlesome brother.

"What are you guys in here fussing and feuding

about?" Kelsey asked. "I could hear you in the other room. Is this the Delacourt means of communicating?"

"Pretty much," Trish reported cheerfully. "Jeb's taunting Dylan, so Dylan's threatening to have Dad send him off to an oil rig. It's the usual stuff. Now that you're here to referee, I think I'll call it a night."

Dylan glanced pointedly at his brother. "You going with her?"

Jeb deliberately stayed right where he was. "I hadn't planned to."

"Change your plans," Dylan said grimly.

Jeb touched a lingering kiss to Kelsey's cheek that had Dylan seeing red.

"Guess I've got to run," Jeb told her. "Don't let big brother here bully you, the way he does us."

"Not a chance," Kelsey told him.

"If you need any tips on handling him, call me. I know all his dirty little secrets."

Kelsey chuckled, then gave Dylan a speculative once-over. "I had no idea you had any dirty little secrets."

"None worth mentioning," Dylan assured her, then scowled at his brother and sister. "Weren't you leaving?"

When Jeb and Trish were gone, Dylan shoved his hands in his pockets to keep from reaching for her. "I wouldn't even try to bully you, you know."

She laughed. "Sure you would. I'm not dumb enough not to know it's your nature to bully the people you care about." She studied him thoughtfully. "And you strike me as smart enough to know that it won't work with me."

"Duly noted." He nodded toward the living room. "Still mobbed in there?"

"It's thinning down some."

"Want me to clear the rest of them out?"

"No, I'm fine. I just can't seem to take my eyes off of Bobby for more than a second. I forced myself to come in here, just so I could break the pattern before it became a habit. Even at three, he'd hate me hovering."

Dylan stepped closer, crowding her. "And here I thought you came into the kitchen to see me."

She laughed again and Dylan realized how little reason she'd had for laughter in the last few days and what a pleasure it was to hear the sound of it.

"You're just a bonus," she told him.

Dylan met her gaze evenly, saw the laughter die on her lips, then the fire of desire in her eyes.

"Do you know how badly I want to kiss you right now?" he asked.

She swallowed hard before answering. "I have an inkling." Her chin rose a notch. "What are you going to do about it?"

The feisty tone made his pulse hum. "Why, Doc, I think you're actually flirting with me. In fact, that almost sounded like a challenge. Is that possible?"

"Try me."

Dylan kept his hands jammed in his pockets as he lowered his head until his lips skimmed lightly over hers. Even so, he felt the shudder that washed through her. It was only a faint imitation of the one that rocked him when she leaned into the kiss, deepened it.

"Oh, baby," he murmured, "I have wanted this for so long."

"We've only known each other a few days," she reminded him before her breath hitched on a sigh.

"Forever," he corrected.

His arms went around her then and his mouth moved

over hers, tasting, savoring, possessing. Heat spread through him with the speed and intensity of a flash fire.

With the one tiny little part of his brain that was still functioning he recognized this as a bad idea. It wasn't the time or the place to go into a passiongenerated meltdown. In the aftermath of Bobby's rescue, Kelsey couldn't be thinking clearly, so it was up to him to do it.

In just a minute, he promised himself as he dipped his head for one more kiss. She had recently had a sip of wine and her lips were still cool, still bore its fruity taste. He doubted he would ever touch a glass of Chardonnay again without thinking of this moment.

He could feel himself growing hard, his erection as urgent and demanding as a randy teenager's, as hot and heavy as a man's. He knew he had to stop before he lost his last fragile thread of control.

Sighing, he pulled back, then stared into Kelsey's dazed eyes.

"Oh, my," she murmured, resting her forehead against his chest. "I've been married. I'm a doctor. I've read all the anatomy and human sexuality books. I understand how this works, but it has never, *never,* felt like this before."

Dylan grinned, nearly gave in to the temptation to swell right up with male pride. He had the sense not to delude himself that this was entirely personal, though. "Darlin', under the circumstances, what with all this adrenaline that's been pumping today, any man could have made your head reel."

"I don't think so."

"Trust me."

"I do," she said at once. "Just not about that."

"We'll try it again in a few days and see what you think."

Still frowning, she drew in a deep breath and gave him a curt nod. "I'll be looking forward to it," she said in a prim, businesslike tone that made him want to ravish her right then and there.

"I've got to get out of here," he muttered under his breath. This was dangerous turf, especially for two people who had a whole lot of thinking to do.

"Don't go," she pleaded. "Everyone will leave soon. Bobby will go to bed. I'm way too wired to sleep. I could use the company."

He scanned her face looking for evidence of just what she wanted the company for.

As if she'd read his mind, she smiled. "Just to talk, Dylan."

He nodded. "I can do that."

But it was going to be a whole lot harder than she could possibly guess.

Kelsey knew that Dylan was struggling with himself, that he wanted her every bit as much as she wanted him. She also recognized the danger in wanting something so badly under the circumstances. She certainly wasn't thinking clearly. Too much had happened in the last few days.

Still, she was reluctant to let him leave, even more reluctant to be alone with her thoughts. Her promise to do nothing more than talk had been made in haste, born of desperation. However, maybe by the time everyone else had gone home, after she'd tucked Bobby into his bed, she would have cooled down enough to stick to it.

"I'd better get in there and start saying goodbye. Maybe they'll take the hint," she said.

"You go. I'll hang out in here for a bit," Dylan said as he grabbed a beer from the refrigerator.

She walked back into the living room, scanning it for signs of Bobby. When she didn't spot him at once, her heart slammed against her ribs. She moved through the living room, then ran up the stairs to check his bedroom. He wasn't there, either. By the time she came back downstairs, her pulse was racing.

"Bobby! Where are you? Lizzy, Sharon Lynn, have either of you seen Bobby?"

Her shout brought Dylan from the kitchen.

"What is it?"

"I can't find Bobby," she said, nearing hysteria. Lizzy rushed over, grabbed her in a tight hug. "Kelsey, it's okay. He's just outside with the other kids. They're playing hide-and-seek in the backyard."

"Are you sure?" she asked, her breathing not yet returning to normal.

"I'll check," Dylan said at once.

She was right on his heels. "I'll go with you."

He took her hand and she immediately felt calmer. But only when she spotted Bobby racing after Lizzy's son did her heartbeat slow. She sank down onto the top step and put her hands over her face. "Dear God, will I ever get past this?"

"Of course you will," Dylan said. "It's only been a few hours, darlin'. Nobody gets over having their kid taken that fast. Stop beating yourself up over a perfectly normal reaction."

She heard Bobby's laughter as he and some of the others tackled Jamey and began tickling him till he pleaded for mercy.

"How can it be so easy for him?" she wondered. "It's as if he hasn't even been away."

"All he knew was that he was away with his dad," Dylan reminded her. "He didn't know there was anything really wrong with that. Now he's just falling back into his usual routine. Be grateful, Kelsey. You wouldn't have wanted him to be traumatized by what happened."

"Of course not."

Bobby spotted her just then and ran across the yard. He flung his arms around her. "Mommy, I love you."

Surprised by the impulsive and increasingly rare gesture, Kelsey squeezed him back, then forced herself to let go. Only after he was out of earshot did she whisper, "I love you, too, baby."

She allowed her shoulder to brush Dylan's as they sat on the back steps watching the kids play. He slid an arm around her waist, gave her a reassuring squeeze, then released her.

"They grow up so fast," she observed eventually. "One minute they're babies, the next they're all but grown...or think they are. Bobby's only three, but already I can feel the time flying by."

Only after her comment was greeted with total silence did she realize the impact it must have had on Dylan. She touched his cheek. "I'm sorry. I wasn't thinking."

"Don't worry about it. It's true. They do grow up way too fast. When I think of what I've missed with Shane, it makes me a little crazy. No more, though," he said with quiet resolve. "I'm not going to miss the rest of it."

She snuggled more tightly against his side, satisfied

for the moment with no more contact between them than that. "Tell me what you remember most about him."

"What a tough little guy he was," he said at once. "There were some bigger kids in the neighborhood, but as soon as he could walk he wanted to play with them. He would fall down, get right back up and run even harder. He was the same way with his brothers."

Kelsey stared at him in surprise. "You mean his stepbrothers?"

"Technically, yes, but that's not how he thinks of them."

"You've seen them together? I thought you hadn't had any contact with him at all since you gave up custody?"

Dylan looked vaguely disconcerted that she had picked up on that. "I went by the house once, just to check on him," he said defensively. "I needed to see for myself that he was okay."

Somehow she found it reassuring that walking away hadn't been easy for him. "Of course you did. Were you satisfied?"

His expression glum, he nodded. "He looked happy. They looked like a real family."

"Was that the only time you saw him?"

"No," he admitted. "There was one time at his preschool. Kit spotted me that day. She sent me a finger painting he had done of his family. I guess she wanted to be sure I got the message."

"Or maybe she just wanted to reassure you that he was fine."

"Maybe."

"Dylan, can I ask you something?"

"Of course. After what we've been through the last

few days, I think you've got a right to ask me just abut anything."

"What was your relationship with Kit like?"

He regarded her with surprise. "Are you sure you want to hear about that?"

"Why not? You know all the gory details of my relationship with Paul."

He nodded. "Fair enough. The truth is we never should have gotten married in the first place, even though we thought we were crazy in love with each other."

"Why not?"

"We were complete opposites in every conceivable way. That's probably why the attraction was so powerful, but in the end we couldn't find a middle ground on anything. We argued over everything. She liked pasta. I liked steak. She wanted to sleep in. I liked to get up at the crack of dawn. She preferred one toothpaste. I refused to give up the one I liked. At least with two tubes, we didn't have to fight over which way to squeeze the stuff out."

"Sounds like the usual marital kinks that get worked out with time," Kelsey said.

"Oh, that was the least of it. There were bigger issues, like my hours, the way I got caught up in a case and forgot about everything else. Before we had Shane, she was more tolerant of that. Afterward, she felt neglected and taken for granted and put upon. She was right. I didn't hold up my end of the marriage. But when she divorced me, I didn't like seeing all those faults listed on a court document, because I didn't want to believe I was to blame for our marriage failing. I wanted to blame her, so I accused her of being selfish and unwilling to compromise. I even tossed in a few accusations about other men. It got ugly."

"Was she seeing other men?"

He shrugged. "None I could prove, but I needed to believe that was the real reason she'd left me. I couldn't deal with the idea that she just didn't want me. When it didn't take her all that long to find someone new and marry again, I was convinced I'd been right all along."

She met his gaze evenly. "Is that really why you gave up custody of Shane? To punish yourself and her?"

"Of course not."

"Are you sure?"

He sighed heavily. "I don't know. Probably. I told myself it was the best thing for Shane and at the time, it probably was. Kit and I couldn't have a civil conversation."

"Maybe now you can," Kelsey suggested.

"I hope so," he said fervently.

"When will you go to see her?"

"Tomorrow. Justin took Jeb out to get my car, so I'll be able to leave first thing in the morning."

The thought of him leaving so soon was disconcerting. "Tomorrow?" she echoed, aware that she sounded dismayed.

He studied her intently. "Okay, Kelsey, what's going on? Why do you sound so worried?"

"I guess I've just gotten used to you hanging around," she said mildly.

Looking very pleased, he looped his arm around her shoulders and planted a kiss on her cheek. "Don't worry, darlin'. I'll be back. That's a promise."

The intensity of his gaze disconcerted her almost as badly as the thought of him leaving. She glanced away, instinctively searching among the children until she spotted Bobby. He looked worn-out, which motivated her to leave Dylan's loose embrace.

"Okay, kids, that's it. It's time to call it a night."

"Aw, Mommy, not yet," Bobby protested.

"Yes. It's way past your bedtime. Everyone else has day camp tomorrow, too."

"I want to go to day camp."

"You're too little," Jamey Robbins pointed out.

"Am not little," Bobby retorted.

Dylan scooped him up before it could turn into a full-fledged battle. "Now you're bigger than he is," Dylan said as he settled Bobby on his shoulders.

"See," Bobby crowed. "I'm the biggest."

"You still can't go to day camp," Jamey told him and went indoors.

"Mommy," Bobby cried plaintively. "What?"

"What's day camp?"

Kelsey bit back a grin. Typical kid. If someone he admired had something, he wanted it, too. It didn't matter that he didn't even know what it was. "Day camp is a place kids go in the summer and learn stuff," Dylan told him. "Sort of like school. If you ask me, you're the lucky one. You get to stay home and play all day."

"Yeah," Bobby whooped. "I get to play!" He tugged on Dylan's hair. "Down. Gotta go tell Jamey."

As Bobby ran off, Kelsey chuckled. "Well, you've certainly given him the momentary edge. Thanks."

Then with Dylan's help she shooed the remaining pint-sized guests inside and matched them with their respective parents. Once the exodus started, it didn't take long to clear the place.

"Up to bed," she told Bobby.

He hesitated and she sensed suddenly that it wasn't

just his usual reluctance to see the day end. "What's up, pal? Want me to come up with you?"

He shook his head, then gazed shyly at Dylan. "Are you gonna be here in the morning?"

"Nope. I'm going away for a few days."

"Oh," Bobby said glumly.

Dylan hunkered down in front of him. "Why? Was there something you wanted to do tomorrow?"

"I was thinking maybe if you were here you could play with me. I got lots of neat stuff in the backyard."

Kelsey exchanged a puzzled look with Dylan. "Why did you want Dylan to play with you, sweetie?"

"So Daddy can't make me go away again," he said simply.

Tears welled up in Kelsey's eyes. She had to turn away to keep Bobby from seeing. She was aware of Dylan quietly reassuring Bobby that his daddy wasn't going to take him again, but all the while her heart was breaking.

She felt Dylan's light touch on her arm and jerked her head toward him. "What?"

"I'm going to take Bobby up to bed and hang out for a minute, if it's okay with you."

Unable to speak around the lump in her throat, she simply nodded. Dylan squeezed her hand and mouthed, "He's going to be fine."

But Kelsey wasn't so sure. Would any of them ever really be fine again?

Fourteen

Dylan spent nearly a half hour talking to Bobby, trying to ease his fears, then tucking him into bed and waiting until he drifted off to sleep. All the while, he kept thinking of all the nights he'd missed doing exactly the same thing with Shane, all the stories he could have read to his son, all the sleepy talks they could have shared. The experience reinforced his decision to see Kit as soon as possible the next day. He wanted his son back in his life. He needed to be a dad again. Even part-time would be better than nothing.

As he went back downstairs, though, his thoughts shifted back to the woman waiting for him. He had seen her shattered expression when Bobby had revealed his fear of being taken away again by his dad. The fact that she had allowed him to step in and reassure the boy, then put him to bed, told Dylan just how distraught she had been. She'd been afraid Bobby would detect her own fear.

Obviously, she had been wanting to believe, just as he had, that Bobby hadn't been affected by the events of the last few days. Now they could no longer delude themselves. He'd been able to step in tonight, but what if

Bobby needed more help than either he or Kelsey could give him?

Dylan walked into the living room to find Kelsey curled up at one end of the sofa. She hadn't turned on the lights and the room was in shadows.

"Is he okay?" she asked, sounding lost and defeated.

"Sound asleep," Dylan reassured her as he crossed the room, sat down beside her and drew her into his arms. She came willingly.

"Oh, Dylan, I wanted so badly for him to have come through this unscathed."

"To tell you the truth, I think he was just worried about leaving you again. I don't think it had anything to do with him being frightened of his father."

"But he saw Paul shoot that gun in the air and tie you up. How could he not have been terrified? I must have been crazy to think he would forget all about it just like that."

"We talked about that. I told him nothing really bad happened, that it was like a game between his dad and me to see who would get to bring him back to you fastest. He seemed to accept that."

"In other words, you lied to him. Is that good?"

"It's better than telling him his dad did a terrible thing that could have had tragic consequences. He'll figure that out for himself when he's older. For now, I think it's better just to ease his mind. Maybe you should talk to a psychologist. See what he says."

"Of course," she said, sounding relieved to have something concrete she could do. "I don't know why I didn't think of that. It's exactly what I'd recommend to the parent of any patient of mine who'd been through a traumatic experience. I'll call a friend of mine in Miami first thing in the morning. I just wish I had some answers now."

"Bobby's sound asleep. The answers can wait until morning." He gave her a knowing look. "But just in case you don't see it that way, my guess is you have a few psych books left over from med school tucked away somewhere around here."

She brightened at the suggestion. "In the attic." She started to get up.

"Not just yet," Dylan said, holding her a little more tightly. "Let's talk about you for a minute. Will you be able to sleep tonight or are you going to spend the whole night running into Bobby's room just to make sure he's there?"

"I'll try to limit it to once an hour," she said candidly.

He debated asking his next question, then decided to make the offer anyway. "Would it help if I stayed here? On the sofa," he elaborated before she could jump to the wrong conclusion.

Her hesitation suggested she badly wanted to resist the idea, that she was used to handling crises on her own and needed to start doing that again. Finally she released a soft sigh. "Would you mind?"

"I offered, didn't I?"

Her gaze clashed with his. "Not on the sofa, though. Upstairs. With me."

Dylan's heart beat a little faster, but he shook his head. "Bad idea."

"Why?"

"We won't sleep, Kelsey, and you know it."

"Would that be so terrible?"

Dylan struggled with himself, with his sense of honor. "I thought we'd decided not to rush into anything."

"It's just sex, Dylan, not a commitment."

She uttered the words so damned bravely, but they both knew better. She didn't have casual relationships, and though he'd had his share, he knew this wasn't going to be one of them. She deserved better from him.

"You're wrong," he told her. "You don't have casual flings and when it comes to someone like you, neither do I. I want to make something of what we have, Kelsey. I don't want to mess it up by getting into something heavy at the wrong time, when you're vulnerable. I don't want you waking up in the morning with regrets."

"I'm stronger than I seem, Dylan. You've seen me at my worst. Believe me, under normal circumstances, I'm perfectly capable of making a rational decision."

He laughed. "Oh, I'm certain of that, darlin', but you're not thinking with your brain just now."

She stared at him indignantly, then chuckled selfconsciously. "Shouldn't that be my line?"

"I'll give you a rain check to use it on me," he promised. "Now scoot before I change my mind and decide I can't resist ravishing you, after all. You can hunt for that psychology book and read yourself to sleep with all that dull, dry material."

She regarded him with obvious regret. "You're not going to be noble forever, are you?"

Dylan laughed, despite the ache that was already building with no immediate relief in sight. "No, darlin'. I think you can count on me getting past this in no time at all."

To Kelsey's amazement, after checking on Bobby only twice and reading just a few pages of the child-psychology textbook she'd found in the attic, she actually fell soundly asleep and slept through the rest of the night. She knew she owed that to Dylan's presence downstairs. While the rational part of her brain knew that Paul couldn't come after their son again, on another level she had feared he would somehow find a way out of jail and do just that. Having Dylan there to stop him had relieved her illogical worries.

The man was definitely one of the good guys. She had recognized his strength from the beginning, but she was just now beginning to understand how deep his integrity ran. Last night she had found his sense of honor inconvenient, but today she was grateful for it. She had been caught up in an adrenaline rush, no doubt about it.

One thing she knew, though, the attraction she had developed toward Dylan Delacourt wasn't going away. If anything, it was growing deeper day by day. Sometimes, with some people, a lifetime of getting acquainted could be crammed into a few short days. It had been with them.

Down the hall she could hear Bobby thumping around in his room, probably tossing half his toys on the floor in search of the one buried deepest in the pile. The sound brought a smile to her lips.

Then she heard Dylan stirring downstairs and her smile spread.

She took a quick shower, tugged on a clean outfit, then poked her head into Bobby's room. He was sitting on his bed, totally absorbed in his favorite picture book, one with lots of fire engines and police cars in it. He gave her a distracted wave and went right back to it.

Back to normal, she told herself with a relieved sigh. At least that was the way it seemed right now. Hard to tell what the day would bring.

Downstairs, she could smell the coffee brewing as

she walked toward the kitchen. She found Dylan with one jeans-clad hip propped against the counter, his shirt hanging open and a cup of coffee in his hand. He looked sleepy and rumpled and indescribably sexy. His expression brightened when he saw her.

"Good morning."

Staring at his partially bared chest, she murmured something that was probably incomprehensible. Finally she tugged her gaze away and looked into eyes dancing with amusement.

"Never seen a male body up close before?" he teased.

"Most of the ones I see are under twelve. Trust me, it's not the same."

"Speaking of that, you aren't planning to go back to work today, are you?"

"I was thinking about going in later. Why?"

"What about Bobby?"

"Hank's invited him out to the ranch after day camp today to play with Jamey. I figured he'd rather do that than stay here with me."

"Are you okay with that?"

"I'll have to be sometime."

"*Sometime* is not necessarily today," he pointed out.

"Dylan, I have to do this my own way."

He appeared to bristle a bit at that. "Well, of course you do, but I was just worried."

"No need for you to worry," she insisted. "Not anymore."

He leveled a look straight at her. "That's like asking me not to breathe. I'm the oldest of five. Worrying is what I do best." He grinned ruefully. "It always drove Trish, Jeb and the others crazy, too. I can't get over it, though, so you might as well get used to it."

"Then add me to the list of those who find it annoying, but endearing," Kelsey told him, then stood on tiptoe to press a kiss to his cheek to take the sting out of her words. "Thanks for caring."

Having someone concerned about her well-being, challenging her independence at every turn, was going to take a whole lot of getting used to. But seeing the flare of heat in Dylan's eyes, feeling the responding warmth steal through her, she knew it was also going to be worth it.

That peck on the cheek was the best Dylan got from Kelsey before he took off, but in some ways it was better than the most passionate kisses they had shared. There was a lighthearted teasing about it, an underlying affection that he couldn't mistake. It was exactly what he intended to build on…as soon as he had his own life settled.

First he drove by the sheriff's office to check in with Justin and assure himself that Paul wasn't going anywhere anytime soon.

"Listen, there's something I've been wanting to talk to you about," Justin said, gesturing toward the chair opposite his desk.

Dylan studied him worriedly as he sat. "You're not still agitating about me coming after Paul yesterday and almost busting into that meeting you had staked out, are you?"

"No more than you're still ticked that I stopped you," Justin retorted.

"Okay, let's call it a draw. What's on your mind?"

"I could use another man around here, someone with real experience and good instincts. Interested?"

"I'm a private investigator. What makes you think I'd want to become a sheriff's deputy?"

"Call me crazy, but I got the distinct impression you were interested in a certain baby doc who's new in town. Am I wrong?"

Dylan hesitated, then shook his head. "You're not wrong."

"What do you intend to do about it?"

"I'm not real sure that's any of your business." Justin scowled. "Kelsey's like family. That makes it my business. You can either answer to me or answer to Grandpa Harlan. Believe me, I'm the better bet. He tends to get real pushy."

Dylan actually appreciated the strength of that particular bond. He knew from his own experience with his brothers and his sister that that kind of protectiveness ran deep. Hadn't he explained that very concept to Kelsey the night before?

"I have some things to work out," he finally admitted. "Then I intend to come back here and see how things go from there."

"Wouldn't that be a whole lot easier if you had a steady paycheck?"

"My business does real well," Dylan said.

"In Houston. How well will it do if you're here?" To Dylan's regret, Justin had a point. "I guess I hadn't gotten quite that far along with my thinking," he conceded. "Give me a little time. I'll consider the offer."

"Take as much time as you need."

Dylan stood up and offered Justin his hand. "Thank you for letting me work with you on this case. I would much rather work with the authorities than butt heads with them."

"Which is exactly why I think you'd fit in here." Dylan thought about the proposal all the way over to Trish's. While it had some merit, he still wasn't sure he was suited to following a bunch of rules and regulations, even with a decent guy like Justin as his boss.

When he got to his sister's, he found her in the kitchen and discovered that Jeb was packing to go back to Houston.

"Where's my best girl?" Dylan demanded as he poured himself a cup of coffee.

"Upstairs with Jeb. Be careful. I think she's defecting. You haven't been around much the past couple of days and I suspect her heart's fickle."

"Not my sweet Laura," he said loudly enough to be heard upstairs.

"Unca Dyl." The delighted cry echoed through the house and was quickly followed by the thunder of tiny feet heading for the stairs.

"Whoa, there, sweetheart," Jeb shouted, pounding after her.

A moment later, he came into the kitchen with Laura sitting on his shoulders. Their niece's arms were already outstretched for Dylan.

Trish chuckled. "Told you she was fickle."

Jeb handed Laura over, then surveyed Dylan. "You look like hell. No sleep?"

"I got plenty of sleep," Dylan told him. "Unfortunately the sofa was too blasted short. I've got aches and pains everywhere."

"And here I envisioned you over there—"

"Careful, pal."

Jeb grinned. "Celebrating, big brother. That's all I was going to say. Where did you think I was going?"

"Never can tell with you."

"Can I hitch a ride back to Houston with you or should I call Dad and ask to have the corporate jet sent over?" Jeb asked, wisely changing the subject.

"I'll take you," Dylan said.

Trish stared at him in shock. "You're going back to Houston today?"

He nodded.

"But I thought…"

"Well, you thought wrong. I have things to do." Her gaze narrowed. "Such as?"

"I'll let you know next time I see you."

"When will that be?"

He frowned at her. "Why all the questions?"

"It's just that I saw how you and Kelsey were together. I was sure something was going to happen."

Dylan sighed. "Saints protect me from the busybodies in this town. You're the second person today who wanted to poke around in my private life."

"Because I care," Trish said huffily. "You certainly don't hesitate to poke and prod when the mood suits you. Never mind, though. I don't have to follow your example. I'll keep my mouth shut from now on."

Dylan exchanged a look with Jeb and they both burst out laughing.

"That will be the day, baby sister," Dylan said, then kissed her. "We forgive you, though. Just rein it in for a few days, okay?"

She seized on that. "A few days? That's it?"

He nodded.

"I can last a few days," she said briskly, then grinned at him. "Can Kelsey?"

Dylan frowned at her. "Watch it, kid."

"Just checking," she said innocently.

Damn, Dylan thought. How was he going to figure out the rest of his life with half the world watching his every move? He realized Justin and Trish were only the tip of the iceberg. He still had to drive all the way to Houston with Jeb in that car, then be subjected to the curiosity of his other brothers, his father and, worst of all, his mother.

There were occasions—and this was clearly destined to be one of them—when he deeply regretted being part of a large family that insisted on knowing everything about his life practically before he did.

Then again, turnabout was only fair play. He'd been doing the same thing to all of them for years.

Fifteen

Kelsey couldn't concentrate. She'd done nearly a dozen preschool physicals since noon, returned nearly as many calls, and organized her schedule so she could catch up on all the appointments she'd missed while Bobby had been missing. Even at that, she kept thinking about Dylan and the promise that had been in his eyes and in his voice when he'd left her.

Could something so important be this easy? Could she possibly fall in love in the blink of an eye in the midst of the worst crisis of her life? Or was she just confusing love with relief and gratitude? Dylan was obviously worried that she might be doing just that and she supposed he was right to be so concerned. It wasn't something to make a mistake about. They both had past mistakes to serve as warnings against making hasty judgments.

She leaned back in her chair and thought about the kisses they'd shared. She was still daydreaming, a smile on her lips, when Lizzy poked her head in. "You ready to grab some lunch?" she asked, then did a double take. "Or would you rather tell me what put that smile on your face?" She came in and sat down, clearly making her own choice about which took precedence. "Dylan, I suppose."

"Why ask when you think you already know the answer?"

"Because, contrary to all the rumors, I'm not infallible. Sometimes my diagnoses are off."

"Not a smart thing for a doctor to admit to," Kelsey teased. "Malpractice suits being what they are these days."

"Don't remind me." Her expression sobered. "How's Bobby doing? I didn't get to see him before I left the ranch today."

"Overall, he's doing a whole lot better than I would have predicted. Even so, first thing this morning I called that child psychologist we liked so much back in med school. You remember the one?"

"Handsome Harry?" Lizzy recalled.

"We liked him because he was brilliant."

"Yeah, right," Lizzy teased. "Who actually noticed that?"

"I did," Kelsey insisted. "And so did you, so stop it. He agreed with Dylan that Bobby's probably more worried about me leaving again than about his dad coming back. Bobby had one bad spell last night right before bed, but Dylan talked to him and that seemed to do the trick. He slept straight through the night."

"Dylan, huh? He's still spending a lot of time around the house, even though his job is done?"

"Don't look at me like that," Kelsey protested. "It's not like he spent the night. Well, he did, but—"

"Oh, really?"

"Lizzy, cut it out."

"He's a great guy."

"Yes, he is," Kelsey agreed. "And he was a rock during all of this, but he has his own issues to deal with and so do I. The timing's all off."

"Today, maybe," Lizzy noted. "How about tomorrow?"

"We'll see." It was as much of a commitment as Kelsey was prepared to make until she and Dylan could have some time together to sort things out.

Dylan sat outside Kit's house and mentally rehearsed what he intended to say to persuade her to have the custody agreement amended. He needed to have every argument in place, needed to remain absolutely calm. Anything else and he would blow his best chance at getting back into Shane's life. He could always go to court, but this way was preferable. Funny how a little maturity could make things a whole lot clearer.

He'd arrived without any advance warning, figuring that the element of surprise was on his side. Kit's defenses would be down and she would be alone without her new husband there to shore up any protests she might have initially.

"It's now or never, pal," he muttered under his breath. He got out of the car and walked across the street. Kit had the front door open before he could knock.

"I was wondering when you were going to decide to come in," she said, meeting his gaze evenly. She didn't seem especially surprised to see him. Nor did she seem as dismayed or angry as he'd anticipated.

"I see your radar's as good as ever," he said, managing a grin to take any sting out of the words. "You look good, Kit. Great, in fact."

"Are you trying to butter me up for something, or

do you mean it?" she asked, studying him thoughtfully. "You actually mean it, don't you?"

He nodded. "Is that such a big surprise?"

"You rarely noticed how I looked while we were married, not after the first year, anyway."

The truth hurt. "I'm sorry," he said, meaning it. She shrugged. "It's in the past. I'm happy now.

How about you?"

"I'm getting there. There's just one thing missing."

She regarded him evenly, then sighed. "I've been expecting this. Come into the kitchen. Can I get you some iced tea or some lemonade? You used to like that."

Relieved that she hadn't gone ballistic right off the bat, he nodded. "Lemonade would be great."

She poured the drink into a tall glass filled with ice just the way he liked it, then handed it to him. Rather than sitting, though, she stood by the counter, watching him warily.

"Okay, out with it," she said.

He was surprised by her demand. "Were you always this direct? I don't remember that."

"No," she said. "I learned from my mistakes. Maybe if I'd told you what I needed a whole lot sooner, we wouldn't be where we are today."

The comment stunned him. It was the first time he could recall her being willing to share any of the blame for what went wrong in their marriage.

"I don't know," he said honestly. "I probably still wouldn't have known the meaning of compromise."

She laughed. "You really were used to being king of the roost in that family of yours, weren't you? Big brother could do no wrong."

"Is that how you saw it?"

"That's how it was," she said without rancor. "And they might fight you tooth and nail over anything and everything, but heaven forbid anyone else should question your decisions. It was daunting."

He tried hard to remember that part of the past, but all he recalled was the mounting tension between him and Kit and his inability to do anything to lessen it.

"I'm sorry for that, too," he told her.

She shook her head. "Amazing. Two apologies in one day, when I didn't think you were capable of any."

"I'm—"

She held up her hand. "Enough. Why are you here, Dylan? It's not to take a walk down memory lane."

He took a deep breath and dived in. "I've been thinking a lot about Shane lately." He looked into her eyes. "Wondering if I made a mistake."

"He's happy, Dylan."

"I know that," he said, fighting against an unreasonable tide of misery. Was he wrong to be asking this of Kit? Of Shane? Was it too late to stake a claim he never should have given up in the first place?

"But you miss him, anyway," she guessed. "Yes. Does that make me totally selfish?"

"No. Sorry. It just makes you human. You're his dad, Dylan. He's the best thing you ever gave me. I'm not surprised you want to know him. I would, if our roles were reversed."

He began to feel hopeful. "Can we work this out? Or is it too late?"

She regarded him with surprising sympathy. "As long as we're still alive, it's never too late to change things. Another lesson learned through our mistakes."

"I don't want to turn his life upside down, or yours and Steve's."

"Oh, Dylan, knowing his real dad loves him isn't going to turn his world upside down. It's just going to bring more love into his life. Steve and his boys taught me that when they accepted Shane and me right from the beginning. You're the one who was so certain Shane would be better off without you. I never thought it. Not really. Neither did Steve, though he was grateful to you for wanting him to be a real dad to Shane. I always hoped you'd realize one day what you'd given up."

He stared at her in amazement. He could tell that she honestly meant what she'd said, that whatever ill will had been between them was in the past. "You're a remarkable woman, Kit. Why didn't I know that?"

"Maybe I did my best to see that you never saw it," she said wryly. She glanced at the clock. "Shane will be home soon. Want to stick around?"

"More than anything," Dylan admitted, then felt panic clawing at his insides. What if he'd waited too long? What if Shane didn't even know who he was? Would he be able to bear it? "Maybe we should do this another day. Shouldn't you talk to Steve first? Maybe a lawyer?"

"This is between you and me and Shane," she said. "The legalities can be worked out later. As for Steve, we agreed from the beginning that if you ever changed your mind, we'd amend the agreement. Frankly, what surprised us both—especially after those surreptitious little visits of yours—was that it took you so long."

He shook his head at her ability to read him so well. "Why didn't you just knock me upside the head back then and tell me what a mistake I was making?"

"Would you have listened?"

"Probably not," he admitted.

"Which is exactly why it seemed like such a waste of time. Besides, I'll admit to being selfish enough back then to want Shane all to myself. I figured you didn't deserve him."

Just then Dylan heard the rumble of what was most likely a school bus outside. His pulse accelerated.

"Is that him?"

Kit nodded. "Prepare to be caught up in a tornado."

Less than a minute later, the front door opened, then slammed shut.

"Mommy!" The excited shout just about raised the rafters. "I'm home!"

"In the kitchen, Shane."

"Baking cookies?" he asked hopefully as he ran into the room, then skidded to a stop at the sight of Dylan. He inched closer to his mother, eyeing Dylan warily. Kit kept a light hand resting on his shoulder, but said nothing. Dylan was at a loss for words.

"I know you," Shane said after what seemed like an eternity. He looked up at Kit. "Don't I?"

She nodded.

"You're the man in the picture."

Dylan felt as if his heart had stopped. "What picture is that?"

"In my room. Mommy told me it was my dad, my real dad. She said Steve adopted me, so he's a real dad, too. She said I'm really lucky to have two dads."

Dylan felt the sharp sting of tears in his eyes and blinked them away. If he and Kit had been alone at that moment, he might have bawled like a baby, he was so grateful to her for keeping him alive in Shane's mind. He glanced up at her and mouthed silently, "Thank you."

Shane tilted his head in a way that was pure Delacourt and studied Dylan. "Am I right? Are you my dad?"

Dylan nodded. "I am." He hesitated, then asked, "Would you mind if I gave you a hug? I've really, really missed you."

"I guess."

Shane said it with the obvious reluctance and distaste of a typical boy his age. It was such a normal reaction, Dylan almost laughed. He knelt down, opened his arms and waited until Shane came to him. If it had been up to him, the hug would have lasted forever, but he knew Shane couldn't possibly understand why such a simple gesture meant so much to him that he wanted it to go on and on.

The instant Dylan released him, Shane turned to his mother. "So, did you bake cookies today or not?"

"Chocolate chip," Kit said, sounding as emotional as Dylan felt. "They're in the cookie jar. Take two."

Shane darted to the counter, climbed up on a step stool and reached for the cookie jar. He came out with a handful of cookies. Grinning, he held them toward Dylan. "You want some? Mom makes the best chocolate chip cookies in the world."

"I remember." He accepted the cookies, then asked, "Are these your favorites?"

"Pretty much. How about you?"

"Definitely." There were a thousand other things he wanted to know, a thousand questions to be asked, but he knew he'd have to ease into this new relationship, give all of them time to adjust.

With Kit staying in the background, they munched their cookies in companionable silence. Dylan felt the situation called for something momentous, but maybe sharing chocolate chip cookies with his son was exactly right. He figured a fireworks display and whoops of joy would have put the boy off. This was—he searched for the right word—this was a beginning, he concluded. He knew, too, that he couldn't have asked for—much less deserved—anything more.

"Mommy, can I go outside now?" Shane asked, already anticipating a positive response and heading toward the back door.

Kit nodded. "In the yard or, if you want to ride your bike, on the sidewalk out front. Nowhere else, okay?"

"Got it," Shane said. At the door, he glanced back at Dylan. "Are you gonna be my dad for real from now on?"

"I'd like that very much."

"Do I have to go away with you?"

"No," Dylan said, thinking of another little boy who'd been taken from his home all too recently. "I'll come here, if it's okay with you and your mom and dad."

"Will you bring me stuff sometimes?"

"Shane!" Kit protested.

"Well, Jimmy's real dad brings him presents all the time."

Dylan winked at him. "Oh, I think you can count on me bringing you things from time to time, if your mom says it's okay."

A smile spread across Shane's face. "Two dads. This is so cool."

And then he bounded out the door, letting it slam behind him.

Just like that, as if in answer to a prayer, Dylan had his son back. And it was all because of Kelsey and another little boy who'd come into his life and made him see what he'd given up.

He knew then that he didn't want to wait, couldn't wait to bring the two of them into his life forever. Waiting could cost a man everything that really mattered. He would never risk that kind of loss again.

Dylan impulsively stopped and bought the biggest diamond in the jewelry store on the way back to Los Pinõs. Kelsey was probably figuring he'd start out slow, maybe ask for a date. He intended to go for the gold right from the start.

He found her at the clinic, surrounded by kids getting preschool physicals. He shuddered at the number already clutching lollipops as proof that they'd bravely withstood their shots. Kelsey caught sight of him in the waiting room and stumbled over whatever she'd been about to say to the mother standing with her. Then she deliberately glanced down at the chart in her hand, gathered her composure and went on as if he weren't there. As soon as mother and child were on their way, she beckoned to him.

"Mr. Delacourt, come on into my office." She smiled at the remaining patients. "This won't take long."

Dylan followed her into her office, then shut the door. He studied her in her crisp white lab coat and decided she looked just as sexy in that as she did in those shorts she'd worn around the house. Apparently he was going to get turned on no matter what she wore. Good thing, too, given what he was planning for their future.

"You're back sooner than I expected," she said, moving behind her desk as if to keep a safe distance between them.

"I couldn't stay away."

"How did things go with Kit?"

"I'll tell you about it later. Have dinner with me."

"I can't," she said too quickly. "I shouldn't leave Bobby again tonight."

Dylan regarded her intently. "You're not getting nervous about being alone with me, are you?"

"Of course not," she retorted indignantly, but there were bright patches of color on her cheeks.

"Tsk, tsk, Doc. Fibbing doesn't suit you."

"You come to dinner at my house tonight," she countered as if that would prove her bravery.

"With Bobby as chaperone? How convenient," he taunted.

Her chin rose at that. "He has a very early bedtime."

Dylan grinned. "Things are looking up. How about you, darlin'? Do you have an early bedtime?" She stared at him. "What has gotten into you?"

"I'm a man on a mission."

The statement clearly disconcerted her. "What sort of a mission?"

"You'll find out soon enough."

"Tell me now. I'm an impatient woman."

"Here? You want me to tell you here, in your office, with all those people just outside?" He followed her behind her desk, leaned down until his mouth hovered over hers.

"Mmm-hmm," she murmured.

"I was thinking more along the lines of something with moonlight and roses, but if you say so…"

She swallowed hard. "Dylan, what…this isn't about… you're not going to…"

He touched a finger to her lips. "Hush. Let me say it."

"I don't think—"

"It's not the time or the place," he agreed. "But what

the heck? We're an unconventional pair. We do things our own way. Why not ask you to marry me in your office, especially now that I've seen just how cute you are in that lab coat?"

"Marry you?" she echoed, clearly stunned. "You're asking me to marry you? Are you serious?"

He waved the jewelry box under her nose, then gestured for her to take it. "See for yourself."

She put her hands behind her back as if she didn't dare. Dylan opened the box instead. Kelsey gasped. Her eyes widened in wonder.

"You are serious."

"Every bit as serious as one of those needles you've been poking around with today."

"Why? What?" Her gaze searched his face. "Dylan, are you sure?"

"That I love you? Yes. Absolutely. Seeing Shane again also made me see that I don't want to waste any more of my life being separated from the people I love. You're one of those people. You and Bobby."

"Just like that?" she asked incredulously.

He nodded. "Just like that."

She shook her head as if to clear it. "Dylan, I can't think."

"Don't think. Feel. What do you feel right now?"

"Overwhelmed," she said at once. "Dizzy."

He tucked a finger under her chin, waited for her to meet his gaze. "And?"

"In love," she whispered. "I don't understand why or how it happened so fast, but it's true. I love you."

"Then can you think of a single reason to wait?"

"I can think of a million reasons to wait," she said,

regarding him with mock severity. Then a smile spread across her face. "But not a one of them really matters."

"Then we're on? You'll marry me?"

"Yes," she sighed against his lips. "Oh, yes."

"If there weren't a whole waiting room full of people out there, I would make love to you right here and now," he told her.

"I could get rid of them," she offered.

"But you won't. You're entirely too responsible. I admire that, usually. I can wait until later."

"Tonight?"

"Or our wedding night," he suggested. "Maybe that should be the one traditional thing we do."

"Tonight," she repeated very firmly.

Dylan laughed at the prospect of two control freaks butting heads from now through eternity. "If you say so, darlin'," he said, proving that he'd very recently learned the art of compromise.

"I say so," she said, seizing the last word.

He figured he'd let her get away with it...this time.

Epilogue

Impulsiveness could only go so far. Kelsey made Dylan wait for two months before walking down the aisle. She insisted there were too many things to be settled, such as whether he was going to accept Justin's offer to work as a deputy sheriff and which brand of toothpaste they were going to use. She wanted all of those pesky little details ironed out before the ceremony. She intended to start their married life in blissful unanimity.

Of course, things got a little crazy when it came time to decide on how big a wedding to have. Harlan Adams won out with his bid for a lavish affair, held in the same church where all of the Adamses had been wed. There were two ring bearers—Bobby and Shane—two maids of honor—Lizzy and Trish—and a whole slew of ushers. Jeb was the best man.

As for the honeymoon, with Bobby staying safely at Lizzy's Dylan had refused to tell her a single thing. He'd swept her away from the ceremony, escorted her to the Delacourt Oil corporate jet, and for most of the trip he'd plied her with champagne and kisses to keep her questions to a minimum. After a while she hadn't much cared if they wound up on a beach in Hawaii or in a snowbank in Alaska. Or stayed at thirty thousand feet. "We are not making love for the first time in a jet," Dylan declared eventually, drawing away with obvious reluctance.

"Why not? The idea of flying high on love doesn't suit such a staid individual as yourself?"

"Staid? Me?" He regarded her indignantly.

She reached for the top button on his shirt and slowly undid it. "Prove me wrong," she challenged. She leaned forward and ran the tip of her tongue over his lower lip. He shuddered.

"Kelsey."

His protest sounded a lot like a moan, so she decided to put a little more effort into getting him to loosen up. She worked the next button loose and caressed his upper lip with her tongue, then dipped inside his mouth until they were both gasping for breath.

There was a lot to be said for surprising Dylan with her inventiveness. It was having a very provocative effect on her own libido, too. She'd never had the time or the lighthearted daring to experiment with her own sexuality with Paul. Dylan seemed to welcome it, even if he was somewhat bemused by it. In fact, he was beginning to look downright dazed.

"Doesn't this fancy jet have a bed?" she inquired, gazing around at the luxurious interior and concluding that this was a life-style she could get used to.

"I doubt there's been much need for one before now," Dylan said dryly. "It's mostly used for business trips."

"Don't the Delacourt men ever rest?"

"Not so you'd notice."

"Too bad," she said, then tried a release button to see just how far the seat would go back. "Not bad," she observed when Dylan was all but prone. His eyes widened as she inched over to join him.

"Kelsey, I really don't think…"

"Ssh." She touched a finger to his lips. "This isn't about thinking. It's about discovery and exploration. Since you're part of an oil family, those terms should be familiar."

"I'm a private investigator," he reminded her, though a smile was building at the corners of his mouth.

"Then investigate," she said boldly, sitting up so she was straddling him.

"Oh, baby," he murmured, but his hands fumbled with the buttons on her blouse, then made short work of her bra.

His heated gaze settled on her breasts with such longing that she could feel the nipples tighten into hard little buds. When his mouth closed over one, she sucked in a shocked breath, then moaned with pure pleasure. "Oh, Dylan," she said with a sigh. "I want you so much."

"Since I could never deny you anything, I guess that means we make love here and now," he said with feigned resignation. "Are you really sure you don't want to wait for fancy sheets and buckets of champagne?"

She picked up her glass and dribbled a few drops of champagne on his chest, then leaned down and slowly licked them up. "There's more than enough champagne right here to make things interesting."

"Kelsey, I've gotta admit this is a side of you I never imagined."

She laughed at his perplexed expression. "Hey, I grew up playing doctor, remember? How about you?"

"Not once," he admitted.

"Then now's your chance. I'll let you know if you're getting it right."

"I'm so glad I have an expert on hand to advise me."

"Something tells me you'll be a very apt pupil," she said as his hands moved from her breasts to her hips, then began working on the snap of her slacks. Desire took away the last of her breath as she gave in to sensation—heating skin, slick caresses, intimate kisses.

She murmured praise and yearning in a mix that quickly turned to almost incoherent pleas as the coil of tension inside her spiraled tighter and tighter. Only when she was at the very edge did Dylan lift her hips, then settle her over him until he was deep inside.

Complete, she thought with amazement. This was what it felt like to be whole, to know the wonder of being one with another person. How had she not known about this in all the years she and Paul had rushed through sex, fitting it into a schedule already filled to bursting with other commitments? That was why, of course. They had had no leisure, no time or inclination for the pure enjoyment of each other's bodies. How terribly sad, she thought right before she gave herself completely to wicked sensation.

Yet how right that she was discovering this now with the man who was her future, the man who had given her back her son, then blessed her with a stepson she was rapidly coming to love.

Dylan looked deep into her eyes and seemed to understand what was going on in her head, seemed to know that she'd been thinking too much about the past. He intensified his movements, made the thrusts deeper and longer until she could no longer think of anything except him and this burning need to reach some elusive goal.

Then suddenly she was there, her whole body quaking with a climax that drove everything else from her head. Dylan was right with her, too, his timing as impeccable as ever.

Completely drained, she snuggled against him. "Do you think it will always be like this?"

"I think I'll probably die if it is," he said. He met her gaze. "What I really think is how remarkable you are."

"Funny, I was just thinking the same thing about you."

"Which tells me that we're both doing entirely too much thinking, when there are far more interesting alternatives."

Kelsey grinned. "Who needs a honeymoon, when there's a very private jet? Think we can just stay up here?"

"At least until we run out of fuel."

"Maybe we ought to consider getting to a hotel, after all," she said with regret. "As nice as this is, I want to know our future is going to last a little longer than a few hours."

"Your call," Dylan told her. "Really?"

"Today, anyway."

"And tomorrow?"

"We'll negotiate."

"Everything?" she asked. "The important issues."

"What about everything else?" His grin turned smug. "I win."

She leaned down and gave him another long, slow kiss. "You already have."

He gave a heartfelt sigh. "Don't I know it. After all, I've got my family now—you, Bobby, Shane."

She thought of something they'd never discussed, something they should have considered before rushing headlong into marriage. "Do you want another child, Dylan? Our baby?"

He cupped her face. "Nothing would make me happier. We can have a dozen more, if you want them."

"One or two ought to do it."

Dylan's gaze skimmed over her. "Want to get started?"

Kelsey sighed and reached for him. "Absolutely."

* * * * *